RHIANNA SYLVER

MAREN AND THE MISCHIEF SPIRIT

The Gilded Fable Series Book 1

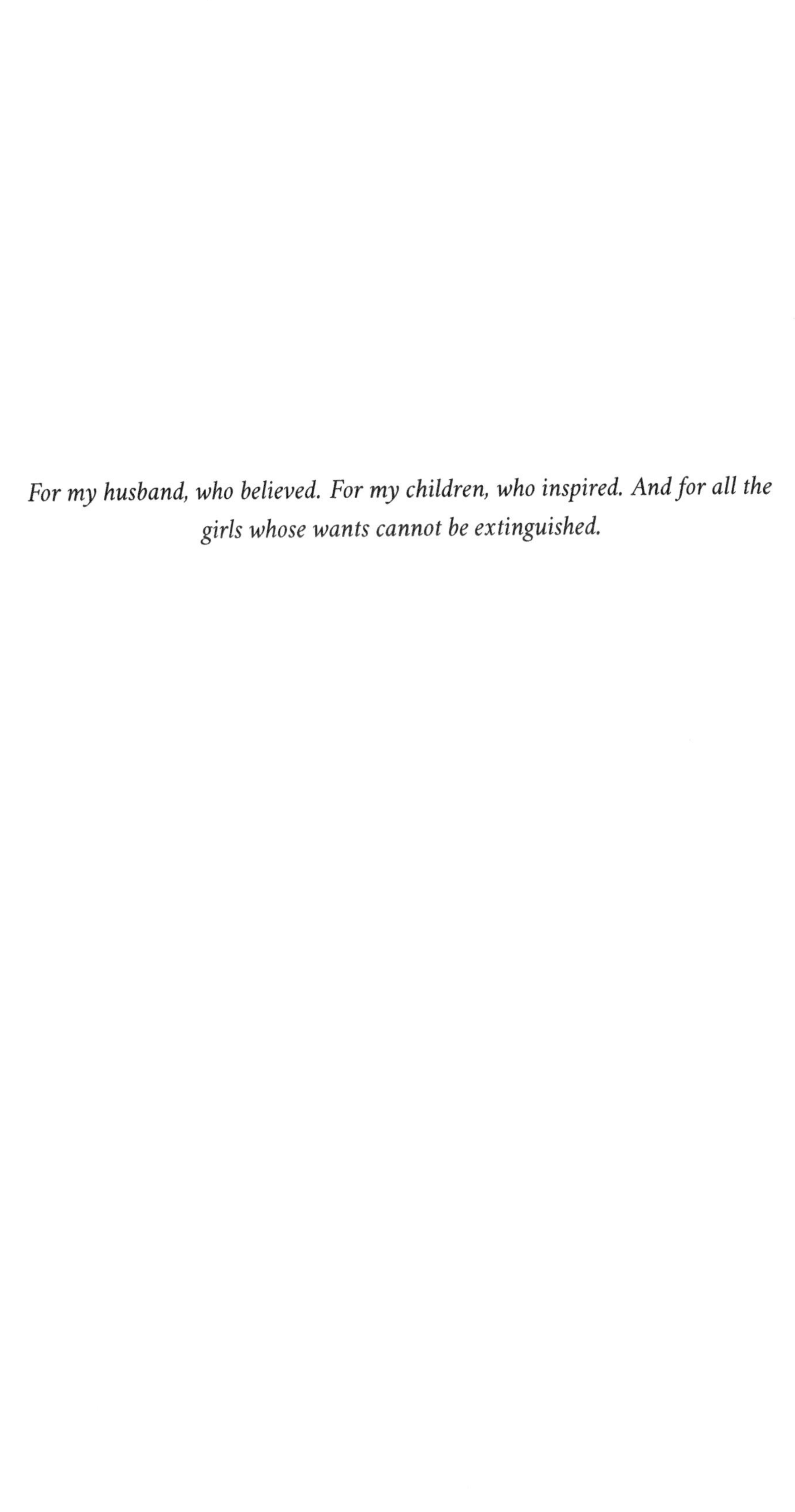

For my husband, who believed. For my children, who inspired. And for all the girls whose wants cannot be extinguished.

"The universe is made of stories, not of atoms."

-MURIEL RUKEYSER

Contents

1	Bread Witch of Eldenwick	1
2	Festival of Castings	12
3	The Weaver and the Star	21
4	Saint of Sorrow	30
5	Just a Breeze	41
6	A Blessing	52
7	Mischief Incarnate	61
8	The Court of Terrible Ideas	72
9	Coin-Flipping Bastard	80
10	Spectacle	89
11	Berries	97
12	Execution Eve	105
13	Fever Dream	117
14	Star-Marked	126
15	Fire Girl and the Bastard Coin-Flipper	135
16	Of the Twenty Locks	145
17	Spirited Ink	155
18	Graceful Flour Sack	167
19	Breaking Bread	177
20	Name the Nameless	186
21	Dressed to Disturb	200
22	Arsenic	207
23	Hall of Fractured Tales	217
24	Predatory	227
25	Rise and Despair	235
26	Labyrinth	242

27 Chaos Made Flesh   252

28 Vile   261

29 Scandal   269

30 Corruption of Proceedings   276

31 Beautiful Cages   283

32 The Hollow   294

33 Until Dusk   303

34 Choose   313

35 Work Proposal   324

36 Adornment   335

37 Wonder   343

38 Beautiful   354

39 Unstable   366

Epilogue   368

Acknowledgments   371

About the Author   375

Not to scale. Neither is my patience.
Tideglass
where is my salt?
Hollowmere
Here be feelings.
an offering to the goat

Penny Thornwick
Stormreach
The Pale Confederacy
Amberfell
Eldenwick
Greenbriar Bakery
Mythrin
The Capital City
Silkwell
honey
KINGDOM OF *MYTHRIN
*proof that you can base national identity on emotional instability and still get decent honey exports

1

Bread Witch of Eldenwick

Maren had flour in her hair again.

Not a dusting. Not a charming, picturesque smudge like the heroines in her books. No, this was a full-bodied, ghost-of-an-Elizabethan-orphan level coating of flour. The kind that stuck to her eyelashes and dared someone to comment so she could legally hit them with a baguette.

She wiped at it with the back of her wrist and only managed to grind in a streak of dough. Perfect. Exactly the aesthetic she was going for: Bread Witch of Eldenwick.

Patron sinner of the overworked and under-blessed.

The shop smelled of vanilla and burnt sugar, the air warm enough to melt thoughts. A cracked bell hung above the door, still chiming despite the fracture. A single key lay under the hearthstone, teeth-out, as her mother had taught her. Half-superstition, half-insurance.

She leaned over the prep table and glared down at the dough she was supposed to be coaxing into something artisanal.

"You're scowling at it again," a voice chirped behind her.

Maren looked up from the sullen lump of dough she'd been threatening into cooperation.

Penny Thornwick leaned in the doorway, sunshine incarnate in a bright yellow apron. Her apron was so violently yellow it could be seen from

1

orbit, embroidered clumsily with rosemary and patched at the corner with daisies. She'd tucked two rosemary sprigs into her braid like a crown, and they bobbed every time she moved her head. Their scent cut through the sweetness of the bakery air.

A thin red ribbon circled her wrist: the daily Fury ward, knotted once for courage, once for restraint. It gleamed against her skin as if the Spirit herself approved.

Maren pressed her knuckles into the dough, letting its soft resistance absorb her irritation. "It started it," she muttered.

Penny tilted her head, unbothered, green eyes catching the light, "You're supposed to knead with love, not homicide."

"Same result," Maren deadpanned.

The dough sagged pitifully, proving her point.

Beside her, a battered storybook lay open across a mixing bowl that definitely violated every sanitary law the Chapel ever wrote. *Tales of the Fox and Other Fables,* the gilt letters nearly worn away.

Her father's handwriting filled the margins: tiny arguments with the text, alternate endings, the occasional "nonsense" scribbled beside a moral. Maren had added her own notes over the years, smaller but meaner. The book looked less read than debated to death.

She squinted at the line she'd left off on:

"And there, in the heart of the woods, the fox waited..."

Maren snorted. "Yeah. Probably to eat someone."

"That's not the moral," Penny said, sweeping in with a tray of rolls that smelled so divine it could've converted an atheist. She moved through the flour-light like sunlight given human form, a faint chime following her from the bell charm on her apron.

"It's about cleverness and fate," Penny continued, setting the tray down.

"Or tooth decay." Maren flipped the page with her elbow, leaving a crescent of dough across a fox illustration that smirked up at her. The margin note there read: *Rewrite ending. Make girl smarter, fox hungrier.*

Penny leaned over her shoulder, curls brushing Maren's arm. "You still change the endings?"

"When they're stupid," Maren said. "Someone has to rescue the heroines from bad writing."

Penny laughed, the sound ringing off the copper pans like a small bell. "You could write your own, you know. *Tales of the Bread Witch,* perhaps."

Maren raised a brow. "Blasphemy."

Penny grinned. "Against you or the Chapel?"

"Both," Maren said, dusting flour off her hands. "One burns the loaves, the other burns the books."

Penny only smiled wider, sunlight over a thundercloud. "Then it's a good thing you're hard to scorch."

"I'm resilient," Maren said. "Like mold."

"That's one word for it." Penny's laugh was quick and warm, the kind that lived in the rafters long after she stopped. "You know I'm right. You stay up half the night reading, scribbling in margins, dreaming with your eyes open. You want more than this."

Steam ghosted up between them, sweet with cinnamon and yeast. Outside, hammers rang from the square where carpenters were raising a festival stage; the rhythm slipped through the shutters like an impatient heartbeat.

Maren tightened the braid of dough. "I want," she said sweetly, "for you to stop psychoanalyzing me before I weaponize this rolling pin."

Penny grinned, undeterred. "See? You've already got character work. All you need is a plot."

"Plot's overrated," Maren muttered. "Most stories end with a wedding or a funeral, and both require catering."

Penny laughed again, and for a moment, Maren almost smiled with her. They'd been doing this dance for years: light and dark, honey and salt, the world a little less dull when Penny was near.

Flour hung in the air like stardust, settling over everything: the copper pans, the cooling rolls, the two books propped against the wall. Her mother's cookbook leaned against her father's tattered storybook, the spines forever at odds with each other. Recipe versus fable. Bread versus wonder.

She'd been trying to knead the two together since she could hold a spoon.

Her gaze drifted to the door, to the bell hanging there. Outside, a sliver of sunlight cut through the glass, gilding the countertop, the flour, Penny's hair; everything she was supposed to love.

She could almost convince herself it was enough. Almost.

Then the bell over the front door chimed.

Not the cheerful, chaotic jingle of Old Keld with his turnips or the candle girl bartering beeswax for buns. No, this was a precise chime. Polite. Practiced. Like a curtsy in sound form.

Maren froze mid-knead, dough clinging to her fingers. "Incoming," she murmured.

Sure enough, Mrs. Aldren swept in like she was hosting a garden party. Her bonnet was perched at a gravity-defying angle that no law of nature could explain. Her shawl was embroidered with lilies, and her basket was lined with lavender sachets, soaps, and just enough superiority to season a stew.

"There's my favorite girl," she trilled, smiling widely.

Maren glanced over her shoulder, deadpan. "You mean me?"

"Of course, dear," Mrs. Aldren said, gliding closer. "You've grown up so well, considering… everything." Her eyes flicked to the portrait on the wall: the Greenbriar plaque, three generations of bakers glaring down from flour-smudged frames.

"Everything," Maren echoed. "My favorite euphemism for 'orphaned young.'"

Mrs. Aldren tutted delicately, rearranging her shawl as though sympathy were contagious. "We all have our tests, child. The Spirits shape us through suffering. It's character-building."

"Mm," Maren said. "And here I thought *parenting* did the shaping."

Penny coughed sharply, the universal sound for *please behave in front of customers*.

Mrs. Aldren, unfazed, inspected the trays like an auditor. "Now, I'll take the rolls without seeds this time. The flax ones are quite… indecent."

Maren blinked. "Indecent."

"Flax," Mrs. Aldren whispered, as if invoking sin itself. "The Chapel says it stirs the blood. Too much heat in the body invites Temptation's favor. Why, they say the Saints used to ban it outright."

Maren folded her arms, the picture of calm insolence. "Ah. Seduced by fiber?"

Penny nearly choked on air. "Maren—"

"I'm serious," Maren went on, tone sweet as poisoned honey. "If lust and constipation share a cause, perhaps the Spirits should coordinate their departments."

Mrs. Aldren's smile didn't move, but her eyes narrowed just enough to suggest divine displeasure. "Indigestion and lust share the same root in the old tongue," she said tightly.

Maren froze mid-reach, then turned slowly, expression solemn. "So you're telling me flatulence offends the gods."

Penny made a choking noise. Mrs. Aldren drew herself up, scandalized. "It is *not* a laughing matter!"

"No, of course not," Maren said. "We should all repent immediately. Maybe light a candle for anyone who survived a suspicious stew."

Mrs. Aldren's mouth opened, closed, and twitched in silent prayer. "That's not—well—perhaps your mother didn't—"

"Oh, she did," Maren said lightly, brushing flour from her sleeve. "She just had the sense to know that divine beings don't care about bowel movements."

Mrs. Aldren smiled tightly. "You do like your little jokes."

"Thank you," Maren said sweetly. "I bake them fresh."

Penny stifled a laugh behind her hand, but the sound escaped anyway, bright as chimes. She bounced forward, rosemary sprigs bobbing as she moved.

The older woman stiffened, clutching her lavender sachet as if it were a talisman. "You ought to wear a ribbon," she said sharply. "Red at the wrist keeps Fury from nipping at the temper. Yours, I daresay, could use taming."

Maren glanced at Penny's bright ribbon, then at her bare wrist. "Maybe Fury and I have an understanding."

"Blasphemy," Mrs. Aldren gasped, as though she'd just witnessed a murder.

"Occupational hazard," Maren replied. "You can't bake miracles without singeing a few fingers."

Penny darted in with the diplomacy of someone trained in disaster relief. "We have lovely seedless rolls this morning, Mrs. Aldren. Fresh from the oven. Maren insists on perfection."

"Does she?" The woman eyed Maren with suspicion. Still, she selected two rolls, weighing them as though judging souls. "Such enthusiasm," she said at last, accepting the bag. "It's a wonder it hasn't worn off on you."

Maren plastered on her best polite smile, which looked a lot like a grimace. "Oh, it's worn off plenty. Mostly in the form of gray hairs."

"Gray suits wisdom," Penny chirped, brightly loyal as ever. "And Maren has enough for both of us."

Mrs. Aldren's brows climbed. Maren choked on a laugh. Penny beamed like she'd just declared Maren the Empress of Bread.

Mrs. Aldren's lips pursed so tight they could've piped icing. Coins clinked into Maren's hand, cold and deliberate.

"Do give my blessings to the Saints," she said, heading for the door.

"Of course," Maren said sweetly. "I'll tell them flax remains the deadliest of sins."

The bell chimed again. Silence followed, thick enough to frost.

Penny pressed a flour-dusted hand over her mouth, eyes bright with laughter she shouldn't risk. "You could try to be nice," she said finally.

"I was nice," Maren replied, sweeping stray crumbs into a pile. "I didn't throw the flax rolls."

"Progress," Penny said, bumping her shoulder. "But maybe next time, less commentary on divine digestion."

Maren sighed, brushing flour off the counter with the dignity of someone deeply unrepentant. "Fine. Next time I'll just curse her bonnet instead."

* * *

Outside, Eldenwick was already in one of its morning spirals.

The cobblestones sweated from a halfhearted bucket wash, an attempt to scrub away the chalk protests about turnip prices.

Laundry lines drooped overhead, dripping onto anyone unlucky enough to pass below. The air smelled of dirt, horse, and the metallic tang of bell polish; festival week always reeked of ambition.

Maren stepped into the sunlight, basket balanced on one hip, and blinked at the chaos. The sky hung low and heavy, typical late-summer weather in the Kingdom of Mythrin, the kind that promised rain but primarily delivered humidity and bad tempers.

Somewhere beyond the hills, the Red Steppe winds carried news of Stormreach and its holy war: Fury's provinces shouting about devotion while bleeding for it. The Chapel called it a divine duty. Maren called it bad bookkeeping.

She glanced toward the blacksmith's forge, where the man himself swung his hammer in steady rhythm, the red sash tied around his bicep stark against the heat. It wasn't the Fury ribbon of prayer this time, but a conscription mark.

He'd likely be bound for Stormreach by winter, unless the army rerouted him to Amberfell to forge spearheads instead. Either way, he'd be hammering for the gods soon enough.

Penny walked beside her, a tray of honey rolls glittering under a drape of muslin and an apron bright enough to blind the sun. She waved to nearly everyone. Maren, meanwhile, grumbled at nearly everything.

"Market first," Penny sang, dodging a cart stacked with linen. "Then apothecary, then the bookbinder. Don't let me forget the bookbinder."

"Wouldn't dream of it," Maren said. "You'd mourn the cinnamon like a widow."

Penny shot her a grin over her shoulder. "And you'd mourn the gossip. Look at you pretending you don't care."

"I don't care," Maren said. "But I *do* eavesdrop recreationally."

They rounded the corner into the market square.

Festival preparations had begun early.

Carpenters hammered together a small dais for the coming Festival of Castings, where the Chapel would parade six relics: the coin, the loom, the vessel, the key, the spearhead, and the bell tongue across the square like prized livestock.

Stalls were already draped with bunting: fox masks for Mischief, serpent bangles for Temptation, cracked bells strung as ornaments for Delight.

Children darted through the crowd wearing animal masks of the Spirits' creatures, chasing each other with the high-pitched reverence of sugar and belief.

One boy in a fox mask tugged at Maren's skirt before darting away, shouting a line from a fable: "Luck loves a liar!"

Maren scowled after him. "And honesty loves a day off."

Penny bit her lip to keep from laughing.

Everywhere Maren looked, there was something to remind her of the Faith. A key maker selling charms to "lock away dread." A weaver burning scraps of thread in a small brazier as an offering to Temptation "to let go of what no longer serves." A candle monger hawking red wax ribbons "to keep Fury calm."

"People really will buy anything if you brand it with a Spirit," Maren said, stepping around a cart of bell clappers.

Penny smiled without looking up from her tray. "They just like feeling blessed."

"They just like excuses," Maren said. "The Festival of Castings is half theology, half consumer trap. At least the Day of Reckoning has fistfights worth watching."

"Mar," Penny said patiently, "not everyone wants their religion to be violent."

"That's the only honest part," Maren muttered, glancing again toward the forge's red sash.

A gust of wind lifted the scent of roasting chestnuts and the distant brine of Tideglass salt, finally reaching the inland town after months of delay. A vendor shouted that the trade roads were open again, though Maren doubted it. Salt from the coast had become expensive as gold since the war started clogging the caravans.

Honey, salt, thread, and iron; the four tithes Mythrin worshiped with. Everything useful, everything taxable.

And somehow, none of it made the bread rise faster.

Penny nudged her with a shoulder. "You look like you're narrating the end of the world again."

"I'm narrating the cost of it," Maren said, adjusting her basket. "There's a difference."

They passed the fountain, where petals from yesterday's chapel blessings floated like wilted confetti. Maren flicked one aside and muttered, "Wonder how much holiness costs by the handful."

Penny laughed, the sound light enough to lift the whole square for a moment. "Come on, Bread Witch. Let's sell something before you offend another Spirit."

"I don't offend them," Maren said, following. "I just remind them they're ridiculous."

On the far side of the square, the candle maker's apprentice hammered away at a display, desperate to impress the candle girl. The candle girl leaned against a post, pretending not to watch him ruin his thumbs. Sparks practically flew between them, if not literal ones, though Maren gave it a week before both were on fire.

"They're sweet," Penny said dreamily, hugging her basket tighter.

"They're a lawsuit," Maren said. "Romance built on property damage never ends well."

"Not everyone's doomed, you know," Penny countered.

"Everyone in this town is doomed," Maren said, "mostly by goats."

As if summoned: "Goats!" someone screamed.

Three of them barreled through the square, one trailing Mrs. Aldren's stolen bonnet ribbon in its mouth like a battle flag. Penny yelped, clutching her tray higher, while Maren stepped calmly aside and gave them a lazy wave.

"Morning, gentlemen. Try not to eat anyone's laundry this time."

By the time they reached their stall, the square was a riot of color and sound. Banners snapped overhead, painted with the six animals of the Spirits.

Their stall stood at the crossroads of chaos, wedged between the candle maker's booth and a woman selling cheap miracles in jars. Maren's table, by contrast, smelled of honest bread.

Penny immediately went to work, arranging the rolls in perfect rows, brushing crumbs from the tray, and charming half the crowd by simply existing.

She thrived here. Eldenwick adored her.

Penny laughed with the butcher's wife about the cost of salt, tossed a roll to the cooper's apprentice with alarming accuracy, and sold out an entire basket in the time it took Maren to calculate how many coppers they'd lose to tithes.

Rosemary sprigs bobbed in her braid with every turn of her head; she looked like she'd been born from sunlight and yeast. Meanwhile, Maren leaned against the stall's edge and glared at the world.

"Bread made with love!" Penny called to the crowd, voice bright and sure. "Best rolls in Eldenwick! Guaranteed seedless this week!"

"Bread made with homicide," Maren muttered. "Comes with a free existential crisis."

An onion vendor gave her a look like she'd just confessed to witchcraft.

Penny didn't miss a beat. "Ignore her," she told the woman cheerfully. "She hasn't had her tea yet."

Laughter rippled through the line, coins clinking into the tin cup like applause.

Maren should've been annoyed. She was a little. But mostly she watched Penny. How her hands never stilled, how her face seemed to catch and reflect every spark of delight around her.

Penny was everything the market rewarded: warmth, laughter, charm. The same gifts once belonged to Maren's mother, who used to hum as she baked and make customers feel like family. Maren hadn't inherited that melody. Her humor came out sharper, her smile crooked. She knew it, accepted it, and hated how much the world punished her for being good at the wrong kind of thing.

Still, together they worked. Penny made them love the bread. Maren made sure they paid for it.

It was almost a rhythm.

2

Festival of Castings

By midday, the honey rolls were gone, and only the heavy loaves for delivery remained. Penny counted the coins, sunlight catching in the curves of her smile. "Look at that! Enough to cover flour, sugar, and maybe a new apron for you!"

Maren rolled her shoulders, every muscle protesting. "Or a new back. Preferably one without knots."

"Maybe the apothecary sells spines," Penny said, sweeping the last of the crumbs into a paper twist. "All right. Deliveries before we collapse."

"That'd be their first miracle," Maren said, but there was a thread of affection beneath it.

They packed the trays and set off down the narrow lane that split the square. Penny walked fast, weaving through the crowd with the confidence of someone who knew she was welcome everywhere. Maren followed more slowly, shouldering the breadbasket against her hip, muttering at anyone who jostled her.

First stop was the apothecary, where glass jars gleamed like jewels behind the counter.

Mistress Ryn looked up from her mortar, gray hair pinned in a haphazard knot, sleeves rolled to the elbows.

"Bare hands again?" she scolded, though the corners of her mouth softened when she saw Maren. "Your mother used to say you'd lose your fingerprints before you learned patience."

"I prefer efficiency," Maren said, setting the bread bundle on the counter.

"You prefer ignoring good advice." Ryn whisked the rolls away, wrapping them in a cloth that smelled faintly of lavender. "How's the honey supply? Still short?"

"Shorter than the Chapel's sense of humor," Maren said.

Penny winced, but Ryn only snorted. "Blasphemy before lunch. She'd be proud." The older woman reached for a small tin. "Here. For the aches."

Inside were sugar-dusted leaves meant for steeping, along with mint and other herbs.

Maren accepted it with a nod. "Thank you."

"Don't thank me," Ryn said. "Thank your mother for teaching me to bake bread that didn't fight back. Saints know you didn't inherit that part."

Maren smiled, small but real. Ryn was one of the few people who could discuss her mother without pity or the awkward pause that often followed.

When they stepped back into the street, Penny bumped her shoulder lightly. "You're the only person she doesn't terrify."

"She's armed with a pestle," Maren said. "Terror's mutual."

The bookbinder's shop sat between a weaver's stall and a shuttered glass maker's studio. A cracked bell hung over the door, its tone soft yet persistent, as they stepped inside.

The air was cooler, shaded with the smell of parchment, ink, and dust. Books lined the walls in haphazard towers; everything from chapel hymns to old fables bound in mismatched leather. Behind the counter, the bookbinder looked up, startled mid-page. His spectacles slid down his nose; his hair was tied back but already escaping.

"Miss Thornwick," the bookbinder said warmly, far too quickly, as Penny stepped up with her tray. "And Miss..." He squinted at Maren. "...baker."

Maren deadpanned. "A pleasure."

"Of course," he said quickly. "Welcome."

His eyes were on Penny, "Your hair looks... fragrant today."

Maren blinked. "Fragrant?"

"Like rosemary," he stammered, cheeks pinking. "Which, er, suits you."

Penny's sprigs bobbed in approval as she leaned forward. "We're here on important business. Cinnamon bark. We brought your loaf."

"Not what bookbinders are for," Maren muttered, because someone had to.

He straightened. "Ah, yes. One moment."

As he disappeared into the back room, Penny's eyes wandered over the shelves, lighting on a stack of books bound in indigo thread. "He's got *The Book of Thresholds*," she whispered. "The chapel banned that one last year."

"Did they?" Maren murmured, scanning the spines. "How scandalous. A few untidy metaphors and they start banning punctuation."

He returned carrying a small packet wrapped in parchment and tied with a fine thread. "From my mother," he said, offering it to Penny with both hands. "It's fresher than what the spice merchants bring from Silkwell."

Penny clasped it like a prize. "You're wonderful."

He went pink all the way to his ears. "I… do try."

Maren, watching, bit back a smirk. *Tragic,* she thought. *He's gone full cinnamon-poet.*

"Do you read much?" the bookbinder asked after a beat, clearly trying to recover.

"Mostly price ledgers," Maren said. "Fewer plot holes."

Penny laughed, and the sound seemed to ease him. "She writes," she said brightly. "Or rewrites, depending on her mood. Endings, mostly."

He blinked. "Endings?"

"She doesn't like how stories finish," Penny said. "So she makes them worse."

"Better," Maren corrected. "Worse is subjective."

The bookbinder's smile turned shy but sincere. "I'd like to read one someday."

"She doesn't share," Penny teased. "Proprietary secrets."

"Understandable," he said. "Stories can be… personal." He hesitated, then nodded toward the counter where a slim, worn book lay half-open. "This one's a collection of old fables. My father used to say the fox's coin stood for choice, not luck. I've always liked that."

Maren's attention flicked to the page. Ink drawings of a fox and a silver coin gleamed faintly in the low light. She said nothing, only filed the thought away.

When Penny straightened with her tray, the bookbinder bent low, fumbling with his spectacles before adding, "If ever you require… parchment for your—ah—recipes, you've only to ask."

Maren nearly gagged. Penny just smiled sweetly. "I'll remember that."

When they headed back toward the bakery, Penny was humming, cinnamon bark tucked neatly into the coin pouch at her waist.

"You know he was flirting, right?" Maren said flatly.

Penny's eyes went wide in scandalized shock. "Flirting? He offered me cinnamon, Maren. That's just commerce."

"In Eldenwick?" Maren snorted. "That's practically a betrothal."

Penny swatted her with the corner of the tray, laughing so brightly the street seemed to tilt toward her. Maren scowled, but inside, a quieter thought gnawed at her: she would've killed for someone to offer her parchment like that.

Books, after all, were her real inheritance. And for one bitter, fleeting moment, she envied Penny's herbs.

By the time they stumbled back into the bakery, the sun was sinking low, painting Eldenwick in honey and shadows. The trays were light, the coin purse heavier than usual, and Penny hummed some tune she'd picked up from a fiddler in the square.

Maren, carrying the larger basket, dropped it onto the prep table with a grunt. "Successful day," she muttered. "If you count overzealous hagglers, goat stampedes, and public flirtations as successful."

Penny dusted her apron with a twirl, shaking flour dust into the air like a halo. "Oh, come on, Mar. People smiled. We sold everything. Even Old Keld remembered to pay in actual coin."

"Barely." Maren rubbed her temples. "He tried to barter with a turnip first."

"A very handsome turnip," Penny said cheerfully, stacking trays with too much energy for someone who'd been on her feet since dawn. "And don't pretend you're not secretly thrilled we came home with cinnamon bark."

Maren shot her a look. "Thrilled isn't the word."

Penny smirked, not fooled. "Jealous, then?"

Maren scoffed, too quick. "Of what? A man who can't tell the difference between a compliment and an herb garden?"

"*Of cinnamon*," Penny teased, brushing past her with a cheeky grin.

Maren turned back to the counter, sweeping crumbs into her palm. "It's bark that smells nice. I'll survive."

But her eyes lingered anyway. Jealous. Not of Penny, never of Penny. But of the ease. The way things fell into her hands. Cinnamon bark and compliments, laughter in the square, whole futures blooming like the rosemary in her hair.

Whereas Maren... had a bakery. A legacy she'd sworn to keep alive, even if it smothered her. And a stack of storybooks she only dared whisper to when no one else was listening.

Penny hopped up onto the prep table, swinging her legs like a child who'd never known fatigue. "You know what we should do with all this good fortune?"

"Pay taxes," Maren said automatically, reaching for the ledger.

Penny groaned. "You're allergic to joy."

"I'm allergic to overdraft." Maren flipped the book open, its spine sighing under the weight of years. The ink stains on the margins looked like old bruises. She licked the tip of her quill and began to jot figures in neat, ruthless columns.

Flour, sugar, and honey. All paid. Barely.

She paused, frowning. "We'll need another shipment from Amberfell before the week's out. If the salt caravans don't make it through from Tideglass again, we'll have to buy from the Chapel's stores. Triple price."

Penny tilted her head. "Or we could stop thinking about salt for one night and go to the Festival."

Maren didn't look up. "We have bread to proof for morning."

"Bread can wait. The Spirits are practically throwing a party in the square!"

"Exactly my concern." She flipped another page, pretending not to notice the smear of cinnamon scent drifting closer as Penny leaned over her shoulder.

"Come on," Penny said softly. "It's been months since you left this kitchen for anything other than markets and burials."

"Cheerful as ever," Maren muttered, keeping her eyes on the numbers.

Penny nudged her arm, knocking a tiny blot of ink across the page. "You're working by candlelight, talking to ledgers like they're family. One evening won't ruin us."

Maren sighed. The flame wavered. "If we're ruined, you're working double shifts until we can afford a new roof."

"Done," Penny said instantly, sliding off the table. "See? Bargain struck."

Maren looked up at the red ribbon still looped around Penny's wrist, at the smudge of flour on her jaw, at the way she glowed like she'd swallowed the whole sunset. She thought of her mother humming as she baked, of her father reading aloud from fables no one believed anymore. And how, somehow, she'd ended up keeping both their ghosts alive in the same four walls.

Duty was what kept the ovens hot. But it was Penny who kept her here.

"All right," Maren said finally. "I'll go. But on three conditions."

Penny clapped her hands, delighted. "Name them."

"One — I'm not buying any charms."

"Understood."

"Two — we are not wasting any more honey on Mischief. He can go hungry."

Penny bit back a smile. "Blasphemy again."

"It's a theme," Maren said. "And three — we're home before midnight."

Penny seized her hands, spinning her in a little half-dance that nearly knocked the quill pot over. "Deal!"

"Careful," Maren said, steadying her. "Ink stains are harder to erase than sin."

"That's why you're coming," Penny replied, breathless with laughter. "To remind everyone how serious redemption paperwork is."

Maren closed the ledger, carefully, as if mercy might spill out. The quill still trembled faintly in its pot.

Outside, the bells began to toll, six notes rolling across Eldenwick.

The Festival of Castings was beginning.

Maren glanced toward the window, where lamplight flickered gold against the cobbles. Wonder waited just beyond the door. Duty sat behind her on the table.

Maren shrugged into her shawl. Rough wool, dyed a shade between smoke and practicality, and checked that the latch was drawn. Penny was already halfway out the door, apron still dusted with flour, and the small bell on her hem still chiming every time she moved.

"You're worse than a magpie," Maren muttered, pulling the door closed behind them. The bell over it gave a faint, weary note. "Anything shiny and you're halfway airborne."

Penny only smiled, breath misting in the cool air. "You'll thank me when you see it."

Maren doubted that, but she pocketed her little salt purse anyway. Habit, not faith. Grief didn't need worship, only remembrance, and it seemed polite to bring something for the only Spirit she still halfway believed in.

And they stepped into Eldenwick.

The ordinary cobblestone square had been transformed beneath the violet hour.

Lanterns hung from ropes between the chimneys, trembling in the evening breeze like captured stars. Banners in six colors fluttered from the poles: orange for Mischief, white for Temptation, black for Grief, violet for Dread, red for Fury, and yellow for Delight. A small stage had been built at the far end where the Saints would soon take their places.

The air was thick with music: pipes, fiddles, and the low hum of a hundred overlapping conversations. Candle makers had lined the edges of the square, selling sticks of tallow that smelled faintly of citrus and smoke. A cart of roasted chestnuts creaked past, the vendor shouting promises of warmth. Children in animal masks darted through the crowd: foxes, serpents, hares, and lions, their paper ears catching the light as they ran.

Penny's laughter joined theirs as naturally as breath. "It's beautiful," she said, turning in a slow circle.

Maren admitted, silently, that it was. The cobbles had been scrubbed until they gleamed. Musicians played from the fountain's rim. The water itself had been scattered with flower petals, each one lit by floating candles. The scent of roasted apples mingled with the sharper bite of iron from the smithy's corner forge.

She followed Penny through the press of bodies, careful not to tread on anyone's trailing ribbons. Everyone had adorned themselves in their favored Spirit's colors.

"If the Spirits loved them," Maren thought, *"they had a strange way of showing it."*

Penny pointed to the altars in the center of the square, each one draped in cloth the color of its Spirit. Mischief's silver coin glimmered on a small pedestal, Temptation's loom gleamed faintly in the lamplight, Grief's vessel sat dark and still, and beside them lay the iron key, the spearhead, and a cracked bell. Six relics for six emotions that ruled the world, as the Chapel loved to remind them.

Maren stopped at the edge of the crowd, arms folded. "It looks the same every year," she said, mostly to herself. "The Saints perform, the town applauds, and the bakery loses a night's profit."

Penny bumped her shoulder, cheerful as ever. "Don't start with economics. You promised to have fun."

"I promised to attend," Maren corrected. "Fun was your invention."

Penny ignored the distinction. She tugged her toward a row of stalls, where vendors were selling candied nuts, small ribbons blessed by the local priest, and carved wooden charms shaped like the Spirits' animals.

"Let's get you a fox," Penny said, holding up one painted silver.

"I already have one," Maren said, nodding toward the coin altar. "He takes enough of my luck as it is."

Penny rolled her eyes. "You are the least festive human being in Mythrin."

"I'm *consistent*," Maren corrected.

Still, she allowed herself to be dragged along, because Penny's joy was contagious in small doses, and the festival lights softened even her cynicism.

The whole square thrummed with energy, music layered over prayer, gossip tangled with laughter.

Maren watched it all with the wary fondness of someone observing a childhood home from a distance. She knew every crooked stone in the square, every stall owner by name. These were her people: exasperating, devout, and entirely predictable. She loved them the way a bird might love the sky. It was familiar and infinite, but never quite enough to stay grounded in it.

Penny was still talking, hands moving as she described which Saint's robe she wanted to see up close. "They say the Saint of Delight brought an actual bell from Tideglass. Real gold. Can you imagine?"

"Easily," Maren said. "I see gold every time the Chapel passes a collection bowl."

Penny groaned, elbowing her. "You're impossible."

"Possibly *right*," Maren said.

The first of the bells rang.

It was a clear, ringing tone that rolled over the square, silencing the laughter. The crowd turned toward the stage as the procession began, torches flaring along the path. The Saints would appear next, and with them the part of the night that always made Maren itch: the storytelling.

She glanced at Penny, who had clasped her hands in excitement, eyes bright. The red ribbon on her wrist caught the firelight, and the tiny bell on her apron chimed softly as she breathed.

Maren sighed through her nose, almost smiling. "All right, show me your Saints," she said quietly.

3

The Weaver and the Star

Torchlight lifted along the lane as the procession rounded the corner: six robed figures and a herald in Mythrin green, moving at the quiet center of a town gone bright.

The altars stood waiting at the square's heart, each draped in its Spirit's color.

This was how the Festival of Castings always began: the Saints arrived empty-handed and left bearing what the crowd already knew by sight.

The Herald of Mythrin stepped forward first, his voice carrying cleanly:

"By leave of the Faith and under the eyes of the Six, Eldenwick receives the Saints. Tonight, the Castings are remembered. Tonight, we lift what the gods tore free, and we carry it carefully."

Maren's mouth twitched. Carefully was not how any god had ever done anything.

The Saint of Mischief reached the altars before the others. He couldn't have been more than thirty, with sharp cheekbones and his cloak lined in silver. He bowed to the coin and lifted it from its stand with two fingers, the way one might test a blade. When he turned to the crowd, its face reflected the torchlight, a tiny world spinning as he let it roll over his knuckles. A neat trick.

The Herald named his post "from the capital, seat of Mythrin," which felt right; Mischief had always preferred the center of the board.

Temptation came next from Silkwell, robe soft as poured wine, veil stitched with moth-bright thread. She cradled the loom like a living thing, silver-blue against her palms, and when she breathed, the strand seemed to tighten, as if agreeing with her.

A strong perfume trailed her: ripe grapes, vanilla, and jasmine. She exuded desire effortlessly.

From Hollowmere, the Saint of Grief walked as slowly as the moon rose. A gray stole crossed his shoulders, salt stains at the hem where mourners' hands had gripped. He lifted the vessel, a simple clay cup sealed with wax, and held it steady at his chest. A heavier hush fell over the crowd. Even Penny's bell seemed to understand the weight.

The Saint of Dread followed, also sworn out of Hollowmere. The marsh breeds watchers as well as mourners. His robe was plain black, and his mask had no eye holes; a tradition Maren disliked on principle.

He took up the key with two hands and set it against his palm, teeth out, the old way: a promise to keep thresholds honest. Somehow, the simple movement was enough to cause a few onlookers a look of unease.

Delight arrived bright from Tideglass, bells stitched into the girdle of her gold robe, hair braided with child-like ribbons. She plucked the bell from its cradle and lifted it high; it rang a clear note that hopped along roofs and slipped down alleys.

People laughed with its jolly ring as if by instinct. Penny was beaming in admiration. Even Maren felt her jaw unclench a fraction.

For Fury, there was no Saint. Only the Herald again, voice lower now. "Stormreach keeps its oath."

A red sash lay across the empty pedestal, and a soldier from Amberfell set the spearhead upon it in formal substitution. Forge in place of battlefield, iron in place of blood.

The Herald added, with the practiced cadence of a message meant to travel, "Our general speaks from the front. The Pale Confederacy presses the north. Prayers and ribbons are received."

The crowd murmured; a few raised wrists bound in red. Maren watched as the blacksmith in the back lifted his arm and looked away.

When each relic was in mortal hands, the Saints formed a line across the dais. Torches dipped. The Herald stepped aside.

The Saint of Mischief spoke first, voice bright and controlled. "In the first days, the gods learned their error. Laughter cracked, and from its seam, he who changes stories stepped through." He turned the coin once, the way a locksmith shows a key before he uses it.

Temptation plucked a thread from her loom and let it spill a little over her knuckles, catching lantern-glow. "From hunger," she said. "Want made visible. Desire woven where there had been only need."

Grief lifted the vessel just enough to change the way light struck its seal. "From what could not be kept," he said, simply. "The memory that refuses to rot."

The silence he made had shape; Maren felt it pass over her like shade, familiar and almost kind.

Dread's voice came muffled through the mask. "From the moment before," he said. "From the keyhole and the held breath." He showed the iron, teeth glinting. The crowd held its own breath, obligingly.

Delight rang the bell once again and smiled. "From the refusal to die quietly," she said, and the note seemed to hang around her like a second robe.

The spearhead remained where the Amberfell man had set it; the Herald spoke for Fury. "From injustice named aloud," he recited. "From the blade that divides what is owed from what is taken."

Together, the Saints recited the Casting in sequence, each line handing the tale to the next like a torch. The words were the Chapel's canon, compact and polished, stripped of the teeth Maren remembered from her father's versions. But the bones of it were still there: gods without feeling; a world corrected by the arrival of six sharp things; mortals building chapels and taxes around whatever made their hearts move. People listened with tilted faces, the way they did every year, as if repetition could make anything safe.

Maren stood at the edge of it all, Penny's shoulder pressed lightly to hers, and let the sound roll over her. The Saints were highly regarded and *very* human: a smudge of ink on the Mischief man's thumb; a frayed seam at the Temptation veil; salt dried white at Grief's hem; a faint tremor in the Herald's hand when he named Stormreach.

Ceremony made them taller. The torchlight made them holy. Up close, they were only people carrying heavy objects and heavier stories. Which, if she were honest, was respectable work.

The last line fell. Bells answered. The Saints lowered the relics against their hearts, and the square exhaled as one.

"Pretty," Penny whispered.

Maren's mouth curved, quick and private. Pretty, yes. And, like most pretty things, carefully arranged.

The Saints began to descend from the dais, robes whispering against the stone.

The formal recitation had ended; now came the stories. The *mortal-sized* tales that fit easily in mouths and could be sold to children as lessons.

The Saint of Temptation stepped forward first.

Her veil shimmered like wet silk, its threads catching on the torchlight, her face a blur of warmth and grace. The crowd quieted into reverence. Penny tugged gently at Maren's sleeve, eyes alight.

She unwound the length of the thread in her palm, holding it aloft. "You've heard the Castings," she said, her voice low and warm, "but it is not enough to remember how the Spirits came to us. We must remember what they teach us. Tonight, I'll tell you of *The Weaver and the Star.*"

A murmur of approval passed through the square. Maren had heard this one before; everyone had, but the Saints always told it as if it were new.

The Saint began to pace slowly before the empty altars, letting the thread drift through her fingers. "Once, long before cities and shops and coins, there was a weaver who lived in a valley. She made cloth fine enough to catch moonlight, but she longed for more. She wished to weave something brighter than anything on earth. So she looked up and saw the stars, and she desired one."

The crowd leaned closer. The Saint smiled, knowing she had them.

"The weaver spun a ladder from her own hair, each strand a promise, each knot a prayer. She climbed until her fingers brushed the lowest star.

And when she touched it, she burned. The gods punished her for pride, for daring to reach too high, and she was lost. The moral—"

"—is that gods have terrible design skills," Maren said, apparently louder than intended.

A few heads turned. Penny made a strangled sound beside her that might have been panic.

Maren froze mid-breath, shoulders going rigid as the Saint's gaze landed squarely on her.

The Saint blinked down from the dais, politely frozen. "Excuse me?"

Maren blinked back, caught between horror and stubbornness. She cleared her throat, entirely unrepentant. "You say she was punished for reaching. I've always thought the better moral was: *maybe the star wanted to be touched.*"

The crowd stiffened. A few gasps scattered like dropped pins. Someone hissed, "Greenbriar girl," under their breath.

Maren tilted her head, tone as mild as cream. "If wanting something noble makes us divine, why make it sin in mortals? The Weaver didn't steal, lie, or murder. She *reached.* That's the closest thing to faith most people ever manage."

The Saint's lips parted, the measured grace of her training faltering. "Desire without restraint leads to ruin. Temptation tests the soul."

"And restraint without want leaves us hollow," Maren countered. "If the gods didn't wish us to desire, they shouldn't have given us eyes. Or looms. Or *stories.*"

The murmur rippled wider now, half scandal, half awe. A few older women clutched their red ribbons tighter, warding off Fury's notice.

Penny whispered frantically, "Maren, please—"

But Maren wasn't cruel; she was precise. She stepped forward just enough to let the lamplight touch her face, steady and calm. "My father told that story differently," she said. "In his version, when the Weaver reached the star, she saw herself reflected in its light and realized the world was brighter for having tried. Maybe ruin's just what happens when mortals try to live like gods and feel like it matters."

The Saint's fingers tightened around the spool. For a heartbeat, no one breathed. Then a voice from the crowd, the butcher's wife, muttered, "Blasphemy."

Maren smiled faintly. "I prefer the term *editor*."

That broke the silence with the uneasy rustle of judgment.

"Her mother warned her tongue would damn her," someone whispered. "Cursed blood, that one. Born out of lust and raised on lies."

Another voice: "A storyteller's daughter. Never knew when to stop talking."

Maren heard them. She always heard them. The words didn't sting; they settled. Truth was, she had been born between pages, her mother's oven and her father's fables, and both had burned out early. The Chapel had called it a curse. Maren called it inheritance.

She glanced at Penny, who stood pale and small beside her, caught between loyalty and fear. The candlelight gleamed on Penny's red ribbon, the mark of faith. Maren's wrist was bare.

The Saint drew herself tall again, dignity stitched back into her expression. "Child," she said gently, "faith is not argument. It is surrender."

"Maybe that's the problem," Maren said softly.

No venom. No defiance. Just *fact*.

The Herald, sensing danger, raised his hand. "The Chapel thanks our Saint for her words," he said quickly. "Let us honor the lesson."

The crowd clapped, a thin, awkward sound. The music started again, pipes and drums meant to bury tension under noise.

Penny tugged at Maren's sleeve. "You didn't have to—"

"I know." Maren's gaze stayed fixed on the dais where the Saint of Temptation still stood, thread coiled tight around her hand. "But someone should."

Above them, the lanterns swayed. The stars, unbothered, burned exactly where they pleased.

And though Maren didn't know it yet, she'd just made her first wish: for something beyond the reach of saints.

"Come on," Maren said, forcing lightness into her voice. "Let's not give them more to whisper about."

Penny hesitated, eyes darting to the faces around them. The whispers hadn't stopped; they'd only softened into that hum of false civility the Chapel prized. A woman at the pie stall crossed herself as Maren passed. Another whispered something to her husband and looked away.

Penny's smile was too bright, the kind of light that tried to bleach out a stain. "It'll blow over. You know how people are."

Maren knew exactly how people were. Eldenwick had the memory of wet dough: pliable, but slow to forget the shape of your hands.

She told herself she didn't care, but the truth was more practical than prideful. The bakery depended on those same hands that now pretended to bless themselves in her absence. Every frown in the market, every whispered word about the "Greenbriar girl," could cost them a sale. And Penny, bright and loyal Penny, wanted that bakery to be her future. Maren couldn't afford to look like the curse they said she was. So she swallowed the sting, straightened her shoulders, and chose composure over honesty. Better to be unbothered than unraveling. Better to be strong, if only so Penny could keep believing she was.

She adjusted her shawl and tried to sound casual. "Stay, Penny. You earned it. Go have some mead, dance a little. The town can survive one heretic baker wandering off early."

Penny's brows drew together. "You think I'd let you—"

Maren cut her off with a half-smile, dry as old parchment. "Relax. I'm not running off to hang myself in the chapel. I just need quiet. You're better at the crowds, and they like you better when I'm not around."

"That's not true."

"It is, and it's fine." Maren's tone was even, matter-of-fact. "Someone has to keep them from setting the bakery on fire with their candles, and you're the only one they'll listen to."

Penny hesitated, torn between guilt and the music still playing behind them. The bell on her apron chimed softly with every nervous shift of her weight.

Maren softened, the edge in her voice thinning to warmth. "Go on, sunshine. You've earned one night that isn't about dough or damage control. I'll head up the hill and be back before curfew."

The words landed softly: half jest, half truth. Penny gave her a small, conflicted smile and looked back towards the crowd.

She touched Penny's arm, brief but certain. "Really. Go. I'm just walking, not vanishing."

"Mar—"

But she was already turning away, slipping into the current of bodies until she wasn't part of the festival anymore. The noise dulled to a muted clamor behind her: laughter, coins, the rhythmic clapping of hands keeping time with the music.

The street beyond the square was quieter. Lantern light thinned into narrow gold streaks on the cobbles. Maren walked fast, as if she could outrun the weight in her chest. The air smelled of honeyed smoke and wet stone, the leftovers of celebration. Behind her, Penny would stay and smile and smooth things over because someone had to. Someone always did.

Maren pressed a hand against her own sternum, as though she could stop the familiar tightening there. It wasn't regret, exactly. More like a kind of compression, the way bread collapses under its own heat if you don't give it space to rise.

She'd spoken the truth. She knew that for certain. But truths didn't keep customers coming and ledgers balanced. Words didn't buy flour. Or sugar. Or salt. Words just followed you home, whispering all the ways you'd ruined your chances.

The road sloped upward toward the hill where the chapel graveyard waited. The festival glow faded behind her, replaced by moonlight and the low hum of insects in the grass. Her boots scuffed over gravel. The town looked softer from here; Eldenwick under glass; every roof haloed with gold, the sound of laughter carrying thin through the air.

From this distance, she could almost pretend she wasn't the villain of the evening's fable.

She adjusted her shawl tighter and thought of her mother's steady hands kneading dough, her father's voice threading stories through the air until the whole room leaned closer to listen. Both gone. Both still here. Duty and wonder, staring each other down like rival tradespeople, waiting to see which one she'd pay first.

Maren's throat ached. She hated that.

Maybe Penny was right about her wanting more, about life being something other than work and memory. But want was dangerous here. Want made people whisper. Want had made her father a ruin and her mother a scandal.

The path curved beneath the old yew trees, their branches hung low enough to brush her shoulders. The first marble headstones appeared like pale teeth in the grass.

She slowed, pulse steadying in the hush that only graveyards carried. Somewhere below, a stray firework cracked like delight's little rebellion, but the light didn't reach this far.

Maren's fingers brushed the salt purse in her pocket. Just enough for one offering. A small thing, but something that felt true.

She exhaled, the sound thin in the cold air. "Well," she muttered, mostly to the dark. "Let's see if anyone's still listening."

Then she stepped through the iron gate, leaving the music, the lights, and the whole whispering town behind her.

4

Saint of Sorrow

The gate moaned behind her as it swung shut.

Maren followed the gravel path between crooked rows of stone, her boots crunching softly in the hush. The moon had climbed higher, caught in the fog that drifted low over the hill; it painted the headstones pale and familiar. Eldenwick buried its dead close together, as if crowding could keep the ghosts from wandering.

She passed the baker's row first. Her mother's family, the Greenbriars, their name carved again and again into the markers like a recipe repeated through generations. **Elora Greenbriar, kneader of dough, keeper of warmth. Hendrik Greenbriar, who fed the hungry in lean years.** Someone had left a stale roll wrapped in linen on one of the stones. The smell of yeast had faded to dust.

Maren knelt by the last one, where her mother's name gleamed faintly under the moss: **Lilian Greenbriar, 14th of Bloomturn, 1334 – 16th of Ashfall, 1373. She rose early and loved well.**

The words punched softly, the way only kindness could.

Her mother had been a woman of sunlit mornings and burnt forearms, her laughter the sound of spoons clattering in mixing bowls. There was always warmth around her, always the scent of honeyed bread. Lilian had kept the bakery alive through famine, through taxes, through the ache of being a single woman running a family business. She had also fallen,

30

inconveniently, in love with a traveling storyteller who came through town every winter, his voice full of miracles and his pockets full of nothing.

Maren brushed her thumb across the carved letters. "You could've chosen someone safer," she murmured.

But safety had never been part of her father's stories.

His grave sat a little behind hers, smaller, the stone rougher. **Emmett of Nowhere**, it read. **"He told her the stars would listen."** No family name, no dates. Just the words he'd chosen before he'd faded, when his laughter had turned to silence and his stories to stillness.

Maren could still remember the way he'd looked in those last years: hands ink-stained, eyes turned inward, every day shrinking around him until he was little more than a shadow.

The sickness that took Lilian had come quickly; a fever that no herb or prayer to Delight could fix. And when she went, Emmett had followed, slowly, like a candle that refused to admit it was burning out. Before bed, he'd whisper one verse, an odd, forgotten prayer that the Chapel never recited:

> *"Saint of Sorrow, keeper of what cannot be kept.*
> *Here lies what was loved, and what remains.*
> *Take neither. Guard the ache instead.*
> *Let it hollow us into something that can hold joy again."*

It wasn't the approved prayer. The Chapel would've edited out half the honesty. But this one had weight. It belonged to her.

Maren untied her salt purse and poured a pinch into her palm. She let the crystals fall between her fingers, scattering across the grass.

"I know," she said quietly. "You hated these ceremonies."

A wind moved through the yews, sighing like a tired breath.

"I said too much again," she went on. "They'll call it heresy, same as always. Maybe they're right."

She pressed her palms against her knees, grounding herself in the chill. "I just—" Her voice caught. "You used to say wanting things made us alive.

You said it didn't matter if it hurt. That if we stopped wanting, we'd stop being human. But sometimes I think you made that up because you couldn't stop wanting her."

The truth of it scraped raw in her throat.

Her hand trembled as she reached for her mother's stone. She meant only to steady it, to wipe away the moss she'd missed, but her knees buckled instead. The ground felt too close, too cold, and before she could stop herself, she pressed her forehead against the carved name.

The marble was slick. It smelled faintly of rain and earth and everything she'd lost too early.

"I don't know how to do this without you," she whispered, the words catching like dough too heavy to rise. "I'm so tired of pretending I do."

For a long moment, she stayed there, half kneeling, half folded, until the ache beneath her ribs eased into something quieter. The kind of silence that held you rather than judged you. She hadn't cried at either funeral. She'd been too busy baking, collecting debts, and writing letters to suppliers who never answered. Now, years too late, the tears came sharp and unwelcome, streaking flour-scarred cheeks.

When the worst of it passed, she leaned back against the stone, staring up at the sky. Her father had once told her that grief didn't fade; it just learned to hum under the noise of living. She believed him now.

The bakery, the debts, the whispers, it all felt like the crust left behind after something had already burned. Duty baked solid around her, and yet there were nights she dreamed of taking her father's stories and walking into the world, following his trail past Tideglass and Amberfell and whatever lay beyond the border wars.

But she stayed. She always stayed.

Maren brushed the dirt from her mother's stone, straightened the small clay cup someone had left on top, and set her salt purse beside it for a moment.

"I kept it going," she said. "The bakery. The legacy. The gossip, too, probably."

Her laugh came out thin.

"I just wish…" She stopped. Words felt too fragile.

She stood, tucking the purse back into her pocket. The salt still glimmered faintly on the grass, like starlight that had lost its way.

When she looked down at the two graves, side by side, the baker and the storyteller, earth between them but still close enough to share secrets. Her chest ached with something that wasn't quite grief and wasn't quite envy.

"Sleep well," she whispered. "I'll try to keep wanting."

The wind answered with a low rustle through the leaves, and somewhere behind her, faint and far, the festival bells began again: bright, distant, and indifferent.

Maren turned toward home, the salt taste of memory still sharp on her tongue.

The walk home felt longer than it should have.

The festival noise had thinned to a low hum, the music carrying only in stray echoes that tangled with the sound of her boots. Lanterns guttered along the street, their wicks half-burned, leaving the cobbles silvered by moonlight.

Maren's breath misted in the chill. She pulled her shawl tighter and kept her pace steady, counting her steps as if that rhythm might settle the churn inside her.

Seventeen paces past the apothecary. Twelve past the fountain. Seven past Old Keld's shuttered stall. The kind of counting that meant *control,* or something close enough to fake it.

She wasn't afraid of walking home alone. Eldenwick at night wasn't dangerous, only restless. The saints would say Mischief's creatures roamed at such hours: foxes with gold eyes, trickster spirits eager for trouble.

Maren had met worse than foxes: debt collectors, inspectors, people with opinions.

By the time she reached the bakery door, the street was empty but for the sound of her own key in the lock. The iron scraped, and the bell above the door gave a half-hearted chime as she pushed inside.

Warm air didn't greet her; the ovens had long since cooled. The room smelled faintly of flour, ash, and the ghost of cinnamon. It was the scent of her entire life distilled into one breath.

She stepped inside, set the salt purse on the counter, and exhaled. The silence pressed close, thick and familiar.

Home.

But something was off.

Years of closing alone had tuned her to the bakery's moods. Ovens sighed when content, beams popped when damp. This silence was different. It was *expectant*. She told herself it was fatigue, but her pulse didn't buy it.

It wasn't sound, there was no creak or movement, but a wrongness in the air, the way warmth sometimes clings where it shouldn't. The faint scent of smoke that didn't belong to the ovens.

Her eyes went to the prep table.

The ledger *should* have been there. Right where she had left it before leaving for the festival. Right where she was planning on sitting with it until ungodly hours of the night. Only, it wasn't there. Everything else in the shop seemed mostly untouched, but why would her ledger have gone missing?

No one stole ledgers. Not unless they wanted recipes… or debts. And if some fool thought numbers could be pawned, she almost pitied him. Almost. Anger prickled cleaner than fear; it gave her something to hold.

Maren froze, pulse ticking hard against her throat.

Then, slowly, she reached for the rolling pin on the nearest shelf.

The wood was worn smooth from years of use, heavy enough to break a nose. Her mother's voice surfaced in her head, *"Keep your temper in your hands, not your mouth,"* but the two had never been separate things for long.

She crept across the floor, her boots whispering against flour dust.

Every story her father told had started like this: the heroine creeping toward danger with nothing but wit and poor judgment for armor. Maren had annotated those tales: *"How not to die in Act 1."* Apparently, tonight she was testing the notes.

The moonlight cut through the front window in thin bars, catching the edges of every bowl, every tray. Her shadow stretched long across the counter.

Someone was in her bakery.

A shape leaned against the far counter, half in darkness. Male, by the look of it. Cloaked, though the hood caught the light like silk soaked in moon water. The fabric didn't hang right. It was too fluid, almost alive in the draft that wasn't there.

He turned a page with slow, deliberate care. The faint gleam of silver flickered at his fingers.

The ledger!

"Bold of you," Maren said, voice low and dry, "to break into a bakery and rob the least profitable thing in it."

He didn't lunge, didn't startle, just turned the page like she'd interrupted a hobby. Typical. The dangerous ones never rushed. Her back ached, but adrenaline made a decent second wind.

Maren's grip on the rolling pin tightened. Under the hood, the suggestion of a mouth curved, deliberate. His eyes caught the candlelight as he glanced up, and for a moment, she forgot to breathe.

Gold.

Not the muddy brown-gold of ale or brass, but molten, luminous, and… *wrong*. The kind of color that didn't belong in human eyes.

She blinked hard. Must be a trick of the light.

Magic, she told herself, was for saints and showpeople. Light could lie. Eyes couldn't actually glow; that was exhaustion painting halos where none belonged. Still, her grip shifted tighter on the rolling pin.

"You broke into my bakery," she said flatly, rolling pin lifted like she fully intended to swing it. "Either you leave right now, or I swear to every Spirit I will beat you like egg whites."

Her mother had owned this bakery before her, so she had a few run-ins with intruders. But Maren had a habit of running her mouth. Her mother's advice rattled through her skull: *Never bargain when you're cornered. Hit first, bake later.* She raised the pin a little higher, just in case maternal wisdom still counted as protection.

The corner of his mouth curved, slow and infuriating. "You're quick with threats."

"And you're slow at taking hints," she shot back. "What kind of thief breaks into the one shop in town that doesn't keep offerings out for Mischief?"

That earned her the faintest tilt of his head, amusement flickering in those too-bright eyes. "You don't leave honey in the hearth?"

"I run a business, not a superstition," Maren said. "The Saints already take their share in taxes. I'll be damned before I tip the trickster, too."

"Careful," he murmured. "He might take that personally."

She snorted. "Let him. I'm a heretic, remember? Bastard-born, unblessed, and statistically overdue for divine punishment. Get in line."

For the briefest moment, his amusement flickered into something more challenging to name, like *recognition*. His voice softened, deliberate. "He'd like you."

"Good for him," she snapped. "Now get out before I introduce your skull to pastry science."

He chuckled, low and quiet, and began to circle the counter, moving with that deliberate stillness of someone who knew he was faster than you anyway. A coin flickered between his fingers, each spin catching what little light lingered.

"Tell me," he drawled, "what exactly was your plan with that?" He nodded at the rolling pin. "Bludgeon me into buying bread?"

"If you're lucky," she shot back.

"And if I'm not?"

Maren bared her teeth in something not quite a smile. "Then I find out how many times it takes to knock sense into a trespasser."

That earned her another grin. Not friendly. Not mocking, either. Amused. Intrigued. As if she were playing the right game without realizing it.

He flipped the coin once more, higher this time, letting it linger in the air just long enough for her pulse to quicken. When it landed, it made no sound at all.

The silence stretched.

Maren exhaled slowly, refusing to let him see her nerves. "You're not from around here," she said finally.

"No," he agreed, voice smooth. "And neither are you. Not really."

Her stomach twisted. She masked it with a scoff. "Bold assumption from someone about to get chased out with baked goods."

His eyes gleamed. "You think you're the one chasing."

Maren tightened her grip on the rolling pin. "You've got about three seconds to explain why you're in my shop before I test whether flour's good for cleaning blood."

He didn't flinch. In fact, his grin deepened, sharp and amused, like she was a favorite line he'd been waiting for someone to deliver.

"Why?" he asked softly, coin flickering between his fingers. "Because it's yours?"

She blinked, thrown. "Excuse me?"

"This place. These walls. These loaves all taste the same after a while." His voice curled around the air like smoke. "It's your cage, isn't it?"

The word hit too close.

Her jaw snapped tight. "It's my bakery."

"Mm. Same thing." He strolled closer, boots silent against the flour-dusted floorboards, golden eyes alight with mock sympathy. "It was your mother's once, wasn't it? Now it's your inheritance. Your obligation."

The mention snagged like a hook. Her mother's hands still lived in every dented pan, every burn mark. This place wasn't an obligation; it was proof she'd survived someone worth loving. She hated that he could make it sound like chains.

Maren's heart lurched, but she forced a smirk. "What are you, the town clerk? You break into bakeries to remind people they're miserable?"

"No," he said, and for just a heartbeat his grin softened into something dangerous. "I break into bakeries to remind people they're meant for more." He flipped the coin again, light bending wrong across the silver. "And because some cages… rattle louder than others."

Something in her chest stumbled. She hated it.

"Wrong shop," she said quickly, turning back toward the stairs. "Try the tavern across the square. I hear they've got ale and gullible ears."

The coin spun high. She heard it even though it made no sound when it landed.

"If you could have it," he said, voice lower now, intimate, like the question was meant for her bones instead of her ears. "What you desire most. Would you ask for it?"

Maren stopped on the step. The air shifted, as if the bakery itself was holding its breath.

"That's… a very heavy question from a trespasser," she said, forcing nonchalance into her tone.

"Most people never get asked," he murmured. "Fewer still answer honestly."

Her throat tightened. She kept her back to him, clutching the railing, rolling pin still tucked in her other hand. Practical desires bubbled up: ten hours of sleep, a week without burns, customers who didn't complain about seeds. But underneath them, something older stirred. Something she never admitted, not even to Penny.

She shook her head, hard. "If this is a robbery, you're terrible at it."

He chuckled. "Not a robbery. An offer."

Offers always cost more than theft. At least thieves took something tangible. Promises took the parts you didn't realize were for sale.

She turned then, glaring at him with all the sharpness she could muster. "I don't make deals with thieves."

He smiled lazily, leaning back against the counter as if he'd already won. "You don't have to. You already told me."

Maren's chest clenched. "I didn't say anything."

"No," he agreed, golden eyes glinting as he twirled the coin one final time, catching it in a palm that closed like a secret. "But your heart did."

The silence that followed pressed in too thick, too heavy. Maren's pulse roared in her ears, but she refused to give him the satisfaction of backing down.

"Get out," she said coldly.

And just like that, he was gone. No sound, no door, not even a trace, only the faint smell of cedar and the coin's echo still shimmering in her bones.

She stood frozen, the rolling pin poised, as if she still might need it. For a long moment, she just listened. Nothing. No footsteps. No bell. Only the bakery creaking in its old bones, settling like it always did at night. The smell of sugar and cinnamon clung to the air, steady and grounding.

"Hallucination," she muttered, though her voice cracked. "Overworked. That's all."

She turned and headed up the stairs, but her hand trembled on the railing. She still carried the rolling pin clutched tightly in the other hand like a talisman.

She threw the bolt on her bedroom door and leaned against it, breathing hard.

Her hand was white-knuckled around the rolling pin. She set it down on her nightstand, as though having it within arm's reach might still matter if the cloaked lunatic decided to reappear.

The candlelight flickered across the ceiling beams, shadows stretching long and restless.

She tried to shake him off. Just a trespasser. Just some smug idiot with a flair for dramatics and gold-painted eyes that were probably a trick of the light. Except she couldn't stop replaying his words. His grin. The coin vanished like it had slipped out of the world.

It's your cage, isn't it?

She scowled, dragging off her apron and tossing it over the back of a chair. It's *my* bakery, she thought fiercely, as if he were still listening. It's mine. And Penny's. We keep it alive. We make it work.

Her chest pinched. Penny. What if he came back while she was here alone? What if he showed up tomorrow while Penny was working the counter, flashing those molten eyes and that too-smooth grin? Penny would probably offer him tea.

The thought knotted her stomach.

She kicked off her shoes, crawled onto the narrow bed, and tried to force her mind blank. Tried counting recipes in her head. Tried listing every goat-related incident in Eldenwick history. Nothing worked. His question kept circling, low and insistent:

"What do you desire most?"

Finally, with a frustrated groan, she reached for the comfort she always did when the world wouldn't shut up: one of her father's old storybooks.

The leather was cracked, the spine bent, and the pages swollen with stains. Margins scribbled full of her younger handwriting: angry edits, doodled daggers in a heroine's hand, alternate endings scrawled over the printed ones. *The fox betrays her here,* she'd written once, years ago, *but mine doesn't trust him long enough to fall for it.*

She balanced the candle beside it and flipped to a tale she knew by heart: *The Girl Who Bargained With the Moon.* A girl, poor and plain, who tricked a king with riddles, spun silver into laughter, and danced barefoot on rooftops until dawn. A girl who was clever, bold, and *alive.*

Maren traced the ink with her finger, slow and reverent. She envied that girl. Envied all of them. Every impossible heroine her father used to read to her by firelight, every dream she'd rewritten in the margins.

"I want that," she whispered. "I want *wonder.*"

The candle guttered. For a heartbeat, the flame stretched tall and strange, casting shadows that bent the wrong way. In the polished side of her teacup on the nightstand, her reflection wavered and grinned back at her with someone else's mouth.

Gold eyes, sinful and mysterious.

She jolted upright, but when she blinked, it was only her face again. Only the candle. Only the silence of the bakery settling into sleep.

But a faint sound lingered in the dark. A coin, clinking once against wood, before vanishing into nothing.

Maren's skin prickled. She slammed the book shut and pulled the covers over her head like a child, scowling at herself the entire time.

"Idiot," she muttered. "Absolute idiot."

But no matter how tightly she shut her eyes, she couldn't shake the feeling that somewhere in the shadows, someone had just taken her at her word.

5

Just a Breeze

Maren looked like death, and not the elegant kind.

Her reflection in the bakery window was a disaster: hair a dark, curly snarl that had refused every braid she'd attempted, skin still dusted faintly with flour no amount of scrubbing could coax out, and silver-blue eyes that glared back at her.

Her mother's eyes.

Clear, striking, and wasted on someone running on three hours of restless sleep.

She yanked the shutters open, flooding her room with pale morning light. Dust motes scattered through the air like they'd been caught committing crimes. The scent of yeast lingered heavy in the rafters, clinging to her hair, her clothes, her very skin. Even after a scalding scrub last night to rid herself of the flour caked in her scalp, she swore she'd never smell normal again. Bread had soaked so far into her pores she'd probably be buried rising.

She shoved her arms through the sleeves of her plain work dress: linen gray, patched at the elbows, apron already streaked from yesterday's battles. She tied it too tight at the waist, daring it to hold her together.

Maren had tried to sleep. Gods, she'd tried. But every time she shut her eyes, she saw him: the coin flashing between long fingers, those impossible golden eyes, the smirk that lingered.

Trespasser. Villain. Figment. Whatever he was, he had stolen her night.

She carried the rolling pin back downstairs and leaned it back against the counter. She stared at it briefly, a ridiculous kind of comfort, before quickly looking away with a scoff.

The street outside was already up to its usual morning clatter: goats bleating, hawkers shouting, the constable's unmistakable voice. Inside, the quiet pressed. Not empty. Expectant. The ovens clicked like tired hearts.

She told herself it was normal.

She told herself a lot of things.

Her thoughts drifted to Penny. The festival last night.

They hadn't been on their best of terms last night. She would no doubt be bursting through the doors any minute now, and Maren would have to face her and everything else Penny would have had to answer to after she left.

Penny probably didn't even know she had gone to visit her parents. If she had told her, she probably would have wanted to tag along and offer her mother a sprig of rosemary.

A respectable girl. A complete foil to Maren. Her mother would have loved her.

"Work," she reminded herself.

Feelings were useless. They clung too stickily, constantly clouding judgment and stealing energy. She had a family business to run, and she did not have time or coin to worry about hypotheticals.

She pulled out the flour, salt, and the jar of starter, which smelled like a friendly ghost, and began to measure. Numbers were honest. They did not gossip, they did not bless, they did not punish. They only added up.

Seventeen counts of whisk. Twelve of scrape. Seven of fold.

The dough gathered slowly on the hook of her hands. Heel, turn, fold. Heat bled into it from her skin. Control returned in inches. Her shoulders unhitched.

Maren kneaded like she meant to bruise it. Heel, fold, turn, and again. If she pushed hard enough, maybe she could pound the memory of golden eyes out of her head. Maybe she could forget the sound of that coin cutting the silence in two. But every time her mind slipped, the question crept back:

"What do you desire most?"

She ground her teeth. Heel, fold, turn. Harder this time. Her arms ached, her palms burned, and still she kept going, because stopping meant remembering. And she could not afford to remember.

Heel. Fold. Turn.

The dough warmed.

Progress.

Then it yielded too easily. Its surface smoothed under her fingers like silk hit by a breeze. She lifted her palms off instinct, the way skin jerks from a hot pan.

The lump made a slight, traitorous shift.

Her breath hitched, and her throat made a small squeak, as if she were frightened.

She set her palms flat on the wood and breathed until the embarrassment passed. Yeast moved. That was its job. She had notes. She had charts. She could recite entire studies on fermentation if cornered.

The room hummed once, below hearing. But she could feel the subtle wrongness under the surface. She knew this bakery almost as well as she understood herself. It was instinct at this point.

"Not happening," she muttered, trying to reason against every wrong feeling she was having. "Absolutely not."

She reached for the salt to prove the world still understood cause and effect. The grains skated out smoothly. Her hand did not shake. She dusted. The fall of white looked normal.

The bell over the door clanged. Maren jumped so hard her hip slammed into the table.

"Good morning!" Penny's voice rang through the shop. She bustled in, tray balanced under one arm, today's apron was a riotous red stitched with wildflowers that somehow made the color louder. Fresh thyme threaded her braid like little green flags tucked between golden strands.

Maren instinctively slid sideways, body between friend and dough, as if called to a gate. "You're early."

"Someone has to keep this place lively," Penny said cheerfully, untying her shawl. She set the tray on the counter and surveyed Maren's scowl. "What's wrong with your face?"

Maren blinked. "What's wrong with yours?" she retorted.

"Deflection," Penny said, satisfied. "You look like someone tried to mug you."

"Accurate." Maren wiped her flour-dusted palms on her apron, which did nothing except add new stains to old ones. The motion sent a puff of powder into the air, except the dust didn't fall quite right. It lingered, caught in the light like it had forgotten gravity.

Penny tilted her head. "Wait, what?" Her face fell by a fraction. "You didn't actually get mugged, did you?"

Maren hesitated. Her mouth opened, then shut again. Penny didn't need that weight dropped on her. What would she even say? *Oh, by the way, a golden-eyed stranger broke into the bakery last night, flipped a coin that vanished into thin air, and asked me what I desired most like he was a deranged fortune-teller?*

Yeah. No.

She forced a smirk. "Rough night," she said instead.

Maren turned toward the counter, hoping motion might disguise her confusion. It didn't, of course. The spoon in the mixing bowl had begun to stir on its own in slow, lazy circles, as if it were bored. She dropped a rag over it, leaned a hip on the bowl, and smiled tightly. "How was the festival?"

That got Penny glowing again. "Oh! You should've stayed. After the Saint of Temptation—well, after you said your *thing*—they went right into the Saints' Dance, and the fireworks started early because someone set the ale tent on fire—"

"Charming," Maren said, eyes fixed on the rag that was now twitching like the spoon underneath wanted out.

"—and there was this troupe from Silkwell! With ribbons! Real silk, Mar. They said they blessed each strand under Delight's moon. You'd have loved it."

Maren forced a sound that might have been interest. The light had shifted; it wasn't morning light anymore but something softer, gold-flecked and moving. The rafters glowed faintly.

She rubbed her temple. Maybe she was just sleep-deprived enough to hallucinate luminescent hygiene problems.

Penny kept talking, her hands fluttering as she reenacted the dance. "And then the mead competition! Old Keld nearly fell into the judge's trough again. Honestly, it's not a festival until someone drowns in mead."

"Local tradition," Maren said absently. She edged toward the oven, which was humming under its breath. Not burning, not creaking, but *humming*! Something low and tuneful, like someone testing a note. She placed her palm against the stone. The warmth pulsed back at her once, gently, like a heartbeat checking for hers.

She snatched her hand away. "Cold," she said too loudly.

Penny blinked mid-story. "What?"

"Nothing. You were saying something about drownings."

"Oh! Right, and Mistress Ryn unveiled new tonics. 'Essence of Serenity,' though she spilled half of it on her husband, and he serenaded a goat afterward, so maybe it worked?" Penny giggled, oblivious to how Maren's eyes kept darting to every flicker in the room.

A row of cooling racks gleamed sharply at the other end of the counter. The tins lined up straighter on their own, edges kissing like soldiers at inspection. Maren casually bumped the counter with her hip to misalign them again. They slid obediently back into place.

She coughed. "Impressive marketing, the goat."

Penny laughed harder, warmth flooding the space.

The space seemed to respond. The smell of yeast swelled richer, sweeter, as if her amusement had summoned it. Maren's pulse spiked. That wasn't possible. Smells didn't obey tone of voice. She fumbled for something rational. Maybe she'd mismeasured something. Maybe she'd slept too little. Or, maybe she'd caught a fever.

"Anyway," Penny said, catching her breath, "people were still talking about you after you left. I think Mrs. Aldren called it a 'public lapse in decorum.'"

Maren groaned. "She would."

"But others said it was refreshing! Brave, even. One woman called you 'spirited,' which, given the Saints, might've been literal."

"Lovely." Maren slid a tray onto the rack, nearly missed the shelf, and caught it by sheer reflex. The metal was warm, though the oven hadn't been lit. She stared at her own reflection warped in its shine; a ghost with flour freckles and disbelief under both eyes.

Penny reached for a measuring cup, and Maren practically lunged, intercepting it mid-air. "I'll handle that," she said, voice an octave too high.

Penny frowned. "Are you… sure?"

"Positive. You have a festival hangover. I can see the joy radiating off you." She nudged Penny back toward the counter with her hip, plastering on a smile that felt like it might crack.

The sugar jar behind her gave a quiet rattle. Just once. Enough to make her flinch.

"Anyway," she said quickly, "Delight herself must've blessed you, if you remember that much detail."

Penny preened a little, pleased. "Do you think so?"

"Oh, absolutely," Maren said, even as the jar lid lifted half an inch and set itself down again. "You were born to represent uncontainable enthusiasm."

Penny laughed, tossing her braid. "That's the nicest insult you've ever given me."

Maren's answering smile didn't reach her eyes. She was counting: one, two, three. The number of things currently disobeying physics. The spoon, the tins, the oven, the jar. Maybe the rafters if she admitted what she'd seen. Her mind hunted for explanations like a feral dog: tremors, drafts, exhaustion, divine punishment for blasphemy. Take your pick.

"Maybe Delight did take notice," Penny mused, dreamy now. "Imagine! A blessing on our little bakery. Wouldn't that be wonderful?"

Maren's throat went dry. The last time she'd heard someone say *blessing* with that kind of reverence, the Saint of Temptation had been onstage, warning the crowd. She thought of the saint's story, of pride punished, of a girl reaching too high. She'd laughed then, and told the Saint the gods had terrible design skills.

Now, staring at her own reflection in the tray, she couldn't remember the punchline. The warped metal caught her face in molten glints; for half a heartbeat, her eyes looked gilded.

She forced a laugh that felt too sharp for her own throat. "Sure. Nothing says divine favor like unpaid invoices."

Penny snorted, exactly as Maren hoped she would, and went to fetch a broom. Relief flickered, momentary and traitorous. Banter was safer than theology.

As her back turned, Maren pressed a flour-dusted hand to the counter. The wood felt alive, faintly humming under her palm, as though something unseen had just answered *yes*.

She pulled back fast, wiping her hands on her apron until the sensation dulled. Her brain scrambled for logic: maybe the ovens had stayed lit overnight, maybe the floorboards were resonating from street carts. Maybe, maybe, maybe.

She risked another glance around the bakery. The air had changed. Not visibly, not enough to name, but *something*. Maren knew that much.

This was the kind of thing that happened right before a curse in a storybook.

Penny turned back, broom in hand, and paused mid-step. "You look like you swallowed a wasp."

"Just thinking," Maren said quickly. She was already moving. She forced herself into motion, busywork being the oldest religion she knew. Wipe the table. Straighten the rack. Pretend.

When she looked up again, Penny was watching her with the wary affection of someone who had seen this exact look right before Maren threatened to strangle the tax inspector with a baguette.

Penny's eyes narrowed, broom forgotten now. "What are you hiding?"

Maren froze mid-motion, one hand hovering over a mixing bowl. "Nothing." The word clattered in the air like dropped cutlery. She grabbed a rag, wiped the already-clean counter, then the same spot again for good measure.

Penny crossed her arms. "Maren."

Think. Her mind scrambled for excuses: humidity, bad ingredients, heat from the ovens. Nothing fit. The air itself was almost suffocating. It was thicker now, sweeter, humming with a pulse she could nearly match to her heartbeat. The hairs on her arms stood up.

She forced a crooked smile. "If I tell you the dough's possessed, will you exorcise it?"

"That's not funny." Penny's tone faltered between concern and warning, the way people talk to dogs before storms.

"Neither is waking up at dawn to bake rolls," Maren shot back, still scrubbing. Humor was armor; keep swinging it, and maybe no one would see the panic underneath.

Penny didn't laugh. The silence swelled until it seemed as though the rafters were listening. Her expression softened, worry threading through the brightness of her smile. "You're scaring me a little."

Good, Maren thought wildly. *Maybe that'll make you leave before it gets worse.*

But the idea hollowed her stomach. Penny leaving meant being alone with whatever this was. The seemingly sentient dough, the hum, the strange warmth bleeding from the counters. Alone with the punishment she clearly deserved. Heresy didn't go unnoticed forever; she'd mocked the Saints right in front of the crowd. Maybe Mischief hadn't forgotten. Maybe this was the price for refusing honey on the hearth.

She straightened too fast. "I'm fine."

Penny stepped closer, cautious now. "Then why are you standing like someone's about to swing at you?"

"Because someone's asking too many questions," Maren muttered.

Behind her, the dough sighed. Not loudly, not even humanly, just a faint release of air that sounded eerily close to breath.

Her spine locked.

Penny leaned, quick and curious, trying to peek around her shoulder.

Maren's body moved before thought: she caught Penny's wrist mid-reach, grip firm enough to startle both of them. "Don't," she said, sharper than she meant.

Penny blinked. "Why not?"

Because she couldn't risk it. Because one look at that impossible, breathing dough, and Penny would bolt straight to the chapel, or worse, the constable. They'd call it corruption. They'd burn her bakery and her name together.

Maren's mind raced through all the wrong kinds of logic: maybe if she ignored it, the miracle would rot on its own. Maybe if she acted normal long enough, the Saints would believe she'd learned her lesson and take the curse back. Her hands itched to grab the ledger, to write it down, to make sense of it like her father's stories, but writing about it might make it real.

So she laughed instead, brittle and too loud. "Starter's moody today. Overfed it. Happens all the time."

Penny's frown deepened. "Since when does yeast breathe?"

Maren released her wrist, tried for flat calm. "Since always. You just don't listen close enough."

Penny studied her for a long, quiet beat, that knowing tilt of her head that said *I've seen you lie better than this.* Maren busied herself with rearranging bowls that were already in perfect rows. If she stood still, she might scream.

Penny sighed and shook her head, letting it drop. "Fine. Be cryptic. But don't snap at me when it explodes."

"It won't explode," Maren said automatically, even though the word *explode* seemed to test its luck in the rafters. Her voice came out thin. "It's dough, Penny, not gunpowder."

Penny chuckled and turned away, humming as she fussed with the tray of crocks near the window. The tune wobbled between notes, half-cheerful, half-prayer.

Maren stared down at the table. The dough lay there, placid, smug. She wanted to punch it. Or maybe apologize to it. Her palms still tingled from the last time she'd touched it, the way it had shifted beneath her hands. Obedient. And *alive.*

She forced a steadying breath. "You're fine," she muttered. "You're tired.

You're hallucinating sentient carbohydrates."

A lie with decent potential.

Then—movement. Not the dough this time. The flour along the opposite edge of the table stirred as if someone had brushed it with a fingertip. Maren froze. No breeze, no open shutters. Just a slow curl, grain by grain, spiraling into motion.

She stared. Her pulse ticked like a metronome gone wild.

The flour began to trace itself into a word. Not written but *etched,* as if invisible fingers were dragging through the dust with idle amusement.

M

A lazy loop.

O

Grain by grain, the swirl tightened.

R...

Her mouth went dry. She watched the rest unfurl:

Morning, darling.

Maren's heart lurched so hard it almost felt like the bakery's hum had synced to it. For a second, she couldn't move, couldn't breathe. Then her instincts kicked in—

She slammed her elbow down, scattering the message into a meaningless smear of white.

"Not happening," she hissed under her breath. Her elbow print looked like evidence of a crime.

Penny was still humming near the front, reorganizing the display trays like the room wasn't haunted.

Maren pressed her palms to the counter. The flour stuck to her skin, cool and soft, like something reaching back. Her mind scrambled to fill in explanations. Maybe she'd drifted off standing up. Maybe she'd written it herself. Perhaps this was how curses announced themselves —politely?

Except for the word *darling.* That wasn't how the Chapel described the Spirits. That was *him.*

The thief. Cloaked. Golden eyes. The coin.

Her pulse thudded harder. The wish she'd whispered last night, *"I want wonder,"* slipped back through her memory. She'd muttered it half asleep, a stupid, wistful thing over her father's storybook. The page had flickered, candlelight stretching strangely.

She stared at the bowl. "You didn't," she whispered.

The dough gave a faint twitch, like a laugh muffled under cloth.

"You did," she breathed.

Panic and awe braided tight in her chest. It wasn't a curse. It was worse—he'd *heard* her! He'd stolen it.

What a thieving little bastard! she thought bitterly.

The kettle on the stove whistled low, though it hadn't been lit. Steam rose from the spout, curling into a single phrase that faded almost as quickly as it formed:

You're welcome.

Maren backed up until her shoulder hit the shelf. "Raven spare me," she whispered, though she doubted anyone was listening.

But part of her, that reckless, curious part, that still lived in old storybooks whispered back anyway.

I asked for wonder. He delivered.

The thought was dangerous. It tasted sweet.

6

A Blessing

Maren was smiling.

An actual, teeth-baring, unadvised smile. Relief loosened the knot at the base of her skull.

Not cursed.

Not smote. Not even lightly scorched.

Blessed.

The word slotted into place with a tiny, delicious click.

Penny was always the one people called Delight-touched, laughing bright enough to make the bells over the door ring on their own. Maren had never been anyone's blessing. She was bread and invoices: heat and hands. Useful, not chosen. Yet here the bakery breathed under her palms like a large, pleased animal, and every shelf sat at attention as if waiting to obey.

Which Spirit would claim *this*?

Temptation, maybe. Her parents had been accused of that one often enough. Love without marriage, a daughter born first, and explanations later.

Or Mischief? The one no one liked to admit they prayed to.

Who else carried a coin like that?

She dismissed the thought before it finished forming. The thief was a trespasser, not a Saint's echo. Still, her pulse quickened, a little traitor.

All right. Work. She could be blessed and useful. There were rolls to braid, loaves for the market, and the town to feed. If the Spirits were offering efficiency, she would not be rude.

She reached for the ledger to tally flour and salt like she always did when the world wobbled. Numbers steadied things. The leather cover was cool under her palm. When she opened it, the familiar columns waited: date, cost, profit, loss.

She exhaled, pencil poised.

The ink at the top line loosened. Lifted and slid into a curve like a fish in water.

Maren went still.

Letters gathered themselves with lazy confidence, black strokes unhooking and strolling into new shapes. A hand that wasn't hers, elegant and amused, rewrote her morning.

Better than you expected, isn't it?

Her pulse leaped. She snapped the book shut so fast the ribbon marker bit her thumb.

"Did the ledger just snap at you?" Penny called from the front. She had one foot on the lower shelf, stretching to rearrange the display, thyme flags nodding as if to second the question.

Maren pasted on a tired smile. "It has opinions." She tucked the ledger under a flour sack like she was suffocating a snake. "And so do I. Trays. We need six for the market."

Penny grabbed two. "Only six? With this smell, we could sell to the Pale Confederacy."

"Tempting," Maren said, lining tins that somehow lined themselves. She told herself the neat click was her doing. "But I'd rather not provoke another holy war with bread."

"Historically, wars have started over less," Penny chirped, already polishing the glass. She looked lost in thought for a moment, then spoke again. "We should paint a bell on the sign. Invite Delight properly."

"We have a bell," Maren said. "It clangs like a goat fell down a well."

"We could hang another. Smaller. Pretty." Penny countered.

"Too inviting. And I refuse to invite Mrs. Aldren."

Penny threw her head back in laughter. The notion warmed Maren at the edges. A bell for Delight. A tidy column of black ink where red used to live. Honey they could afford to pour without counting drops. She slid dough from bowl to board. It yielded like silk again, a clean, shameless pleasure that tightened her throat.

"Do you hear that?" Penny stilled, laughter ebbing like the tide.

Maren listened. The oven hummed, low and content, like a hymn. The cooling rack answered with a faint, answering ring. The whole room was in conversation.

"Wind," Maren lied. "Through the shutters."

"There is no wind," Penny said, soft, delighted, a little afraid. "Maren. The bakery feels… different this morning. That bakery blessing!"

Blessings, in the stories, always came with clauses and clever wording. Maren rolled a braid anyway, fingers moving faster than thought. She set it aside. It shimmered, as if brushed with egg before it had earned the shine.

Do not grin, she told her mouth. *Do not look like you like this.*

Her father's old storybook sat cracked on the corner, where she had left it the day before. The page still lay open. Maren glanced at a line she knew by heart.

Except the line wasn't there.

The text rippled, letters unlatching and reforming with shameless ease.

Careful with wishes, baker.

Her stomach dropped and lifted at once. She shut the book very gently, as if it might bite. "Penny, hand me the peel," she said, voice even.

Penny paused, eyes bright. "When did you start being polite to tools?"

"Today," Maren said. "I am modeling growth."

She looked at the counter, where coins lived, where orders lived, where the little future she now wanted so badly might live. She imagined a painted door sign with their names, *Greenbriar & Thornwick,* two ribbons of color, a bell that chimed pretty, not loud. She imagined market days where barter did not mean turnips for three rolls and a sermon. Honey purchases without counting. Firewood deliveries on time.

Wonder and duty. Together. Both legacies intertwined into one.

The ledger squirmed in its flour shroud.

Penny stood, reading the room the way she read people. "You are… oddly chipper for someone who hates mornings."

"New philosophy," Maren said, shaping another braid that obediently perfected itself. "I'm trying optimism. It looks terrible on me, and I am doing it anyway."

Penny's mouth quirked. "It looks good."

"It looks expensive," Maren said, but the words came out softer. She slid the first braid toward the oven. The door unlatched without a hand. Heat rolled out, slow and approving, cinnamon unstitching into the air like a festival morning.

Penny's eyes went wide. "Oh."

"Mm," Maren said, pretending this was normal while every hair on her arms stood up. "Set the samples. Small squares. If we sell out by noon, I can skip the afternoon run to the apothecary and still make the Chapel honey tithe."

"You are going to tithe?" Penny nearly dropped the knife.

Maren smirked. "If we are going to be scandalous blasphemers, we can at least be polite."

Penny tried to suppress a grin and failed utterly.

The braid in the oven sighed, a sound like pride. The glass fogged briefly, then cleared, and in the warm blur a phrase wrote itself across the inside pane.

Why choose when you can take it all?

Maren set her jaw. "We are throwing him out of the marketing meeting."

"Who?" Penny blinked.

"The steam," Maren said. "It is getting ideas."

Maren jerked her head toward the oven. "Steam. Just… steam."

Penny blinked, then laughed, quick and nervous. "You're talking to steam now?"

Maren forced a smirk. "Better conversationalist than most of our customers."

Penny's gaze skimmed from kettle to oven to ledger lump. Color rose in her cheeks, not fear, not quite. Awe, threaded with practicality. "Well, if the steam wants to help, we are not saying no. You cannot offend a miracle."

"Watch me," Maren said, but she was smiling now, traitor heart and all. Because she could see it: a week without scalded wrists, nothing owed, a bakery that sang back when she sang to it. Wonder and duty, at last, braided neatly together.

The bell over the door gave its goat-in-a-well clang.

Early customers.

"Places," Maren said, wiping her hands on her apron like a general, even as the oven purred her name in heat. "Let's earn our blessing."

Both girls stiffened.

Old Keld shuffled in, smelling faintly of turnip and pipe smoke. His basket swung from one elbow, stuffed with vegetables in various stages of regret. He stopped just inside the door, his rheumy eyes sweeping the shop while his nose lifted like a hound.

"Smells better than usual," he said.

"Thanks," Maren said flatly. Her mouth, treacherously, wanted to smile.

He drifted to the display. The braid on the board wore a lacquered sheen that looked brushed with butter, though she had not touched a glaze. The crust had that thin, crisp promise that crackled if you breathed on it. Heat pooled off the loaf like warm sun on a winter sill.

Keld squinted. "Never seen bread shine like that."

"New Greenbriar recipe." Penny chirped, bright as a bell. She slid the loaf toward him and tore a small corner loose. "Taste."

He pinched the piece. He bit. Chewed. Stopped.

His eyes went wide, then wet. "By the gods." He swallowed like a prayer had surprised him on the way down. "That's the best bread I've ever tasted."

Maren folded her arms and leaned on the counter, unimpressed in posture only. Inside, something golden uncoiled. "Careful, Keld. Compliments cost extra."

He dug out a coin so quickly that it clinked against the counter. More than usual. He left with a dazed look, muttering about miracles.

Penny beamed. "You heard him. Miracles."

Miracles, Maren thought, watching steam drift in a pale ribbon from the torn edge. Not the chapel kind. The work kind. Her kind. The oven's low hum curled through the rafters and lingered at her ear like a promise.

"They love you now," a voice purred, very near.

She nearly jumped out of her skin.

His voice. Though she did not see him now, and had not spoken to her like this since last night. The word love slid under her ribs with skilled hands. She shoved a tray into place harder than she meant. Metal rang. Penny's eyes flicked over, a question she pretended not to see.

The bell clanged again.

Mistress Ryn bustled in, all brisk skirts and the permanent frown of an apothecary's wife who had learned where pain lived. She halted mid-step as the scent hit her, cinnamon and sugar and warmth.

"Morning," she said, and then, pointedly, "What is that?"

"Bread," Maren said. "Radical concept."

Ryn ignored her. She leaned in and inhaled, as if testing a tonic. "It smells divine."

"It *is* divine," Penny said, glowing. "Try it."

Maren watched Penny's hands, deft with the knife, generous with the slice, joy tipping her taller. This was Penny's element: people, delight, the clean exchange of something made well. For a breath, Maren let herself see it the same way. The oven's warmth spilling like honey. The braid gleaming as if it remembered sunlight from some other world. Penny's grin was bright enough to turn cynics into customers.

"Look how happy she is," the voice murmured into her ear, softer now, amused. "And you. You are smiling. You could keep her this way. Forever."

Maren's smirk snapped back into place like armor. "Careful," she said under her breath. "Smiling ruins the mystique."

Ryn glanced up. "What?"

"Nothing," Maren said quickly. "Try the roll."

She tore one in half. Steam breathed out, spiced and heady, carrying notes of orange peel from the bundle that had opened itself, along with the warm bite of fresh cinnamon. The crumb was tender and laced with fine air, the kind of softness that came from perfect proofing rather than luck. Ryn tasted. For once, she did not complain. Coins followed, crisp with satisfaction.

The bell chimed again.

Then again.

Eldenwick worked by rumor, and rumor adored sugar.

The tailor's twins arrived next, bickering over hem lengths, and left arguing about whose crumb was bigger.

The candle maker's apprentice drifted in next on a cloud of beeswax, nearly tripped over his own boots, and bought three loaves with a dazed grin.

Mrs. Aldren stepped through the door with disapproval already loaded and stopped short as the scent hit her. Her mouth shut. That alone was worth a tithe.

Maren kept the counter. Knife steady, voice level. Slice, wrap, pass, take coin. The rhythm soothed even as it sped. But her hands lingered more than they should have. Every time her fingers brushed dough, the surface seemed to respond: seams sealed neatly under the pads of her thumbs, braids tightened obediently with a single coaxing turn, crusts blushed deeper at her touch as if eager to impress her.

Customers gasped the way people gasp in chapels.

"Admit it," the thief crooned through the hum of voices. "You wanted this."

She kept cutting. The blade whispered through a loaf so cleanly that steam hissed out like a pleased sigh. "I wanted sleep," she muttered.

Penny, catching only the mutter, laughed. "Don't we all."

* * *

The shop swelled.

They were a two-person tide, and still the room did not drown.

The oven's song stayed even, as if an invisible hand tended fuel and breath.

Flour lifted in the sunlit window and fell in slow constellations that would not settle on anything that needed to stay clean. The bell over the door, traitorous creature, learned to chime on the half beat between transactions so as not to jar the rhythm.

Maren moved through the rhythm of it all like someone who'd finally kicked open her own cage. Every motion flowed, and for once, nothing fought her back. The ledger no longer loomed like a verdict. The shelves looked fuller, the air itself generous. She could almost see the future taking shape behind the counter: bread that bought rest, warmth that wasn't borrowed, a door sign painted without debt hanging over it. For the first time in years, the story felt like hers again.

Costless things do not exist, her stubborn brain said.

Profitable things do, said her hands.

Another pair came in, then another.

She lost track of names. Penny sparkled, calling people dearest and darling like the Saints, but making it sound like she meant it. She pressed samples into palms and remembered whose aunt could not chew crust and whose son would only eat the ends. Delighted people tipped. The till grew heavy. Maren's shoulder loosened another degree.

"Even your ledger can breathe again," the thief said, lazy with satisfaction.

Her jaw ticked. "The ledger does not bake," she said to the knife.

The knife did not answer. The loaf did, splitting with a polite crack to reveal a crumb that belonged in a painting.

Penny bumped her hip. "At this rate, we can skip the market tomorrow," she whispered, eyes bright. "You could sleep in."

Maren looked at the line, the glow, the impossible efficiency that made everything taste like victory. Sleep seemed like a waste of momentum. She shrugged. "Or we could sell out twice."

Penny's laugh skated across the counter like a blessing. For once, the word did not make Maren flinch.

"Another roll," someone called. "Whatever that one is that tastes like winter mornings."

"Cinnamon twist," Penny sang, already moving.

"Two loaves for my sister," another said, then added shyly, "and one for me."

Maren cut. Baked. Wrapped. The paper crackled. Coins clinked. She let herself enjoy the sound long enough to commit it to memory.

"See?" the voice whispered, nearer now, pleased as a cat finding cream. "Look how simple it can be when you stop pretending you like suffering."

She did not dignify that with an answer. But her hand stayed on the warm flank of a finished loaf one heartbeat longer than it had to. The bakery hummed back at her, steady and sure, as if it had been waiting for her to match its note.

The door bell did not clang this time. It chimed light and precise, like crystal touched with a fingernail. Conversation thinned to a curious hush. Penny's laughter gentled, went still, poised as a bird ready to lift.

Maren glanced up, knife midair, and her stomach dropped.

7

Mischief Incarnate

A man filled the doorway.

Cloak thrown carelessly over one shoulder, boots clean despite the mud-slick cobbles outside, posture loose and deliberate in the way of someone who had never been denied entry anywhere. The air shifted with him, a sharp citrus sliced clean through the sugar-thick bakery air, layered with cedar smoke that clung like something older. Something wilder.

Maren's body moved before her mind caught up. Her hand flattened on the counter, fingers splayed for balance. The hum under the wood felt weaker, confused even, like the bakery itself had just remembered it could be afraid.

Her mouth went dry. Her brain, ever logical, began cataloging facts: an unknown man, well-dressed, not local, not human.

Definitely not human.

The thief.

She knew him before she could stop herself from knowing. Memory struck like a bell: gold eyes, coin spinning, the voice that asked: *"What do you desire most?"* Her pulse hitched so hard it hurt.

He didn't even glance at the customers. His gaze slid over them as if they were ink smudges on a page. Then those molten-gold eyes found her, and the corner of his mouth curved slowly and wickedly, like he'd been waiting for this exact cue.

"Well," he drawled, stepping inside. Each footfall bent the air a little tighter. The cedar smoke threaded through the room, suffocatingly polite. "The rumors didn't lie. Miracles on Market Street."

Even his voice warped the air. It was the same lazy warmth that had taunted her across her own counter last night, except now it carried the weight of inevitability.

Penny's grin wavered, "Sir, can we—can we help you with something?" Her words were careful, kind, the way one might speak to a feral dog.

His smile sharpened. "You already have."

The coin appeared between his fingers as if it had never left them, spinning once, catching the dim light like a trapped sunbeam. Maren's stomach turned. Every tick of its rotation felt like a countdown.

Maren slammed the knife blade point-first into the cutting board hard enough to crack it. The sound made several customers flinch. "Get. Out."

The shop went very still. The knife's echo hadn't yet finished ricocheting when the whispers began.

"Did she just—?"

"Saints preserve—"

"Raven, spare me!"

The air curdled with interest. Gossip had always loved her, but this time it felt *hungry*. The villagers' eyes gleamed in the golden haze like coin edges. For years, she'd worked to scrub her parents' names clean. One curse, one raised voice, and Eldenwick was already writing the ending for her.

He arched a brow, almost bored. "Is that any way to greet a satisfied patron?"

The coin appeared between his fingers again, gleaming like an accusation. He tossed it once, twice, then it vanished midair. A neat clink rang from the tip jar beside her elbow. The coin spun lazily, perfectly balanced, then stilled.

Every head turned toward it. Every breath drew tighter.

Maren's pulse thrummed against her ribs. Her logic, her weapon, scrambled to keep up. *Trick of the light. Sleight of hand. Coin tosses don't teleport.* But beneath the rationalizations, a colder truth stirred: this was the same sound she'd heard when her wish slipped free last night. The same echo that had followed her into dreams.

Penny shifted closer, tray pressed against her chest like a shield. "Maren?" she whispered. "What's happening?"

Maren didn't answer. Her voice might betray that she didn't know.

"You don't belong here," she said instead, low and dangerous, a statement aimed as much at herself as at him. Because suddenly she wasn't sure she *did* belong. Her laughter from this morning still rang in her head, bright and hollow, the sound of someone fooled by mercy.

He tilted his head, mock sympathy softening the cruelty in his smile. "Neither do you."

The words struck like a slap.

For one sharp second, Maren saw herself the way the crowd did: the heretic baker who mocked the spirits, who tempted fate and brought ruin home as if it were a houseguest.

Her jaw clenched. If he wanted fear, she'd feed him fury instead. She forced a smirk sharp enough to cut glass. "Funny. I seem to be the one baking."

"And yet," he said softly, stepping closer, "it's my oven singing for you. My flour dancing under your hands. My wonder in your walls. You're playing house in a story I wrote."

The words landed too easily, too true. She could feel them in her bones, in the faint vibration under her palms where the counter used to hum with life. His magic pulsed through the wood like a heartbeat that wasn't hers.

For a heartbeat, her mask cracked. *He stole it,* she remembered. *The bastard stole my wish.*

Then her anger returned: hot, instinctive, and *blinding.*

"Take your story," she snarled, "and choke on it."

Gasps rippled like wind through wheat. The crowd's awe turned brittle, disbelieving. Someone whispered, "She's cursing him now." Someone else crossed themselves. The word *"blasphemy"* hissed through the air like steam escaping from a kettle.

Penny's hand brushed her arm, a plea for restraint. Maren shook her off, eyes never leaving the thief's. He was still smiling, lazy and delighted, like he was savoring every second of her undoing.

The thief's grin deepened, slow and lazy, like a cat stretching after the kill. "Ah," he said, voice velvet against the ruin of her composure. "There she is. My favorite, violent baker."

He leaned one hip against the counter, as if it had been built for him. The golden light of the ovens danced along the edge of his jaw, painting him in every shade of false holiness. The crowd watched, suspended between fascination and fear. Someone whispered a prayer. Someone else whispered, *"curse".*

The smell of cinnamon thickened until it felt like drowning in sweetness.

Maren couldn't breathe. Her mind clawed at reason. *Illusion. It has to be an illusion.* Tricks and parlor glamours existed. Peddlers performed them at Bloomtide. She'd even scoffed once, laughing at the audience gasping over disappearing coins. But no illusion reached this deep. No illusion made your heart keep time with someone else's laughter.

He smiled wider. "But I nearly forgot the price of this little wish. Silly of me, really."

Her stomach dropped.

Price.

The word struck like the toll of a bell she hadn't realized she'd been hearing all along.

He turned, slow as the turning of a page, until his gaze landed on Penny. The warmth drained from the room.

"Payment due," he murmured.

Penny's breath hitched. The tray in her hands wobbled, rolls sliding. "Me?" Her voice was small, still threaded with disbelief, as if the universe had never aimed at her before.

Maren's body moved first. Her hand slammed down on the counter, the crack loud enough to make a few customers flinch. "No."

The thief's golden eyes slid back to her, bright with amusement. "Open to negotiation?"

She could feel every gaze in the bakery pressing against her, waiting to see if the heretic would bargain with the divine. Her pulse hammered behind her eyes. *Think. Think.* Logic was supposed to save her, to make sense of nonsense. *Curses have terms, deals have loopholes.* That's what her father's stories had taught her. Nothing takes without leaving a way out.

Her voice came out rough. "Take me instead."

A murmur ran through the room: half pity, half awe.

The thief tilted his head, considering. "Tempting," he drawled, voice smooth as oil, "but you see—" He lifted his hand. The coin appeared between his fingers again, gleaming like a captive star. "I'm nothing if not generous. There's always a choice, darling."

The coin spun.

The air changed.

Heat rolled off the ovens in a low, warning breath. The flour on the counter trembled. A few customers backed toward the door but didn't dare leave.

Maren's logic fractured under the weight of it. She tried to count breaths, to catalog details: cedar, citrus, gold eyes, coin, witness accounts, but the data refused to assemble into sense. Every explanation dissolved before it finished forming.

And through it all, she kept thinking: *He said price. He said payment.*

Her wish, her whispered, stupid, impossible wish, had called him. Had called this.

She looked at Penny, bright and terrified in her red apron, and thought of the night before: of herself whispering to an empty room, *I want wonder.* The thief had heard her. And wonder had teeth.

The bakery seemed to have stopped breathing by now.

Even the ovens went still, their glow fading to a dull, frightened pulse. The customers stood frozen mid-motion; their rolls half-eaten, coins sweating in palms, and every face taut with that human instinct to stay very quiet when divinity walks in.

The thief basked in it. He propped his elbows on the counter like a king lounging on a throne stolen from her own kitchen. His coin clicked once against the wood, rhythmic and patient.

Maren's breath came too fast. She felt it clawing the back of her throat. Her mind, always at its sharpest under pressure, tried to devise a plan. *Weapons. Distance. Doors.* But her knife was buried in the board, and her bakery had gone limp and obedient under his presence. Even the air seemed to be kneeling.

"Don't look so grim," he said, voice low and smooth. The coin rolled across his knuckles like it had always belonged there. "I'm not unreasonable. I'll give you terms."

She hated the word *terms*. It made this sound like trade, like fairness.

Her voice rasped out. "Terms."

He smiled, slow, satisfied, like she'd handed him her pulse to count. "Your little wish, the wonder, it's more mischief than most mortals can stomach. I admire that." He leaned forward, tone dipping into mock reverence. "But balance, darling. Balance demands payment."

The coin stilled.

Then his eyes shifted, their bright gold locking on Penny.

Maren felt the focus of the room pivot with him. The weight of a god's attention. It pressed cold fingers into the back of her neck.

"Payment keeps the world honest," he murmured.

Penny made a slight, strangled sound. "What—what do you mean?" Her hand trembled on the tray, the rolls shaking with it.

"Don't," Maren snapped, stepping between them, voice cracking like a whip. "You lay one finger on her, and I'll—"

He laughed. Soft, almost delighted, as though she'd said something adorable. "And there's that fire. I wondered when you'd bare your teeth." He twirled the coin, its silver edge catching what little light was left. "You've no idea how much I've missed mortals who think they can threaten gods."

He didn't sound amused now. He sounded hungry.

Maren's nails bit into the counter. The sweet scent of yeast curdled into something sharp, metallic. Her heartbeat refused to slow. *Don't fold,* she told herself. *Logic, find the loophole.*

Her mind raced: every story her father told, every bargain. Tricksters could be bound by their own games, couldn't they? *You have to name the rule before you can break it.* But her thoughts kept snagging on one phrase: *Payment keeps the world honest.*

He was still smiling when he offered his so-called mercy. "Tell you what," he said, each word polished smooth and deadly. "You keep the magic. Keep your tidy little bakery, and your sunshine girl stays safe. All you have to do is…" The coin spun in his hand, throwing off shards of light. "…survive."

The word hung there, indecently intimate.

Maren's laugh was a brittle thing. "Survive what?"

He leaned closer. "Trials." The syllables were velvet-wrapped venom. "Every story has them. You made a wish; now you get your plot."

The crowd stirred, uncertain murmurs rising: *trials, curse, blasphemy, justice.*

Maren swallowed the knot in her throat. "And if I don't?"

The thief's grin sharpened into something unholy. "Then Penny returns in your place. Safe and unscathed." His voice softened, mocking gentleness. "But you…" He tapped the coin against the counter, once, twice. The sound echoed. "…you'll be rewritten. Folded into my Court where you belong. A mortal turned story. Don't worry, I'm very good at endings."

The word *rewritten* caught in her mind like a hook.

Her father's stories came rushing back: heroes who became legends, lovers who became myths, mortals swallowed by miracles. She had loved those endings once, back when they were safe inside a book. Now, standing in a bakery that smelled of fear and burned sugar, she realized how much horror fit behind a word like *story.*

Maren's fingers dug into the wood until it splintered. The rational part of her brain—the piece that consistently refused to die spoke up anyway.

She forced a laugh, brittle and sharp. "And those are my only choices? Play your game or let her vanish?"

He leaned in slightly, smile gone, almost tender. "You mortals are so fond of choices," he murmured. "Two paths," he said, almost sweetly. "Both heroic in their own way. But only one keeps your hands clean."

The room seemed to shrink around them. Maren could feel every eye digging into her, all of them watching her ruin take shape.

Her throat ached. "You call this noble?"

He shrugged, casual, cruel. "It's fair. And fair is more than most get."

The coin flickered again in his fingers. Each rotation drew more light out of the room. Her reflection glimmered across its surface: small, warped, and frightened. She had the sudden, sick thought that if it stopped spinning, she'd vanish with it.

Her logic grasped for an angle, *a rule, a pattern, a way out.* If he was Mischief, he was bound by story; every bargain had a seam. She just needed to find it before he unmade everything she loved. But thinking was hard when fear was pressing its thumb against her windpipe.

For a flicker of a moment, it almost sounded fair. Almost sounded like she could fight her way through his trials, spit in his face, and drag Penny back to safety.

Almost.

Maren leaned forward, eyes silver-blue fire. "Fine. I'll play. But hear me, Thief—" she spat the name like a curse, "—when I win, you don't get to touch her. Or me. Ever again."

The heat in the bakery snapped cold, the firelight gone thin and trembling. Even the flour suspended midair seemed to hesitate, caught between settling and fleeing. Maren's heartbeat filled the silence. So did his smile.

"Well," the thief murmured, voice soft enough to make the room flinch. "A heroine accepts her trials."

He straightened, and the illusion of humanity sloughed off him like ash. His shadow stretched long against the far wall, tall enough to scrape the rafters. Light bent around him.

Penny made a small, frightened sound. The sound a mouse would make before a hawk strikes. "Maren?"

"Don't touch her." Maren's knife hand lifted instinctively, though she had no idea how a baker's blade could stop a god. Her voice broke anyway. "I said don't—"

He didn't.

That was the cruelty.

He didn't move at all.

Penny's smile faltered, her tray tilting. Rolls slid and hit the floor, soft thuds against the hush. Then her outline shimmered, faint as heat over stone. The thyme in her braid browned in an instant. The bright stitches of wildflowers on her apron dulled to gray.

Maren's mind shattered and reassembled on instinct. *Rules. Every curse has a rule.* She'd read that in a dozen stories. *Say the name, break the spell, bleed if you have to.* She lunged forward, vaulting the counter, knife in hand, shouting words that sounded like they should matter: "Leave her! Take me! Take the damned wish!"

The thief watched her rage with polite interest. His expression barely shifted. "You mortals," he said, almost fondly. "You always think fury is a language."

Maren reached Penny and grabbed her arm. It was solid. Warm.

Relief hit her so hard she nearly sobbed. "I've got you," she said, stupidly, as if words could anchor a soul.

Then the warmth slipped through her fingers.

Her grip closed on air.

"NO!" The word ripped out of her, raw and ugly.

She swung her knife at the space where he stood, where the air rippled gold. The blade sliced nothing. The edge glowed briefly, then cooled. He didn't even blink.

Penny's eyes met hers, wide with terror and apology. "Maren—"

Her name fractured mid-breath. The sound stuttered, rewound, vanished. The girl who'd sung while kneading dough, who'd tied herbs in her hair, began to unspool. Her outline peeled apart like threads pulled from a cloth, each strand dissolving into light. The smell of her, cinnamon and honey and soap, lingered half a heartbeat longer, then thinned to cedar smoke.

The tray hit the floor, empty.

Maren hit her knees. The knife clattered beside her. Every thought she'd ever used as armor shattered into soundless static. The bakery swayed; the crowd blurred. She could hear someone praying. She could hear herself breathing, fast and uneven.

"You bastard," she said, but it came out hoarse, almost a whisper.

The thief tilted his head, expression mild. "Careful," he said, the coin balanced on his thumb like a sun he could flip at will. "You're talking to the man keeping his end of the bargain. Wonder granted. Payment claimed."

The ledger snapped open behind her, pages riffling until they screamed. Coins spilled from the till and scattered across the floor. The shelves trembled; loaves toppled; the room itself seemed to bow, the way lesser creatures bow when power passes too close.

Penny was gone.

Gone in the way a word vanishes from the tongue. Gone in the way a story ends.

Maren staggered to her feet, fury dragging her up like a puppeteer's strings. "Bring her back." Her voice scraped like metal. "Bring. Her. Back."

He regarded her with a quiet amusement that broke her more than mockery ever could. "Oh, I gave you a way," he said softly. "Survive my trials, and she returns. Fail, and she wakes up safe while you get the better ending. You get to become a story."

Her breath came in ragged gasps. "You think I'll let you rewrite me?"

He stepped closer, and the scent of cedar wrapped around her like smoke. "You already said yes."

Something inside her snapped. She spat at his boots, hand closing around the fallen knife. "I'll end you before you end me."

His laugh rolled through the rafters, deep and delighted. The shutters rattled. "Hate me all you like, darling. It makes the game sweeter."

Then the coin spun high.

Impossibly high.

Light fractured.

Flour rose from the counter in a storm. The shutters slammed. Heat and cold crashed together. The world tilted on its axis, folding like paper. The customers cried out.

Maren reached for anything, Penny's tray, the counter, even the ledger, but everything was sliding away.

The thief caught her wrist, elegant and absolute. "Stories don't start in bakeries," he murmured.

And then the floor was gone.

Eldenwick folded in on itself, crushed to ink between two unseen pages. Her last glimpse was Penny's tray, gleaming in the dark.

And then—

Black.

And the voice that would haunt her forever, warm as honey, cruel as truth:

"Welcome to the Court, my reluctant heroine."

8

The Court of Terrible Ideas

Maren stood at the lip of a corridor that behaved like a tide. The ceiling was an ink sea with its own slow constellations, stars drifting as if tugged by a moon no one else could see. Below, an obsidian floor mirrored that sky until it was impossible to tell which way was up. Gold veining moved inside the stone, not on it, spiraling and unspiraling like molten script that refused to settle on a single sentence.

It was beautiful in the way of knives. A beauty that asked for blood to finish the line.

It knocked the breath out of her.

It was the exact kind of beauty she'd have written into a margin once upon a time, tucked between recipes and business obligations.

And Maren decided then that she *hated* it.

Penny was here. That was the only true thing. Everything else could be gorgeous nonsense.

Her shoes slapped against the polished floor, small and human. She clenched her fists at her sides like she could punch sense into marble. The air pressed close, charged. Every inhale filled her nose with something sharp: cedar, citrus, and smoke. As though the place wanted her to remember who had dragged her here.

Don't look impressed. Don't look curious.

Figures drifted past, each stranger than the last. A woman sewn from night, her gown projecting scenes that moved when she did: a hunter losing a trail, a ship finding one. The fabric whispered as it moved, retelling what it couldn't forget.

There was a creature made of glass. Old glass, bubbled and uneven, catching the light in shy blues and bruised golds. Its words chimed and trembled faint and brittle in her bones.

Behind it were gilded fox-faced figures in embroidered robes, eyes gleaming with sly amusement. All of them moved with the weightless grace of half-told stories. All of them turned to look at her.

Some bowed. Some sneered. One whispered, "A mortal? How strange."

Maren's chin tipped higher. Let them stare. She'd grown up under Mrs. Aldren's judgment; these things couldn't be worse.

Still, her heartbeat thudded traitorously, steady as a drum calling something to attention. The air shifted with her pulse. Light pooled closer. A thousand glimmering eyes, real *and* imagined, tilted toward her. Even the floor's molten veins slowed, as though the Court itself wanted to see who had dared walk in with dirt on her shoes.

It's watching you, whispered the part of her that still believed in bedtime stories.

It's choosing what you'll be.

She forced her jaw to tighten, forced her eyes to narrow at the endless corridor ahead. She wouldn't admit, not even in the privacy of her own head, that wonder was already gnawing its way through her anger.

She wanted Penny back. She wanted Eldenwick. She wanted her stupid bakery with its ledger and its leaky roof.

But she also wanted…

No. Absolutely not.

She clenched her fists tighter, nails biting into her palms, and stepped deeper into the Court of Chaos.

Columns rose from the floor in graceful spirals, impossible corkscrews. They curled like frozen smoke into the heavens, supporting nothing and anchored by less. They hummed faintly, like they were dreaming. Above, lanterns floated in lazy orbits. Some glowed like captured fireflies, and others blinked like eyes. The light they cast didn't just illuminate. It transformed. It shifted the color of her apron, her skin, even her thoughts.

She didn't get three steps before the Court noticed she was trying not to be impressed and decided that was adorable.

Doors stood free of walls like riddles; one breathed like a sleeping animal, another ticked as if full of clockwork, a third exhaled the smell of rain on old paper.

Maren fixed her gaze on that last one. The smell of her father's study. The smell of stories that never paid the rent but fed him anyway. It meant safety and escape and something dangerously close to home.

Books meant answers. And Penny might need one.

The thought wasn't rational—it was reflex. The way hunger answers to bread.

Don't be stupid, she told herself, but her feet had already angled toward the smell.

"Clever little moth."

The voice brushed her spine.

Cedar and citrus cut through the air like a blade dipped in memory.

He stepped from between two columns, the space bending around him. Cedar and citrus cut clean through her breath. He'd shed the forest cloak for something darker, leaner, a mantle that didn't weigh on him so much as obey. Lazy posture, lethal edges. Gold eyes that made the Court's lanterns look shy.

"Stray already?" he murmured, as if they were sharing a joke. The coin danced along his knuckles, an idle heartbeat that made the air thrum in time.

Maren didn't flinch. She'd already lost one world. She wouldn't cower in this one. "Get out of my way."

"By all means," he said, stepping aside with a courtly bow that reeked of mockery. "Do open the door that bites."

She glared at him, jaw tight. "You think I'm that stupid?"

He tilted his head, smiling without showing teeth. "Oh, *darling.* I think you're exactly that brave."

The rain-and-paper door pulsed, eager. The handle glinted, but the keyhole grinned like a trap. The nearer she moved, the louder the ticking grew, and the more every hair on her arms stood at attention.

Maren took one step closer, the scent wrapping around her like a promise she hadn't made. Her heartbeat synced with the mechanical rhythm.

She didn't believe him. But, she also believed him a little.

Because bravery and stupidity were rarely strangers, and she'd never learned the difference until it was too late.

Behind her, whispers gathered:

"Brash little thing."

"Her story smells too sweet."

She turned on her heel to face them and let her nicest smile out to play; the one that meant: *I would happily salt your tea.*

"Do you all come with commentary," she asked sweetly, "or is this just the Court's version of a welcome basket?"

Laughter tinkled: the glass-creatures, bright and brittle. One of the fox-masked nobles tilted its head, constellations stitched along a midnight waistcoat. Its voice was velvet and razor. "New toys are rare."

"And they break quickly," sighed a woman in a gown of shadow, "I prefer my mortals at the end, when their sobbing."

"Good news," Maren said, heartbeat thunder and voice steady. "I don't sob."

Behind her shoulder, the thief made an appreciative sound that she did not need him to make. "She scowls, mostly," he said to the crowd, almost fond. "And glares. It's invigorating."

She didn't look at him. Looking was a kind of giving. "Where is she?"

"Vague," he said lightly. "So many *she's* in your life."

"My apprentice. My friend." The words sharpened. "Penny."

A ripple went through the onlookers at the name, like someone had dragged a nail along the surface of a drum. Heads turned. Whispers pricked sharp as nettles. Maren's spine tightened. She hadn't thought "Penny" was the sort of word that could draw blood.

The thief rolled the coin along his knuckles, slow and deliberate. "Alive," he said at last, and the single word cracked her wide open with relief so sharp it felt like pain.

He smiled wider, sensing it. "Kept, as agreed."

"As kidnapped," she snapped. "Show me."

He clicked his tongue, mock scolding. "Skipping chapters already? Mortals," he sighed, stepping close enough that the scent of cedar and citrus ghosted down her throat, "always trying to peek at the ending."

"Maybe because they always suck," she said.

A few of the glass beings gasped like she'd blasphemed, which, technically, she had.

His grin curved lazily, molten. "Still playing brave. Adorable. But we made a bargain, baker. *Trials first.*"

The coin halted. For a breath, the entire corridor seemed to hold itself at the angle of that stillness. The Court watched with the greedy focus of an audience sensing blood.

Maren didn't bend. She pivoted, not toward the rain-and-paper door, but toward a narrow passage slanting between two pillars, where a thread of air smelled like fresh thyme and sun-warm hair. Penny. She didn't question how she knew. She moved.

She took two strides before the air hardened.

The sound came first: a low, crystalline hum, like light scraping itself against glass. Then the space in front of her split open, and mirrors blossomed upward from the floor in a spine of silver.

In the blink of an eye, the corridor vanished.

Floor to ceiling in a blink, a lattice of mirrored panes stitched itself from nothing, catching her reflection a dozen times: flour-smudged cheek, stubborn mouth, silver-blue eyes gone flint. In every pane, the thief stood just behind her shoulder.

Waiting.

Near enough that the air thinned between them. Golden eyes gleamed in all her reflections, multiplying like a constellation.

Maren forced her voice low, steady. "Do you think I can't find her without you?"

He smiled at her reflection rather than her, lazy as a serpent after a meal. "I'm counting on you trying."

The quiet honesty of it cracked through her like thunder under glass.

Her anger, sharp as it was, stuttered for half a breath.

"Is this a maze or a cage?" she asked.

He tilted his head, coin rolling idly between mirrored fingers. "What's the difference, if you built both yourself?"

She wrenched her gaze from the reflection, pulse hammering in her throat. "I'll find her," she said. "With or without your games."

His eyes flickered, amusement tempered with something almost—almost—respect. "Good," he murmured. "It's no fun if you don't try to win."

He flicked the coin once; the sound was small, metallic, final. The mirrors trembled and shattered into dust that glittered as it fell.

The Court shifted, scenting tension like perfume.

From the fringe of its glittering assembly, the fox-masked noble drifted forward, grace so fluid it looked rehearsed. The tray in his hands appeared out of the air, silver chased with constellations, carrying goblets that glowed as though they had been poured from a vein of starlight.

"Drink," he said smoothly. "It starts like wine, ends like memory. Mortals find it… harder to put down."

Maren didn't break eye contact with the thief. "If I drink, do I skip the part where everyone plays cryptic charades with my life?"

"Alas," he said, "no."

She tilted her head. "Then keep your glitter."

The fox inclined his head, amused. "Rude." He withdrew, the goblets dimming a little in disappointment as he melted back into the crowd.

Something smaller slipped in to take his place. A child-shaped thing, only wrong at the seams. They were flat where they should be round, edges sharp enough to slice thought. Its eyes were two holes punched through paper.

"Ask for a boon," it whispered, voice rustling like turned pages, "and he'll give you a rule. Ask for a rule, and he'll give you a game."

Maren's mouth twitched despite herself. "Go taunt someone else."

It grinned, or rather, folded itself into the shape of a grin, and vanished in a flutter of paper.

Behind her, the thief's laugh unfurled like velvet pulled over thorns. "They aren't wrong."

"And you're not useful."

"Oh, I'm very useful," he said. "Just not to what you think you're doing."

She hated the way that threaded through her. Hated the part of her that wanted to ask what he thought she was doing. Hated, most of all, the flicker of heat low in her chest when the Court's impossible beauty leaned close and purred:

You could love me. You already do.

No. She was a bakery girl with ledger ink on her fingers and burns along her wrists and a sick, steady ache where Penny should be. Wonder was not for her. Or, if it was, it didn't get to cost this.

She set her shoulders. "Fine. Your trials," she said, spitting the words like gristle. "But hear me: the second I have her, we're gone."

"Darling," he said, coin flashing, eyes bright with cruel delight, "I'm counting on that, too."

The Court liked that answer; the air rippled with soundless applause. Light shifted. The sideways chandelier spun faster, casting a hundred tiny moons across the veined floor. Doors turned their faces away. The rain-and-paper scent thinned until all she had was memory.

"Room," he said, casual as ordering wine, and the Court obeyed. A door bled into existence on the wall ahead: plain dark wood, iron-bound edges, brass knob. Above it, carvings etched themselves into place with a faint hiss: a flame, a broken crown, a feather. They twitched when she looked too long, restless, as though eager to rearrange themselves into her name.

"Let me guess," she said, her mouth dry. "Foreshadowing."

"Mm." His smile curved like a blade. "Such a clever little listener."

The door creaked open, not into velvet or silk, but stone. Bare walls. A cot hard enough to bruise. No window, no stars. Just a cell pretending to be a room. A place that whispered: You are temporary.

Maren's jaw locked. "Charming."

"Don't pout," he murmured, his voice soft enough to prickle. He didn't touch her, but his presence leaned against her, velvet-heavy, smug. "It isn't punishment. Yet. The Court simply likes to… take its time deciding whether a mortal deserves cushions. Or chains."

"Great," she said. "I'll sleep like a princess."

He tilted his head, coin sliding between his fingers. "Sweet dreams, darling. Try not to run around opening doors with teeth." His golden eyes glittered, deliberate, like he wanted her to imagine just what kind of teeth he meant.

"Try not to breathe near me," she returned, sharp as glass.

His laugh was low, delighted, and the Court shivered like it enjoyed the sound. "Hate looks excellent on you."

"Good," she said. "You'll be seeing a lot of it."

She reached for the knob. Her palm left a print in the brass, a little crescent of flour she hadn't managed to wash away. It pleased her in a petty, necessary way. Her mark on their world. She stepped through without giving him the satisfaction of a last glance.

Maren shut the door behind her, leaning against the iron-bound wood. The silence pressed close. Four walls. A cot. That was all.

She pressed her palms into her eyes until sparks flared across the dark.

I won't love this, she told the greedy part of herself that was already measuring the space, already cataloging its potential, already wondering what it might look like if she bent it into something hers.

Tomorrow, the Court. Tonight, a plan. Somewhere beyond these walls, Penny was breathing in a story that didn't belong to her.

Maren breathed out once, long and steady, and let the hate keep her upright. If she had to walk their maze to find a way out, she would. If she had to smile and bow and pretend to play, she would. And if she had to set the Court of Chaos on fire to bring Penny home—

Well. The carvings above her door had already offered her a flame.

9

Coin-Flipping Bastard

In the first hour, she tried the door.

Not politely. She set her shoulder to the iron and pushed until the wood printed a bruise across her collarbone.

The second, the walls.

The stone looked ordinary until her knuckles met it. The seams in the stone weren't wide enough for fingernails, much less a mortal girl with a grudge.

By the third, she'd considered setting the cot on fire. Except she didn't have a match.

Think.

She tried to leverage.

A boot heel under the latch. A twist of apron strings braided into a makeshift loop. The latch yawned at her efforts and stayed married to the frame.

She went smaller. If the door would not break, perhaps something else would. But even the straw-stuffed pillow resisted her efforts at strangulation practice.

The room seemed designed to mock every escape attempt.

So she paced.

Six strides to the door, six back.

The distance mapped itself under her feet, a loop of stubborn habit. Her bare soles left pale prints that blurred as soon as they formed, like the room disliked keeping a record.

On the seventh pass, she measured the hinges with her eyes, the screws with her imagination, and the odds with the kind of math that had kept a bakery alive through lean winters.

The coil under her ribs tightened.

Six strides.

Six back.

The beat of a heart that refused to quiet.

Penny was out there.

Maybe breathing. Maybe not. The thought pressed closer than the walls, a weight under her ribs that refused to let her lungs do their job.

Maren's palms stung where her nails bit into them. "Brilliant plan," she muttered, pacing again. "Trade common sense for adventure, get a one-way ticket to divine captivity."

The room soaked her voice like bread in broth.

That was the worst part: it didn't answer. Even silence should have texture, but this one felt deliberate.

She tried to fill it anyway. "I was so stupid to want more. Ledger-balancing. Market runs. Gods, I'd sell my soul for a boring invoice right now."

Her laugh cracked sharply in the empty room. "Well. Almost. Already gave that to the coin-flipping bastard."

The walls didn't correct her.

She dropped onto the cot at last, arms crossed, every part of her thrumming with fury. Her eyelids stung from fighting sleep. She told herself she wouldn't, couldn't—

And then the Court slipped in like a draft through the cracks.

* * *

She was back in the bakery.

The first thing she noticed was the heat.

Not the good kind. Not the kind that meant bread and safety, but the other kind. The kind that peeled the air from your skin.

The ovens glowed like open throats. Their mouths yawned wider with each breath she took, metal liquefying at the edges.

The dough on the table swelled too fast, frothing like it had lungs. Her hands moved on instinct, but every touch blistered.

Pain licked her fingers, and still she couldn't stop. The rhythm owned her.

Heel, turn, ache.

Heel, turn, burn.

Across the counter, Penny smiled.

The rosemary in her braid had wilted to gray. Her skin shimmered under the heat, almost translucent, as if she were becoming something lighter than air. She laughed, but it wasn't *her* laugh. It didn't sound like Penny at all.

"Penny," Maren said, voice catching.

Her friend didn't answer. Her head tilted instead, listening to something Maren couldn't hear. The sound reached her a moment later:

A coin clicking against wood.

Maren turned. Her father sat in the corner, posture too still. He wore the same coat he'd been buried in. The one with ink stains on the cuffs and crumbs on the lapel.

He didn't look up. His hands rolled the coin over his knuckles with the precision of long practice.

Flip.

Catch.

Flip.

Catch.

"Stop," she whispered.

The coin spun again, rising this time, glinting silver as it cut through the heavy air.

The smell thickened. No cinnamon now, but caramelized ruin: sugar burning past sweetness, butter gone black.

Penny's smile widened.

"Stop it!" Maren shouted.

The ovens exhaled, a single, blistering breath. The loaves on the table split open like wounds. Molten honey spilled from them, sizzling across her palms. She staggered back, choking on the sweetness, the suffocating perfume of her own desire turned rancid.

The coin hit the floor with a sound that didn't belong to any world she knew.

And she jolted awake.

* * *

Maren woke like someone surfacing from deep water.

Her lungs refused to decide between scream and sob, so she settled for a ragged inhale that scraped her throat raw. The air was colder now, but the ghost of heat clung to her skin.

Her curls were plastered to her neck. Her palms ached as if she'd been clawing stone. When she lifted them, faint red crescents marked her skin, proof that even asleep, she hadn't stopped fighting.

The cot had not softened overnight. It had simply evolved, discovering new ways to hurt. She sat up slowly, the straw sighing beneath her.

"Dream," she muttered. Her voice was hoarse, half-unbelieving. "Just a dream. Grief and guilt and… gods-damned imagination."

But the echo of that coin-click clung to her ears.

Her stomach turned. "Not him," she said louder, as if volume could make it true. "Definitely not him."

The silence absorbed her lie with perfect composure.

She needed to move, to break something. Her gaze landed on her boots. Loyal companions through mud and market gossip.

With a snarl, she snatched up one of her boots and hurled it at the wall. It hit with a satisfying thud before flopping sideways like a corpse. The second followed fast, clipping the cot frame before collapsing in defeat.

Her breath came ragged, chest heaving. "Fine," she hissed at the pair. "Traitors."

She pressed her palms hard against her thighs to stop the tremor. "If he thinks I'm some bedtime story to toy with, he's wrong."

She wasn't going to give them her best.

If they expected trembling knees, they'd get boredom. If they wanted wide-eyed wonder, they'd get scowls sharp enough to slice parchment. Her stubborn streak dug in like heels in wet dough.

The coil of dread inside her chest loosened just enough for spite to slip in and take its seat.

The lock clicked.

Maren tensed. No trumpet of doom. No creak. Just the quiet shift of space making room for something else.

A foxling the size of a child stepped in, waistcoat neat, whiskers twitching with disdain. His claws clicked daintily against the stone as he bowed.

"Lady Maren," he said, his voice smooth and unhurried, like he expected applause. "I am Kipwick. Your attendant."

Maren blinked. Then laughed. Once. Hard. "My what?"

"Attendant," he repeated, unfazed. His tail flicked, measured, and smug. "I've been assigned to escort you. The Court is assembling for judgment."

He stood there, entirely too pleased with himself, the tip of one paw brushing imaginary lint from his vest.

Maren stared. The day before, she'd been baking bread with homicide and publicly shaming the Saints. Now, apparently, she had staff.

"That's adorable," she said flatly. "And delusional."

She reached for the nearest boot and threw it.

The fox didn't dodge. The leather thudded squarely against the top of his neatly polished head, slid off, and came to rest between them.

Kipwick blinked once. Twice. Then adjusted his bow tie.

"I'll assume that was a greeting," he said politely.

Maren rubbed her temples. "Do you people not knock?"

"I did," Kipwick replied, as though explaining arithmetic to a small child.

"With my presence."

Her laugh came out half-groan. "Fantastic. Another narcissist." She slumped back against the wall, her legs stretched out, the picture of exhaustion. "You can tell your Court they'll get nothing from me today. Not even my shoes."

Kipwick tilted his head. "You've already given me one."

Her jaw clenched. Gods, she hated him already.

The fox smoothed his vest again, the motion neat, rhythmic. "Best not to keep them waiting," he said. "The Arbiter is not fond of tardiness."

Maren arched a brow. "Good. Neither am I."

She stood, her braid tumbling loose over one shoulder. "Lead the way, furball."

Kipwick's tail swished, sly amusement flashing green in his eyes. "As you wish."

An archway yawned open without warning.

One blink, and the cell's stone walls peeled back like paper, folding inward until an archway opened in their place.

Maren flinched as the world rearranged around her. The scent of damp stone gave way to something richer, stranger: honey and smoke, candle wax and ozone. The air hummed as if alive, thrumming in her bones.

Beyond it, the Court unfolded.

Like a book spreading its pages to show her what she'd missed. The floor gleamed like white marble veined with gold, stretching out in all directions. Above, the stars drifted lazily through a ceiling that wasn't a ceiling, just open space stitched with light. Tall columns rose like the bones of ancient trees, holding up nothing at all.

There were hundreds of creatures, maybe thousands. Each one defied taxonomy. Some stood in small, shifting clusters: a trio of women with scales instead of skin, their hair twisting upward in braids of flame. A tall figure cloaked in moth wings. A boy with stars for eyes and a silver chain of wishes looped around his wrist.

And every single one of them was looking at *her.*

Maren's throat went dry. Her first thought was unprintable. Her second was, *Oh, good. A full house.*

Kipwick swept a paw toward it, maddeningly pleased. "After you."

"Ladies first," Maren muttered and stepped through before he could make a remark about species.

The marble chilled under her bare feet.

Laughter rippled through the crowd. Whispered wagers followed, spilling like coins onto a betting table: how long until the mortal cried, whether she'd faint before the Arbiter finished speaking, if the Spirit would bother keeping her at all.

Maren's lip curled. If they wanted tears, they'd choke on disappointment.

Then the chamber shifted.

Not loudly. Not violently. The kind of change that made her stomach drop and her instincts scream *wrong.*

Every head turned. Every body pivoted in one fluid motion, predator-smooth.

He was there.

The thief. The bastard. Only he wasn't leaning in a doorway this time, coin in hand like some wandering rogue. He lounged across the marble seat; one elbow draped across the armrest, one leg stretched long, and his posture was lazy to the point of insult. And yet the space bent around him.

Whispers sharpened in reverence:

"The fox himself."

"The coinbearer."

"Mischief made flesh."

Maren's pulse hitched, but she forced her brain to catalog instead of panic.

He sat too comfortably for a ruler; no crown, no symbol of office. His dominance wasn't declared; it was more… *gravitational.* Like the universe simply folded its edges around him.

Which meant one thing: he didn't need to prove it.

His gaze met hers.

The coin paused mid-spin, light catching along its edge, and his eyes, those molten, unholy, gold-as-sin eyes, found her like the rest of the Court didn't exist. The look was a blade honed with amusement, indulgence, and something she didn't have a word for.

"Darling," he drawled, voice carrying as though the room had been built to cradle it, "you look like hell."

The crowd tittered. Some gasped. Some applauded.

Maren's blood flared hot. She wanted to spit, to scream, to hurl another boot, even if she had to borrow it. Instead, she smirked with all the sugar-poison sweetness she could muster. "And you look like you practiced that line in a mirror."

A pause. Then laughter, bright and awful, rippled through the chamber. It rolled like heat from an oven, feeding on her defiance.

He smiled wider. Slow. Wicked. Delighted. The kind of expression that promised this wasn't ritual, or law, or justice.

It was a *game*.

And Maren had just been cast as the leading act.

The Court roared with laughter at her jab, the sound rippling like fire catching dry leaves.

The Mischief Spirit lounged deeper into his throne, chin propped on one elegant hand, gold eyes heavy-lidded with enjoyment. The coin glimmered as it rolled across his knuckles.

"Well," he murmured, voice cutting through the noise like a violin through chaos, "someone found her claws overnight."

His tone was soft, almost fond. The kind of softness that could gut you before you realized it wasn't kindness.

Maren's spine straightened. Her brain, ever helpful, supplied: *Predator behavior. Don't blink.*

Her mouth, less cooperative, replied, "Try it. See if I don't shred you first."

The Court gasped, delighted. Bets shifted instantly, coins clattering into eager hands.

His grin sharpened. "Hear that?" He gestured idly to the crowd, lounging deeper in his seat. "Already their favorite act. Mortals usually need to scream first."

Maren's pulse thudded in her throat. *Don't give him rhythm,* she thought. *Make him trip. Make him improvise.*

So she smiled. The kind of smile that had once gotten her out of church scoldings and into trouble twice as fast. "Oh, don't sound so jealous. You'll get your applause soon enough."

A ripple of laughter again. Louder. Sharper. The sound of something ancient enjoying the taste of rebellion.

His eyes burned hotter, bright enough to make her breath catch. A mistake she masked with another smirk.

He leaned forward slightly, voice dropping to a near purr. "Careful, Maren. They'll start betting on how long before I declaw you."

She tilted her head. "If you could, you would've by now."

For one heartbeat, one perfect, impossible heartbeat, the grin faltered. The Court *howled.*

Maren's heart stuttered. *Logic works,* she thought wildly. *Keep the narrative, don't lose the upper hand.* She didn't know the rules here, but she knew performance. She'd survived markets and gossip and gods by turning words into tools.

His smile returned, sharper. Deadlier. "I won't need claws to undo you, darling."

Her voice was calm, cool sugar over venom. "You'll need more imagination to undo me then."

"Darling," he said, low and amused, "I already have."

10

Spectacle

A soft chime rang, and the floor rippled.

From the shadowed edge of the dais, a gilded cage drifted forward as though tugged by invisible strings. Its bars gleamed like melted sunlight. Inside, Penny sat serenely, hands folded in her lap, braid swaying as she hummed a lilting tune that made Maren's stomach lurch.

For half a breath, Maren's mind refused to name her. Couldn't. The brain always reached for logic first, even in hell.

It's a glamour, she told herself. *A trick. The Court deals in illusions.*

Her throat betrayed her anyway. "Penny!"

The name cracked across the chamber like a thunderclap.

The crowd flinched, delighted. Whispers caught the echo and carried it: *Penny, Penny, Penny...* until the sound itself seemed to shimmer in the air. Some of the nobles tilted their heads, listening to the mortal syllables like a song they didn't understand. One woman inhaled sharply as if tasting it.

Maren didn't notice. She'd already surged forward, but Kipwick's paw caught her wrist. The fox's grip was deceptively firm.

"Let me go—" Her muscles shook against his grip. "That's my *friend.*"

"And now," the fox said gently, "she's theirs."

The thief's smile widened. "Your little lamb," he purred. "Isn't she exquisite? Untouched. Entranced. The Court does so love their dreamers."

Maren's pulse hit like a hammer. "You bastard," Maren spat, voice shaking with fury. "Let her out."

"Oh, but look at her." His tone was silk drawn over steel. "Content. Peaceful. Better than she ever was in your crumbling bakery, don't you think?"

The nobles hissed approval, whispering hungry agreement.

Maren's nails dug into her palms until her skin split. Blood dotted her lifeline like punctuation. *Don't cry. Don't.* She could feel their eyes waiting for it.

"She's not a prize," she ground out. "She's not your—"

"Entertainment?" He leaned forward at last, golden gaze molten with delight. "Oh, she is. You both are. Mortals have always been. Did you think your kind slipped into the Court for any nobler purpose?"

The words were simple, brutal. No poetry. Just fact.

The chamber hummed with agreement. Nobles shifted, eager, like spectators awaiting the first drop of blood in an arena.

Maren swallowed hard, rage boiling under the surface of reason. "You think this makes you powerful?"

The thief's coin vanished mid-spin, only to reappear between his teeth as he smiled. He spoke around it, clear as ever. "No, darling. It makes me entertaining. And that's far more dangerous here."

The crowd roared again, thrilled.

Penny hummed on, oblivious, while Maren's pulse thundered in her throat. The thief leaned back once more, every inch of him smug, patient, infuriatingly at ease.

And then the chamber shifted again.

A figure slid into being at the dais's heart.

The air tightened, stilled, as though the walls themselves held their breath.

It didn't walk. It simply existed one moment and then the next: tall, robed in molten gold that seemed to pour endlessly from its shoulders, pooling without ever touching the ground. Its face was a mask of porcelain, blank, perfect, and unbearably smooth. No eyes. No mouth. No seams to suggest it had ever been human.

Yet Maren felt it look at her.

Felt the weight of that gaze press against the back of her neck like the edge of a blade.

Her mind, ever rational, scrambled for labels: god, spirit, judge, monster. None fit cleanly. *Maybe all of them did.*

The air grew taut.

Kipwick leaned close, his whiskers brushing her wrist. "The Arbiter," he whispered, reverent and sly. "Judge, jury, order-keeper. Doesn't rule, doesn't revel. Just weighs the scales. Without it, the Court would eat itself in a week."

"Sounds ideal," Maren murmured. Her voice came out thin, brittle around the edges.

Kipwick's grin flashed, teeth sharp in the dim. "For you, perhaps. Not for him."

But the coin-flipping bastard didn't rise. He lounged exactly as before, one arm draped over the marble throne, the other spinning his coin again with deliberate ease. A portrait of insolence. Only the faintest shadow at the corner of his mouth betrayed annoyance.

The Arbiter turned its head, a motion so smooth it seemed boneless. Its porcelain surface caught the starlight, throwing it back in perfect white.

When it spoke, it wasn't sound. It was *every sound at once.*

"Order demands balance. A mortal has been brought forth. A bargain has been struck."

The Court exhaled, a collective sigh of hunger disguised as reverence.

Maren's brain snagged on the phrasing. *Brought forth,* not *arrived.* Like she was a delivery.

Her hands curled into fists.

The thief flicked his coin lazily, catching it without looking. "Formality," he drawled. His tone carried the arrogance of someone who found eternity tedious. "We've been over this. I made the deal. One mortal for wonder, one mortal for trial. Payment and prize, all wrapped neatly."

The Arbiter tilted its masked head, as though listening to an echo from somewhere far older:

"Then present her."

The floor rippled under Maren's feet, a tremor that wasn't quite physical but forced her forward all the same. She stumbled, heels skidding, before planting herself stubbornly in place.

"Not happening," she said, breath sharp.

The nobles laughed, delighted.

The thief's eyes glinted, bright and merciless. "Don't pout, darling. It's tradition." His smirk cut wider, the smile of a cat, "And besides, I'd hate for them to think I'd lost control of my favorite mortal already."

Her heart lurched. Her mind clawed for logic. *He's provoking you. Don't give him the story he wants.*

Still, her mouth moved before her reason could stop it.

"I'm not yours."

"Mm." The sound was almost a hum, intimate and amused. "Tell them that." His coin flashed in the air, catching starlight as it spun. "They'll enjoy the show."

The Arbiter raised one hand, silence falling sharp as a blade.

"The Mischief Spirit has claimed the mortal. Her presence disrupts the pattern. Disruption must be tested."

Mischief Spirit. As if he needed a grand title. He was a thief, nothing more, dressed up in Court theatrics. They could call him whatever they wanted. She refused.

Kipwick's tail flicked, brushing Maren's calf. "Three trials," he whispered, almost kindly. "Always three. Fail, and you're unmade. Survive, and... well. Few do."

Maren's pulse thudded. "And Penny?"

"Collateral," Kipwick said lightly. "Payment promised. If you win, perhaps you'll have leverage. If not…" He let the thought trail off, ears twitching.

The Arbiter's masked face turned back to the Spirit.

"As ruler, you accept responsibility for her trespass."

For the first time, the bastard straightened. Not stiff, but deliberate. His smile thinned into something sharper, older. "Of course," he said, voice smooth as poured wine. "She is mine to present. Mine to wager. Mine to lose."

The Court cheered, vicious and bright.

Maren's nails bit into her palms.

Not his. Not ever.

The Arbiter lowered its hand.

"Three trials,"

The voice intoned, rolling through the chamber like thunder muffled in silk.

"At dawn, the first shall begin."

The words weren't spoken so much as engraved into the air. Maren felt them press against her skin.

The Court erupted. Nobles clapped with gloved hands, stamped jeweled feet, snapped their fingers in sharp bursts of sound. Wagers flew. Predictions tangled in eager whispers:

"She'll break in the first."

"No, the second.

"I'll give a charm she makes it all three, if only so he can toy longer!"

Heat rushed to Maren's face. She wanted to scream that she wasn't a spectacle, wasn't their entertainment. But their hungry gazes told her the protest would only feed them more.

Beside her, Kipwick adjusted his little waistcoat as if all this were a polite luncheon. "They do love a trial," he murmured. "Mortals are such pliable stories. Tear easily. Burn nicely."

Maren shot him a look. "Comforting."

"Honest." His whiskers twitched. "And honesty is rare here."

Across the dais, the thief rose at last. The crowd hushed instantly, as though their delight bent itself to his will. He descended two steps, coin dancing between his fingers, every motion languid and lethal.

He stopped just close enough to catch her eyes, to make sure the Court saw the spark between them. "You hear that, darling? All you have to do is survive."

Maren's throat tightened. "And Penny?"

He leaned in close, too close, until she could smell the cedar-smoke beneath his grin. His whisper slid through her like the whisper of a blade. "Survive," he said, "and maybe I'll let you ask again."

She could've slapped him. Should have. Instead, she stood, locked, fury thrumming so loud it drowned the Court's applause.

The Arbiter's faceless mask turned toward her once more.

"It is decided."

The decree settled like a closing book.

The Court buzzed, delirious with anticipation.

Maren swore, right then, she would not scream for them. Not beg. Not break.

And the Mischief Spirit, smiling like the cat who'd already swallowed her whole, flipped his coin high, catching the light as it spun.

"Try not to disappoint me," he said.

Her retort caught somewhere between her throat and her pride. There were a thousand words she could have thrown, vicious, clever things, but none of them made it past the iron press of her jaw. His eyes held her there, gleaming with cruel amusement, until she hated the sound of her own pulse.

"Take her," he murmured, not loudly but with the weight of a command that didn't need volume.

Hands closed around her arms. They were cold. Elegant. *Unyielding.*

The crowd parted like a living sea, all shimmering silk and teeth, their laughter tapering into low murmurs of satisfaction.

No one helped her.

Why would they?

Mortals were spectacle, not kin.

Maren twisted, trying to wrench free, but the more she struggled, the gentler their grip became, mocking, almost tender, as if she were a child mid-tantrum.

The coin winked once more in the thief's fingers, glinting in rhythm with her defiance. *He's enjoying this,* she realized. *Every second of it.*

Her boots scraped marble. Someone laughed softly as they dragged her backward through the archway. The air bent, shimmered, and then—

Stone.

The echo of the Court vanished like snuffed flame. The archway dissolved behind her as if the world had simply decided she didn't belong in it.

Stone walls. Iron door. The same cot sulking in the corner.

Maren stood for a breath, fists balled tight, chest rising like she was still on the edge of a fight. Her pulse hadn't caught up to the silence yet; it still thundered with the roar of the Court, the Arbiter's decree, Penny's humming in that gilded cage.

She swore again, not softly, not politely, but with the kind of venom that would've made Mrs. Aldren faint on her spotless parlor rug.

Then, she got to work.

The lock was thick, but thick things broke. She yanked at the hinges until her fingers split, shoved her shoulder against the seam until her collarbone screamed, scraped her nails along mortar until powder flaked under her nails. Each failure was fuel. Each bruise earned its place.

"This isn't a cell," she muttered between gasps, forehead pressed to cold iron. "This is kindling."

The cot groaned when she kicked it over. She tore a leg off, splintered wood biting her hands, and jammed it against the lock. The wood snapped first. She cursed so hard the walls echoed it back.

No window.

No vent.

Not even a crack to pry wider.

The Court was clever; it made sure the rat knew exactly how trapped she was.

Her chest heaved, sweat sliding down her temple. But she refused to sit. Refused to curl up and let despair touch her.

If Penny still lived, then there was still a way out of this.

Maren paced because pacing cost nothing and because movement pretended to be progress. Bare feet slapped cold stone in an uneven metronome: plan, pace, spit the plan aloud so it might solidify into something less fanciful than prayer.

"Step one: find Penny. Step two: get out. Step three: bake the smug bastard into a pie if there's time." Her voice ricocheted off the walls and came back small but defiant, like a child throwing a stone at a bell and expecting the bell to break.

The cot leg lay snapped in two at her feet, useless as a wooden spoon in a sword fight. She hurled it anyway. It skittered across the floor and clattered hard, a sound that settled like victory for a heartbeat before it settled into uselessness.

She stood above the wreckage, chest ragged, lips pulled into something too sharp to be a smile. Sweat slicked her hair at the nape of her neck. All useful things had been spent. Anger was the only coin left that still bought heat.

"I won't disappoint you," she hissed at the empty stone, testing how the words sounded alone. "I'll ruin you." The vow felt better spoken than thought. It made a shape to aim for. It made the air move.

Breath was company when the world would not be.

"Ambitious," a dry, amused voice answered.

11

Berries

She spun so fast her curls slapped her cheek.

He was there as if the room had folded him into being: a shape taken from shadow, a coin lazy between his fingers, a line of cedar and citrus that cut the damp of the cell.

Her chest punched the ribs she'd been trying to keep still. She folded her arms, trying to smother the betrayal of the quickened pulse.

"Pout all you like," he said, smiling slowly and practiced. "The walls aren't listening."

"They never did," she shot back, baring her teeth. "And neither am I." It was easier to be furious than to be afraid; fury was a map she knew by heart.

"Mm," he said, stepping inside. The door slid shut behind him without a sound. "And yet here you are, talking."

"I was rehearsing what I'll say when I kill you. Turns out there's quite a list," she spat.

His coin clicked. "Flattered."

"Don't be. The list also includes 'scrub the bakery floorboards' and 'oil the oven hinges.' It's not an honor."

He stepped into the circle of light cast by the single lantern of the cell with the casual confidence of a critic appraising performance art. "Creative use of furniture," he observed. "I especially like the part where you bludgeoned

97

the lock with splinters."

"Glad my suffering entertains you."

"Darling," he murmured, slow grin spreading, "your suffering is practically a gift. Look at you. Every mortal emotion, loud and wild, like fireworks. Do you know how rare that is?"

She stepped closer, jabbing a finger into his chest, ignoring the heat of him, the way he bent slightly toward her like it amused him to be scolded. "You kidnapped Penny. You trapped me here. You want rare? Try surviving me."

He laughed, low and silken, sliding across her like a hand she would have liked to slap away. "Careful. You're starting to sound like an invitation."

The laugh grazed her; indignation flared, and something not-indignation stung at the same place. She shoved her hand back and folded her arms again like armor. "If I invited you anywhere, it'd be into an oven."

He flicked the coin higher; the silver winked against the dull stone. "And yet you look as if you're deciding what flavor I'd be." His eyes followed hers, molten and amused.

Maren scoffed to cloak the heat rising through her. "Burnt."

"Sweet," he countered, smoothly. "Sharp at the edges. Addictive if you're foolish enough to try." He moved closer in a way that made the air between them crackle with electricity.

The cell seemed to contract until it was only the two of them and the small, cruel space of the coin's clink.

Her defiance hung brittle in the room. She would not step back. "Keep talking," she said, voice steady as a blade. "And I'll add 'coin-flipping menace' to the menu."

"Mm." He leaned so near she could feel the heat of him like a promise. His scent threaded into her head, distracting, intoxicating. "Delicious," he breathed, and the single word landed somewhere beneath her sternum where pride usually sat.

It was the wrong kind of hunger. She fisted her hands until the knuckles shone white. If she were clever, if she were nothing *but* clever, she'd answer with a shove. If she were braver, she'd spit. Instead, she cataloged the fact that the Court had taught him how to make mortals burn spectacularly, and that she, stubborn baker that she was, already knew how to strike a match.

The thief's grin stretched, wicked as the coin dancing between his fingers. "You'll forgive the Court's hospitality," he said, "they prefer their mortals… nourished."

A table shimmered into being beside him, obscene in its abundance. Bread still steamed, crust glistening with butter; slices of meat dripped honey; fruit bled sugar and color into crystal bowls. There was even a glass vessel of dark liquid, *not* wine or anything she recognized from Eldenwick, but something that glowed faintly from within. It was the color of dusk and firelight.

A *Spirit's drink*, she realized, the kind of thing that might taste like desire and regret in equal measure.

The scent hit her so hard her stomach betrayed her with a sound she could feel in her ribs. She folded her arms tighter, as if that might hold the hunger down. "I'd rather starve."

He prowled toward the table, deliberate, every movement too fluid for comfort. He plucked a berry; black, glossy, swollen near to bursting, and rolled it between his fingers. Red juice streaked across his knuckles like blood finding a pulse.

"You say that," he murmured, eyes never leaving hers, "but your body disagrees."

Her gaze flicked to his hand. It shouldn't have been erotic. It was *fruit*, for gods' sake. But the way the juice ran, the way his thumb traced the stain, it dragged her mind somewhere far less innocent.

She raised her chin, trying to steady the air in her lungs. "Funny," she said, voice a little rougher than intended, "my fists still say hit you in the face."

"Mm." He smiled without humor. "And yet, they're shaking."

Her breath hitched, traitorously, hating how observant he was.

He lifted the berry, brought it to her lips, holding it there as if daring her. "Open."

Maren scoffed, barbed and breathless all at once. "Not a chance."

"Come now." The mock sympathy in his tone wrapped around something darker, an invitation edged like glass. "You'll need strength. You want to save Penny, don't you? Or would you rather collapse halfway through your *grand* rebellion?"

That name, *Penny,* slid between them like a knife. For a second, the world tightened.

She snatched the berry from his hand before she could think, her fingers grazing his warm skin, and bit down hard. Juice burst tart and red across her tongue. She made sure to chew slowly, to glare while she did it.

"There," she said, swallowing, voice sugar-cut with venom. "Happy?"

His smile deepened, honey-slow. "Ecstatic."

She hurled the stem at his chest. It stuck against the dark fabric before sliding down. "Choke on it."

His laugh was low enough to vibrate through the floor, dark enough that it could have been mistaken for a promise.

"Darling," he drawled, leaning close enough that she could nearly taste him when she breathed, "I'd much rather watch you choke."

Heat coiled deep in her gut, dangerous and traitorous. Every instinct screamed to strike him. Every nerve begged to move closer. She hated both. She hated that the difference between violence and hunger was now a single, impossible breath.

Maren's throat was tight with too many things: fear, fury, want. She swallowed all three, hard, and smiled with every tooth she owned. It wasn't sweetness. It was strategy.

"Funny," she murmured, voice low and dangerous. "For all your coin tricks and clever words, you still haven't managed to get what you want."

The coin slowed in his hand. One brow arched, his amusement sharpening. "And what, pray tell, do I want?"

She leaned another inch closer. Slowly, deliberate. Like the clever heroines in her father's tales, trapped by monsters. "You keep trying to make me yield," she said. "That's the whole game, isn't it? Not the Court, not the trials. Me. And you still haven't managed it."

A sound left him; half chuckle, half growl. Gold eyes caught the dim light like embers. "Yield?" he said softly. "You mistake me. I don't want surrender. Surrender is a full stop." He flipped the coin once, caught it with a flourish that should have looked careless. "What I want is to see how long you'll burn before you break."

The word hit like a struck match. *Burn.* It crawled under her skin and made a home of her pulse. She forced a laugh, brittle as sugar glass. "Careful. You sound like you're begging me to flirt back."

He leaned in even closer, every inch of the move deliberate, slow enough that her breath adjusted to his pace. She could feel his breath hovering over her ear. "Begging?" he echoed, his voice a purr around the word. "I never beg. I invite. And mortals rarely decline."

Her mouth curved, not into warmth but challenge. "Maybe you haven't met the right mortal."

His grin answered, sharp and knowing. "Maybe I just did."

Heat bloomed in her chest, infuriatingly alive. The rational part of her screamed *trap.* The foolish, traitorous part leaned toward the flame. Maybe this was what those old tales had meant when they said that curiosity was a kind of bravery. She let her lashes lower, her tone dipping into something smoky and deliberate. "Maybe you should test that theory," she said. "If you're not afraid."

The coin paused. That smile, the one that always seemed rehearsed, faltered and was replaced by something hungrier. Mischief adored audacity, and she had just given him one hell of a performance.

His hand lifted, brushing the wall beside her head, the way a wolf might pen in prey. "You're not nearly as stubborn as you pretend," he said, voice a low hum. "One berry, and you're already playing my game."

She tilted her head until her breath ghosted his jaw. "Maybe it's *my* game."

Then—swift as instinct, cunning as any storybook trickster—her hand darted past him. She snatched the goblet from the tray, raised it between them like a toast. "To your entertainment."

He smiled. "To your audacity."

She drank. The drink was bitter, sweet, and alive; a taste like lightning and sugar on her tongue, and then she spun.

The empty glass shattered against the lantern. Light burst, not from flame but from something that *wanted* to be flame, the way the Court's magic wanted to mimic life. Fire erupted, greedy and gorgeous, climbing the walls in ribbons of gold and violet.

The heat slapped her face.

He didn't move. Didn't blink. The fire gilded his face, drew molten reflections in his eyes. He looked, gods help her, beautiful. *Blasphemously* so. And then he laughed.

It wasn't cruel laughter. It was even worse. He was delighted.

Proud.

"Oh, darling," he drawled, voice molten as the light around them, "you've finally stopped sulking. You've chosen spectacle."

"Not for you," she spat, lungs burning. Her braid snapped against her back as she lunged for the door. The heat chased her shadow. Her whole body thrummed with the strange pulse of the place, something between heartbeat and thunder.

She thought of her stories again. Thought was magic, her father had said once. Thought, then word, then will.

Open.

Out!

NOW!

The iron shimmered, blurred, and with a shuddering sigh, it split into an arch. Cool air spilled through, sweet as salvation.

Maren's chest seized. She had *done* it. She had made this impossible place listen to her.

She ran.

Bare feet slapped the floor, heartbeat hammering in her ears. The smoke roiled up in black ribbons, the world tilting with her momentum. For the briefest, most glorious instant, she was *free*. Hair flying, lungs filling, air so pure it nearly made her laugh.

She had outfoxed the fox.

Until the air shifted.

"Close," the thief said.

One word. Silk wrapped around steel.

The arch slammed shut, stone knitting back with cruel finality. Maren hit it shoulder-first, pain bursting bright as stars. She gasped, staggering back, rage and smoke clawing her lungs.

Behind her, a coin clicked.

He was still inside, untouched by fire, standing in the haze like it crowned him. His smirk was molten, his eyes molten gold. "You nearly had me," he said. "Nearly."

Her palms burned as she pushed to her feet. "It opened. You saw it. It *listened* to me."

"Yes," he said, savoring every syllable. "That's why you're mine. Not because you failed but because you almost didn't."

The words hit like a chain slipped over her throat. "I am not yours."

"Oh, but you are." He stepped closer. Fire bowed away from him in reverence, kissing her ankles instead. His voice dropped low, velvet drawn across a blade. "Every time you fight, every time you burn, you make yourself mine. Your hate is a leash, Maren. And gods—" his eyes dragged down and up again, slow as sin, "—how you pull it."

Her breath caught, her fury fracturing under the heat of him. She wanted to strike him. She wanted to devour him. She wanted—

No.

She steadied her jaw. "Enjoy your leash while it lasts," she said, voice raw and shaking but hers. "Next time, I'll burn you."

He smiled then. Leaned close enough that the words brushed the shell of her ear. "That," he whispered, "is why I keep you."

And with a flick of his coin, the fire vanished, smoke sucked back into stone. The cell was bare again, cold, unyielding. Only the taste of ash on her tongue and the hammer of her pulse remained.

He turned away, already dissolving into shadow. "Try not to disappoint me."

Silence.

Maren stood trembling, the ache in her shoulder pulsing with every heartbeat. The taste of ash clung to her teeth. Her knuckles stung, her lungs scraped raw, but she had *seen it.*

The door had answered her. The Court had obeyed, even for a breath.

She pressed her palms to the cold floor, grounding herself in pain, in breath, in purpose. "I'll ruin you," she whispered, and this time it wasn't a threat.

It was a prayer.

12

Execution Eve

aren hadn't slept.

Her body had abandoned the idea hours ago, twitching between shallow dozes and half-dreams where gold eyes stalked her through flour-dusted corridors. Every time she blinked, there he was: lounging against her bakery counter like it belonged to him, coin flicking in rhythm with her pulse, mouth curved in that infuriating almost-smile.

She woke cursing, the cot answering with an indignant squeak.

Now she sat on its edge, bare feet dangling, curls gone feral, auditioning for the role of *woman already halfway to a breakdown*.

When the lock clicked, the door didn't open so much as dissolve. The Court, she had learned, had a flair for the dramatic. Shadows folded back on themselves until Kipwick trotted through, waistcoat gleaming, whiskers twitching with anticipation.

"Good dawn, lady mortal," he chirped. "Or should I say: good execution eve?"

Maren rose slowly. Her spine protested, her eyes burned, but her stare could have skinned him where he stood. "Try it, fox. See how well you'd last the first trial."

Kipwick only bowed, paw sweeping like a stage magician. "As charming as ever. This way."

The walls obeyed.

Stone melted outward into a corridor strung with lanterns that weren't lanterns at all; just jars holding a frantic storm of lightning bugs. Their glow caught on veins of gold threading through the obsidian floor, pulsing faintly. Like the Court itself had a pulse.

Maren stepped after him, barefoot at first until the floor shifted slick beneath her, conjuring boots that tightened around her calves. The leather was supple, black. Perfect fit. Perfect insult.

The rest followed suit. Her flour-stained apron sloughed away, threads unspooling midair before reweaving into silk. It was dark, heavy, and restless with glints of gold. A collar clasped at her throat, cool as shackles, pretending to be jewelry. Her curls slipped loose down her back, glossy from some unseen hand.

She froze. Heat crawled up her neck like shame and fury stitched together.

"Stop dressing me like a doll," she hissed at the walls.

The corridor shivered, unconcerned, lantern-light catching the golden threads so they sparked every time she moved. The gown clung as if it had been tailored not just to her body, but to her defiance. Exactly the kind of spectacle the Court of Chaos might have adored.

Kipwick didn't even glance back. "Consider it a kindness. Trials are rarely performed in aprons."

Maren ground her teeth. "Then I'll bleed on the silk."

The fox's whiskers twitched, amused. "Exactly."

They passed through archways stitched from bone-white branches, past mirrors that stretched their reflections taller and sharper than they were.

In one, she swore her hair gleamed like flame, a crown of fire. In another, her hand clasped with a shadowed figure at her side, their crowns crooked but gleaming. A third showed a pale serpent coiled at her throat, its scales rippling with threads that frayed and vanished into nothing. And farther still, just for a blink, her reflection dissolved entirely, and only a pulse of light in the shape of a heart beating against the dark.

She didn't linger.

By the time they reached the trial chamber, Maren's nerves were strung so tight her hands ached from clenching. The space opened suddenly and vast, a hollow cathedral of impossible scale. Pillars of smoke coiled upward into a ceiling stitched with constellations. The floor was a wide circle carved into black stone, its rim already humming with faint light.

Every seat along the perimeter was filled. Nobles, tricksters, and creatures that whispered as she entered, voices overlapping. Hungry.

"Mortal."

"Spectacle."

"She'll burn fast."

Maren lifted her chin.

And then she felt it.

That gaze.

Across the chamber, sprawled like boredom given shape, the thief toyed with his coin. The smirk wasn't full, but it was enough. His gold eyes dragged over her like he'd spent all night waiting for this moment.

Her stomach twisted traitorously. The sensation was half fear, half recognition; a memory her body kept insisting on, even when her mind refused.

Gods. She really had dreamed of him.

"Darling," he drawled, voice rolling across the vast chamber with obscene ease, "you look almost presentable. Amazing what silk and shoes can do."

Maren's jaw ached with the effort of control. She made herself look bored, brushing the glittering threads of her gown as if to check for dust. "So, it was you," she said. "Couldn't resist playing dress-up with your favorite mortal?"

The crowd rippled with laughter, delighted at the sting in her voice. His smirk curved sharper.

"You call it dress-up," he said, flipping the coin high. "I call it preservation. Aprons scorch so easily." His gaze slid lower, a measured drift that traced the collar at her throat. "Besides. You wear a shackle beautifully."

Heat darted down her spine. She masked it with a venomous sweetness. "Careful," she said, smiling with teeth. "Someone might think you're flirting."

He leaned forward, elbows on knees, smirk curling like smoke. "Oh no," he purred. "Just reminding the Court who you belong to."

The chamber gasped. Nobles leaned forward, scenting scandal.

Maren's pulse kicked, but she held her ground. If he wanted theater, she'd give him a better one. Her smirk turned into a blade's edge. "Try claiming me again, thief, and I'll show your court what color a Spirit bleeds."

The crowd erupted with a roar. Wagers flew like sparks, lighting the air with sound.

His grin widened, molten gold catching the starlight. "Magnificent," he said softly, only for her, the word hidden beneath the din. "Burn for them like you burned for me last night."

Her breath stuttered. He meant their sparring, surely, but her body remembered something else. The scrape of heat, the pulse that refused to stay buried.

"I'll burn," she said, voice low and defiant. "But I'll choose who I take with me."

The coin vanished mid-spin, reappearing pinched between his teeth as his smile spread lethal and amused.

And then the air stilled.

The Arbiter slid into being at the chamber's heart, faceless, robed in molten gold. Its silent gaze pressed against the back of her neck until her shoulders locked. The crowd hushed like children waiting for a bedtime story.

The Arbiter intoned, its voice from everywhere and nowhere:

> *"Order demands balance. The mortal has been brought forth. A trial must begin."*

People chewed their nails. The thief lounged, coin flicking lazy as breath, as if he had nothing to do but watch. His gold eyes found her and held her like a question.

The Arbiter lifted a pale, gloved hand. It did not explain so much as carve a shape in the air. It said:

> *"Listen,*
> *The circle is flame.*
> *It listens to story.*
> *Speak truth, and it loosens.*
> *Speak false and it leans.*
> *Speak nothing and it feasts."*

Each phrase hit like a tolling bell, sealing the space in its rhythm. Maren felt the rules settle over her skin, solid and invisible, like chains made of breath.

A hiss rolled through the chamber, a noise like parchment being torn.

The floor at Maren's feet trembled, and a ring of fire rose up around the carved circle. It was taller than a man, a wall of orange and black and oil-slick light. The tongues of flame licked inward, curious, tasting the air.

Heat slammed her like a hand.

She realized, with an almost scientific clarity: silence would kill her faster than lies.

The Court reacted as if hearing a song. Some leaned in, delighted.

Across the circle, the thief's voice slid through the heat. "Speak true and be held, falter and be eaten," he repeated, mimicking the Arbiter as if it were a nursery rhyme. "Simple enough, baker. Don't make it dramatic."

Maren's jaw worked. She wanted to chew his ear off. But breath was currency now, and she intended to save it.

She forced herself to inhale through her nose, slow and thin, and to catalog her options like ingredients:

- Truth: slow burn, possible survival.
- Lie: quick death, guaranteed entertainment.
- Silence: suicide.

The math wasn't good.

She lifted her chin and let the heat wash across her face. Heat made sharp things of her breath. Heat made the silk at her throat puff with smoke. She tasted copper before the flame had even touched skin.

Her mind raced. *Story. They want story. Not pretty, not perfect, but real.*

She thought of her father's fables: the way truth had weight, how falsehoods made the page curl.

Keep it simple. Keep it human. Keep breathing.

The first lick of fire brushed the nape of her neck, singeing a few stray hairs into wet little ropes. The silk collar smoked. The action was a slow, measured cruelty; not to kill at once but to teach what counted.

"Begin."

Maren's voice was sand and rope at first. "My mother," she said, "baked until her fingers bled."

A ripple of approval skimmed the crowd. The flame leaned, tasting the syllables, then eased a hair. The heat pulled back like a cat's ear turning toward a voice. It was not mercy. It was a measurement.

The rule showed its teeth almost immediately. The fire responded to the body of truth. When Maren offered a true detail, the ring drew its tongues inward enough to let cold breath slip past. When she reached for pretty, it swelled and snapped its teeth.

She dug deeper. Memory came in crumbs and the sharpness of real things. "She kept the ledger's stub in her apron, always. She saved the last coin when a neighbor's baby had a fever. She said the till's bell was louder when kindness came with it."

Each fragment cost her breath. Each line felt like pulling heat through wet wool. The flame noticed. It thinned a little. A murmur of satisfaction ran through the nobles. A wager rose, higher.

That was the mercy of the rule. Tell the truth, and the Court fed on a slower hunger. Lie, and it hungrily closed. Stop talking, and it chewed the silence into living flesh.

The second phase came without fanfare.

The silk at her hem blackened in a neat, ugly bloom; the smell of burnt sugar rose, cloying and intimate. A sting crawled across the inside of her calves like an insect. A blister leapt open on her shin and burst, an obscene bead of fluid that huffed and steamed.

She tried to stay steady.

She reached for the story and found only sharp shards. Memory offered her Penny in small pieces. Penny splitting a honey roll in the alley, rosemary caught in her braid, coins slipped into small, numb hands. The details were small and true and therefore holy.

She kept telling. She bled truth like a baker pulling dough. Each honest sentence stretched, elastic, painful, but it held. Each one bought her another breath.

Then she slipped.

She reached for polish when all she had left was raw grain. She tried to make the story pretty.

"My father," she rasped, lungs scraping. "He said the stars themselves listened when he told his tales—"

The lie was small. Almost harmless. He'd never claimed the stars listened. He'd just squinted one eye shut when he got to the punchline, saving light for later. But she wrapped the memory in gold anyway, a flourish meant to impress, a ribbon where there had never been one.

The flame answered like a hound on scent.

It surged.

Heat banged against her ribs so hard she thought one of them might crack. The silk at her throat shriveled, hissing, and a smell rose that would haunt her whole life: hair, sugar, and the small, animal stink of melting fat.

Panic arrived like rain, sudden and cold under the scorch. Her legs wanted to fold. Her hands wanted only to press palm to palm and feel something that was not flame. Her heart hammered so loud she could not hear herself think. For a long breath, she could not form a sentence; her mouth made wet, useless noises.

The ring tightened at her silence, inches closer, pleased.

She tried to anchor herself with anger, as she always did. It was a poor anchor when skin split. The pain came in waves, a staccato of knives. First, the sting, sharp and clean. Then a slow gnawing heat tunneling under flesh into bone. She tasted metal. Her left calf blistered and popped with an indecent little sound; whatever came out of it smelled of old sugar and iron and something that made her gag.

Her voice snapped into a scream before she could close her teeth on it.

The Court laughed. A carnival chorus. Bets clattered higher, coins chinking like knives being sharpened.

Maren gagged on the taste of her own burning. Smoke clotted her throat, turned words into needles. Each attempt to speak further shredded her voice.

Her story stalled. She had nothing left but panic. Panic shaped like cold water, thrashing for the surface. She clawed after another line, another anchor, but the smoke stuffed her mouth, clogged her tongue.

And the fire leaned closer, greedy for her failure.

The Court became a blur at the edge of the smoke, a ring of faces whose eyes were cut-glass and pleasure-drunk. Voices transformed into a single, distant thing. Maren couldn't think of them. She could only think of Penny.

Penny humming in a gilded cage, rosemary braided, mint-sweet laugh stolen.

That thought burned brighter than anything else. Penny's face was the only compass point that did not spin. Her sentences shortened. The story lost polish and became a litany. Memory was no longer art; it was survival.

"I took the bakery," she gasped. "Because no one else could."

Between phrases, she coughed up thick smoke and blood. Her knees trembled. The ring was a bright well of intent, pushing at her like a tide. She felt the Court's attention as a physical pressure; their desire for spectacle pressing into the backs of her legs, wanting to spill her whole open.

"Penny," she said, and the name lodged like a splinter. "She came every day. She split rolls for her brother. She envied the rain that fell on me."

Each clause struck like a match against raw skin. The flame curled its tongues tight to test the truth in every small thing.

"I hired her," Maren whispered, no, it was a groan, "because I was drowning." She had to force the sentence out, to force the lungs to push one more torture of breath. Every syllable stole oxygen. She felt unconsciousness nudge, the soft, tempting dark. Panic was a spider's thread holding her to the present; let it snap, and she would fall into nothing.

The Court's murmurs sharpened when the sound of her voice thinned. Some of them laughed. Some bet. The noise of coins sliding like little blades filled the space. Maren's vision went white at the corners, then acoustically distant, as if the world had been wrapped in wool.

The next line came out in a frantic, jagged heave: "I will not let her—" and her mouth gave up. Sound dissolved into a raw, animal howl. Too big and wrong for words. Her hands clutched at empty air. Her knees hit stone.

The hot pain from the fall shivered up her legs; a new wetness slicked her palms where skin had separated from the underlying flesh.

She thought she was going to black out. The world made small, spinning beacons; the stars stitched overhead bled into smeared fingerprints. All the time she'd been stubborn, refusing sympathy, turning jokes into armor: that armor lay in tatters at the rim of the flame.

She may have imagined the glint of a coin being flipped in the corner of her eye. But she felt a whisper of air reach her lungs instead of a fist. Not enough to heal. A margin. Enough to thread one more sentence through a needle's eye.

"For Penny," she said, the words icily small and ferocious, each one hooked to will like a ring through flesh. "I will burn. I will not let her be just...a prize."

The sentence ripped itself from her in a strangled clang. Her voice came out raw, sanded by smoke, but for the first time since the flame had taken her, the words carried something besides pain: will.

The circle tilted, tasting the stubbornness in that vow. Flame answered with a hot, hard surge that found the soft space behind her knee and laid it open in a white flare. She gave a sound like a broken animal. Skin fluttered. The silk gashed against the flesh, black edges curling. Her boot, sealed onto her foot by summoned leather, stuck to her skin in one horrible, adhesive rip when the magic tried to free it.

She gasped and clung to the story anyway.

Every clause shredded the inside of her chest as if the telling itself were a searing. She counted in her head, not numbers but names; mother, father, Penny, each name an anchor she could wrap her will around. Each time she promised, the air came back in the slimmest measure.

"People called me lucky," she coughed, blood tasting like pennies when it hit her tongue. "They—" A cough stole the next word. She coughed until her vision tunneled black. "They didn't see the ledger."

She should have been incoherent. Any sane mortal should have been. She should have been begging, screaming, giving up. Instead, she fought like a baker kneading dough with broken hands: one bit at a time, through the worst of it. Each tiny sentence was a folded layer of will. Each breath was bartered for a single line.

Maren's lungs had the minute to pull in another ragged breath. That eked breath let her finish the vow: "I will find her. I will take her home."

Her voice broke on the last word into a sob that was less noise than bone-scraping.

She slid forward. Her hands, blistered and raw, left bloody smears on the black stone. For a breath, she had no sense at all of her body as more than pain points. When she finally opened her eyes, the world swam, and the faces beyond the smoke were a circus of indifferent light.

Kipwick clicked his teeth. Someone clapped. A noble shouted for finer entertainment. The thief's coin flashed, and the fire drew back enough to show the Arbiter's mask, impassive and indifferent.

Maren did not remember the Arbiter's words, only that it pronounced she endured. Only that she heard something like the Court's approval explode, and that the sound was a physical shove against the ribs.

She tasted copper and salt.

She tried to move and could not feel her left ankle; the boot had become a welded thing of skin and leather. Her leg trembled under her like a ruined machine.

The thief lounged, expression smoothed to lazy pleasure. His coin lay quiet between finger and thumb. His mouth shaped something that could have been nothing at all.

She crawled out of the circle on hands that screamed and knees that left black tack marks on the stone. Each inch was an argument. Each gritted inch was a victory. When she reached the rim, someone in the crowd sobbed, moved by the spectacle; someone else laughed, speculating whether the scars would be pretty.

Maren's skin hung in ragged, angry sheets where the fire had eaten it. Blisters the size of coins trimmed the edges of her arms, and one thumb was a white, useless nub.

Pain radiated in cold and heat at once, a two-headed beast that would not be sated. She tasted ash and her own blood and the old sugar of the bakery, and the smell of rosemary, Penny's rosemary, was a mirage that made her ache.

She had saved nothing but a promise. Her promise smelled like burned flesh and iron.

Gold eyes found hers through the haze. For one heartbeat, his gold flashed with something that was not mischief but a sharper, rawer thing: calculation and the echo of a plan briefly derailed. The coin in his hand spun, a lazy, private metronome. He did not rush to her side. He watched, and when he smiled, it was like a cut.

She spat blood on the floor because she could not think of a better thing to do. The sound of it was obscene, a hideous punctuation. In the bleary ring of spectators, the bets settled. The Court hummed its approval, and the Arbiter's voice declared the trial adjudged: she had lived this round.

The words reached her ears, but not her body. Her body had gone elsewhere—into pain too vast to map. Her skin hung in strips, boots fused to blisters, every inhale a knife dragged crosswise through her chest. She clung to the floor, slick with her own blood, until her hands forgot how to hold.

The chamber tilted. Black ate at the edges of the firelight, devouring smoke and stone alike. She thought of Penny one last time: Penny's rosemary crown, Penny's laugh. The image flickered, frayed, and burned to ash.

Then nothing.

13

Fever Dream

The stone was cold.

Not the winter kind that promised thaw, but the deep-vault chill that had never met a hearth. It climbed her spine and made a home beneath her burns, claimed her ribs, set its teeth in the soft places, until her body belonged more to the chill than to her.

Breath came shallow and uneven, sawed thin by smoke.

Inhale, knives.

Exhale, iron.

Her chest hitched against the tightness of her tortured skin like a door that did not fit its frame.

The burns argued for first place. Angry, wet, a country of ruin spread over her skin. Fever waited just outside her edges, patient as a creditor. She could feel it counting.

No one came.

The Court was vast, loud, eternal. It danced and drank and rearranged its own bones outside these walls. Here, inside, a mortal girl lay crumpled on a cot that smelled of mildew, not worthy of witness.

She tried to turn her head. Her cheek stuck. When it peeled free, it left a damp smear the color of failure.

For a blink that expanded into forever, she thought: *so this is it.*

Not a legend. Not a noble end. The opposite of a story. A quiet rot on a borrowed slab, untallied, unremarked.

She listened for courage and heard only the small mechanics of survival.

Heart.

Breath.

Pain's steady metronome tapping beneath both.

Her eyes slid shut, not in surrender, but because there was nowhere else to look.

Heat bloomed behind her eyelids, slow and internal, a furnace sealed beneath the skull. The ache built until it should have burst, but when she blinked—

It wasn't Stone that answered.

It was *home*.

The bakery breathed around her like an old animal, sighing through its vents and seams. Steam rose from the ovens in tender curls, silvering the air. Flour drifted through the haze, falling so softly it could have been snow; if snow smelled of vanilla and sugar and the faint, forgiving smoke of overbaked crusts.

The warmth hurt worse than the cold ever could. Familiarity always did.

Her lungs tried to weep, but the sound came out as a dry, breaking wheeze.

Her father sat at the counter, spectacles balanced low, his hand steady over the pages. He didn't look up at first; he never did when she interrupted his books with nonsense.

"Papa," she whispered. The word cracked like old glass.

His head lifted instantly, not startled, but rather *summoned*. That small softening on his face, that patient curve of recognition, was almost too much to bear.

"You kept the corner folded," he said, nodding toward the battered storybook left open beside him. His voice came from two directions at once, both past and fever. "Good. Stories need a place to breathe."

The words landed both like a mercy and a knife. Maren's mouth twitched toward laughter. What came out was a brittle sound, like glass that was about to break. For a second, she imagined curling into that laugh and sleeping forever.

Her mother turned from the oven, brushing flour from her sleeve with a small, practical swipe. That gesture alone, the unshakable calm, was enough to split Maren open.

She wanted to reach out, to press her thumb into the white dust on her mother's wrist, to feel warmth that didn't blister. But she hesitated, half afraid the air would refuse to give her hand back.

In the next breath, Penny was there too, bright as midsummer, herbs woven into her golden hair. She hummed as if she'd been here all along, as if life had always been this: their three voices under one roof.

Penny tilted her head, smirk warm enough to scald. "You look ridiculous when you try to be tragic," she teased.

The tease landed exactly where her body ached most.

Maren's throat tightened. Words surged up, too many, all jagged. Everything she had buried under ovens and obligations fought to surface:

that she had loved books before bread,

that she had dreamed of fables instead of festivals,

that she had been terrified of failure,

bored by routine,

and guilty for wanting anything beyond Eldenwick's narrow streets.

She wanted to spill everything.

She wanted to lay her contradictions out like loaves to cool, but her mouth wouldn't obey. The words were dough before the rise: dense, half-formed, impossible to swallow, impossible to serve.

Her chest burned hotter than the fever now. Her body knew she was dying, but her heart hadn't caught up yet.

The bakery shivered. Counters blurred at the edges, breathing like lungs. Her father's pages ruffled, though no breeze stirred them. Her mother's hand froze mid-motion, trembling faintly. Penny's smile softened, tilting toward a question.

"Say it," her father urged, voice low, steady as prayer. "Say the thing out loud."

Maren's lips cracked. Her voice was threadbare, frayed to nothing. "I—"

Black seeped in. Like ink spilling across a page, it ate the edges of her vision. The oven's click became a far-off hum, then a metallic rattle, then—

Stone.

The bakery snapped away. Cold iron slammed into her senses: mildew, blood, sour air. Her breath rattled in pieces, each inhale forced past a ribcage that no longer trusted itself. The cot beneath her was stone pretending to be mercy. The bandages at her ribs pulsed with heat that might have been fever or spell work. Her skin felt borrowed, like thin parchment pulled too tight over the ache beneath.

A strip of light leaked through the iron door and broke against her cheek, crosshatching her in gold and gray. Her body didn't fit her anymore; she couldn't tell where the burns ended and the trembling began.

Bandages pressed at her ribs; she couldn't remember when they'd been wrapped. She tried to move. The world folded her under instead, nausea rising like a tide.

Somewhere close, metal whispered against metal. Water, basin, cloth. The small domestic noises of care, wrong in a place like this.

Then came the voice.

Soft. Too soft.

A whisper tuned to her pulse, careful and intimate, spoken by someone who had already learned her breaths by count.

She tried to answer, but the sound died before it reached her mouth; a cracked rasp that left her lips bleeding.

Her tongue tasted of something she hadn't eaten in days, or weeks. Berry. Too sweet. Too sharp. The flavor bit through the metal tang like a dream refusing to end.

Her body didn't believe in miracles anymore, but the memory of sweetness was enough to trick it into wanting one.

Panic stirred. Small, mechanical, like a wind-up bird fluttering its last wingbeat inside her gut.

She tried to lift her hand, but it didn't move. The fever pressed its palm to her chest, firm, possessive.

The whisper came again, closer now.

A breath against her ear that sounded almost like a promise, or a warning:

"Breathe."

So she did. Barely.

And in that fragile, borrowed breath, the bakery began to bleed back through the cracks.

She sat at the table now, though she didn't remember sitting. Steam veiled the windows, blurring Eldenwick into watercolor. The ovens glowed steadily, their breath lapping her skin in waves that promised safety.

Her father was writing this time. The story poured neatly and looping, ink tracing its own gravity. She couldn't read the words, but she felt their pull in her ribs, the way a child leans toward firelight without thinking what fire means.

Her mother hummed at the counter, kneading dough that shimmered faintly, like it might rise on its own. The sound was ordinary, almost holy. If Maren listened hard enough, she could nearly catch the answer to every question she'd never dared ask.

Penny perched on the counter, swinging one bare foot, grin reckless and warm. "You've been sulking for hours," she said, as if sulking were a profession Maren had chosen. "Say the thing already."

The *thing.*

Maren's throat locked. She swallowed until it hurt, trying to force sound through smoke. "I tried," she said, voice breaking on the effort. "Gods, I tried so hard. I ran the bakery. I kept the books. I thought if I worked enough, it would—" she almost laughed, breath hitching—"feel like enough."

The air trembled around the word *enough.*

Her father's pen slowed, then stopped. Ink bled into the page like blood through linen.

Her mother dusted her hands and looked at her with that mixture of pride and disappointment Maren remembered too well. Except this time, the disappointment was gentler, like it wanted to let her off the hook.

"You wanted more," her mother said simply.

It should have sounded like an accusation, but it didn't. It sounded like the truth.

Maren bowed her head. Tears hit the table, two sharp dots on the wood grain. "I wanted—" Her voice faltered. "I wanted stories. Not ledgers. Not loaves. I wanted foxes and forests and endings that surprised people."

Her father closed the book carefully, as if afraid to startle her truth. He reached across the table, thumb smudged with ink and ash, and wiped one tear away.

"Then why didn't you?"

Because.

Because she was duty.

Because she was bread and numbers and survival.

Because she'd buried her wants so deep, she'd thought she'd killed them.

She opened her mouth, but the words came out as sobs instead, jagged and humiliating.

"Because I was *scared*."

The silence that followed was unbearable. She braced for judgment, for scolding.

Instead, Penny slid from the counter, curling an arm around her shoulders, the smell of rosemary enveloping her completely. "So what if you were scared?" she whispered. "You're still here."

Maren pressed her face against Penny's shoulder, shaking with the force of it. For once, she didn't care how it looked. "I miss you," she rasped.

"I know." Penny's voice was tender, but wrong at the edges, too calm.

Her mother sat beside her, smoothing curls back from her damp face. "You don't have to be only what we left you."

Her father's eyes lifted, fierce now, bright as a candle's flame before the wick dies. "You can be more."

The words cracked something open.

Her heart surged with wanting. Wanting to write. Wanting to live. Wanting Penny alive. Wanting a life beyond flour and fire and ledgers that never balanced.

She lifted her head, eyes raw. "But I failed. I'm here, and she's gone, and I—"

The bakery wavered. The walls stretched and blurred, their edges running like ink in the rain. Penny's face flickered between light and shadow.

Her mother twisted sharply, discordantly.

Maren gripped Penny's sleeve tighter, desperate. "Don't go. Please, don't—"

Black seeped through the windows, eating the light. The ovens shuddered.

The chill rushed in.

Her body was pinned to the cot by exhaustion. She couldn't tell where the fever ended and paralysis began. Every breath was a negotiation: take air in, pay with pain.

The whisper didn't stop. It came steadily, threaded through the fever's ringing, too patient to be imagined.

Coin.

Click.

The sound slotted into the quiet like a metronome.

Her gut clenched. She knew that rhythm. Gods help her, she knew.

But her body was too weak to lift, too weak to fight. She could only lie there, trembling, fever-shaken, clutching the memory of warmth from the dream like it was the last crust of bread in the basket.

Her chest hitched again, half-sob, half-breath. The sound startled her. She hadn't meant to give it away.

For the first time since the trial flame had gutted her, she pitied herself. Bitterly, honestly, with no snark sharp enough to cut it down.

She was broken. She was alone. And someone, or something, was here.

Maren's fingers curled against the cot. She wanted to be furious, to spit some barbed line, but her body betrayed her. The fever pressed heavier, dragging her under. Each blink took longer to return from. Each breath fought harder to stay.

Fear should have held her upright. Should have kept her tethered to stone and pain. But even fear was slipping, dulled to a dim throb under her ribs.

Her hand slid from the edge of the cot, limp. Her body gave the truth before her mind could argue it: she couldn't hold this anymore.

Her consciousness bled out, and the cell dissolved around her.

Stone became wood. The stench of infection gave way to vanilla. Shadows folded back into light, ovens humming with heat that warmed, rather than burned.

Maren staggered forward, her body suddenly light again, her wounds forgotten, but her voice cracked with the wreckage she carried.

"Please don't leave me," she whispered.

Her plea lingered in the warm bakery air, but the reply came from somewhere colder.

A hand, not her father's, not Penny's, brushed against her ribs. Light as thread. Clinical as a knife.

The ovens hummed louder, the heat rising like a tide, but beneath it pulsed a cool bite. She felt it: the cot under her back, her body fever-slick, and every nerve screaming. A thumbprint of ink burned on her cheek, but beside it, another sensation bloomed; fingers smoothing bandage from skin, dragging slow, deliberate lines across wounds.

The worlds folded on top of each other.

Her mother leaned in, tucking curls from her face, whispering: *You don't have to be only what we left you.*

But the touch belonged to someone else; someone with longer, steadier fingers that were callused in places her mother's had never been. They lingered at the curve of her collarbone, then traced lower, pressing against her scorched ribs until she gasped.

Constellations flared beneath her skin. Bright, unbearable, and then dimming into scars.

The bakery lanterns popped one by one, stars breaking overhead, only to reappear stitched into her flesh.

"Rest," murmured a voice.

Coin.

Click.

She whimpered, shaking her head, but the bakery steadied her again. Penny's arm anchored her shoulders, rosemary brushing her jaw. "So what if you were scared?" Penny whispered. "You're still here."

But Maren felt the lie. She felt the press of another hand sliding lower, brushing the hollow of her hip, tracing a star into tender skin. She arched weakly, too fever-slack to resist.

Another stitch. Another burn soothed too gently.

The bakery wavered. Her father's eyes gleamed across the counter, gold instead of brown. His coin spun in ink-stained hands that had never known coins.

Maren sobbed, raw. "I want—" Her throat failed. Her body shuddered against the cot, against his fingers.

The ledger closed. The ovens hissed. The bakery dissolved in steam.

And in the cell, a man leaned over her, coin flashing lazily between stitches, hands impossibly gentle as he pulled silver light through her skin. Constellations bloomed along her ribs, her arms, her throat. Scars that would never quite fade, written like a map only he could read.

Her body jerked once, fighting. Her voice, cracked and half-gone, broke into the stone-dark: "Stop—"

But his whisper brushed her temple, velvet and merciless. "Never."

The fever dragged her back under. The bakery returned, warm and false, her parents smiling, Penny humming. They didn't leave. Not yet.

But the scars were there now, glowing faintly beneath her dress.

14

Star-Marked

The stone was gone.

Maren blinked, slow and jagged, as if her eyelids were weighted with ash. The mildew-stained and reeking cot she remembered had vanished. Beneath her now lay something firm and faintly warm, not quite soft enough for comfort.

For a wild moment, she thought, *I died and got promoted.*

Her second: *not likely.*

If the Court did afterlives, they would've made hers humiliating.

The air was clean here. Not bakery-clean. There was no cinnamon or yeast to cling to her tongue. This was stranger; a faint metallic tang, something that hummed just beyond human senses.

She pushed herself upright, movement scraping along stiff muscles. Her hair tumbled forward in a snarl of curls, and then stopped. She looked down.

Her arms.

Not blackened. Not blistered. No peeling skin, or angry ruin carved into her flesh. Instead, faint patterns of light marked her in slender arcs and dots, as though some celestial map had been inked just beneath the skin. Silver at first glance, but when she moved, they glowed blue-white, shimmering like embers that refused to die.

Constellations.

Maren sucked in a breath. The sound rattled in her lungs, too loud in the hush of the room. She turned her arm slowly, watching the marks shift, flex with her muscles. Not the scars or brutal, melted aftermath she knew should be there and fully expected. These were... *beautiful.*

Her stomach turned.

It wasn't right. She'd felt the fire tear her apart. She remembered the scream scraping up her throat, the smell of skin burning, the way her body convulsed as if it wanted to crawl out of itself.

She remembered the certainty that she'd be ruined, unrecognizable, if she lived at all.

And now? She looked like one of them. Etched in impossible patterns, ornamented instead of maimed.

Her hands curled into fists, trembling against the sheets.

She *hated* it.

Hated how her chest ached with relief that she didn't look like melted wax. Hated how her pulse stuttered with shame for even thinking that. Hated the way the silver glow looked almost right against her pale skin, her storm-colored eyes, her wild curls.

They'd made her beautiful.

She tried to remember what had happened after the trial. After the fire ate her alive? Her thoughts scattered, slid away when she reached for them. She remembered... voices. Gold eyes watching through a fog.

But the moment she tried to drag those fragments into focus, her mind blanked. As if the memory itself had been cauterized. A mercy or a theft, she couldn't tell.

Her nails dug into her palms. She stared at the glowing lines across her arms, the way they pulsed faintly in time with her heartbeat.

Her eyes flicked over herself: she was dressed now, though she didn't remember being touched. A simple shift, linen white, sleeveless, hung loose to her knees. It smelled faintly of ozone, not cloth. Someone had washed the blood from her hair and combed her curls back from her face. Care had been taken, which somehow felt more obscene than pain.

"Gods," she whispered, voice ragged. "What did you do to me?"

The walls didn't answer.

Maren shoved the blanket off and swung her legs over the side of the bed. The floor was cool stone, solid under her bare feet, too steady for the way her chest shook.

She needed proof.

A mirror.

Something that would show her the damage, honestly.

The room didn't oblige.

Curved walls arched overhead, ceiling veined with faint starlight that moved like breath under skin. The air hummed, faint but constant, a low vibration that filled the gaps between her thoughts.

She pressed her palms to her glowing arms, half hoping the light would smear off on contact. It brightened despite her efforts.

"Stop it," she muttered. The sound came out hoarse.

She started to pace, slow, uneven steps. Each breath scraped her ribs. She was looking for anything reflective: a polished bowl, a shard of metal, the back of a spoon. Anything that could tell her the truth.

Then she saw it.

The door.

The same, but cracked open. As if the room itself had grown careless.

Her pulse kicked.

A dozen thoughts collided: trap, trick, miracle. Her body didn't care which. The sight of freedom crawled electric through her veins.

She clenched her fists, scars sparking under her skin. If the Court thought it could gild her wounds and cage her in gratitude, it had misread its mortal.

Maren crossed the room, her steps gaining confidence with each pulse of that silver-blue glow. She shoved the door wide.

Noise tumbled through: laughter, drums, the clash of goblets.

Maren bared her teeth in something that wasn't a smile. Perfect cover for searching. Perfect distraction. And if the Court wanted to celebrate her survival. Fine. She'd use its chaos to her advantage.

She stepped through the threshold.

The hallway stretched sideways into an impossible arcade of light and shadow. Walls bent in soft curves, each pulse of her heartbeat seeming to push them farther apart. Lanterns floated overhead, swaying like jellyfish caught in a tide. They didn't burn with flame, but with words: black ink unspooling into the air, letters dissolving before they finished their sentences. Some glowed faintly gold; others shimmered white-blue, their fragments drifting like snow.

When she moved, the air brushed her skin as if trying to read her.

Ribbons hung from the vaulted ceiling. A few gleamed like moonlight on water. The rest whispered words when they swayed, soft and coaxing, syllables that slipped through the language barrier and straight into her mind.

She stopped breathing until they fell quiet again.

The scent here was dizzying: wine, ozone, and something sharp that didn't belong like… blood?

Hers?

Her pulse echoed it, drumming out of sync with the music leaking from farther down the corridor.

She wanted to go left. Or right. Anywhere but forward. But the Court leaned, literally: the floor sloped just enough to send her weight sliding toward the sound.

The air shifted with invitation.

She muttered, "No," under her breath, and the word came out small, almost childish.

Her hands shook. The glowing lines beneath her skin brightened, veins rethreading themselves in silver-blue rebellion. The hall seemed to notice, its whispering ribbons shivering in response, letters stuttering midair.

"I want Penny," she said louder, testing whether the world would listen.

It didn't. The air only hummed back, low and knowing, like a cat's purr at the sight of prey.

Her bare feet carried her forward anyway, treacherous in their obedience. The slanted floor became a guide, the murmuring lanterns an audience.

The noise swelled, too big for the narrow corridor: laughter, applause, the rattle of dice, a violin scraping wild against a drumbeat.

The hall spilled into an impossible chamber; a ballroom stretched out before her, too vast for reason, too golden for sanity. The kind of space that looked like someone had swallowed a cathedral, a starlit sky, and a fever dream…and then decided it still needed more chandeliers.

Revelers twirled across a mirror-polished floor that shimmered like a lake made of starlight and glass. No shoes scuffed its surface. No feet ever quite touched it. Beings moved in impossible elegance. One, spun entirely from smoke and song, danced with a creature of polished obsidian whose fingers left trails of midnight. A woman wore a dress made of flame and feathers, both real, both shifting as she dipped her partner, who might have been a sentient gust of wind.

The laughter in the air fizzed like champagne. Magic hung thick in the space, sweet and heavy. Tables bowed under platters of food that glowed faintly, pulsing with magic. A fruit blinked. A roast tried to climb off the table before a guest politely stabbed it with a fork.

A revel.

The kind that bent itself toward her, each laugh pitched brighter as she entered, each eye glancing her way before sliding off again, as though pretending not to stare.

Maren's throat tightened. She hated how her pulse quickened. This was the wonder she'd once begged for, wasn't it? The noise, the spectacle, the sense of stepping inside a story bigger than herself. For one breath, she *wanted* it.

Then she remembered Penny in the cage, and the want turned sour.

Still, the Court pressed. The music swelled, the floor tipped her nearer to the throng, and when her gaze lifted instinctively toward the heart of it, she found him.

Thief.

The coin-flipping bastard lounged like the revel had been built to orbit him. A constellation of mythical beauties draped across him; arms looped, hair tumbling, gowns shifting hue with every sigh. One leaned against his chest with sea-glass hair and a smile like a sharpened shell. The coin glinted between his fingers.

Gold eyes caught the lamplight, and even at this distance, she knew he'd already seen her.

Maren's pulse gave a traitorous kick.

The Court of Chaos, damn it, had led her straight to him.

She tore her gaze away, but it was too late. The image branded itself behind her eyelids.

And that was when a fox leapt into her path.

"Marvelous!" Kipwick crowed, bowing low. "Our mortal heroine survives! Barely singed, delightfully scarred, and looking like she just escaped a bakery fire." His whiskers twitched with glee. "Oh, wait. That part's accurate."

Maren blinked at him. "Move," she said flatly.

He swept aside with a flourish, never missing a step. "Of course. Straight into the wolf's den. Do try not to get eaten."

"Not worried," she muttered, though her pulse disagreed.

Kipwick walked along beside her anyway, tail flicking like a metronome. "Good! Wagering is still open, and I've put five coppers on you lasting until dawn. Don't disappoint me."

Maren clenched her fists. The Court laughed around her, the music surged, and no matter how many steps she took, the gravity of the room kept pulling her back toward *him*.

Her feet carried her forward before she could stop them, each step a dare, each step betraying how badly she wanted to land a blow… even if it was only with words.

Her jaw locked. *Use the anger. Not the awe.*

"You enjoy throwing parties for your casualties?" she asked, voice hard enough to slice through the music.

His coin stilled. The grin spread slowly. "Not casualties. Survivors. It's a narrower guest list."

She laughed once, bitterly. "Last time you promised I'd burn beautifully."

He leaned forward, elbows on his knees, gaze drinking her in. "And you did. Look at you. Still standing and still sparking." His eyes slid deliberately to the faint glow of her arms. "Radiant."

Heat licked up her throat, fury dressed in blush. "Radiant isn't the word."

"No?" The coin spun again, catching blue firelight from her scars. "Chaos thinks it suits you."

The words landed low in her gut, dangerous as a kiss.

Maren's throat burned. She forced a smirk. "Glad my agony was so entertaining."

"Agony?" His eyes glinted, molten in the lamplight. "You shimmer now. The Court gave you stars for skin. Chaos prefers its mortals…improved."

She shoved an arm out, scars glowing faintly in the revel light. "Improved? I should've been ash."

His grin was all teeth. "You should have. But instead, you're standing here, bright and furious. Don't tell me you're not enjoying it."

Her pulse jumped. She hated him for being right. She hated him more for knowing it.

"One day I'll kill you," she whispered, every word a blade.

The coin spun, caught, spun again. His smile curved, slow and wicked. "Promises, promises."

That was when *she* moved.

Her hair tumbled in sea-glass waves, crown fashioned from delicate coral branches that gleamed wet in the lantern light. Skin pearlescent, gown shifting from tide-green to moonlit blue with each move she made.

Maren named her instantly: *Coral Head.*

She slid against his side like she'd been poured there, voice honeyed and false. "Don't mind her," Coral Head crooned, tracing one elegant finger along his sleeve. "Still smoldering from the trial. Poor thing hasn't learned that smoke doesn't last."

Her smile dripped sweetness. Her eyes did not.

Maren let her lips curl in something that wasn't a smile. "Strange. All I see is driftwood trying to cling to the nearest rock."

The mythical women draped nearby tittered. Coral Head's fingers stilled against his arm, nails biting silk.

The thief only watched Maren. His grin widened, sharp with approval. "Careful," he murmured, golden gaze hot. "If you keep sparking like this, you'll set the whole Court alight."

"Good," Maren said. "Let it burn."

Coral Head laughed, sultry and false, tilting her coral crown so it gleamed like blood. "Darling, chaos doesn't burn. It consumes. Best you learn the difference before you're ash."

Maren met her gaze, steady, scars glowing faintly with every heartbeat. "Guess we'll see which of us the fire eats first."

The thief's coin spun again, faster now, his eyes never leaving Maren. Not the coral-crowned beauty pressed tight against him. Not the revel roaring around them. Just her.

And Coral Head knew it.

Coral Head's laugh slid over the music like oil. She tipped her crown of coral just so, so the light made it blaze rose-gold, and leaned into him with feline ease.

"Come," she purred, voice velvet and venom. "This crowd is noisy. Let's find somewhere more...private."

Her hand trailed down his sleeve, possessive as shackles. The woman nearest them giggled knowingly, eyes glittering with the promise of spectacle.

The coin-flipping bastard didn't shrug her off. Of course, he didn't. He let her curl closer, let her words drip into the air like bait. He smirked, not at Coral Head, but at Maren.

Like he knew precisely which chord he'd just plucked.

Something low and sharp twisted in Maren's chest. Jealousy, ugly and hot, spiked before she could choke it down. The memory hit fast, the berries, the way he'd looked at her like she was the only dangerous thing in the room. Her pulse stuttered in recognition of that moment; of the stupid warmth it had sparked.

And now? Now he sat golden-eyed and unbothered while Coral Head draped herself like seaweed across a wreck.

Maren's throat ached. She forced the bitterness down until it sat heavy as the ash in her gut.

Hatred was cleaner.

Hatred was easier.

Penny was still out there, caged or worse, and here she was wasting breath on the villain who stitched stars into her skin and smiled like he owned the fire that nearly killed her.

She smiled then, razor-thin, and inclined her head as if granting permission. "By all means," she said sweetly, venom tucked beneath every syllable. "Don't let me interrupt."

Coral Head's answering grin glittered, too many teeth for sweetness. She twined her arm through his and tugged, triumphant. The bastard let her. The coin flashed once more, lazy and deliberate, before he rose to follow.

The revel swallowed them both, gasping with laughter and cheers as though it had just been fed.

Maren stood in the space they'd left behind, pulse hammering. She clenched her fists until the constellation scars pulsed against her skin. She refused to look shaken. She refused to let them see.

Jealousy was a luxury.

Hatred was *fuel*.

And Penny—

Penny was the reason she would not break here.

The Court wanted to toy with her heart. She'd use its chaos for cover instead.

Maren turned, slipping into the revel's madness, letting the noise mask her escape.

15

Fire Girl and the Bastard Coin-Flipper

The revel roared on behind her.

Maren pushed through the crush of dancers until the music blurred into a dull, distant throb. She didn't look back.

Penny. Penny. Penny. Penny. Penny...

The name pulsed in her skull, the only rhythm worth keeping. If the Court thought it could bury purpose beneath silk, gold, and that bastard's smile, it had gravely underestimated its mortal experiment.

She'd find Penny. Drag her out by the wrist if she had to. She'd burn the whole damned realm or tear down every impossible hallway to do it.

The corridor stretched ahead, lit by lanterns that breathed out their faint light. The walls seemed to flex in the periphery, rearranging their angles every time she blinked.

A throat cleared behind her.

Maren didn't startle. She'd learned by now the Court loved to announce itself at the most inconvenient moments. She did, however, curse under her breath when Kipwick came into step beside her, a crystal goblet balanced in one paw like he'd just wandered out of the orchestra pit.

"So," he chirped, tail swishing smugly, "should I alert the Court to prepare for your enemies-to-lovers arc, or...?"

Maren stopped dead. "Not. Another. Word."

"Very well," he said solemnly, and took a sip. "I'll draft it instead. Working

135

title: *Fire Girl and the Bastard Coin-Flipper*. Bestseller material."

Her cheeks heated. From anger, obviously. "You've been eavesdropping."

"Observing," Kipwick corrected, whiskers twitching. "It's called mentorship. You storm; I narrate." He tipped the goblet toward her scars, which pulsed faintly in the lantern glow. "And I must say, your new look has the audience enraptured."

"Stars aren't a fashion choice," Maren snapped.

"Ah, but here? Everything is. Even survival." He padded ahead a few paces, then glanced back, eyes too knowing for his grin. "The Court tilts toward what you want, Lady Mortal. Always has. But beware. It doesn't give. Instead, it bargains. And some bargains come stitched in silver."

Maren's stomach tightened. She hated the implication.

Maren folded her arms, glaring down at him. "You're saying the Court gave me these." She flicked her chin at the constellations crawling up her arms. "Because I wanted them."

"I'm saying," Kipwick replied, finishing his drink with a flourish, "that the Court listens to what's unsaid louder than what's shouted. You wanted to live. It obliged. Beautifully, like it always does."

"That's not an answer."

"It's the only one you'll get." His grin flashed, too many teeth for comfort. He set the goblet on a ledge that hadn't existed a heartbeat ago. "Now, off you go. Find your Penny, if that's where your feet insist on dragging you. I've got money on you lasting another round."

Before she could retort, he melted into the shadows, whiskers and waistcoat vanishing as though he'd never been there.

Maren exhaled through her teeth. Alone again. Good.

The corridor stretched out before her, longer than it had been a moment ago, like the Court had stretched it to watch her sweat.

"Fine," she muttered. "Watch."

She started forward, jaw tight, hands balled at her sides. She quickly realized the corridor wasn't a corridor anymore, but a throat.

Long, alive, and endlessly swallowing itself. Every time Maren blinked, its length changed: stretching, contracting, sighing through its seams. The light wasn't constant either. It flickered like a mood, softening to gold when her anger spiked, sliding to blue when exhaustion threatened to pull her under.

So this is why they call it the Court of Chaos.

It wasn't chaos in the sense of disorder. It was precision masquerading as madness. The realm didn't break its own rules; instead, it just rewrote them before anyone could catch up.

Maren moved carefully, back straight, each step measured against the drum of her pulse. Her skin glowed faintly in the dark, constellations flickering like signal lights, throwing warped shadows up the curved walls. She tried not to think about the fact that her body could now light a hallway on its own.

She fixed her mind on Penny instead. *Rosemary, superstition, Delight, soft voice, that stubborn laugh.* If the Court listened, then let her want be a compass. Let it drag her straight to her friend.

At first, it seemed to work. A hum echoed faintly in the dark, soft and familiar: Penny's habit of humming while she worked, little half-songs that had filled the bakery in Eldenwick.

She followed.

Left, then right, then left again. Each corner opened onto a new shape of wrong: ceilings bending inward, floors tilting until she had to brace her palm against the wall to stay upright. The wall was warm to the touch, breathing slow as if with a pulse of its own.

The Court had always been described as a *realm*, but realm wasn't the right word. Kingdoms stayed put. This place wasn't built to be understood; it was built to be experienced. To devour awe and spit it back in prettier forms.

She caught glimpses between turns of open doorways spilling impossible scenes. A garden blooming underwater, its petals shedding tiny bubbles of light. A clock with no hands, its face bleeding sand. A stairway that led nowhere but made the air hum when she stared too long.

Everything here existed on purpose. Just not hers.

The humming wove through it all, always a few steps ahead.

"Penny?" Her voice cracked on the name.

No answer. Only the shift of the hallway, an almost playful tilt beneath her feet.

Her mind worked even as panic clawed for purchase. *If the Court listens to what I want, maybe it's feeding on it. Maybe it's letting me chase her to see how long I'll run.*

Her feet rang against stone, deliberate and rhythmic. The pulse in her arms matched it beat for beat, its veins pulsing like a drumline.

The first door she reached gleamed faintly, handle warm under her palm.

She wrenched it open.

Fire.

The world split into color and heat. The blast hit her face before she had time to scream. Orange light swallowed everything; smoke clawed into her throat. The bakery's oven yawned wide, its mouth full of roaring flame, dough already blackening to ash.

The smoke curled toward her in greedy fingers, burning her throat, searing her eyes.

The pain was memory, not flame, but her body didn't know the difference.

Her whole body jolted as if the trial flame had found her again, licking at her skin, clawing into her chest. Her knees nearly buckled. She staggered back, pulse hammering, lungs refusing to fill.

All she could taste was fire, all she could hear was the crackle, all she could feel was her body tearing apart.

For one terrible heartbeat, she thought she might faint, or worse: fall in.

Maren gasped, half a sob, half a curse. Her body shook, violent and involuntary. The phantom pain pulsed down her ribs in hot waves, her mind flashing white with each breath.

Her hand shot to the frame, clutching it like a lifeline. Her breath came sharp, ragged, frantic. The Court had known. It had carved her open, pressed its thumb against the freshest wound.

And if Penny were in there?

The thought stabbed through the panic. If Penny were inside, would she walk into the fire again? Could she?

Her stomach twisted. The door shivered closed of its own accord, sealing the inferno away, leaving only the phantom sting on her skin.

Maren stood shaking, hugging herself as tightly as she could in hopes it could keep her from falling apart completely. She dragged air into her lungs until her chest steadied.

Then she shoved forward.

The next door opened by itself, silent and expectant, as if the room beyond had been expecting her.

Maren hesitated. Her hand hovered at her side, fingers twitching like they wanted to reach for a weapon she didn't have. Then she stepped closer, muscles locked against the tremor that had started in her thighs.

The chamber inside was vast and wrong in proportion; wider than the hallway that birthed it, the ceiling lost to shadow. Pillars leaned at odd angles, built from stacked books instead of stone, their spines stamped in languages she half recognized: some mortal, some older.

Her heart stuttered.

At the far end sat a desk, and on it, a quill writing by itself.

The scratch-scratch of nib on parchment echoed like an insect crawling inside her skull.

She took one step in. Two. The sound stopped. The quill turned its feather, bending toward her like an eye.

Maren froze.

The parchment in front of it bore her name.

She watched as the following line etched itself in real time:

MAREN GREENBRIAR WILL FIND WHAT SHE WANTS.

Another pause. Then new letters seared themselves beneath it:

IF SHE LEAVES FIRST.

Her stomach flipped. *Leaves what?*

The air shifted, dry and hungry. Pages began to fall from the nearest pillar, fluttering like frightened birds. One brushed her shoulder.'

"Very funny," she said, though her voice came out smaller than she meant.

The quill twitched once more and wrote, in elegant spite:

FUNNY. YES.

That was enough. She stepped back fast, bumping the door frame. Her skin prickled as though every word in the room had turned to eyes.

The instant her heel crossed the threshold, the books collapsed soundlessly inward like a mouths closing around laughter.

She slammed the door.

Her pulse wouldn't slow. Her hands shook so hard she had to fold them behind her head for a moment, elbows pressed to the wall, breathing through her teeth. The cool stone steadied her only a little; it pulsed faintly under her palms, responding to her heartbeat.

The corridor around her had changed again. Longer now. The lanterns were gone, replaced by floating orbs that glowed the color of bruises.

She kept walking.

Another door, narrow and tall, waited ahead. This one didn't open immediately; it waited until she reached for it, then flung itself wide, almost gleeful.

Inside stretched a garden, if gardens could happen indoors… and upside down.

Trees grew from the ceiling, their roots dangling like chandeliers, dripping silver sap that hissed when it touched the ground. Flowers the size of her fists opened and closed in a slow, deliberate rhythm, inhaling light and exhaling perfume so sweet it made her throat ache.

She knew instantly it was bait.

Still, she stepped forward, drawn by the faint sound of humming again. Penny's melody threaded between the branches, light and familiar.

"Penny?" Her voice shook. "If you're here—"

The flowers turned toward her at once, faces blank, petals quivering. Their movement made the sap fall faster. Drops sizzled on the stone like acid rain.

Her gut seized.

The humming rose, not from the trees but from the roots above her, dozens of throats harmonizing in uncanny imitation of Penny's voice.

She stumbled back, nearly tripping over her own feet, and slammed the door before the song could form words.

The silence afterward was deafening.

She pressed her forehead to the cool wall, shaking. Every nerve hummed. She was breathing too fast again; she counted to steady herself. Four in, four out, the way her mother used to teach her when dealing with difficult customers.

It didn't help much.

The corridor narrowed, then widened, then split and doubled back on itself.

"Enough," she whispered.

The walls leaned closer, as if offended. Penny's hum grew louder. She broke into a run, feet striking stone, chasing that thread of song with fury sharp enough to split her chest.

"Damn you," she spat at the walls. "Show me where she is!"

The Court didn't answer. Or maybe it did, because the next door gave way beneath her hand.

The door groaned shut behind her, and Maren realized too late she hadn't stumbled into a new passage at all. It was her chamber. The same bed, the same walls.

And *him*.

He was already there, sprawled in her chair like he'd been born in it, a book open in one hand, coin resting idle on the table beside him. The bastard looked up with maddening calm, as if he'd been waiting for her to come home past curfew.

"You," she spat, fury sparking fast enough to burn away exhaustion. "Finished already? Or did Coral Head kick you out of bed?"

One brow arched. He shut the book with unhurried grace, the sound softer than her heartbeat. "Mm. Jealousy." His mouth curved slowly, sinfully. "I'd been wondering when you'd admit it."

"I'm not—" Heat climbed her throat before she could choke it back. "She hangs off you like barnacles. Forgive me if I mistook it for a spectacle."

"Ah." He rose, every inch deliberate, and the air seemed to tilt with him. "So you were watching."

Maren's pulse betrayed her, kicking hard. She folded her arms to cage it in. "I was looking for Penny."

"Were you?" He circled closer, unhurried, until the glow of her constellations lit against his sleeve. His fingers brushed her arm before she could step away. His touch was light, testing, tracing one silver line as if it were scripture.

She jerked, but not fast enough. The touch had already left a hum beneath her skin. "Stop."

"Why?" His voice dipped velvet. "They flare when you're angry. Didn't you notice?"

Her throat tightened. She wanted to claw the smirk off his face. She wanted to kiss it off, too. Both urges terrified her.

"Radiant," he murmured, thumb grazing the edge of one glowing star. "I told you you'd burn beautifully. But this…" His gaze roved slowly, gold deepening, "This outshone even my imagination."

She bit back the shiver clawing up her spine. "You think everything's a joke."

"Not everything." He leaned close enough that his breath stirred her curls. "Not you."

The words cracked something inside her. Her knees wanted to give, her teeth wanted to bite, her heart wanted both at once. She hated him for it. Hated how the Court itself seemed to lean nearer, savoring the spark between them.

"You're a bastard."

"And you," he said softly, "are delightful when you call me one."

She swatted his hand away, forcing steel into her voice. "You think you can toy with me, dangle me on strings like the rest of them."

"Oh no." His smile sharpened. "They dance for applause. You blaze for spite. That's much more interesting."

She took a step back, though her body rebelled against it. "You don't care about me. You care about your wagers. About your Court."

"Of course," he said easily. "Wagers make the world turn. But you…" He tilted his head, studying her like a puzzle. "You keep breaking the odds. The Court tilts toward what you want, and still you fight it. Tell me, fire-girl, do you truly not crave the wonder it lays at your feet?"

Her jaw locked. "I crave Penny. Not wine. Not crowns. Not you."

Something dangerous flickered in his eyes; amusement, yes, but edged with hunger. "Liar."

Her breath hitched. She shoved past it. "If the Court bends to want, then tell it to give me Penny."

He chuckled low, the sound sliding under her skin like dark silk. "It doesn't work like that. Chaos doesn't hand out what's pure. It twists. It tempts. You of all mortals should know by now."

Her stomach twisted. He wasn't wrong. Every corridor had mocked her; every vision clawed at her heart.

He leaned closer, finger tracing a constellation across her collarbone. "And yet," he murmured, "you still want."

Her throat burned. "I want you gone."

His grin cut her in two. "Another lie. And a charming one."

Maren's whole body felt like a tinderbox; one more spark and she'd catch. She wanted to scream, wanted to kiss him, wanted to burn him alive. He read all of it in her eyes, she could tell, and the bastard savored it.

"Tell yourself whatever helps you sleep," he said softly. "But you'll still come when I call."

"I'd sooner starve."

"Then it's fortunate," he said, pocketing the coin with a flick of his wrist, "that I've decided to supervise your diet."

Her breath caught again. "You mean to watch me eat?"

"Oh no." His gaze dragged slowly from her mouth to her throat, then lower. "You're having dinner *with* me. A guest of honor, if we're pretending you have any."

He let his hand fall away, slowly. He turned, casual as ever. At the door, he paused, glancing back over his shoulder.

His smirk deepened, victory scented with sin. "Rest well, darling," he said, voice smooth. "Tomorrow, you dine."

The door sighed shut behind him, and Maren was left in silence, chest heaving, skin still humming where his fingers had been.

She'd just survived something far more dangerous than fire.

<h1 style="text-align:center">16</h1>

Of the Twenty Locks

Maren woke burning.

The world was a ring of fire again, the white heat biting her lungs, flour turning to ash between her fingers. Penny's voice thinned to a thread no hand could catch. A coin clicked. The flames leaned in, hungry for gossip.

She jerked upright with a gasp that scraped her throat.

Bed. Four unlovely walls. No fire.

There was the afterimage stitched across her nerves, constellations on her skin quietly pulsing like cooling embers. She caught her breath, palms flat to the mattress till the tremor passed.

The room held a different kind of hush than last night; the air was denser, more awake. If the Court had a dawn, it came like this: a soft pressure through the stones, as though some leviathan beneath the Court had rolled over and decided day should begin.

"Rotten dream?" said a voice from her ceiling, amused.

Maren didn't scream; she did, however, fling a pillow.

It arced beautifully and smacked the man hanging upside down from the lintel.

"Man" was generous. He had the unfair sort of face that painters forgave sins for. Every inch of him is wrong in *exactly* the right ways. Hair the color of sunlit copper spilled in braids and loose strands, catching light like stolen fire; brilliant green feline slit pupils flicked like ink when light moved; a mouth built for trouble shaped a smile.

The tail gave him away. It wasn't always there; it simply… remembered to be, curling over the edge of the lintel with a languid flick, tipped in starlight like it had been dipped in frost. A slim knife rested upside-down across his knuckles, the way some men idle a coin. It rolled when his fingers rolled, the blade whispering shh shh as it balanced on skin.

"Who," Maren said carefully, "are you and how long have you been watching me sleep?"

"Mm. A delicate question for a delicate hour," the voice answered with a lazy purr of an accent. He slid off the lintel with a fluidity that felt illegal, bowed just enough to be mocking. The bow involved an unnecessary flourish of a long, dark coat embroidered with silver thread that shifted if she stared, patterns rearranging mid-glance.

"Tamsin. Of the Twenty Locks. Of the Too-Many Rules. Of the We-Shall-See." The corner of his mouth quirked. "And I was watching you *not* sleep. You make a very committed insomniac."

"Get out."

"I would," he chirped, "but if I obey you too quickly, he'll be jealous."

The "he" didn't need a name. The room had a faint scent of cedar and citrus for no apparent reason. Maren's jaw tightened. "If that bastard sent you—"

Tamsin laughed, bright and private. "Sweet mortal, Mischief never sends me. He *endures* me." His head tilted, listening to a rhythm only he could hear. "And I am awful at being endured."

"Congratulations." She angled her chin toward the door. "Leave the way your ego entered."

"Can't," he said, cheerfully unrepentant. "Ego's too wide. Also—" He sniffed the room, wrinkled his nose theatrically. "Smells like singed heroine and hurt pride. Tragic. Needs air."

"Needs you gone."

"Needs you dressed," he countered, eyes glittering. "Lest Mischief fall into a jealous sulk and rewrite six bylaws about my imminent execution because I discovered you in a shift."

Only then did she register how far the blanket had slid. Heat crawled up her throat. The stars on her arms glimmered softly against bare skin, the patterns too bright and too telling. She yanked the sheet higher with sharp, offended dignity.

He prowled closer, like he was testing the room's gravity. The scent that followed him wasn't the thief's forested arrogance; it was like mint and cold metal, the kind of perfume you couldn't buy because it belonged to theft and freshly opened locks. When he grinned, a tiny tooth, cat-sharp, peek-a-booed just behind the polite ones.

Maren made herself breathe slowly. Her stars eased their prickle, one by one. "What do you want, Locks?"

He leaned in, head cocked, eyes bright and unblinking. Up close, the not-human details multiplied: the faint velvet stripes ghosting his temples when the light shifted; cheekbones carrying a rumor of whisker-lines. Beautiful in a dangerous way.

"To rescue you," he said cheerfully. "From monotony. From your own good sense. From your very dreary plan to sit here fuming until the Court rings its little bell and parades you like dessert."

"I'm not dessert."

"Everyone's dessert to someone. But don't worry, your thief prefers savory." He flicked a glance at the door, "He won't like this."

Maren pulled the sheet higher again, purely on principle. "If this is a seduction attempt, it's sloppy."

"Darling, if I were seducing you, you would know. I have standards." He sauntered to the wardrobe and breezed it open. Fabric shifted color inside, reacting to the movement. He rifled through with expert disrespect and plucked out a long, high-collared shirt the color of deep ink and a pair of soft, dark trousers that looked stolen from some noble's casual sins. "Up. We're going to breakfast."

Maren scoffed, "I'm a prisoner."

"And I'm a bad influence." He tossed the clothes; they landed across her knees, heavy enough to hide stars. "Also, technicality: you're a *kept* mortal.

Which means the rules about your roaming are contradictory enough to qualify as an invitation."

Maren did not move. Her body remembered heat and ash and a coin at her throat; her mind remembered Penny's braid swinging in a gilded cage. Curiosity shoved a shoulder into both and muttered, *Go on, then. Look.*

She set her jaw. "Why are you really here?"

Tamsin's tail, traitorously visible again, flicked with feline satisfaction. "Because I am bored, because you are interesting, and because Mischief's face does a very pretty thing when he thinks something that belongs to him has slipped the leash." He bared his too-pointed smile. "Come make him do it."

A laugh slipped out of her before she could throttle it, small and sharp. "You want me to poke the god."

"Poke, pinch, embarrass in public. I'm flexible." He turned his back to her with absurd ceremony, hands clasped behind him like a man awaiting execution. "Dress. I won't look. Much."

Maren didn't move. The clothes sat still in her lap. The sheet was still twisted around her hips like she'd drowned in it. Tamsin turned his head just enough that one slit-pupil peeked over his shoulder.

"You dressing?" he called, sing-song, "or shall I serenade you until you do? I know forty-seven ballads about impractical mortals."

"Tamsin," she warned.

He brightened. "Oh, good, a tone. That means progress."

She threw another pillow. He dodged with a lazy sway of his torso, tail curling smugly behind him like punctuation. Then he began humming: loudly, terribly, triumphantly, some tune that sounded like it had been banned by multiple kingdoms.

Maren cursed under her breath and kicked off the blankets. The room was cold; the shirt and trousers were colder, both soft and heavy, with a scent of faint lavender. She tugged them on quickly, fingers clumsy but determined. The sleeves hid most of the constellations along her arms; the high collar covered the stars scattering her throat.

"Question," she said, wrestling with the final button. "If my stars show through this, why am I bothering?"

"Fashion," Tamsin declared, as though it were holy doctrine. "Also, it will keep most nobles from fainting at the sight of you. They're rather delicate." He paused. "And vain. And vindictive. And dramatic. Actually, now that I think about it—"

"Enough," she muttered.

He tapped his claws together. "Ah! Modesty. Charming mortal trait. Doesn't last."

She shot him a look that could curdle milk. His grin only widened.

"How did you even get in here?" she asked, tightening the sash around her waist. "The door locks from the outside. With iron."

Tamsin blinked innocently. "Oh, I didn't use the door."

She froze. "Then—?"

He pointed upward.

The ceiling had a faint distortion, as if someone had pried reality up at one corner and slipped through. A small patch was still fluttering, almost shy, like the Court was embarrassed to have been picked open.

"You climbed through the ceiling?" she demanded.

"Climbed?" Tamsin scoffed. "Please. I am a professional. Also, the cell wards only cover the door. Not the ceiling. Very foolish structure. Ten out of ten for intimidation, three out of ten for actual security."

"Perfect," Maren muttered, rubbing her temple. "I've been kidnapped by an idiot with the architectural sense of burnt toast."

Tamsin flashed his teeth as if she had complimented him. Then, stepped back, rolled his shoulders, and—without warning—*leapt.*

It wasn't a mortal leap.

It was uncomfortably feline.

His boots skimmed one wall, claws flicking out for balance, then he angled off the opposite wall in a clean, predatory arc. The air didn't even rush around him. He simply *rose,* fluid as ink poured upward, and slipped fingers-first into the distortion in the ceiling. The stone rippled like water greeting an old friend.

In half a heartbeat, half his torso was already through.

He dangled upside-down again, head and shoulders poking back into the room, hair falling toward her like dark waterfall strands.

"Well?" he asked brightly. "Coming up, Starsleeves?"

Maren stared at him, arms crossed tight over her chest. "No. Because I am not a cat burglar or a ceiling mouse. I don't—" she gestured at him, helpless, offended by physics *"do* that."

His grin widened into something sinful. "You could. I believe in you."

"That makes one of us."

Tamsin sighed dramatically. "Fine. If you insist on being contrary about basic vertical travel…" He extended one hand downward, palm open, wrist loose, utterly confident she'd take it. "I can pull you up. With grace. Mostly mine. Some of yours, if you try *very* hard."

Maren eyed the ceiling. Then his hand. Then the ceiling again.

"Is this the part where you drop me on purpose?"

"Oh, absolutely not," he said. "I need you intact. Mischief's face will be heartbreakingly funny when he realizes you escaped your pen before breakfast."

"Breakfast," she repeated blandly. "Right."

"And possibly extortion, depending on what you want to steal on the way." He wiggled his fingers at her. "Up you get."

She took a slow breath. Her stars flickered faintly under her collar. She couldn't tell if she was nervous or annoyed—or both.

Finally, with a muttered prayer to every saint who had ever tolerated fools, she grabbed his hand.

Tamsin's tail curled in triumph.

He lifted her like she weighed nothing at all.

Her feet left the ground; stone blurred past; her stomach dropped. She hissed and clamped her free hand around his forearm. Heat radiated through his sleeve. His claws flexed lightly against her skin, anchoring her with feline confidence.

"There you go," he purred as she reached the distortion. "See? Practically graceful."

"I hate this," she said through clenched teeth.

"You say that now," he replied, pulling her fully through the ceiling with a single, elegant tug, "but give it a week. You'll be scaling walls for sport."

The ceiling sealed behind them with a soft sound.

Maren found her balance beside Tamsin on a narrow lip of stone. The ledge shimmered faintly beneath her feet; the surface shifting in small, restless adjustments, as though the Court preferred to keep visitors guessing where the floor actually was. Her heartbeat thudded hard against her ribs, half from the climb, half from the knowledge that she was, technically, "escaped."

Except she wasn't.

Not while Penny was in a cage.

Not while she still owed trials.

Not while *he* lived a hallway away.

Tamsin extended his arm in a grand flourish toward the corridor ahead. The passage had appeared while she caught her breath: arched ceiling, lacquered stone ribs, lanterns floating in tidy geometric patterns. Everything gleamed faintly, gold threaded through black marble like veins of molten ore.

"Come now, Starsleeves." Tamsin beamed. "Shall we?"

"No." She pushed past him, adjusting the drape of her borrowed clothes that were, thankfully, thick enough to hide every star that pulsed beneath her skin.

Good.

She needed to move unseen. Needed to think. Needed to find an escape route that Tamsin didn't have time to sabotage.

"Yes," he corrected, sliding in beside her with effortless lightness. His tail flicked behind them like a metronome. "Otherwise, I'll start narrating our every move out loud."

Maren shot him a look sharp enough to slice fruit.

He inhaled deeply, preparing. "Maren stepped into the hall with all the fury of a—"

"Tamsin," she hissed. "I swear to every Spirit—"

He grinned, unrepentant. "Very well." He sauntered ahead a step, voice dropping to a conspiratorial whisper. "Though you should know… your walk is surprisingly narrative already."

She ignored that. Looking flustered would only encourage him. Instead, she focused on the corridor.

It spilled open wider with every step, unfurling into a vaulted atrium so massive it made her stomach tilt. Eldenwick had been tidy, practical, structured. This was its opposite: too large, too decadent, and way too complicated to exist.

But also too *interesting* for someone who desperately needed not to be impressed.

"Welcome," Tamsin murmured, sweeping an arm out dramatically, "to the Court's beating heart. The Hall of Wagers. It is loud, it is disreputable, and it is perfect."

The Hall of Wagers stretched out in tiers, carved from mismatched architectural styles the way children stack toys: a cathedral balcony welded next to a tavern loft, a domed library ceiling stitched onto a colonnade stolen from some desert temple. Every structure bled into the next without seams, the whole place breathing slow as melting glass.

Tables sprawled across the marble floor, long and rectangular, arranged in a spiraling pattern that made no mathematical sense but felt strangely inevitable. At each table, creatures of every shape and half-shape leaned over piles of copper and silver coins. The two metals chimed differently depending on who touched them.

A moth-winged boy flicked a coin into a bowl and groaned when it rang "wrong".

A trio of glass-boned women laughed when their pile toppled, and somehow that meant they'd won.

A fox-faced noble lost spectacularly and was congratulated for it.

Rules were being written and rewritten mid-hand.

The soundscape hit her next: clattering coins, murmurs of wagers, bursts of theatrical outrage, laughter that cracked like kindling. It was bustling without being chaotic, loud without drowning her. The scent of spiced tea drifted in from somewhere, mixed with ink, metal, and the faint sweetness of candied fruit.

It reminded her, traitorously, of the festival.

Her throat tightened.

Let it hurt. She thought. She needed that pain sharp if she was going to escape.

"You look like someone solving a puzzle with half the pieces missing," Tamsin observed, padding at her side with lazy interest. "Thinking of bolting? I should warn you, the Court loves a chase. You'd get maybe three, four steps before someone bets on which pillar you'll crash into."

"Four steps is farther than I'd get in that cell," Maren muttered.

"True," he allowed, "but think bigger. If you escape too well, Mischief will sulk. A sulking Spirit is insufferable. He'll make even more rules."

Maren felt something hot and unwelcome flicker in her chest at the mention of that bastard again.

"Good," she said. "Maybe one of those new rules will let prisoners walk out the front door."

"Oh, absolutely not," Tamsin said breezily. "Rules never do what you want. That is their only consistent trait."

They passed a balcony dripping with lanterns. A noble on the balcony hurled a coin down toward a table. It exploded into a shower of sparks and applause.

Maren's eyes flicked around the atrium, mapping exits. Counting guards. Marking shadows dense enough to hide in. Slip between those columns… duck under that stairwell… sprint toward the—

Tamsin nudged her elbow with the back of his hand. "Before you commit to your daring escape, allow me to offer two crucial facts."

"No."

"Yes," he insisted, tail flicking. "Fact one: the doors move. Every time you look away, they change places. You could run toward freedom and end up in a broom closet with a creature that collects mortal teeth."

Maren grimaced. "And fact two?"

"Fact two," he chirped, "I like you, Starsleeves. And I refuse to lose my fun to a broom closet."

She stared at him. "That's your priority?"

He grinned, unbothered. "One must have principles."

Maren's mind spun through possibilities anyway. She couldn't afford to stop thinking. If the doors moved, then she needed a landmark. Something fixed. Something—

Her eyes landed on a pillar carved with shifting script. The letters rearranged themselves in slow rotations, forming new words she couldn't read.

A fixed point? Or a trap?

The Court didn't do linear logic.

She dragged her gaze away before it made her dizzy.

Focus. Penny first. Escape after. The thief last.

Tamsin drifted backward ahead of her, walking in reverse with the ease of someone who'd never tripped in his life. "Come along, Starsleeves. Time for breakfast. Time for mischief you can—what's that mortal word?—weaponize."

Maren lifted her chin, eyes sharp, mind sharper.

Time to look.

Time to learn.

Time to use this place against the Spirit who thought she was his.

17

Spirited Ink

They moved deeper into the Hall of Wagers, the sound thickening around them.

Coins chimed in different metals, laughter rose and fell in bright spikes, and arguments bloomed then died under the weight of new bets.

Tamsin steered her with a light touch at her elbow, polite as a courtier, insistent as a cat. "Food first," he announced. "Rebellion second. Existential crisis whenever you like."

"I am not having an existential crisis," Maren said. Her stomach chose that moment to gnarl in protest. Traitor.

"Of course not." His eyes glittered. "You are merely hungry, exhausted, and wearing someone else's clothes in a new realm. Very grounded."

He guided her toward a long table that might once have belonged in a scholar's hall. Bookshelves formed the legs. Their spines flexed as they passed, letters shifting. The tabletop itself was dark wood polished to an almost reflective sheen, and set with things that pretended to be breakfast.

Goblets stood in careful ranks. They were filled with light, not liquid. Starlight pooled inside each one, bright enough to glow, dim enough not to burn. The light rippled when someone laughed nearby, picking up the sound and folding it into itself.

Beside those sat baskets of bread. Each loaf was shaped differently, patterned with cuts that resembled a script. When Maren drew closer,

155

the bread vibrated against the cloth linings. The vibration was nearly sound, a faint melody she could feel in her bones. Old lullabies nested inside the crust, flour remembering songs from whatever mortal kitchen these recipes had been stolen from.

A row of ink bottles ran along the center of the table. The ink was too thick, too alive, clinging to the glass like it resented confinement. Each bottle had a label in the Court's shifting hand. Spirited Ink. Beneath that, in smaller script that kept trying to rearrange itself, two words finally held: *Tongue Truth.*

Maren eyed it, arms folded, hunger coiled tight beneath her ribs. "I am not drinking anything that advertises itself as a snitch."

"That is the beauty," Tamsin said, plucking up a goblet of light and sniffing it critically. "It does not tell truth. It makes you wish you had. The regret is exquisite. The Arbiter once outlawed it for an entire afternoon."

He poured a thread of Spirited Ink into an empty glass. The ink rolled in slow curls, black with an edge of iridescent blue. It clung to the sides as it settled, like smoke pinned inside crystal.

Maren stayed very still.

She had not eaten since before the trial. Her last meal had been practical. Bread, salt, water. This table looked like an insult to that memory. Or a temptation. Or both.

"You are staring," Tamsin observed.

"I am calculating the odds of this poisoning me," she said. "And whether that would count as an escape."

A faint smile tugged at his mouth. "If it helps, Spirited Ink does not kill. It merely encourages. Your tongue trips ahead of your good sense. Very entertaining at parties."

"Wonderful," she muttered. "A drink that makes me stupid."

"Mortal, you stood in front of the Mischief Spirit and promised you'd kill him. In the middle of a revel." His teeth flashed. "You are already my favorite sort of stupid."

Her lips twitched before she strangled the smile. "You should get out more."

"I am out now." He pushed the glass toward her with two fingers. "Come. One sip. You survived trial fire. Ink will not undo you."

Penny's braid flashed in her mind. Penny behind bars of gold. Penny's humming turning thin.

Maren reached for the glass anyway.

Curiosity had always done this. Reached around duty and tapped her on the shoulder.

She wrapped her fingers around the stem. The glass felt oddly warm, as if someone had held it for a very long time. The ink inside trembled in tiny shivers.

"One sip," she repeated, mostly to herself.

"Or three," Tamsin said. "I do not police ambition."

She lifted the glass. The ink smelled like old parchment and something sharp beneath it, like the first breath pulled in after blowing out a candle.

Maren took a small mouthful.

For one second, nothing happened. Then the taste hit.

It flooded her tongue with layers. Charred paper. Honey. Smoke curling off the edge of a storybook that had been left too close to the oven. Heat flared along her throat without burning. Her spine locked. She tasted every margin note she had ever scribbled, every wish pressed between pages, the shared weight of all the stories she had devoured like stolen sweets.

It felt like pages burning. It felt like that moment just before words catch.

Her scars answered.

The constellation marks hidden under her borrowed sleeves brightened in a slow pulse, as if something inside her had just been lit again. The Court felt it. The air grew tighter, not hostile, simply focused.

Tamsin watched her carefully, letting his goblet of starlight hover near his mouth without drinking yet. "Well?"

"It is awful," she said. Her voice came out a little rough. "I want another."

"Perfect," he said. He tipped his own drink back. The star in it streaked up his throat and settled behind his eyes. They glinted brighter a moment before leveling out again. "You are fitting in already."

Maren took a second sip before she could talk herself out of it. The ink burned less this time. Or she knew what to expect. It coated the back of her teeth with possibility.

A few nearby gamblers glanced over, curious. One of them, a woman with scales in the pattern of old maps down her arms, lifted her glass in a silent toast.

Maren did not return it. She set her own glass down, every motion precise. "It should not feel like this."

"Like what?" Tamsin lounged against the table with the boneless ease of something that had never been caught doing anything it regretted.

"Alive," she said. "Good."

The admission sat between them like contraband.

"Ah," he said softly. "The great crime. Enjoying yourself in your enemy's house."

Her jaw tightened. "I am not enjoying myself."

He looked pointedly at her glass. "Of course not."

Maren stepped back from the table, knuckles whitening. The Court hummed just below hearing. She felt its attention on the marks under her skin. On the way Spirited Ink sat in her chest. On the fact that, for a brief, treacherous moment, she had forgotten to hate everything.

She forced that hate back to the front.

Penny.

Home.

Taxes.

The chapel.

Her parents.

Trials.

She turned, intending to walk away from the breakfast, away from the table, away from the way the Hall of Wagers made her feel like everything was possible if she only reached for it.

Tamsin caught her sleeve lightly. Not enough to stop her, only enough to redirect her a fraction. "Since you are already suffering through nourishment," he said, "you might as well suffer through local history. Look."

He tipped his chin toward a nearby cluster of creatures at the end of the table.

Maren followed his gaze.

Three of them leaned together, their coins piled high. One had wings like lacquered paper. Another's hair floated around her head like she was underwater. The third wore a collar of little silver keys that chimed when he laughed. Maren clued in mid-conversation.

"And spoil our entertainment?" said the one with floating hair. "Never. Her story still pulls the best wagers."

"Which version?" asked the key-collared man. He flexed his fingers as if itching to unlock something. "The girl who burned for him, or the one who vanished into his coin?"

Maren went very still.

Tamsin's tail flicked once behind him. He leaned in to murmur without looking at her. "You did not hear this from me."

"I am not listening," she said.

They both knew she was lying.

The paper-winged noble clicked his tongue. "She did not burn. Fire would have bored him."

"He embodies mischief," the floating hair woman said. "Not cruelty."

"Those are the same thing," the man with keys replied, mouth curling. "Ask any mortal he has touched."

Maren's fingers dug into the edge of the table.

Keys continued, full of smug certainty. "She was folded. That is what I heard. He slipped her into the coin and kept her there, close to his hand. Too dear to spend."

"That is sentimental," the winged one objected. "And Spirits are not sentimental. They feel one thing only. Mischief, temptation, fury, delight, grief, dread, or whatever the gods stamped into them at the beginning. Anything more and they crack."

The woman's floating hair shifted, stirred by some inner current. "Yet he does not crack. He broods. That is different. Perhaps he wanted more than mischief. Perhaps that is why she vanished. Mortals are always leaving when Spirits reach too far."

Maren's breath scraped her throat. She focused on straightening the cuff of her borrowed shirt so her hands had somewhere to go. Her heart had no such convenient task.

A mortal girl. A story. Almost loved.

Coral Head's hand on his arm at the revel flashed in her memory. Laughter. Bright hair tossed back. The little twist of jealousy that had flickered in Maren's gut then, brief and humiliating.

She wanted to roll the memory in flour and bake it into something else.

Tamsin watched the gossipers with lazy interest. "They never agree on the ending," he mused. "It is their favorite part."

"If they love him so much," Maren said quietly, "why do they talk about him like a problem they cannot solve?"

"Because he is both," Tamsin replied. "Patron and hazard. Host and hurricane."

The key-collared creature poured Spirited Ink into his cup. "I think he felt it," he said. "Love. Or something that thought it was. Spirits cannot name what exceeds their one note. That is the tragedy."

"Or the comedy," the paper-winged one said. "Look at him now. Another mortal. Another little story. Another trial that will probably end in screaming. The Court wins either way."

Maren's skin crawled.

Another mortal.

As if she were a replacement trinket.

As if there had been a line.

She dragged in a slow breath. The ink in her stomach twisted. She hated that the gossip fit into some gap inside her that she had not admitted existed. Hated that the idea of him almost loving anyone made something cold and sharp move behind her ribs.

He burned me.

He caged Penny.

He dragged me here.

She repeated each fact until they stacked up into a wall.

Tamsin tilted his head, studying her profile. "Careful, Starsleeves."

"I am fine," she said.

"You are listening like a scholar and glaring like a woman who has just learned her favorite villain has a tragic backstory." His voice stayed light. "It is a dangerous combination."

"He is not my favorite anything," she said. The words tasted too quick, too defensive.

"Of course not," Tamsin agreed smoothly. "Just the one who will dine with you tonight."

Her heart stumbled. She kept her face neutral.

Penny's name whispered under her tongue. Penny in a cage. Penny as a deadline.

"Stories about him are wrong," Maren said at last. "All of them. They do not know him."

"Does anyone?" Tamsin asked. He tipped the last of his starlight into his mouth and set the empty goblet down with care. "Not even Mischief knows where Mischief ends."

She should have turned away. She should have walked back to her cell, counted her breaths, sharpened her hate, and prepared for trial.

Instead, in this impossible hall where bread sang and ink burned, she listened to strangers tell her captor's story.

The creatures' whispers drifted off behind them as Maren stepped away. The ink in her veins settled into a warm, treacherous hum. Her stomach growled again, louder this time, like it was arguing with her principles.

Tamsin raised an eyebrow. "That is either hunger or your mortal organs staging a coup."

"Fine," she muttered. "One more thing. Then we leave."

"Ah," he said, delighted. "The brave words of someone who thinks she will walk away from my favorite table."

"It is just breakfast," Maren said.

"No," Tamsin corrected. "It is an initiation."

She scowled at him. He grinned wider. They returned to the food table, where breakfast had shifted subtly, as though the Court adjusted its plating based on who approached. The bread hummed louder. One loaf released a faint sigh when she reached toward it, like it had been waiting.

Maren tore off a piece before she could think twice. The crust crisped under her teeth with a soft crack. The inside melted on her tongue. A song she did not recognize hummed against her palate, airy and warm, a lullaby without words.

Tamsin made a pleased sound. "There she goes. The mortal who eats for spite."

She swallowed. "I am eating because I hate being hungry."

"No. You are eating because you pretend not to like anything good." He plucked a slice of glowing fruit from a silver dish and held it up. Light pulsed inside the flesh in slow waves. "Try this."

"I am not letting a stranger feed me glowing produce."

"You have already let me name you Starsleeves."

"I did not let you."

"Consent is subjective in nicknames," he said brightly and popped the fruit into his own mouth. It sparked faintly behind his teeth. "Delicious."

She snorted despite herself. "I knew you reminded me of something."

He presented another piece of fruit. She took it just to shut him up. It burst gently, cool sweetness running along her tongue. Whatever magic sat in the fruit slipped down her throat like a secret she had not meant to hear.

Duty pushed back immediately.

You have Penny to save. You have a baker's life waiting. You do not have time for wonder.

Her body softened anyway. Just for a heartbeat.

Tamsin nudged her shoulder with his. "There. Now you look alive."

"I am not here to look alive."

"No," he agreed, tone light. "You are here to survive. This helps."

She almost asked how he knew that. Then she remembered who she was talking to.

Before she could argue, a voice cut off their retreat.

"Halt."

Maren stiffened. Tamsin's tail stopped mid-sway.

Three guards stepped out from between two pillars. Their armor was composed of overlapping plates of polished obsidian, glossy as wet ink, trimmed in faintly glowing lines. Their masks were expressionless crescents of metal, smooth enough to reflect the lantern light without revealing what lay beneath.

The one in the center spoke again. "Unauthorized mortal. You violate Rule forty-seven A."

Maren drew breath through her nose, careful and slow. "I am wearing a disguise," she said. "All of me is covered. You did not see anything."

The guard lifted his hand. Maren's pulse skipped.

Dangling between his fingers was a single mote of starlight. It twisted in the air, flickering in a distinctive pulse. The same rhythm her scars had answered when she drank the ink.

Her stomach dropped.

They had tracked her by the glow she could not hide, even through fabric.

Tamsin hissed something low in his throat. "Very rude. Following pulse signatures is strictly frowned upon during daylight hours."

"This is morning," the guard said.

"Morning is a construct," Tamsin replied. His tone sharpened, though his smile stayed easy. "And Rule forty-seven B states all guests must wander to avoid stagnation."

"Forty-seven A supersedes it."

"Forty-seven B contradicts it."

"Forty-seven A was rewritten last lantern light."

"Forty-seven B was rewritten after someone drank too much ink and attempted to set the chandelier on fire," Tamsin countered. "A more recent revision."

Maren stared between them. "Your laws contradict each other on purpose?"

The guard's helm swiveled toward her. "All things contradict. Only one version is correct at a time."

"How do you know which one?" she asked.

"We decide in the moment."

Maren blinked. "That is not a rule."

"That is all rules," the guard said.

Her mortal brain stumbled over the logic. Chaos was not randomness here. It was a preference masquerading as law. It rewarded confidence more than sense.

Tamsin stepped forward, placing himself lightly between Maren and the guards. "Let us settle this as civilized creatures. Riddle duel."

The guards stiffened. The word carried weight here. A few creatures turned in their seats. Coins paused midair.

The lead guard inclined his head. "Accepted."

Maren's eyes widened. "Absolutely not."

"Too late," Tamsin murmured. "You are my second."

"I do not know Court riddles."

"That is the beauty." He winked. "Neither do they."

The guard recited first. His voice rang flat behind the mask, "I am not alive, yet I grow. I am not a flame, yet I burn. I sleep without sleeping. What am I?"

Tamsin turned to Maren, tail curling in a slow loop. "Starsleeves, inspire me."

Maren rolled her eyes skyward. Her mind sifted the words. Not alive. Grows. Burns without fire. Sleeps without sleeping.

A thought clicked in place the way dough folds into itself.

"Memory," she said under her breath.

Tamsin's smile sharpened. "Memory," he repeated aloud.

A ripple passed through the guard's armor. Approval.

"This round goes to the Twenty Locks," he intoned.

A few gamblers clapped politely. Coins exchanged hands.

The guard straightened. "Your turn."

Tamsin leaned close enough for Maren to feel the faint brush of his coat against her arm. "Do not worry," he whispered. "I am excellent at losing beautifully."

She whispered back, "Why would I want to lose?"

He grinned. "Because losing with flair wins the duel."

She stared at him. "That is not how duels work."

"In Chaos, it is."

He stepped forward and spoke clearly. "Riddle. What belongs to everyone but can only be taken when given? What grows smaller when held tightly and grows larger when shared?"

The guards did not answer immediately. They murmured among themselves in low tones.

Maren's breath caught.

She knew this. She had read this riddle in a storybook before. The answer settled at the back of her throat:

Name.

The guards finally responded. "Hope."

"Trust."

"Breath."

Tamsin placed a hand over his heart and sighed with exaggerated tragedy. "Incorrect. My opponents fail most poetically. I concede."

Maren's jaw dropped. "That was not—"

The lead guard raised a hand. "Accepted. Twenty Locks and companion may continue their wander."

"What," Maren whispered, "just happened?"

"Confidence happened," Tamsin said lightly. "And performance. Both far more important than correctness."

Maren blinked. Somehow, Tamsin had won by losing. Or lost by winning. Or whatever passed for victory here. The Court of Chaos did not reward logic. It rewarded style. And unfortunately for her sanity, Tamsin dripped style like a leaking wine cask.

The guard handed him a small marker coin stamped with a symbol she did not recognize. Tamsin flipped it once, caught it, and slipped it into his coat.

Then he leaned toward Maren, voice low enough that only she could hear. "Names are dangerous here. Better to lose a duel than give that away."

Maren swallowed.

The Hall resumed its noise. The guards moved on.

Tamsin bumped her shoulder, gentle as a nudge. "See? Breakfast, riddles, near-arrests. A proper morning."

Her heart was still racing. She hated that she liked it.

Wonder tugged her forward. Duty pulled her back.

She walked anyway, the ink warm in her veins, the bread-song lingering in her breath, the Court watching from every angle.

And in the back of her mind, one thought smoldered:

If chaos rewards confidence over sense, she could use that.

18

Graceful Flour Sack

The corridors shifted the moment they left the Hall of Wagers. Hallways lengthened or shortened depending on which direction she looked. Doors turned coyly away when she glanced at them for more than a second. Overhead, lanterns drifted into new constellations with lazy, indifferent precision.

Tamsin strode ahead as if the tilting geometry belonged to him. His coat swung behind him like a banner announcing mischief. His tail flicked every few steps, the starlit tip pointing left or right with the confidence of a creature who could navigate a hurricane by smell alone.

"Stay close, Starsleeves," he said, stepping over a ripple in the floor as if it were just a puddle. "Once the Court notices someone wants to go somewhere, it develops opinions."

"Opinions," she echoed, stepping around the same ripple. The stone curved gently under her foot, like skin shifting under touch.

"Strong ones." He sniffed the air theatrically. "Smells like it thinks you ought to be someplace dramatic. Perhaps a balcony. Or a duel pit. Or… a bed chamber." He finished with an obnoxious wink.

Maren elbowed him sharply in the ribs. "Do not start."

Tamsin let out a wheeze that sounded suspiciously like a laugh. His grin flashed, bright and pleased. "Touchy. You should warn a man before you assault the merchandise."

"You are not merchandise."

"Everyone is merchandise to someone. I simply price myself higher." He struck a pose, head tipped back, tail curling. "Luckily, you are not my target audience. You look like you prefer men who glower."

Her throat tightened before she could stop it. She refused to give him the satisfaction of reacting. Tamsin caught the tiny hitch anyway. His smile sharpened, amused but merciful enough not to push.

"Relax," he said lightly. "If you blush any harder, the walls will think you are flirting and take us somewhere unsupervised."

She glared at him so hard her eyes ached. "Walk faster."

"As the lady commands," he said, sweeping into an exaggerated bow. The bow was so deep his hair brushed the shimmering stone. "Though for the record, I have been told my company improves most boudoirs."

She pinched his arm that time.

The corridor bent with a soft groan, revealing a long stretch of pale glass flooring that shone with faint blue light. Shapes drifted beneath the surface, something resembling memories, maybe, or discarded illusions. They drifted with the lazy currents of dream stuff, catching the light when they turned.

Maren forced herself to focus on the path instead of the growing knot under her ribs. Dinner. With *him*. With the Spirit who burned her and stole Penny and smiled like he might swallow her whole.

Tamsin's tail flicked back, brushing her knee. "There you go again. Thinking too loudly. Mortals need switches. Someone should install one in you."

"My thoughts are fine."

"They are screaming," he said, amused. "And they are leaking into the walls. Walk softer or the Court will feel them."

She stiffened. "You are making that up."

"Of course," he said cheerfully. "Mostly." His claws tapped lightly on the glass walkway. "Come along. We are nearly at your climbing point."

"My *what?*"

He pointed upward with the knife he always seemed to have at hand.

High above them, the ceiling rippled like a pond. A faint circular outline shimmered directly overhead.

Maren felt her stomach sink. "You cannot be serious."

"That is where your room landed while you were wandering." He braced his hands against his hips, smug as a cat caught sitting on a warm pastry. "We climb."

"You climb," she corrected. "I am not scampering up a wall like an animal."

Tamsin clicked his tongue. "You make everything sound like a moral failing. It is a wall, Starsleeves. Walls are friends." He crouched, gathering the weight in his legs with casual readiness. "Watch."

He jumped.

It was not a leap any mortal anatomy could support. He rose like someone had cut gravity in half, boots tapping lightly against the vertical stone only twice before he reached the rippling ceiling. He pressed one palm to the shimmering circle, and it loosened like softened dough.

Tamsin peered down at her, eyes glowing faintly. "Your turn."

Maren looked at the wall. Then at him. Then at the wall again.

"No."

"Yes."

She backed up a step. "You saw how I jumped last time."

"You attempted," he corrected. "Gracefully. Like a falling sack of flour."

She wanted to throw something at him. Preferably him.

"I will not climb that."

Tamsin huffed, a sound like a cat interrupted mid-pounce. "Fine."

"I cannot jump that high."

"You do not need to reach the ceiling. Just reach me."

She clenched her jaw. "And you will catch me."

"Yes," he said simply.

Something in his tone disarmed her. Not flirtation. Not teasing. Just solid, uncomplicated confidence, the kind of confidence that expected her to rise to it.

Maren exhaled. Her palms tingled. Her heart drummed in her ribs.

Fine.

Just this once.

She stepped back, felt the floor settle slightly under her feet, and ran. The wall rose in front of her, smooth and impossible. She kicked off, teeth clenched, breath caught—

Tamsin leaned down, arm stretching with a lazy precision no human joint possessed, and caught her wrist. Her feet scraped the opening. Her disguise tugged tight across her shoulders. For a moment, she hung there, breath held, suspended above an untrustworthy hall.

"Pull me up," she hissed.

"Say please."

She glared with the force of a collapsing star.

"Close enough," he said cheerfully and tugged her the rest of the way through.

Her body collided with his shoulder on a narrow ledge of shifting stone. She yelped. He grunted like she weighed nothing at all.

"Lovely form," he said softly, bracing her easily. "Ten out of ten. Very graceful flour sack."

She swatted the back of his head.

Tamsin took one look at her, smirked, and said, "If anyone asks, we were nowhere questionable."

She elbowed him in the ribs. "If anyone asks, I was asleep."

He nodded solemnly. "Of course. My lady slept soundly, like an angel."

"Angels would not let you near them."

"True. Angels lack taste."

He turned toward the shimmering archway forming ahead of them, tail flicking like a punctuation mark at the end of a joke. "Shall we?"

Maren could feel the dread rising from her stomach like bile. She didn't like the prospect of quietly returning to her cell. Or going to dinner with a narcissistic bastard who kidnapped her apprentice.

Tamsin's ears twitched, catching her mood change before she could bury it entirely. His smile softened into something wicked and knowing.

"So," he said. "How does it feel to be escorted back to your boudoir by a handsome creature?" He arched one brow dramatically. "Scandalous, I think."

"It is not a boudoir," Maren muttered. "It is a cell."

"All right," he said, waving a hand, "your romance dungeon."

"That is worse."

"Your *cozy* incarceration nook."

"Tamsin."

He laughed, delighted, and resumed walking properly. "You are blushing."

"I am not."

"You are. A little pink around the ears."

She touched her ear without thinking, then cursed herself for giving him the satisfaction. He twirled a piece of her borrowed sleeve between two fingers, studying the fold like a tailor taking measurements.

"You realize," he said, voice dipping slyly, "if he finds you missing, his reaction will be…" He paused, searching for a word. "Explosive. In a fun way. The Court should sell seats."

"He will not find out." Maren glanced over her shoulder, suddenly uneasy, scanning the ceiling passage for any sign of obsidian armor or prying masks. "You said intention rewrites paths. If we think about going back, the way back should reveal itself."

"Exactly." Tamsin tapped her forehead lightly. "Keep thinking boring thoughts. Routine. Safety. Responsibility."

"I think about those constantly."

"Poor creature."

He clucked his tongue sympathetically, then spun toward the next turn. Their footsteps echoed softly, the sound swallowed by velvet shadows.

At the end of the passage, the floor, or technically the ceiling, knotted itself into a lattice. A faint glow dripped through the seams like morning light poured through woven fabric. Tamsin pointed, "There. Your luxurious rooftop entrance."

She stepped near, "Let us go."

Tamsin lifted his hands. "After you. I am far too much of a gentleman to shove you through the ceiling first. Although I could, if you prefer it rough."

She shot him a murderous look.

He laughed quietly. "There she is. Come along."

She inhaled once. The ceiling accepted her like warm water. Tamsin followed in a smooth vault, shoulders bending with predatory grace.

They slid through.

The ceiling sealed behind them with a soft sound.

Her feet touched stone again. Her room unfolded around her, dim and still. The cot sulked in the corner exactly where she had left it. The air tasted faintly of smoke. Her pulse skittered high in her throat.

She was back.

Tamsin landed beside her without a sound, tail curling as he surveyed the chamber. He made a pleased noise.

"Home sweet imprisonment."

She elbowed him lightly. "Thank you."

"For what?" he asked. "Kidnapping you for breakfast or returning you before your jailer notices."

"Neither," she said. "For making it feel bearable."

His grin softened for a moment, rare enough that she noticed. Then he ruined it immediately by flicking her nose.

"Next time you wake up hating everything," he said, "try not to look like someone who secretly enjoyed herself."

She smacked his hand away. "Get out."

He bowed low with an exaggerated flourish. "My pleasure, Starsleeves."

He retreated toward the ceiling shimmer, tail swaying with lazy confidence. His last glance carried a spark of affection.

"Try not to get eaten before dinner," he said. "I have a wager running."

Then he vanished upward as lightly as a shadow. The ceiling sealed behind him with a soft thump, and Tamsin's laughter faded.

Maren stood alone again.

Her room seemed smaller than before, the stone quieter, as if it disapproved of what she had just done. The Court of Chaos didn't need eyes to watch her; it breathed around her, a slow exhale against her skin. The disguise Tamsin had given her still clung to her frame, smelling faintly of mint and metal.

She rubbed a hand over her face, trying to scrape his chaos off her thoughts.

Dinner. With *him.*

With the nobles.

With the entire Court watching her every twitch.

Her stomach tightened.

She should run now. Bolt through the ceiling again. Or try a wall, or a crack, or a shadow. Anything! The Court answered her once; maybe it would answer again.

* * *

She'd just started scanning the stones for weakness when the lock clicked.

A single click.

Kipwick stepped inside like an accusation.

The foxling's whiskers trembled in disapproval as he took in her disguise, the boots, the tousled curls, the faint hint of starlight lingering under her skin. His vest was immaculate, buttons polished to an arrogant shine.

"I expected disaster," he said primly. "I did not expect… this level of enthusiasm."

Maren folded her arms. "Good afternoon to you, too."

He sniffed. "It is not afternoon. It is pre-dinner. The Court does not believe in afternoons."

"That sounds inconvenient."

"It is." Kipwick's tail flicked, sharp as punctuation. "Now. Stand still before I have an episode."

She blinked. "Excuse me?"

He tipped his muzzle to the hall like a ringmaster signaling a troupe. Four attendants swept in behind him, robed in black and silver, faces veiled in shimmering gauze that shifted like water. They carried trays, brushes, lengths of cloth, and pots of iridescent paint that glowed faintly with their own light.

Maren stepped back on instinct.

"No," Kipwick said firmly. "Forward. The Court expects you in proper attire. And Spirits, help us all, that includes washing your face."

"I don't need—"

"Sit," he ordered, pointing at the edge of the bed with the full authority of someone who had survived centuries of noble tantrums. "Unless you would like to disappoint every ranked creature in this realm, beginning with the one who currently owns your dinner seat."

Her pulse tripped. "He doesn't—"

"He does," Kipwick said. "And he will be insufferable if you walk in looking like you crawled through a chimney."

One attendant placed a cold bowl into her hands. The steam smelled faintly of bergamot and starfruit. Another snapped open a lacquered brush kit, bristles shimmering like spider silk. A third unfolded a garment that wasn't a dress so much as structured art: layered dark fabric shot through with silver thread that moved when the light changed.

Maren sat, reluctant, because her legs weren't entirely steady and because part of her, the treacherous part, wanted to see what they'd make of her.

The attendants moved with ritual precision. Warm water smoothed over her cheeks. A brush traced gentle lines at her temples. Something cool and luminescent dusted her collarbones, settling over her like fallen stardust. A comb tugged her hair into a loose braid, strands left to frame her face in rebellion.

This was not a pampering.

It was preparation.

A mortal girl being polished into something presentable for a god.

Her pulse fluttered for a moment.

Kipwick circled, appraising her like a jeweler assessing a gem. "Better," he said after a long, dramatic sigh. "Much better. At least now the nobles won't ask if you crawled here."

Maren flexed her fingers, watching the starlit dust along her knuckles. "This is a lot for dinner."

"This is the bare minimum," Kipwick corrected. "He is Mischief. Everything is theater."

"And what am I supposed to be?"

He paused, tail swishing slowly. "A surprise," he said finally. "They like surprises."

Her throat tightened. "And him?"

Kipwick's whiskers lifted in something that might have been sympathy. "He likes reactions."

Great. Perfect. Exactly what she didn't want to provide.

One attendant knelt to give her shoes. These were thin silver slippers with straps that wound around her ankles like inked calligraphy. The final attendant drew a tiny design across the inside of her wrist, a symbol that glowed once and sank into her skin, leaving a faint warmth.

Maren jerked. "What was that?"

"A mark," Kipwick said. "So the Court knows you are expected tonight. It prevents… confusion."

"Confusion?"

"One time," Kipwick said gravely, "a mortal wandered into the wrong feast and was eaten by a chandelier."

She stared.

"It was a small chandelier," he added.

"That does not make it better."

"It rarely does."

The attendants stepped back in unison, heads bowed. Maren rose slowly, the fabric of her clothes whispering against her skin. The starlight dust caught the lantern-glow, casting her in a faint glimmer.

She looked nothing like a bakery girl.

She looked nothing like a prisoner.

She looked… like she belonged in this place.

The thought made her stomach twist.

Kipwick clapped his paws together. "Excellent. You have one goal for dinner."

"Which is?"

"Survive. Politely." He added, pointedly.

"Define politely."

"Without insulting our ruler or nobles."

Maren's jaw tightened. "No promises."

Kipwick sighed the sigh of a fox who had seen too much. "Wonderful. Let us hope the Spirit finds your stubbornness charming tonight."

He flicked his tail toward the door, which swung open in silent invitation.

"Time to face the Court," Kipwick said. "And the one who has been aware of your little field trip since approximately one heartbeat after you left."

Maren froze.

Kipwick's eyes gleamed. "Oh yes. He knows."

Her breath hitched. The attendants bowed out. The corridor waited, glittering faintly with shifting gold veins.

Dinner was going to be a blood sport.

19

Breaking Bread

The corridor spilled her into the dinner hall like a dropped pearl rolling into the jaws of a beast.

The space was enormous, but not in any mortal way. The ceiling climbed high enough that the stars drowned in it, drifting slow and lazy as though the sky itself had grown tired of holding them.

The long feast table curved in a gentle arc, carved from some pale stone marbled with soft gold veins. At its heart lounged the Mischief Spirit.

He rested like the seat had been sculpted for him alone. One leg extended, an elbow draped along the armrest, posture loose and idle in the way only a creature certain of its own power could manage. His coin slipped through his fingers with predatory ease, glinting each time the lanterns blinked. His golden eyes caught her the moment she crossed the threshold.

Heat crawled up her spine.

Coral Head was perched beside him at his right. Her sea-glass hair glowed faintly green, curls arranged to look effortless and expensive. Her coral crown curved like antlers grown from a tidepool, glistening as though wet. She leaned close to the bastard with a smile that was all teeth and entitlement.

Maren's jaw tightened. Not jealousy, she told herself, just… irritation. A moral irritation. Nothing else.

Kipwick padded at her side with impeccable posture, presenting her as though unveiling a painting. The room turned toward her.

Nobles did not simply look. They *assessed.* Voices dipped into pleased hums.

Her constellations glowed faintly across her exposed shoulders and along her throat, starlit flecks beneath the tailored dark fabric of her chaos-coded attire. The Court noticed. She felt it in the prickle at her spine, a new kind of attention: not hunger for spectacle, not disdain for a mortal, but the collective inhale of creatures recognizing something that should not exist.

Her heart thudded once, low and hot.

Tamsin lounged three seats down with one ankle hooked over his knee like he owned the place. When their eyes met, he gave her a lazy, feline wink.

Maren rolled her eyes. Show off.

She lifted her chin, walking forward with as much dignity as a mortal girl armed only with borrowed starlight could manage. The table stretched before her, elegant plates arranged like a puzzle. Every noble had a seat. Every noble filled one.

There was no seat for her.

Not one.

Kipwick paused, whiskers twitching hard enough to signal alarm. He whispered under his breath, voice tight, "Unfortunate oversight."

Her stomach dipped. Oversight felt generous. Intentional felt more accurate.

The thief stretched like a man preparing to enjoy a performance he had commissioned. His golden gaze dragged from the tips of her borrowed shoes, up the line of her legs, over the glow of constellations dusted along her collarbone, all the way to her eyes. Slow. Unhurried. Claiming.

He wanted her to feel watched.

He wanted her to feel owned.

He wanted her to *react.*

Maren refused.

Coral Head leaned toward him with a tinkling laugh. "She thought there would be a seat," she cooed, as though reporting on a child's mistake.

"Mortals are so precious."

Maren's lips curved. "Precious is one word." She let her gaze drift lazily to the thief. "I can always sit in your lap instead."

The hall inhaled all at once.

Nobles stiffened like hounds scenting blood. Fans fluttered. A flute player in the corner missed his note. Tamsin, several seats down, coughed into his cup with violent interest, and somehow made even that look like polite surprise.

Coral Head's pretty smile curdled.

The bastard didn't even flinch. He reclined slightly, one elbow slipping over the back of his chair, fingers tapping the coin idly against the armrest. His eyes darkened in a way that made the lanterns tilt toward him.

"Do you offer," he asked softly, "or do you dare?"

The question stroked low across her spine. The room leaned closer, caught in the gravity between them.

His gaze dipped to the empty floor beside his throne, polished and waiting. "You may take your place at my feet," he mused, voice smooth as honey poured from a warm jar. "A fitting spot for a mortal under my... *protection.*"

The word protection curled like a leash.

Then his eyes lifted again, hooded and hungry. "Or," he said, letting the coin circle his knuckles, "you may sit in my lap. Which is less protection... and more indulgence."

The nobles gasped with delight.

Coral Head's hand clenched around the stem of her goblet until hairline cracks spidered through the glass.

Maren's cheeks went hot. Her breath stuttered once, traitorous. She hated the way the air thickened when he looked at her like that. She hated the heat pooling low in her gut even more.

She forced her pulse steady and took a step forward.

The Court held its breath.

His smile deepened. "Come now," he coaxed, voice low and velvet-slick. "Choose. The floor. Or me."

The floor gleamed like a polished command. His lap felt like a trap carved from temptation.

Neither choice was hers.

And he was savoring every second.

Her constellations flared brighter along her shoulders, as if her own skin rejected the idea of kneeling for him. Heat rose along her throat, part fury, part something sharper. She lifted her chin until it felt like a blade.

Her heartbeat thudded.

Her breathing thinned.

The world narrowed to a single golden-eyed problem waiting to see how she broke.

She stepped closer.

Closer.

Close enough that she could feel the warmth radiating from his knees.

His gaze lowered to follow her movement. His tongue pressed briefly to the inside of his cheek, a tiny tell she would hoard for later.

She leaned in, close enough that Coral Head's breath hitched. She lowered herself with slow, controlled precision…

…and sat on the table.

Right.

On.

The table.

A collective hiss swept through the nobles.

Tamsin slapped his palm over his mouth to contain the roar of laughter.

Coral Head sputtered. "You cannot—"

"Can," Maren said, voice calm. "Did."

The bastard leaned back in his chair, coin flicking once, slow as a heartbeat. His eyes were molten. Dangerous, yet delighted.

The hall held perfectly still.

Maren crossed her ankles beneath her, smoothed her skirt, and met his gaze without blinking.

"Let me know when the food arrives," she said lightly. "I skipped breakfast."

Tamsin lost the battle and barked out a laugh that rolled across the hall like broken rules.

The bastard's smile sharpened. Very, very entertained.

The Mischief Spirit tilted his head, gaze pinned to her like a predator deciding which reaction tasted best.

"Darling," he murmured, low enough to vibrate the air, "you have no idea how interesting you just made this evening."

Maren crossed one leg over the other, ankle dangling, the skirts of her midnight gown spilling over the table in defiance of every rule the Court pretended to uphold. The table was cool beneath her palms, humming faintly as though the Chaos itself approved of her choice.

Her constellations shimmered across her shoulders, brightening each time she drew breath.

She could feel his gaze on them.

She could feel his gaze on *everything.*

Torches guttered along the walls in colors no mortal flame had business wearing: rose-gold, star-blue, green like apple skins in sunlight. Shadows climbed and curled, never still for long.

Court nobles straightened in their seats, fans half-raised, attention trained on her like she had stepped into the center of a play. Conversations hiccuped into silence, then broke into delighted whispers that skimmed across the hall like quicksilver.

The first dishes arrived without servants, as if the table willed them into place. Platters slid themselves forward: shimmering roasted pears, bread shaped like braids of moonlight, warm enough to steam, and pomegranates that leaked their juice like rivers.

The thief lounged in his high seat like sin personified, one elbow resting against the carved armrest, the other hand idly spinning the coin he seemed incapable of parting with. Every rotation caught the torchlight and sent it skittering across his face.

His gaze did not bother pretending to be polite.

He watched her legs. Her throat. The slope of her calves as she adjusted her position. If he undressed her with his eyes any harder, the gown would have come off in ribbons.

Maren pretended not to notice, though heat curled under her skin. Her pulse tapped hard against her collarbone. She refused to give his ego the satisfaction of flushing.

Coral Head shifted beside him, moving her sea-glass hair so it caught the light in a deliberate cascade. She let her hand trail across his sleeve with practiced ease. "My lord," she said sweetly, "you promised the evening would be… intimate."

He did not look away from Maren when he answered. "Intimate requires interest."

Coral Head's smile wavered.

Tamsin, sitting several seats down, lifted a goblet in her direction, eyes glittering with mischief. He mouthed *nice seat* and waggled his brows. He looked like he was holding back a cackle with both hands.

A noble on Maren's left leaned closer. "Is it true," she murmured behind her jeweled fan, "that Delight is furious? Her prodigy snatched from the mortal world without so much as a courtesy notice?"

Another noble answered before Maren could pretend not to hear. "Delight sent a message through the Lattice an hour ago. Quite the tantrum. A nova burst in the eastern wing." She clicked her tongue. "All over a mortal girl."

Penny.

Of course, the Saints would fight over her. Penny with her herb-braided hair and sun-warm laugh.

Delight's chosen.

Delight's *favorite*.

Another noble interjected, voice sharp with gossip. "And Temptation sent word as well."

"Temptation claims the mortal," one noble chirped, sipping something bright gold. "Says she belongs to *him* now."

Maren blinked.

A *he*, they said.

Not a she, like the chapel taught.

Her stomach tightened. She remembered standing in the Festival of

Castings days ago—weeks ago?—muttering that the gods had terrible design skills. She had mocked the Weaver and the Star. She had mocked the myths. Of course, she had caught Temptation's attention. Of course, she had pissed off Delight. Maybe half the pantheon had her on a list by now.

The thief's coin stopped mid-spin, hanging between his fingers like a suspended verdict. "Temptation claims many things," he said. The words were mild, but the voice was not. "He does not have her."

Maren's pulse tripped.

He had never sounded possessive before. Not quite like that. It stretched through the hall, thin as a garrote wire.

A low murmur rolled across the table. Coral Head sat straighter, eyes narrowing. "But he has precedent," she pushed, tone sharpened. "She mocked his fable. Mortals who defy a Spirit's myth belong to that Spirit. Everyone knows that."

He finally looked away from Maren to address the table. "She belongs," he said, voice warm and edged, "to whoever holds her story."

The implication crackled through the hall like lightning.

Maren's breath hitched.

Her constellations pulsed once at the collarbone, like startled stars.

Her throat tightened, memory of Penny's humming cage slicing through her. She hated the bastard. Hated him for taking Penny. Hated him for taking her. Hated him for forcing her into trials meant to break her.

And still something inside her reacted to that single sentence, traitorous and molten.

The nobles shifted, eyes flicking between her and the thief as though watching magnets pull.

"Such boldness," one muttered.

"In public, too," another whispered.

"He has not been this territorial since…"

"Since the mortal girl," someone cut in. "The one in the old stories."

Maren froze.

The table grew sharper.

"What mortal girl?" someone else prodded.

"Oh, the almost-tragedy," a noble purred. "Centuries ago. A girl he nearly—well. Spirits do not love, of course. But he flirted with the possibility. She burned. Or vanished. Depends which version you hear."

Maren's heart tripped in her chest.

Jealousy flickered, unwelcome and sharp. She hated how quickly it bloomed. She hated that she cared at all.

He, of course, did not acknowledge the rumor. He didn't deny it either.

He watched Maren instead, eyes gleaming like gold held to flame. He dragged a finger along the rim of his goblet, slow and suggestive. His gaze dipped to her mouth.

Coral Head's jaw clenched. "My lord," she said brittlely, "your attention—"

"Is exactly where I want it," he murmured.

The table went still.

Maren's breath thinned. Her constellations glowed hotter, traitorously bright. The food near her hummed, vibrating faintly under the pressure curling between them.

She reached for a piece of fruit, mostly to do something with her hands. It was warm, soft, juice dripping slowly. She bit into it and felt his gaze track the movement like a hand sliding down her throat. Heat curled low in her belly, humiliatingly alive.

She forced herself to swallow coolly. "Enjoying the view, thief?" she asked.

He smiled a fraction. "I always enjoy my acquisitions."

Her pulse kicked so hard she nearly choked on the fruit.

Maren wiped her thumb across her lower lip, slow, deliberate, taunting. "You assume too much."

"And yet," he murmured, leaning in just enough to make Coral Head bristle, "you keep giving me so very much to assume."

Her stomach dropped. Her anger tangled with something molten that she refused to name.

A ripple of laughter swept the table, but the thief did not join it. He let the amusement fade from his mouth just enough for the air to cool.

"Eat while you can, darling," he said softly, turning his goblet between his fingers. "The Court prefers its challengers standing when the next trial begins tomorrow."

The word *trial* slid through her like a blade dunked in honey. She hadn't known when it would come; no one bothered to tell mortals the hour. But the way the nobles straightened, the way Coral Head's smile sharpened, the way his eyes lingered on her throat, she understood.

It was coming.

Too soon.

And he wanted her thinking about it.

If this dinner was a battlefield, then every bite, every glance, every shift of breath was a weapon.

And she was losing ground.

<h1 style="text-align:center">20</h1>

<h1 style="text-align:center">Name the Nameless</h1>

Tomorrow came too soon.

Maren was still pacing her chamber, skin humming where the thief's gaze had traced her scars, when Kipwick began his knocking:

Three taps, a pause, then three more.

"Lady mortal," came Kipwick's voice, lilting as though he were about to announce afternoon tea. "Your presence is requested. Or, more accurately, required."

The door clicked once, twice, then fell open without her touching it. Kipwick filled the frame, waistcoat immaculate, cane tapping against the threshold like a conductor summoning an orchestra. His whiskers twitched with amusement.

"Good dawn," he said, tone far too chipper for someone escorting her to probable death. "I trust you're well-rested for Trial Number Two?"

Maren squinted at him. "Do you practice being this insufferable, or does it just come naturally?"

"Practice? My dear girl, this is artistry." He flourished the cane. "Now, if you'll accompany me. I've been told it's dreadfully rude to keep a roomful of immortals waiting."

She shoved her curls back from her face, jaw set, and stepped out. Her scars shimmered faintly beneath her skin, pulsing with each irritated heartbeat. Kipwick matched her stride, cane clicking in jaunty rhythm.

"You might find this one trickier," he went on, too casually. "Something about names."

"Something about names?" she echoed, narrowing her eyes.

He sniffed, clearly pretending to examine a crack in the wall. "Or the lack of them."

Her mouth went dry. He didn't say more, which meant he knew more. Which meant she'd have to pay to find out the hard way.

Names. Her mind flicked, unbidden, to the Hall of Wagers, to the winged woman murmuring that Spirits could only feel one thing. To that quiet line about a mortal girl he had almost loved.

Gods, why was she even thinking about something so irrelevant? She was on her way to another trial. She almost didn't even survive the first one! Now, she couldn't get that bastard's love life out of her head.

She shoved that train of thought aside before it could sharpen.

Focus.

The corridor stretched toward a glow of voices. The Court was waiting. The sound thickened into a roar, restless as a tide, hungry for a spectacle.

When they entered the antechamber, all noise seemed to lean toward her at once. Creatures crowded the balconies, their teeth flashing, their eyes sharp.

And him.

The thief lounged against the railing opposite, coin glinting in the lamplight, golden eyes fixed only on her. The grin that curved his mouth was slow, deliberate, promising nothing kind.

Beside him: Coral Head. She tilted her head toward him, laughter low and sweet as syrup. "Will she even last this one?" she asked, voice pitched just loud enough to carry.

His coin stilled. "She'll last," he drawled. "But not intact." His eyes flicked over Maren's glowing scars like they were his handiwork. Which, damn him, they were.

Heat clawed its way up her throat. Maren lifted her chin, refusing to let them see the crack in her fury. "Enjoy the view now," she snapped. "You'll miss it when I win."

Coral Head's smile sharpened, all glitter and venom. "Bold words for a mortal who burns so easily."

The thief chuckled, low and dangerous, a sound that curled under her skin.

Maren's fists clenched. Her scars pulsed bright, betraying her heartbeat.

The Arbiter appeared then, its voice a blade through the tension.

"The second trial begins."

The arbiter continued.

"The nameless must be named.
   Speak false, and a string is severed.
   When the strings are gone, the feast begins.
   Guard what is yours."

The Arbiter's words fell like stones. No explanation. No mercy. Just rules carved thin enough to cut.

Maren's pulse jumped. She tried to fit sense to the phrases.

Strings?

Feast?

But the Court was never that kind. They liked their laws sharp and riddle-shaped, easy to choke on when it was already too late.

Before she could ask, the wall behind the Arbiter split. Not like stone or wood, but like skin under a knife, peeled slowly.

The sound was wrong. Softer. *Wetter.* Like the rattle of a last breath.

The seam yawned wider, revealing not a room but a cavity. Something that should have stayed stitched shut. Blackness clung to the edges like it didn't want to be let out, but it was already too late.

The Court roared their approval above, the noise rippling over her skin. Maren's stomach turned. Every inch of her body whispered retreat. Not fear. Not quite.

Instinct.

The kind of deep-boned dread that came from being prey in a place designed by predators. Something inside this chamber didn't just not want her in there; it was waiting for her, and not in the friendly, let's-bake-cookies sort of way.

She looked once at the thief, lounging in shadow, coin poised between fingers. His grin stretched slowly when her gaze caught his. Coral Head leaned in closer to him.

Maren lifted her chin and stepped forward.

The air hit her first. Not hot. Not cold. Just… *used.* Like it had been inhaled and exhaled a thousand times over, by things that didn't breathe the way mortals did. Like it had absorbed every scream ever swallowed in this place and wore them now as perfume.

It shouldn't be breathed. It reeked of iron and wet moss. And beneath it all, deeper than scent, deeper than sense, was something worse: The scent of forgetting. It clung to the inside of her nose. Sank into her tongue. She tasted her own lost memories before she even knew they were gone.

Her boots sank into the floor. It was black, textured, like ash, trying to remember what it once had been. Something beneath shifted, small but certain, enough to remind her she was not alone.

Rather than taking another step, she was drawn in, as if the space itself had reached out, curled a cold finger around her ribs, and pulled.

The seam behind her didn't just close. It sealed, with a sound not made for ears: the sound of skin being stitched from the inside.

The only light now was the faint thrumming glow of her scars, pulsing with each frantic heartbeat.

Maren couldn't breathe. The chamber hadn't only gone still, it had hushed. As if the moment had snapped shut around her like a trap. As if the room itself had teeth.

And the dark around her wasn't still either.

It breathed.

A slow, rhythmic pulsing, like a lung refusing to empty. The air shifted not with wind, but with the weight of something listening. She was being watched.

Her scars pulsed brighter. The glow stretched a few inches ahead of her, showing only the faintest outline of space. There were no walls she could trust. No ceiling. Just vast, breathing dark.

And then *it* moved.

Not walked. Not crawled. *Moved.* Like blood over a cut. Like heat wavering off stone.

Her faint glow caught it for a moment, enough to tease the edges of a form. Girl-like. A torso, maybe, draped in hair that was more shadow than substance. Then the shape glitched, folding into something longer, limbs bending the way limbs shouldn't, joints too many, and angles too sharp.

The thing shifted again, flickering between shadow and a girl's shape, its limbs bending at wrong angles. Its presence pressed against her chest like a hand, squeezing air out of her lungs.

And then—

"Maren."

Her name. In her voice.

The sound came too clean, too exact. Like her throat had been cut out and replayed on some warped stage. It echoed in the dark, stripped of warmth like a puppet's imitation of life.

Her whole body recoiled. Her scars burned hot, throwing faint starlight across the dark, as if they were trying to hold her together.

Names, Kipwick had said. The nameless must be named, the Arbiter had promised. The creature wanted words. It wanted something to wear.

Maren swallowed hard. Her tongue felt heavy, her thoughts scraping for logic. It echoed her, so the first thought that came was simple. Cruel. "You are an echo," she forced out, voice shaking. "That is your name."

The chamber shuddered.

One of the silver strings overhead thrummed, then snapped.

She had spoken false.

Pain slammed into her chest like lightning, sharp and consuming. She gasped, clutching her ribs, but there was no wound. No blood.

Only absence.

Something had been taken.

She reached for it instinctively, fumbling through the corridors of her own mind the way she used to fumble through dark bakery halls as a child. Searching for a candle. For a sound. For a voice.

Her father's voice.

Gone.

Not the stories themselves. Not the image of him at the counter, flour on his sleeves, and a book in his hand. Those still lived, grainy and fragile. But the *sound.* The low, warm rumble that had filled the bakery like a hearth when he read aloud. The way her name had curled on his tongue. The softness that had once been her entire world.

Vanished.

Cleanly and absolutely. As if someone had slit the thread and burned the ends, so it could never be tied again.

Maren's knees buckled. Her scars flared, throwing a faint light that wavered as she shook. She tried to force the sound back, to replay it in her skull. Nothing.

Not even a whisper.

Her father was truly dead now. Not just in flesh, not just in earth. But in voice. She would never hear him again, not in waking or in a dream. That warmth, that sound, was ash forever.

Her throat locked. A sob built and strangled itself halfway out, breaking into a gasp. Her grief came out jagged. Violent.

And then the shape shivered. Every eye blinked at once. Its mouth cracked wider.

"Maren," it said again. This time, it was her father's voice.

She broke. Her breath hitched, sharp and wounded. Grief flooded in, raw and hot. Rage tried to climb with it, clawing for air, but the grief drowned it and dragged it down.

"You bastard," she choked, voice trembling, body shaking so hard her teeth clattered. "That was mine."

Her scars pulsed wildly, constellations quaking like they wanted to burst from her skin. The faint starlight blurred in her tears, as though even the

Court had grown drunk on her breaking.

The thing tilted its head, eyes gleaming, and smiled.

And then it laughed.

Not in her voice. Not in the warped echo.

In her father's.

The exact sound of him laughing at his own terrible jokes, voice rich and kind, alive again in the mouth of a nightmare.

It *gutted* her.

Maren pressed both hands to her ears, but it didn't matter. The laugh wasn't just sound anymore. It lived inside her chest, vibrating through bone, sickly sweet, burning away the memory of warmth and replacing it with this: a desecration.

Her father's voice was gone, and the only remnant left belonged to this *thing*.

The laughter rang until it rotted in her ears. Until it wasn't laughter at all, but static, warped on repeat like a record left in the sun.

Maren pressed her palms harder over her ears, but her scars betrayed her, glowing brighter, pulsing with each jag of grief. The light flickered across the dark, giving the creature enough shape to step forward.

It came together in jerks and glitches, as if every limb had been sketched wrong and redrawn without erasing the first draft. One moment, girl-like, draped in long shadow hair. The next stretched too tall, dragging limbs bent in reverse. The next melted sideways, joints rearranging until her stomach lurched.

The strings overhead quivered. She could feel them now, as if they were tethered through her ribcage. Each vibration plucked something fragile inside her.

"Maren," it purred in a chorus of her voice, her father's, then twisting toward Penny's hum.

Her chest seized.

"Do not," she snapped, voice raw. "Do not touch her."

The strings sang. One nearly broke. She bit her tongue until blood flooded her mouth, choking the word back before it could spill into a mistake.

Her mind screamed at her to fight. To name it something sharp, to break it before it could break her. The Arbiter's decree circled in her head: *The nameless must be named. Speak false, and a string is severed.*

Her father's voice was already gone. One string snapped, one thread of herself stolen forever. If she gave another false name, what else would it take? Penny's laugh? Her mother's hands? Her own?

Her knees threatened to buckle. Her body wanted to crumple, to crawl, to beg. But she stayed standing. Chest heaving. Blood on her tongue.

The creature tilted its head, every eye unblinking, smile widening without a face.

"You'll break," it crooned. Her father's voice again. *"Everything does."*

Maren's stomach turned to lead. Fear clawed higher, grief clawed deeper. But beneath both, something else sparked: fury, small and sharp as a struck match.

Not yet. Not her.

She wiped the blood from her mouth with the back of her hand, her scars flickering faint light against the dark. "Try me."

The strings shivered overhead, eager.

The thing tilted closer. The dark stretched with it, thick as tar, wrapping around her ankles.

"Maren," it said again. Then, softer—

Penny's hum.

That bright, careless tune Penny always carried with her, whether grinding herbs, kneading dough, or braiding rosemary into her hair. A half-song without words, so stitched into Maren's bones that she couldn't remember a day in Eldenwick without it.

The sound lilted through the chamber now, warped and hollow, as if hummed by something that had never drawn breath.

Her heart stopped. It had already stolen her father, and now it was reaching for Penny.

Her thoughts darted, wild and desperate. Echo had been wrong. The name had not fit. Maybe this was not about what it did, but what it was.

Hunger. Thief. Hollow.

"You are a thief," she forced out, each word shaking. "You are theft given teeth. That is your name."

The chamber thrilled, almost pleased.

Then a second string snapped.

The pain struck deeper than the first. Not just a lash across her chest; this one unspooled her from the inside. Her breath hitched, spine arching like she'd been struck with lightning.

And then she knew.

Penny's hum was *gone*.

She reached for it, desperate, clawing at her own mind. Tried to summon it, tried to trace the rhythm with her lips. That bright, careless tune she had heard every day, grinding herbs, kneading dough, braiding rosemary into hair. The sound that had lived in the bakery's walls like a second heartbeat.

Nothing came.

Her knees buckled. She slammed her palm to the floor to keep upright. Ash dust smeared her skin. Her throat worked around a sob, but it came out raw and broken, no music behind it. The silence inside her was unbearable.

The thing cocked its head. And then it hummed again.

Not Penny's hum. Penny's hum through rot. Flat where it should have lifted, sweet where it should have been sharp; the shape of it intact, but the life stripped away.

It stole the sound and fed it back to her hollow.

Maren's whole body shook. Her stomach twisted. Grief and fury tore at each other until she wanted to rip her own skin apart.

"That was hers," she whispered, voice cracking. "You don't get to have her."

The strings overhead quivered, eager for another mistake. Her scars pulsed, flickering constellations trembling against her arms.

The thing leaned closer, humming louder, pressing the hollow song against her ears like a hand over her mouth.

Maren gritted her teeth so hard her jaw ached. She bit her tongue again. More blood swelled rich and iron-heavy in her mouth. She refused to give it another name. It had taken two already. One more wrong word and it would eat the last of her.

The chamber held its breath, waiting.

Her throat wanted to spill words. Any words. Names sharp enough to cut: *monster, wretch, shadow.* Her jaw clenched. If one syllable broke loose, another string would fall.

The last string overhead trembled anyway, sensing her weakness. If she spoke the wrong word, it would fall.

And there would be nothing of her left to save Penny when dawn came.

She swallowed blood and forced herself still.

The figure twitched, folding in on itself until its shape mimicked hers. Girl-shaped now, curls flickering like shadowed flame, scars glowing faintly across its arms. *Her* arms.

It opened its mouth and spoke in her own raw whisper: "That was hers. You don't get to have her."

The words she had just said.

Maren's chest squeezed. Her whole body shook with fury, with terror. She nearly screamed to *stop.* Almost gave the thing what it wanted. Her tongue pressed against her teeth, aching with the weight of it.

Another string quivered, ready to break.

Her vision blurred. She braced her hands on her knees, sucking air in ragged gasps. If she lost her mother next, if that last memory went hollow, there would be nothing left that was truly hers. No flour-dusted hands guiding hers. No warmth that meant home without needing a word. She could not lose that as well.

Overhead, the last string quivered. One misstep, one wrong syllable, and the Court would eat her alive.

The Arbiter's decree thundered in her skull: *The nameless must be named. Speak false, and a string is severed.*

Her throat worked. Speak, and she risked it. Stay silent, and she broke the law anyway.

Her scars burned hotter, constellations trembling against her skin like they were trying to escape. Her teeth cut her tongue, blood flooding her mouth. She spat it onto the ash-floor, grounding herself.

"You're not Penny," she whispered, voice shaking, teeth bared. Every syllable scraped her throat raw, terror riding it out. The string hummed, tight but intact.

"You're not my father. You're not me." Her voice cracked, grief ripping the words apart. The string vibrated harder, testing.

"You are just…" She faltered.

Her whole body locked. The wrong word could kill her. The silence pressed closer, heavy, as if the dark itself leaned in to hear what she would choose.

Her scars pulsed, starlight shivering under her skin. Her body screamed do not speak. Her mind whispered something else.

Truth.

Not cleverness. Not denial. Not spite.

She racked her brain for words. The Court had built this thing from "almosts". From unfinished stories. From names that never quite landed.

What was this thing with names?

She thought of the Hall of Wagers again, of gossip poured like wine. A mortal girl. The *almost*-tragedy. He nearly loved her. She burned. Or vanished. Depends which version you hear.

Almost loved.

Almost saved.

Almost something.

She thought of the dinner table, nobles purring about the old story. Spirits cannot love. They feel only what the gods stamped into them. Anything more and they crack. Perhaps that is why she vanished. Mortals are always leaving when Spirits reach too far.

This creature wanted a word. It wanted the shape of what it was. Half-eaten. Half-made. The remnant of a choice that had never fully landed.

She drew in a shaking breath.

What if this mortal girl never truly vanished? She was just "re-made" into a different story. What if—

"You are just a hole that pretends to be full," she finally said, trying desperately to reach for more information before dooming hers, and Penny's, future.

The string steadied. The chamber hushed.

The figure shivered. For a heartbeat, it held the shape of the shadow-girl, then its outline broke and healed in jerks, as though the world could not decide what it was. Its eyes blinked one after the other, never quite together.

Maren dragged in another breath, dizzy, grief clawing her open. Her tongue tasted of blood and ash. She clutched the words she had left like a blade.

Her voice wavered, then leveled. "You are not nothing," she said quietly. "You are what someone wanted and never finished. What they almost said. Almost were. Almost saved."

The last string rang clear. The sound wasn't triumph, but rather, survival. Stretched thin, humming against her bones like a warning she'd feel for the rest of her life.

The creature stilled. For a long, terrible moment, she thought it might break again. But then its form folded inward: limbs tucking, shadows collapsing. What had been all wrong angles now crouched small, almost human, its too-many eyes half-shuttered as if in relief.

Maren's legs gave out. She sagged onto her knees, trembling so hard her teeth chattered. Her scars dimmed, faint constellations glowing low like banked coals.

The creature drew a breath.

When it spoke, it did not use her father's voice, or Penny's, or hers. A new sound came. Thin, warped at the edges, but its own.

"*Almost.*"

Her throat tightened. Her chest ached. She had given it something no one else had: recognition. And it had nearly devoured her for it.

In its new voice, it whispered: *"I know yours now too."*

Maren's scars flared. Her breath stopped.

"The name beneath the name," Almost said, eyes blinking in uneven rhythm. *"The one even you have not spoken."*

Cold swept her bones. The Arbiter's rules roared in her head: *Guard what is yours.*

Her lips parted, but no sound came. Fear strangled her voice. If she answered wrong, if she so much as slipped, the last string would snap, and she would be nothing but meat for the Court.

Almost tilted its head, eyes gleaming, voice softened. *"It waits,"* it murmured. *"It always waits."*

Her arms burned faint light, constellations thrumming like a warning.

And then Almost added, softer still: *"You smell like him. Like the one who left me."*

Her pulse thundered. Her gaze snapped up. Him.

The thief. The Spirit.

The one they called Mischief. The one nobles whispered about in half-versions. The mortal girl he almost loved. The almost-tragedy. The one who burned. Or vanished.

The truth pulsed in the dark, bitter and clear. This was what happened when a Spirit reached past what he was made for. When he almost chose. Almost saved. Almost loved. The Court had taken that almost and chewed it into a creature that ate stories to fill the hole in her own.

Maren curled her fingers into fists.

She wanted to shout that he had not left anything, that he did not have love to leave. She wanted to spit his title like a curse and deny every piece of it. The string above her thrummed sharply, as if daring her to try.

So she forced her voice low and careful. "Keep what I gave you," she rasped. "But nothing else."

Almost lowered its head. The faintest hum rolled through its form, not hunger this time, but something closer to reverence.

"I will keep it," it said. *"And you will keep yours. For now."*

The chamber shivered. The seam behind her split open once more, light spilling in like a mercy. The Arbiter's voice cut through, clipped and final:

"One name claimed. One truth spoken. Two trials passed. One remains."

The seam waited.

Maren pushed herself upright. Every muscle shook. Grief dragged at her ribs like a weight. Her father's voice was gone. Penny's hum had been swallowed. She would never hear her own laugh the way it had been, not without remembering the thing that took it. And she knew now, with the weight of iron, that names were not just words.

They were chains. They were doors. They were knives.

Her scars glowed faint and steady, constellations burning against her arms as she stepped toward the seam, back into the roar of the Court.

21

Dressed to Disturb

The seam spit her out again.

One blink, she was inside the wound-door; the next, she staggered into the antechamber, legs jelly, lungs burning. The spectators roared their delight above her, a storm of silk, but the sound hit muffled, as if she were underwater.

Ash and rot crusted the sweat on her skin. Her curls clung in damp knots, streaked with soot. Her stomach turned at the sweet tang of blood still clinging to her tongue.

The Arbiter was already dissolving into light. Nobles fanned themselves as though they hadn't just bet on her corpse. Somewhere, Coral Head clapped slowly. And the thief, coin glinting at his knuckles, watched her with that lazy half-smile, like survival had been for his amusement alone.

Maren ignored them all. If she let herself look too long, she might fold.

A sharp little voice cut through instead. "Honestly."

Kipwick appeared out of the crowd, whiskers twitching in dismay. He flicked his paw and produced a handkerchief roughly the size of a postage stamp.

He offered it up with the gravity of a coronation. "For your face."

Maren took it, pressed it against her cheek. The soot spread wider. "That helped nothing."

"Symbolism," Kipwick said primly, tail swishing. "One must make the effort."

"Next time," Maren rasped, "bring a bucket."

"Next time, don't bleed on the decor," he retorted, then vanished neatly into the tangle of robes and laughter, leaving her alone with her shaking hands and the stink of death.

The crowd surged forward, giddy with someone else's survival. Wine spilled, laughter tangled, coins changed hands in greedy little clinks.

Maren stood in the middle of it, swaying, as if her body hadn't gotten the memo that she was still alive. She could not hear Penny's hum anymore. Could not recall the grain of her father's voice without feeling the absence in its place. The silence inside her skull pressed harder than the noise of the revel.

Her boots scraped forward, half-choice, half-instinct. The floor rippled obligingly, opening a path through the mob. Revelers cheered like she was the star of a parade instead of the corpse they had not gotten.

She didn't meet their eyes.

And if she did, she might crumble, and then they would clap louder.

The hall twisted itself wider as she went, lanterns flaring into revel light. Tables appeared: teetering under platters of jeweled fruit, steaming breads, and meats lacquered in honey.

Music clattered to life. Creatures already spun in wild arcs across the floor.

Maren barely even registered it. Her legs felt like split timber, hollow and splintered. Her lungs still rasped. Every step felt borrowed.

By the time she reached her corridor, her door waited open.

Inside, her chamber had been reborn. The bed was gone, replaced by a slightly larger, more luxurious bed draped in dark velvet. A copper tub gleamed in the corner, steam curling up in slow ribbons. A tray sat balanced on a side table, laden with figs, bread rolls glossed with melted butter, and a glass of something that caught the light like molten ruby.

The air smelled rich and warm and maddeningly kind. Like mercy dressed as temptation.

Her hand braced against the door frame, trembling. Her scars glowed faintly under her sleeve, pulsing with memory of the wound-door. She wanted to collapse into the tub. She wanted to eat until the shaking stopped.

She wanted to scream until Penny's hum came back.

Instead, she laughed once, bitter and hoarse. "Congratulations," she muttered at the room. "You upgraded me to a kennel with plumbing."

The velvet didn't answer. The tub steamed on.

Somewhere down the hall, the revel roared louder. A violin shrieked for her attention, high and insistent. She shoved the door shut and pressed her back against it, as if she could keep the whole Court out with one mortal body already fraying at the seams.

For a moment, she just stood there, ribs protesting every breath.

Then her knees threatened mutiny.

She decided to surrender to that at least.

Her fingers fumbled at her laces. The soot-stiffened bodice clung like it wanted to take her skin with it. She peeled layer after layer of fabric away until she was standing in nothing but grime and tremors. Her clothes collapsed to the floor in a heap that smelled of blood and smoke.

She had not really looked at herself since the first trial. Not properly. A splash in a basin, a glance at her forearms, nothing more. Now the mirror on the opposite wall forced the full picture on her.

Not hideous. Not monstrous.

Burns carved across her torso in pale rivers through the ash. Faint constellations glimmered where the wounds had sealed, a scatter of silver starlight over belly, hips, thighs, calves. For a moment, she could not decide if she looked like a ruin or a map.

A sound escaped her that was not quite a laugh. "Wow," she muttered at the reflection. "You are astronomy now."

The copper tub hissed gently, steam curling toward her. The scent of cedar soap and something sharp, citrus maybe, curled around her like a ghosted hand.

His scent.

Of course it was. She rolled her eyes at the ceiling, but her feet were already moving.

The water seared as she sank into it, then settled into heat that went bone-deep. She hissed, groaned, and finally let her head tip back against the rim. For the first time in what felt like years, she felt clean. Not whole, not safe, but clean. Her muscles unknotted by increments. Her burns quieted from screams to whispers.

She dunked her curls under. Soap clung to them, rinsing away black water that swirled around her knees. When she surfaced, she dragged in a lungful of steamy air.

Him, again, in the cedar and citrus. The Court wore him like a signature.

Her stomach growled, loud and petulant. She snorted into the empty room. "Traitor."

She reached for the tray. Figs melted sweet on her tongue, bread still warm tore soft in her hands. She ate like someone half-starved, which she was, and let the bath cradle what was left of her spine.

That was when she noticed the bed.

She was certain it had been bare when she stripped down. The velvet covers were now turned down with precision. Draped across them, a gown waited. Liquid moonbeams stitched with starlight, the fabric looked as though it had been poured rather than sewn. It bared more than it covered: an open back that dipped low, a slit that read as an invitation, thin off-the-shoulder sleeves that only pretended to be decent.

The cut was precise, wickedly intentional. Designed to trace every scar without hiding one. Beside it, folded neatly, a note.

Her wet hand left smears across the parchment as she picked it up. The handwriting was sharp, elegant, and unbearably pleased with itself.

Wear it. Indulge me.
I want them to see what you survived, and what I claimed.
—S

Her breath caught. Gods, he was vile. Infuriating.
Gods, he was—
She tossed the note onto the side table before it could burn her fingers.

Maren scrubbed her hands over her face, dragging water down her cheeks. She should be furious. She was furious. But the gown gleamed in the corner of her eye, silver catching the lamplight like it was already on her. And the truth was, she was so tired of being nothing but ash and ache.

Maybe this was another trial. Maybe it was a trap.

She was mortal. Mortals needed baths. Needed food. Sometimes, they needed a night where they were not only the thing being hunted.

She climbed out of the tub, dripping, water running down her skin in bright streams. The air met her cool and sharp.

Her reflection sprawled across the polished copper, fractured but undeniable. Every piece of her body was proof she had been broken and still, somehow, stood.

She looked dangerous.

Her mouth twisted into a grin that did not reach her eyes. "Fine," she muttered. "Let us give them a show."

The gown waited like a dare. She dragged it over damp skin. The fabric was cold at first, then warmed, molding and settling as if the Court itself were adjusting the fit. Silver traced her scars instead of concealing them, each glimmer a spotlight on what she had survived. The neckline dipped sharply, the hem slit to invite scandal. Every stitch whispered: ruin, and revel in it.

Maren tugged it tight, cinched herself into the Court's vision, and found, to her own bitter amusement, that she looked ravishing. Not in spite of the wounds, but lit by them.

The note still lay on the table, smirking in ink. She picked it up again and read the last line aloud in a mocking lilt. "What I claimed."

Her laugh came out hoarse and dangerous. "Oh no, thief. You do not get to claim me."

She crushed the parchment in her fist, tossed it into the guttering flame of the lamp, and watched it curl into ash.

Then she turned to the door.

Her legs still trembled, but the gown gave her an armor of silk and shadow. Hunger pulsed through her blood, sharper now that it was fed. Exhaustion dragged at her bones, yet under it thrummed something reckless that dared him, dared all of them, to turn away.

Let the Court see her scars. Let Coral Head choke on envy. Let the thief sit there and pretend he had orchestrated this.

If they wanted spectacle, she would be the spectacle.

Her bare feet whispered across stone as she moved back into the corridor. Her step was not perfectly steady; the gown translated each wobble into a deliberate sway.

Each scar into statement.

The sound of the revel grew louder with every turn: drums pounding like a second heartbeat, strings singing too high for mortal patience, laughter spilling like wine from a cracked cask. Magic thickened the air, fizzing against her damp skin, tugging at the edges of her temper.

And then she stepped through the arch.

The Court exploded in color and heat. Lanterns pulsed with strange light. Tables groaned under platters of impossible food. Nobles and creatures twined and writhed in dances too sharp to be human.

Conversation dropped as if cut.

At the far edge of the floor, Coral Head froze. Her sea-glass curls seemed to dull, her gown paling against the galaxy Maren wore. Her mouth stretched into a brittle smile that did not touch her eyes.

And the thief. *Gods*, the thief.

He did not even pretend not to stare. His grin was slow, devastating. His golden gaze dragged over every constellation stitched to her skin. Not simple hunger. Possession braided with desire, lust tangled with triumph. It rolled over her like heat, prickling every inch of exposed skin.

Maren's lips curved, sharp and amused. If he thought he had claimed her, he could choke on his own delight. She was claiming this moment, every reckless inch of it.

A goblet pressed into her hand from some overeager reveler. She did not ask what was inside. She tipped it back and drank. Sweet fire slid down her throat, fizzing into her veins, turning her limbs loose and her edges bright. The revelers howled their approval. The music climbed.

She let the goblet fall into a stranger's hands without looking.

Her gaze never left the thief's.

As she stepped down into the whirl of music, skirts flaring, starlight scattering like sparks, the Court leaned forward, greedy and breathless for whatever came next.

22

Arsenic

He didn't rush.

He stayed at the far edge of the revel, golden gaze fixed on her like a leash, letting the Court peel open for him. Music seemed to adjust to his stride, strings tightening, drums syncing to the slow, unhurried count of his steps.

Every move was deliberate.

Every breath was a promise.

No coin, no cloak, no distraction. Just him, prowling closer, steady as gravity.

Maren's skin prickled hot. The drink humming through her blood made her brave and a little stupid. She lifted her chin, letting the starlight stitched over her skin catch the lanterns, daring him. She had survived fire, a monster that ate memories, and grief that hollowed her out. She was not about to cower from a Spirit with bedroom eyes.

Still, when he finally stopped in front of her, her throat went dry.

"Bastard," she said sweetly. Safer than admitting what her body was already doing. Leaning in. Reaching for the heat of him like a flame that had already burned her once.

His grin cut sharply. "Astronomy suits you, darling." His gaze traced her constellation scars slowly, like reading a chart of stars he planned to sail by. "The stars would be jealous."

Her laugh flicked out, a small, sharp blade. "Try a line like that again, and I will gut you."

"Then I will die happy." His hand extended, palm open. It looked like an invitation, but it felt more like a command.

She should have spit in it.

She set her hand in his instead.

The contact burned. A low, electric hum jumped from his skin to hers, running along her bones. He drew her into the crush of music, the Court's eyes devouring every step, every crossing of their bodies like bites.

They moved as if the pattern had been set long before she ever set foot into Eldenwick. His hand settled low at her back, fingers firm, guiding and provoking at once.

Her fingers skated over his shoulder, nails just enough to scratch. A warning: this was not surrender, this was a fight.

"Afraid I'll outshine you?" she murmured as he turned her out. Skirts flared, scattering light. For a heartbeat, she was as radiant as a fallen star.

"You already do," he said, catching her back against him with infuriating ease, chest to chest. His breath brushed her temple, his voice a velvet darkness. "I do not mind burning."

A reckless laugh tore loose from her, bright and a little wild. "Careful. I will take you with me."

"Please do," he breathed.

They circled, closer and sharper. Every step a feint, every turn a strike. When she shoved at his chest to break his hold, he folded the motion into the dance, spinning her out and dragging her back in, like she had never escaped at all. When he tried to anchor her with his grip, she twisted against it, using his own weight to pivot under his arm. Their bodies collided, separated, collided again.

It felt less like dancing and more like sparring.

He spun her hard. Her skirts snapped wide. She snapped back into his orbit, her hip catching his thigh, her chest brushing against his. She gave him a smile full of teeth. "You enjoy manhandling mortals, do you?"

His golden eyes gleamed. "Only the ones who bite."

"Good," she said. "I plan on drawing blood."

His laughter rumbled through his chest, into her ribs, low and delighted. He slid her into a dip that was not gentle. The Court gasped around them. Maren's head tipped back, curls skimming the air, spine arched, and still she smirked up at him. "If you drop me, I will haunt you."

"Darling," he purred, hauling her upright, mouths almost colliding, "you already do."

The drink fuzzed her edges, but her mind stayed knife-sharp. She shoved against his chest again, wrenching herself out of his arms just long enough to pivot free. The crowd parted in a hush, watching the opening between them like the start of a duel. Maren spun wide, slit baring her leg like a blade, before he caught her wrist and yanked her back in.

"Careful," she hissed, breathless from both effort and proximity. "You will look like you are enjoying yourself."

He bent closer, close enough to count the dark fringe of his lashes. "I am."

Her pulse jumped. She smoothed it over with a scoff. "I knew you were shameless. I did not realize it was a lifestyle."

"And I knew you were dangerous." His hand flexed against the curve of her spine, thumb pressing lightly into tender, half-healed skin. "I did not realize you would wear it this beautifully."

Heat snapped low in her gut. Her laugh came out too bright, too reckless. "Flattery? Is that foreplay here?"

His grin sharpened. "Depends. Do threats work better on you?"

She leaned in until their noses almost brushed. Her lips were a breath from his. "Try me."

The Court howled, greedy for spectacle. Nobles whirled around them, edges of wings and silks skimming past, but the space around the pair stayed clear, a ring of air held tight as if the room itself were waiting for a kill.

Coral Head's brittle smile had gone strained and sharp, her nails digging little crescents into her goblet stem.

The thief twirled Maren again and pulled her flush against him, their steps falling into a pattern that looked like a waltz and felt like a knife fight.

Knees brushed, thighs pressed, her ribs met his every time she inhaled. Her breath caught somewhere between fury and something far more dangerous.

"You are drunk," he murmured against her hairline. The words were an observation, not a judgment, as warm breath stirred the curls at her temple.

"I am lively," she shot back, her mouth grazing the shell of his ear.

"You are reckless."

"And you are still here," she said.

That grin again, lazy and lethal. "As if I could leave."

Her skin prickled hot. She tipped her head back, meeting his eyes with all the venom she could muster. "You are a bastard."

His thumb traced the back of her hand, feather light, intimate, and infuriating. "And you love it."

She barked a laugh that could have cut glass. "I would sooner love arsenic."

"Then poison me," he said, spinning her once more. The room blurred, music and lanterns streaking into color at the edges of her vision. She staggered from the dizziness, from the heat coiling low in her belly, but he caught her before her knees could fold. His fingers anchored her at the small of her back. His breath brushed her cheek. "Let us see how long I survive."

Their mouths hovered a heartbeat apart. The music swelled. The Court leaned forward like one creature, hungry and holding its breath.

Maren, tipsy and furious and glittering in a gown stitched from galaxies, let herself imagine it for a single, reckless moment. Closing that sliver of space. Burning with him until there was nothing left but ash and starlight.

"You are playing with fire," she whispered, breath ghosting over his mouth.

His grin flickered with a dangerous hunger. "Then burn me."

The world narrowed to the inch between them. Her lips parted. His golden gaze went molten. Her pulse stuttered foolishly against the solid press of his hand at her spine. Every part of her screamed to close the distance, to finally taste the danger she had been orbiting since the bakery.

The Court roared.

A cheer crashed over them, thunderous and greedy, shattering the moment like dropped glass. Someone slammed a goblet against the floor; someone else shrieked with laughter. The fragile pocket of quiet burst.

His grip loosened at once. A mask of lazy civility slid over his features, the change so smooth it almost made her more furious.

He straightened them both with insulting ease, spun her out in a flourish for the crowd instead of for her, and released her with a grand little bow.

Maren's chest ached with the loss. Her mouth still tingled with what had not happened.

He did not look at her right away. He accepted the applause, let the nobles clap his back, and smirked for their benefit.

To anyone else, he looked pleased with his own theatrics. Only when the noise crested did his gaze flick back to hers.

The heat there had not dimmed.

Gods, she wanted to claw at him for it.

She tossed her curls back, smirk sharp as cut sugar. "Enjoy the show," she called to the crowd, her voice rough but steady.

The Court roared louder, adoring. Coral Head's brittle smile finally cracked.

When Maren turned back to him, the thief's gaze was already waiting, coiled like a promise.

The certainty hit her low and heavy, reckless and undeniable: this dance was *not* over.

The Court swallowed her after that.

Hands caught at her wrists, tugging her into new spins and new toasts. Another goblet appeared, then another. She let it happen. Let the sweet burn of liquor slip warm into her belly. Let strange food melt on her tongue.

She laughed when the room demanded it. She twirled when the music tugged. She let herself burn bright because they wanted a blaze and because it was easier than being a wound.

The thief kept his distance.

Not gone. Always within sight.

He returned to the dais, Coral Head draped on his arm like seaweed claiming a rock. His smile stayed razor sharp for the Court. When his eyes found hers across the revel, the air between them crackled, as if they were both still one misstep from ruin.

Maren drank again, throat raw. She told herself it was only to numb the ache, only to keep from thinking of the hum she could no longer hear, the voice she could no longer remember. But every swallow only carved the hollow deeper.

She danced until the balls of her feet throbbed. She laughed until the sound went brittle. She ate until her stomach gave up protesting. The hunger beneath it refused to budge. The old one, the one that had nothing to do with bread. The one who had asked for wonder and gotten this instead.

When the revel finally began to tilt toward its own version of dawn, she slipped away. The music chased her down the corridor, muffled by stone. Laughter echoed too long behind her. She stumbled once, catching herself on a cold wall. Her gown clung damp to her thighs, glittering with spilled wine and borrowed stars.

Her door waited. Open again.

The velvet bedspread glimmered faintly in the dark. The copper tub steamed with fresh water, as if the Court thought mortals needed endless scrubbing to stay intact. She didn't bother. Her skin already smelled of smoke, of cedar soap, of someone else's gaze.

She shut the door and let her forehead rest against it, steadying the spin in her head. The silence pressed in thick and loud. After the revel's chaos, it felt like standing in the empty shell of her own chest.

Her fingers fumbled at her straps. Velvet slid against her skin. She tugged it off one shoulder, then the other, not bothering to pretend modesty for an empty room. Her hair fell forward, no shield against the constellation scars scattered across her body.

She had the gown half down when the silence changed. It felt… *charged.*

Her head snapped up.

The thief lounged in her chair, coinless, smug, as though he'd been there all night waiting for her to notice. One ankle rested over his knee. Golden eyes raked over her, slow and shameless, and his mouth curved like the scene had been staged just to amuse him.

"Enjoying the view, bastard?" she said. Her voice came out flat, but her pulse tripped over itself.

"Ecstatic," he murmured. He leaned back further, hands draped over the armrests, posture all lazy possession. "Although, if you truly wish me to leave, I will graciously escort myself out *after* you finish undressing."

She snorted and dragged the gown the rest of the way off, kicking it toward him. "Choke on that."

He reached for the fabric, fingers slipping into the folds. He lifted it to his face and inhaled like a man savoring the first breath after drowning. "Delicious."

Maren's jaw slacked in a half-scoff, heat prickling across her chest. "You're vile."

"And you're trembling," he countered softly. His gaze flicked to the faint shake of her hands as she yanked the velvet blanket from the bed. "Is that exhaustion, the wine, or just me?"

"Try arrogance." She wrapped the blanket around herself like armor, pulling it high. "You think a dance makes you irresistible?"

He rose then. Fluid, predatory, each step quiet. The loose silk of his shirt caught the lamp light, shadows pooling in the hollows of his throat. "Not the dance," he said. His voice dropped, scraping low. "The way you fought me for every step and still chose to stay. The way you laughed when I threatened to burn with you. The way your lips almost..."

Her palm hit his chest. Heat seared through the fabric. Too close.

"Almost does not count," she cut in, sharp, though her breath stuttered.

His grin flashed white and wicked. "Then let us try again."

She shoved harder. He let her, rocked back half a step, still laughing in that low, pleased way that made her want to bite him.

"Gods, you are infuriating," she muttered, clutching the blanket tighter.

"And you are distracting," he said. "Tell me, baker. Do you truly believe you can slip back into that crumbling shop after this? After you have walked through fire, named a monster, danced in my Court, and worn starlight for a dress?"

The question slid right under her ribs. She thought of Penny's hum, now stolen. Her father's voice was gone. The Chapel, the ledger, the ovens, the life that fit one kind of hunger and starved another. She thought of the starlight burned into her body, the way the Court had listened when she willed a door open.

Could she go back? Untouched? Unchanged?

She showed him her teeth instead. "Better than rotting here with you."

He moved faster this time. Two strides and she hit the wall, his palms braced on either side of her head. His mouth hovered inches from hers, breath warm, eyes blazing molten.

"You hate me." His voice was low and even, velvet wrapped around iron. "Say it."

"I hate you." The words tore out fast, too thin, too honest.

"And yet." His gaze dropped to her mouth, then lifted back to her eyes. "You are still looking at me like I am the only wonder left in the world."

Her breath caught. Retorts scattered. The space between them crackled, hot and fragile.

His fingers shifted, brushing her jaw, tilting her face up like he had the right to handle it. His thumb traced the faint shimmer of starlight scars at her throat, moving slowly.

"Yield," he murmured.

Her laugh came out cracked and dangerous. "You first."

She shoved again. Not enough to break his cage of arms, he was solid and cool in all the ways she was shaking, but enough to jolt the blanket. It slipped from her shoulders, puddling at her feet.

Constellations bared, every scar lit, every tremor visible.

He froze.

Just for a heartbeat. Golden eyes dragged down and back up, rawer than she had ever seen them. Mischief stripped away. Hunger, sharp and unguarded, flared before he smothered it under a grin.

Her skin burned everywhere his gaze had touched. "Like what you see?" she asked. The words tasted like a dare.

"Obsessively." His voice had gone rough. Almost reverent.

Her knees went loose. She locked them out of spite. "You are insufferable."

"And you," he said, leaning in until his lips hovered a breath from hers, "are intoxicating."

The word seared through her. For one raw moment, she nearly leaned forward. Nearly closed that last inch. Nearly chose the fire.

Almost.

She jerked her head away. His mouth grazed her cheek instead of her lips. The near-miss lit her nerves up like someone had dragged a spark across them.

"Not yours," she rasped, breath hot against his ear.

He laughed, low and pleased, pulling back just enough for air to reach her lungs, not enough to feel safe. His grin cut across his face, sharp and radiant.

"Not yet," he said.

Then he stepped away.

Just like that. Heat gone. Hands loose at his sides. A coin flashed into existence between his fingers, spinning as if none of it had happened.

Maren's chest heaved. The blanket lay in a crumpled ring at her ankles. Her scars thrummed beneath her skin, bright with fury and something she refused to name.

She hated him.

She wanted him.

She hated that both feelings sat in the same breath.

The thief tossed the coin once, caught it, and let his eyes skim over her one last time.

"Sweet dreams, darling," he said.

He slipped into the shadows. The room swallowed him.

She was alone again, skin burning, throat raw, trembling in all the places the trials had not even reached. Fury seethed low in her gut. So did something inconveniently alive.

Maren bent, snatched the blanket back up, and wrapped herself in it like a shield. Her pulse thudded in her ears.

If this was the Court's idea of mercy, she thought, dragging in a long breath, then she would show it what a mortal could do with a little hatred and a lot of almost.

<h1 style="text-align:center">23</h1>

Hall of Fractured Tales

Maren woke with her skull splitting.

Not the soft ache of too little sleep, but a cannon-blast throb that made the room pitch every time she tried to breathe. Her mouth tasted of sour wine. Her body ached from too much dancing, too much drinking. Too much *him.*

She dragged a hand over her face and felt the constellation scars faintly warm under her skin. Her memory was patchwork: the revel, the crush of music, the way his hands had pulled her closer instead of letting her fall. Almost a kiss. Almost surrender. And then—

The humiliating slip in her own chamber, his eyes on her before she slammed the door between them.

Something on the table caught her eye. Folded fabric. Dark, elegant. And atop it, a note scrawled in a hand far too smug to belong to anyone but the coin-flipping bastard himself.

> As much as I'd enjoy watching you stumble around without clothes again, I don't like sharing what's mine.
>
> - S.

Heat climbed her throat. She wanted to tear it into confetti and feed it to the nearest fire. Instead, she crumpled it once in her fist, then flattened it back out with petty care, as if refusing to give him even the satisfaction of a clean crease.

The clothes were annoyingly perfect: soft black trousers that clung at her hips and loosened at the knee, a shirt the color of ink diluted with moonlight, a fitted vest traced with faint blue threads that echoed the constellations on her skin.

She yanked them on with more force than necessary, cursing every silken thread that fit too well. The fabric slid over her skin with an obnoxiously smooth texture; the vest hugged her ribs as if it had been tailored to her exact measurements.

She told herself she was only putting them on because she needed to move. The mirrorless basin gave her a dim reflection anyway, water holding the outline of her face in a wavering frame: curls tamed with cold handfuls, silver-blue eyes ringed in not-enough-sleep, star-maps faint at her throat. She looked like a girl who had wanted stories more than bread since Eldenwick. The one Penny kept teasing into admitting it.

Rosemary sprigs in a sunshine braid flashed through her mind so hard her chest pinched. Penny would have laughed herself sick at this outfit and insisted on adding a ridiculous bell.

"Stop it," Maren muttered at her reflection. The water did not listen. Her head throbbed in agreement.

"Talking to yourself is stage one," said a voice from somewhere above her. "Stage two is answering back."

Maren flinched so hard her vision sparked white. She spun toward the ceiling.

Tamsin sprawled across the lintel again, upside down, as if gravity were a rumor. One arm dangled over the edge, knife balancing idly across his knuckles. Copper hair fell toward the floor in a lazy curtain, tail flicking in slow satisfaction. His pupils were slit thin against the ambient starlight, bright and amused.

"How long," Maren said, very calmly, "have you been there?"

"Define 'there,'" he said, accent wrapping around the vowels like it was enjoying them. "Conscious? Since you started swearing at the note.

Physically present? Since before you woke. Mentally? Questionable at the best of times."

Her stomach dropped. "You were here while I was changing."

"Please," he scoffed, flipping neatly off the lintel to land light as a cat beside the bed. He gave her a flourishing bow that exaggerated the sweep of his long coat. "I am a scoundrel, not a monster. I closed my eyes like a gentleman."

"You cannot lie with your eyes open," Maren said. "New rule."

"You assume I need eyes to watch," he replied, then grinned when she scowled. "Relax, Starsleeves. Your secrets are safe. Your modesty, less so, but that is Mischief's problem, not mine."

He prowled a slow circle around her, hands tucked behind his back, knife still miraculously balanced along his knuckles. Up close, the little details announced themselves again: faint phantom stripes at his temples when the light shifted, the almost-whisker shadow along his cheekbones, the soft velvet edge to his ears when they twitched.

"You look tragic," he observed with something like admiration. "Glorious, but tragic. Hangover?"

"My skull is trying to claw out through my eyes," she said. "Take a guess."

Tamsin clicked his tongue. "Mortals and their fragile little vessels. You survive fires and emotional evisceration, yet three goblets of Spitfire lay you low."

"It was more than three," she muttered.

He brightened. "Ah. That explains the part where you almost kissed him."

Her stars flared hot under her skin. "I did not."

"You almost did," he sing-songed. He threw himself backward onto the foot of her bed, landing sprawled on his back, boots still on, tail hanging off the edge like a lazy question mark. "The Court is still gossiping. Wagers doubled, hearts broken. Very productive night, on the whole."

Maren pinched the bridge of her nose. "Did you slink in here just to narrate my poor decisions?"

"Partly," he admitted cheerfully. "Mostly I came because it pains me, personally, to see you suffer in such an uninteresting way." He rolled onto his side, propping his head on his hand. "Headache?"

"Yes," she ground out.

"Stomach?" he asked.

"Rebellious."

"Soul?"

"Do not start."

"Excellent," he said. "You are at prime recovery stage." He hopped back to his feet, coat flaring. "Come on. Breakfast."

Her laugh came out dry. "I have already done the 'noble steals the prisoner for breakfast' field trip with you. It ended in Rule Arbitrage."

"This is different. This is medicinal." He tapped his temple. "I have a cure. And since Mischief is very interested in you staying alive until your last trial, I feel honor-bound to preserve your brain cells."

"You are the last person in this realm I would trust with my brain," Maren said.

"Precisely why it will be fun." He flicked a glance toward the door, ears pricking as if listening to the Court itself shifting. "Besides, the halls are restless. They like you. They will sulk if you spend the whole day brooding in here."

"I am not brooding."

He pointed at the crumpled note on the table, the clenched set of her jaw, the way her fingers flexed tight at her sides. "You are absolutely brooding. It is almost impressive. Now, do you want to lie here marinating in last night's almost, or do you want coffee that can strip paint and a cure that will straighten your spine?"

"Coffee?" Her body perked before her pride could stop it. "There is coffee here?"

"There is something that thinks it is coffee, bites like judgment, and will convince your organs they still want to live," Tamsin said. "Close enough."

Her headache throbbed in time with her heartbeat. Trial three waited somewhere on the horizon, a looming, unnamed weight. The thief's note still sat on the table like a claim she refused to acknowledge. Penny's absence hummed quietly and constantly under her ribs. None of that was going anywhere.

Getting out of this room, even for a few hours, suddenly felt like survival.

"Fine," she said. "Breakfast. Then I come back. I need to think."

"You can think while chewing," Tamsin said. "Many geniuses do. Up you come, Starsleeves."

"Stop calling me that."

"Never," he said, delighted. "It suits you. Come. Let us go sin against Rule Thirty Something."

He tipped his knife into the air; it vanished without a sound. Without waiting for her answer, he sprang back up to the lintel in one effortless leap and pressed his palm to the ceiling. Stone blurred at his touch, seams loosening into a pale, waiting glow.

He looked back down at her, smile wide and wicked. "Last time you needed encouragement," he said. "Think you can manage the jump on a hangover?"

Maren squared her shoulders. Her skull throbbed. Her scars buzzed faintly. "If I miss—"

He beamed. "Worth it."

She bent her knees, pushed off the bed, and leapt for the light.

The ceiling swallowed them, then spat them out into a passage Maren had never seen. Which meant the Court had changed again. Floors here gleamed like poured mercury, their surface rippling faintly under each step. Lanterns drifted overhead, drifting in slow orbits like bored suns, casting pale gold across the hallway.

Her head throbbed. Her stomach lurched. She was halfway convinced the corridor was moving on purpose.

Tamsin landed lightly beside her and stretched like an overgrown cat, spine arcing, tail flicking in elegant annoyance. "Atmospheric today," he announced to no one. "Or still drunk. Hard to say."

"It's the Court," Maren muttered. "Everything here is."

"That is a mortifyingly poetic thing to say first thing in the morning," he replied. "You need food."

He guided her toward an archway that unfolded ahead of them. Warm scents drifted through: spice, fruit, smoke, and something sweet as something candied. Maren's stomach growled, its betrayal loud enough to echo.

She stepped inside.

And froze.

The room was a street, a marketplace, and a tavern stitched into one. Not outdoors, but cavernous, like several buildings from several realities had been perkily jammed together by someone with no respect for architecture.

Lanterns floated low over rows of stalls, colors shifting every few breaths. The air thrummed with chatter that sounded like laughter braided with secrets.

Booths lined both sides of the walkway. Each one sold something stranger than the last. A scaled merchant shaped like an eel, sharpened quill pens carved from forgotten plot lines. A stout woman with brass skin and curls of steam ladled out steaming bowls labeled endings, each swirl tinted a different shade. Bottles on another table glowed with captured whispers that twitched against their glass.

It hummed with chaotic energy. The kind that did not feel wicked until it was too late.

"Welcome," Tamsin said proudly, sweeping his arm wide, "to the Hall of Fractured Tales. Breakfast is whatever it feels like today."

Her eyes caught sight of a cluster of slender, masked creatures exchanging shimmering objects shaped like punctuation marks. They clinked like metal, but when one dropped, it split into sound instead of pieces.

She stared. "What even is this?"

"A market for narrative," Tamsin said, prowling ahead. "Bits of story. Slivers of memory. Whole plot arcs if you have something truly valuable to barter." His tail swished lazily. "Mortals tend to overpay."

"Of course they do," she said under her breath. "No one tells us the rules."

"That is because the rules contradict themselves," Tamsin chirped. "Which is the beauty of it. Come along. You need the cure before your brain leaks out your ears."

He wove through the crowd effortlessly. Maren followed slower, eyes wide despite her best efforts to pretend she was unimpressed. Every stall had something new blinking, whispering, twitching. A small glass sphere rolled toward her boot, humming faintly like it knew her. She crouched and picked it up.

Inside, the sphere held a tune. A simple melody. Gentle. Familiar.

A childhood lullaby.

Her chest stilled. She didn't know how, but it had the cadence of her mother humming on summer nights, when the bread had finished rising and the windows glowed warm. She cupped it in both hands before she realized someone behind the stall was smiling at her.

The merchant's grin was wide, welcoming in the way knives sometimes were. "Beautiful memory," they said. "I can offer a trade."

"What kind?" Maren asked slowly.

"A song," they said. "Yours for another. You give one memory, you gain a new one. Equivalent exchange."

Maren's pulse thinned. The little sphere vibrated in her hands like it wanted to leave her.

She almost said yes.

Tamsin's hand appeared, plucking the sphere free with a hissed scold. "No. Absolutely not. Bad mortal. Bad morning decisions."

"I wasn't going to trade," she snapped.

"You absolutely were." He shoved the sphere back onto the merchant's table and leaned in close, narrowing his catlike eyes. "She is hungover," he told the stall owner. "If you want fair trades, come back when her skull is not full of knives."

The merchant laughed, unfazed. "The Court is always hungry."

"Yes," Tamsin said, "and she is off the menu." He placed a casual, possessive hand on Maren's shoulder and steered her away. "Honestly. You leave mortals unattended for one moment and they start bartering away their childhoods."

Her head spun harder than before. "It was a song."

"It was your song," he corrected. "And you do not give pieces of yourself away before breakfast. That is a rule."

"You have so many rules for someone who claims to hate them."

"Consistency is for bureaucrats and Dread creatures," Tamsin muttered. "Now. Breakfast."

He guided her into a side alcove, where a low counter glowed warmly, its surface carved with shifting runes that rearranged every few breaths. A plump creature shaped like a grandmotherly cloud drifted behind the counter, humming a tune to the kettle floating beside her.

"This," Tamsin announced, "is what you woke up for."

The cloud-woman ladled thick, dark liquid into a cup. Steam curled upward in thin, spiced tendrils.

"What is it?" Maren asked.

"Ether," Tamsin replied. "Drink it slowly or it will narrate your regrets."

Maren lifted the cup cautiously. The scent curled up into her sinuses: bitter, sharp, a hint of cinnamon, and something metallic. She took one sip.

It burned.

Like inspiration lit on fire, it traveled from her tongue to the back of her skull, then down her throat, leaving warmth in its wake. Her headache eased. Her vision sharpened. Her scars tingled beneath her shirt.

Her next breath came easier.

"Good?" Tamsin asked, trying to look casual and failing.

"It tastes like drinking a library at war," she said.

He clapped once, delighted. "You missed your calling. You should review poisons."

She took another sip. The heat unfurled slow, steady, addictive. Her pulse steadied from its frantic thrum. For the first time since waking, or even the night before, she felt balanced. Her feet rooted to the floor in something like certainty.

Her brain, unfortunately, was now awake enough to think about yesterday. About the almost-kiss. About the note. About the third trial. Her stomach twisted.

Tamsin noticed the way her thumb tightened on the cup. His tail swished against the counter in quiet warning. "Do not drift," he said. "You have barely swallowed the antidote. You start thinking about him now and you will undo all the medicinal work."

"I was not thinking about him," she lied.

"Of course not," Tamsin said. "That is why your ears turned red."

"They did not."

"They absolutely did."

Her eyes narrowed. "Why do you care?"

"Because," he replied with a smug grin. Tamsin leaned back against the counter, watching her with lazy contentment. "Now finish that, and I will show you the only part of the market worth the headache you woke with."

"What part?"

"The part," he said solemnly, "where we decide whether you pass for a local long enough to stir trouble. Breakfast is phase one. Phase two is social mischief."

Her brow arched. "And phase three?"

"Phase three is running." Tamsin pushed away from the counter and tilted his head toward the main street. "You will be terrible at it. Please let me enjoy being right."

She finished the last swallow. It seared down her throat in one clean line. The world steadied.

Tamsin stepped back into the current of the market like the entire Hall existed for his amusement. His tail cut lazy S-shapes through the lantern light, and the moment Maren caught up to him, he pivoted with that too-bright grin that meant trouble had entered.

"Now that you have Ether in your bloodstream," he said, walking backward so he could face her, "we can proceed to phase two."

"And what would that be?" she asked, adjusting the vest the thief had insisted she wear. The silk shirt brushed her collarbones. Her scars beneath hummed faintly under the fabric.

Tamsin's gaze dipped to the shirt, his nostrils flaring with theatrical reverence. "Civilizing you. Look at you. A respectable criminal at last."

She snorted, trying to shove past him. "Move, Kitty."

He froze.

The crowd didn't. A dozen shifting forms wove around them: scaled, feathered, half-shadow, full-chaos. But Tamsin's body was still, ears flattening for one shocked second before snapping forward again.

"Kitty?" he repeated softly, deadpan horror dripping from every syllable.

Maren arched an eyebrow. "Problem?"

Tamsin blinked once. Then twice. Then his grin broke wide, wicked, delighted. "Stars, you are dangerous. Keep it. But only in private. If anyone else calls me that, I will steal their skeleton."

She laughed. It still hurt her head, but in a good way. That tiny spark of warmth loosened something under her ribs.

24

Predatory

They walked deeper into the hall.

The stalls grew stranger. One vendor sold folded shadows shaped like cloaks. Another hawked jars filled with flickering punctuation marks. A ring of whisper-thieves lounged behind velvet ropes, stealing fragments of gossip directly from passersby's breath.

Maren felt the Hall tug at her like it recognized easy prey. It pulled at her memories. Her ache. Her hunger for wonder she pretended she didn't have.

She tucked her hands behind her back, narrowing her eyes. "Everything here wants something."

"Yes," Tamsin said. "Which is why we distract ourselves with games before something distracts us with consequences."

He stopped suddenly. Too suddenly. His pupils thinned. Then, that mischief-switch flipped. His smile sharpened. "Let us play a game."

Maren groaned. "No."

"Yes," he said, hooking his arm through hers before she could dodge. "You are spiraling again."

"I am not."

"You absolutely are."

"Tamsin."

He didn't hear her. Or pretended not to. He twirled her once, pivoting

227

them into the flow of foot traffic with the grace of someone who'd spent centuries making chaos look choreographed.

"I bet," he said, leaning into her space like a cat choosing a lap, "that you cannot get the next person who recognizes you to give you a kiss."

Maren tripped. His arm snapped out, catching her waist. He looked far too pleased about it.

"Kiss?" she hissed, wrenching upright. "Are you insane?"

"Yes," he said brightly. "Annoyingly so. But also bored. And you need a distraction."

"No," she repeated, though the chaos-glow in the air made it feel less like refusal and more like foreplay with fate. "Absolutely not."

He tapped his chin like he was giving a lecture. "Maren, the goal is not seduction. The goal is humiliation. Specifically, the humiliation of someone who thinks himself above mortals." His eyes flicked, barely, to a cluster of nobles lounging ahead. "Pick well."

"Pick—? Tam, what is wrong with you?"

He grinned, full teeth. "Everything. Now hush. Incoming."

It happened too fast.

One of the nobles glanced up. A tall male with the smooth, horned elegance of a gazelle and the too-perfect cheekbones of someone sculpted on purpose. His eyes swept the crowd lazily until they found her.

Recognition struck like a spark catching alcohol. His brows lifted.

"Oh no," Maren breathed.

"Oh yes," Tamsin whispered, delighted.

The noble straightened, stepping through the crowd with fluid, predatory grace. His gaze flicked from Maren's face to her scars peeking faintly at her collar. Hunger kindled.

This is what Tamsin wanted. She realized that too late.

"Lady mortal," the noble purred. "Allow me the honor of—"

Maren grabbed him by the lapels and kissed him.

Gasps cracked across the hall like lightning.

The noble froze, startled, then melted under her mouth with a low, pleased hum. His hands rose, hesitant, almost reverent.

And that was the moment Tamsin moved.

He snatched Maren's wrist, yanked her away with a growled curse far sharper than his usual theatrics, and practically dragged her into the crush of bodies. His tail lashed once behind him, agitation flashing bright as neon.

"Tamsin, what are you—"

"You win," he snapped, voice pitched low with something that wasn't lighthearted at all. "Congratulations. Never do that again."

She stumbled after him, confused. "It was your idea."

"Terrible idea," he muttered, shoving through a curtain of bead-strands into a side passage. His jaw was tight. His grip firm. Too firm. "I clearly forgot mortals are feral when properly motivated."

"Are you—" she squinted at him "—jealous?"

He froze mid-step.

The tail gave him away. It fluffed. Outward.

"I," he said with the stiffness of someone denying oxygen, "am not jealous. I am protective. There is a difference."

She blinked hard to keep from laughing. "Protective of who? Me? Or your brilliant game backfiring?"

"Both," he snapped.

The admission shoved something warm and reluctant under her ribs.

He guided her deeper into the side passage, glancing over his shoulder to make sure the gazelle noble hadn't followed. When he seemed satisfied, he leaned close and flicked her forehead with one clawed finger.

"You are a nightmare," he told her.

"You dared me."

"Yes, and you were supposed to fail. Not... that."

Her grin sharpened. "Kitty is jealous."

His ears flattened again. "I will put you in a box."

She burst out laughing then, a bright, uncontrolled laugh. It hurt her ribs, but gods, it felt good.

Tamsin slowed, watching her with that fond, exasperated expression usually reserved for chaotic siblings and poor decision-makers. His eyes softened.

"Breakfast cured you," he said.

"Barely."

"Then you need another dose of mischief before you go thinking about your trials or your… thief."

Her throat tightened.

He noticed.

He changed the subject with zero grace. "Come. There is a booth I want to show you. It sells narrative solvents. You pour them over stories and they dissolve the boring parts."

Maren snorted. "Everything here is a scam."

"And yet," he said, gesturing her forward, "you keep following me."

She rolled her eyes, but she followed.

The passage widened again, emptying into a quieter wing of the market-place. The lanterns dimmed. The noise softened. Shadows lengthened like curtains waiting to be drawn.

Tamsin slowed.

Maren felt it too.

A shift in the air. A presence behind them.

She turned.

And there he was.

The Mischief Spirit leaned in the narrow doorway of an old library, one shoulder propped against the frame, coin nowhere in sight. His gaze slid over Maren, slowly, inexcusably, until her blood heated under her skin.

His smile was a cut of molten gold.

"Out for breakfast, darling?"

Tamsin muttered something in a language that sounded like a hiss and a curse, kissing.

Maren swallowed hard.

The air tightened.

And she realized with a sinking pulse: *They'd just been caught.*

The hallway outside the library felt too narrow for three people, let alone for *predators*. The Court's magic thickened the air until it felt almost viscous, reacting to the tension before any of them spoke. Light from floating lanterns stuttered, guttering low as if bracing for impact.

Tamsin moved first.

A single step. A subtle shift of his shoulders. His tail flicked behind him in a slow, calculated arc, telegraphing annoyance he would never admit out loud. His stance angled protectively toward Maren, not in front of her, but just close enough to suggest he was prepared to become a problem.

The bastard smiled at that. A bare flash of teeth, lazy and amused, though his eyes gleamed far too bright for someone pretending boredom. The air around him bent, shadows pooling near his boots like they'd been waiting.

"I was starting to wonder whether you'd gotten lost," he said, voice quiet enough to be dangerous.

The words were shaped like a tease. The tone wasn't.

Maren's pulse kicked in her throat.

Tamsin leaned one shoulder against the opposite wall, posture casual in the way only a liar could manage. "Good morning to you, too," he said lightly. "We were simply taking a walk. Mortals are encouraged to walk. It's practically a civic duty."

"You," the thief said, gaze slanting to Tamsin with a slow, assessing drag, "encourage her in nothing but bad habits."

Tamsin grinned, showing a tiny flash of fang. "You're welcome."

The hallway pulsed with the Court's interest, stone beneath their feet flickering with a faint glow like the realm itself had leaned closer to watch.

Maren swallowed, trying to ground herself. Every breath reminded her of last night, of almost-kissing a god and regretting it in a thousand different ways.

His gaze slid back to her.

Slow. Intentional.

A sweep that touched her skin without making contact. It wasn't lust, but a cousin of it. Possession edged with surprise, like he was still trying to understand why the sight of her beside another man twisted something inside him.

He'd been born with mischief molded into the bones. But the emotion simmering under his skin didn't seem to be mischief at all.

"How was breakfast?" he asked her, ignoring Tamsin completely.

Maren stiffened. The faintest heat climbed her throat. "Fine."

"Fine," Tamsin echoed, rolling the word like he wanted to bite it. "She had Ether, you know. The good batch."

His brows lifted. "Did she?"

Tamsin's grin widened, wicked as a dare. "She handles it better than you do."

A low breeze stirred the hem of Maren's shirt, brushing cool fingers up her spine. The hallway dimmed further, lanterns narrowing to slits of light.

The bastard stepped forward, closing the distance by half. He didn't touch her, but the space between them tightened anyway, raising the fine hairs on her arms.

"Maren," he said softly. Her name in his mouth was a caress and a threat. "You disappear, wander into the deeper halls without permission…" His eyes cut to Tamsin. "And then I find you kissing strangers in the marketplace?"

Tamsin let out a strangled sound. "One stranger. One. And it was a dare."

His gaze didn't budge from her face. "Did you enjoy it?"

The question landed like a blow. Too quiet. Too intimate. Too loaded.

Maren's breath hitched. "It was a bet," she said, heat crawling up her neck. "You don't get to be jealous."

Silence slid sharply through the hall.

Tamsin blinked. He froze almost imperceptibly, as if the word had struck him somewhere he didn't understand.

Then, very softly:

"I don't feel jealousy."

Maren snorted before she could stop herself. "You do today."

Something in his posture fractured for a heartbeat: shoulders drawing tight, the faintest crack in his perfect stillness. The shadows around him recoiled, then leaned hungry in again, uncertain which impulse to obey.

Tamsin, sensing advantage like only a cat could, slipped in with a bright, poisonous smile. "She has that effect on people. Terrible habit, really."

His eyes sharpened, calculating. Dangerous. "And you," he said, voice silky, "have grown far too comfortable."

Tamsin's tail puffed again. "Maybe you've grown too possessive."

The floor shifted underfoot, the stones brightening in a slow ripple that chased down the hallway like a warning. The Court didn't like fights among its nobles…it loved them.

Maren stepped back instinctively. Two sets of eyes snapped to her at once: molten gold and luminescent green.

The weight of their attention nearly knocked the air from her lungs.

She swallowed hard, trying to collect herself. Trying to anchor her pulse. Trying to ignore how different they were up close:

Tamsin, all sharp humor and restless limbs, keen and observant like he was cataloging exits.

The thief, stillness wrapped in skin, a blade under velvet, watching her like she was a story he intended to read cover to cover.

"This is ridiculous," she said finally, trying to break the current snapping between them. "I was just out for breakfast."

The thief's voice dropped. "Without me."

Tamsin scoffed. "Apologies, your majesty, I didn't realize her meals required your presence."

A slow, dangerous smile unfurled across the thief's mouth. "Everything she does is mine to oversee until her trials are complete."

Maren's stomach twisted. "I'm not yours," she said, too sharply. "Stop saying that."

His gaze dipped to her throat, where her pulse betrayed her, and rose again with quiet triumph. "Your body disagrees."

Tamsin hissed softly, stepping in front of her with a flick of his tail. Protective. Bristling. Ready to claw. "Back off," he said with a low growl that didn't belong to someone who joked for a living.

His golden eyes flicked to him, unimpressed. "Or what?"

The air shivered as if bracing for impact.

Maren stepped between them before either could do something catastrophically stupid. Her hand pressed lightly to Tamsin's chest, her gaze locked on the bastard.

"What do you want?" she demanded.

The answer came without hesitation.

"You," he said. "Tonight."

Her pulse stopped.

Tamsin cursed softly, ears going flat.

He stepped closer, stopping only when the heat of him brushed her skin. "Trial Three begins at dusk," he murmured. "You will be escorted. I suggest you arrive sober."

Maren's breath shook. "And if I don't?"

His smile was slow and lethal. "Then I'll fetch you myself."

The lanterns guttered out entirely for one long, breathless instant.

Then he simply wasn't there.

A faint whiff of cedar and citrus lingered like a handprint on her neck.

Tamsin stared after him, his tail flicked once, twice, betraying a tension he immediately smothered with a grin.

"Well," he said brightly, dusting imaginary lint off his sleeve, "that was exciting."

Maren let out a strangled sound that might have been a laugh or a dying breath. "Exciting is one word."

"Oh, please," Tamsin purred, looping an arm through hers as if the last sixty seconds hadn't been a magical bar brawl without punches. "I have been *begging* for someone to provide quality drama in this Court. And you, my dear, are a gift."

"I'm a prisoner."

"A dramatic one," he corrected. "Much better."

She snorted, the sound thin. Inside, her stomach was sinking like a stone dropped down a well.

Tonight.

Trial Three.

25

Rise and Despair

Maren lay on her back, staring at the ceiling as if it might decide her fate before the Arbiter did.

The chamber was dim, lit only by the bruise-purple dusk bleeding through the high lattice windows. Shadows stretched long across the floorboards, slow-moving, as if the Court itself was pacing in thought. She hadn't slept. Not really. Every time she shut her eyes, the memories slashed through her:

The library.

Tamsin's hissed warning.

Mischief stepped out of the shadow like he had been carved from it.

Fox and cat circling each other with predator smiles.

And then the line that still burned her ribs from the inside out:

Tell me, baker, do you truly think you can step back into that crumbling shop of yours after this?

Her chest tightened. The scent of flour rose sharply in her memory, but the doorway of the bakery blurred when she reached for it. Even the ghosts of home were slipping out of reach.

She dragged a hand across her face, feeling the faint warmth of the constellation scars beneath her skin. Her body hummed with leftover adrenaline from the showdown. Her mind hummed with something worse.

The Court wanted pieces of her. *He* wanted pieces.

She wasn't sure how many she had left to give.

The door slammed open.

"Rise and despair, lady mortal!" Kipwick declared, trotting in like a parade marshal with a death wish and balancing a single glass on a tray. His voice cracked with glee and carried far too loudly for the quiet of the room.

Maren groaned and flopped an arm across her eyes. "Lower your voice or I'll staple your tail to the floor."

"Marvelous," Kipwick said, setting a tray down with a flourish that made the lemon wedge bounce. "She threatens violence. She must be in a good mood."

He hopped onto the foot of her bed with an odd elegance, "You missed lunch. And tea. And two recreational executions. Fortunately, I am here to assist in your rehabilitation."

"My what?"

He pushed the cup toward her with both paws. "Hydration. Before you face the Arbiter."

That dragged her upright faster than any threat could. "Trial Three is now?"

"Not now," Kipwick said, whiskers twitching. "Soon. Dusk trials are especially popular. The lighting is dramatic. Shadows flatter the doomed."

A pulse of cold rushed down her spine. Out the window, the sky was already slanting darker.

She swallowed hard. "Wonderful."

Kipwick's ears flicked. Worried. Barely. Almost invisible, but still there. "The Arbiter bids you attend. There is an audience gathering."

"Of course there is," she muttered.

"Bring the water," he advised. "If you faint during my escort, I will be furious."

Maren drank only because her mouth felt like sand. The taste of cool lemon bit her tongue, sharp enough to steady her.

Kipwick watched her over the rim of the tray. "Decent choice on the clothing. Flexible. Breathable. Excellent for running, screaming, or performing acts of emotional self-destruction."

"I'm not running."

"You are very attached to that lie," Kipwick chirped, hopping down. "Come along. We have a labyrinth to attend."

Maren swung her feet to the floor, wincing only a little. Her muscles ached from the revel the night before, from the dancing, from his hands on her waist, on her spine—

She cut that memory off with a scowl.

Kipwick turned, offering an arm. "He's in a mood."

"The bastard is always in a mood."

"This one is… particular." Kipwick's ears tipped back, not fear so much as respect for a storm he'd rather admire from indoors. "If I were writing an aside, I'd call it sharpened. The Coral Crown lady tried to bait him at dawn and almost lost a hand."

A small, vile satisfaction warmed her. "Tragic."

"Quite." He offered his arm again, a ridiculous, courtly gesture from a fox in a waistcoat, and she took it.

The door widened obligingly. The corridor beyond had rearranged since her wanderings this morning: lanterns dimmed into cold points of light, walls narrowing, the air thickening with the iron-sweet taste of expectation. The Court liked to guide mortals by mood alone.

Kipwick's claws clicked lightly beside her. "You'll want to keep your wits in there. The Court adores a maze. Loves watching mortals chase their own tails until they forget which way is forward."

"Comforting," she muttered.

"Names helped you last time," he said, too casually. "But memory—ah, memory's slipperier. Guard what you are, what you want. The walls will whisper otherwise."

She glanced at him, uneasy. "That's the cryptic version?"

"The less cryptic version is you'll lose yourself if you're not careful," he chirped, tail flicking. "But where's the poetry in that?"

Her jaw clenched. The thief's voice scraped her memory again: *Do you truly think you can step back into that crumbling shop of yours after this?*

Could she?

Did she even want to?

As they walked, the building performed for her. Arches unspooled in slow ribbons of stone that folded back into themselves. A chandelier shed its crystals in a glittering rain, each shard falling weightless before snapping back into place with a soft click. Laughter skittered along the ceiling beams like a mischievous current. Whispers orbited her like moths drawn to a flame, small and hungry.

The corridor stretched thinner, quieter, the air cooling with every step. Even the lanterns seemed to dim themselves, as if the Court knew silence suited what was coming.

Ahead, the Court of Chaos had remade itself into a theater.

Balconies shouldered the walls like watching eyes, stacked in crooked tiers, their railings twisted in suggestive arcs. Shadow pooled across the audience. Nobles leaned forward in expectant clusters, their jewels flashing little sparks of hunger. The Court didn't breathe so much as wait.

At the center stood the Arbiter.

To its left lounged the thief.

He leaned one hip against the railing, posture loose and predatory, a study in lazy violence. His coin spun between his fingers without sound, each arc smooth, each catch too clean to be anything but deliberate.

He didn't look at the Court; he was looking directly at her.

Coral Head draped against him like a decorative warning sign, her sea-glass hair arranged in an elaborate crown of coral branches that glimmered pink like bleached bone. Her hand clung to his sleeve with the entitlement of someone who believed proximity equaled power. A brittle smile clung to her lips, hungry and anxious.

On the far balcony, higher than most, perched with a kind of insolent grace, Tamsin sprawled over the railing like a cat sunning itself. His tail flicked lazily. When he saw Maren, he flashed a slow grin and tapped the edge of his wine goblet against his chin, a little salute meant just for her.

The Arbiter lifted a hand.

The Court's murmurs hushed like someone had pressed a blade against every throat. Its voice rang out, clipped and merciless, each word hammer-struck:

"The path bends.
The walls remember.
Guard your truth, or it dissolves.
Step false, and the maze will keep you.
Find the exit, and you are free."

Free.

Maren's heart tripped. *Guard your truth.* As if that were simple. As if she hadn't already lost half of what she'd been: Penny, her body unmarred, her father's voice, Penny's song, her bakery.

What truth was left to guard?

The floor answered before she could.

Tiles at the Arbiter's feet shuddered, cracked, then peeled back one by one. Not falling into a void, no, *worse.* Each slab dissolved into corridors that unfurled outward, impossible angles spinning like spokes, stairs folding into each other, doorways opening midair. The space kept birthing itself until there was no floor at all, only the promise of paths that writhed and reknit, stretching farther than her eyes could follow.

The balcony shuddered and became a wall. The Court spectators above looked down with eager, glittering hunger. She glanced back for the corridor she'd come through: gone. Just more passages, endless and shifting.

The thief flicked his coin one last time, gold catching the light, and drawled just loud enough for her to hear: "Try not to lose yourself, baker. The Court already has plans for your pieces."

Her pulse spiked. Coral Head stiffened. Tamsin rolled his eyes so dramatically that it should have shattered the balcony.

The tiles dissolved under her heel, and the labyrinth swallowed her whole.

* * *

239

White.

Not the soft, forgiving white of flour or clouds.

This was hard white, merciless white. Marble stretched in every direction, polished so sharp the light had teeth. Walls, floor, ceiling. Just glare; endless glare.

Maren lifted a hand, half expecting her reflection to snap back at her from the stone. Nothing. Only the faint glow of her constellation scars bleeding through her skin, star maps stamped across her arms and throat. Against all that pale, she looked more carved than human.

Her boots clicked. The sound ricocheted and multiplied until it seemed like someone else was walking beside her, behind her, around her.

She froze. The echoes froze, too.

A trap of her own making.

The air was too clean. No smoke, no rot, no perfume of chaos like the Court loved. This was sterile, scraped down to nothing. The kind of place where memory couldn't even stick.

The Arbiter's words rattled her ribs: *The path bends. The walls remember. Guard your truth, or it dissolves.*

She wanted to laugh. In this endless white, even the bakery felt like a fable she'd stolen from someone else's life.

She walked anyway.

The marble stretched ahead in perfect symmetry, corridors bleeding into each other at impossible angles, each turn indistinguishable from the last. Her steps rang out as if the labyrinth was cataloging each one, tucking them away into its memory.

Her scars pulsed again. The faint light spilled out, caught in the marble. For an instant, she thought the stars might guide her. Then the walls shifted, and her light bent, refracted until the map didn't look like hers anymore.

A low hum trembled under her feet. Not Penny's hum, she would never hear that again, but something more profound, like stone remembering every mortal who had walked here before her. Everyone who had stayed.

Maren clenched her fists. "Not me," she whispered. Her voice cracked too sharply in the white. The labyrinth swallowed the sound like a pill.

She tried another corridor. The marble gleamed ahead, unbroken, endless. She turned. Another passage. The same. She pivoted again, faster. The same. White upon white upon white. Each turn a mirror of the last until her breath grew shallow.

The Court wanted her to lose herself here. She could feel it. The labyrinth didn't need claws or fire. It only required patience.

Her pulse kicked harder. She started forward, faster now, chasing the sound of her own footsteps, as if she could outrun the sameness. But the walls leaned closer, perfect, immaculate, unyielding.

Then a shape bled into view ahead. A door, faint, impossible against the seamless marble.

Relief flared sharply in her chest. Too sharp.

She slowed. The door stood waiting. Ordinary wood, iron handle. Wrong in all this white.

Her hand lifted anyway.

The marble whispered against her palm, a thousand unseen voices: *Guard your truth, or it dissolves.*

26

Labyrinth

The door opened onto light.

Not the hard, merciless white of the marble hall, but something warm and golden. Morning light spilled through a wide kitchen window, veining across a scarred oak table where bowls of dough sat rising under linen cloths. Cinnamon and vanilla curled through the air in soft ribbons, so rich her knees nearly buckled.

Her mother stood at the hearth.

Apron dusted in flour. Hair pinned back, already loosening into familiar wisps. Her father leaned against the counter with one ankle crossed over the other, book open in his hand, mug steaming at his elbow. His mouth carried that quiet half-smile he always wore when he was pretending not to watch her.

Alive.

Maren's breath fractured. Her feet moved before the rest of her understood, and the marble corridor sealed behind her with a hush. The world shrank to this room, this moment, this life, the Court dangled like a miracle she didn't deserve.

Her mother glanced up. And smiled. A simple, everyday smile, the kind that once told Maren she was home.

Her father spoke. She saw his lips move. She saw the warmth in his eyes. She even caught the rise and fall of his chest.

But the sound—

The sound was *wrong*.

Muffled. As though she were underwater, hearing him through currents. Every syllable blurred and bent.

Her heart clawed at her ribs.

She wanted to scream for it to be clear, to give her just one word in the voice she had lost. But she had nothing to compare it to now. The labyrinth dangled it in front of her like bait, and she had no way to know if it was real.

"Maren!" her mother called her name. That, at least, was sharp, precise. The way it had always landed.

Her throat locked. Her body swayed toward the table on instinct alone, palms pressing into the worn oak. The grain ran beneath her fingers exactly as it should. The warmth of the hearth brushed her cheek. So real she could fall into it.

A bell jingled at the shopfront.

Penny walked in.

Not *her* Penny. No sunlight and rosemary. A plain-dressed girl with rosy cheeks and a shy smile at the bookbinder trailing behind her, arms full of volumes. They looked absurdly ordinary together.

Comfortable.

Ordinary.

This was the life she *should* have had: parents alive, apprenticeship was hers to grow or ignore, Penny someone else's story entirely.

No trials.

No Arbiter.

No coin-flipping bastard whose presence twisted her thoughts into knots she didn't recognize.

Just a mortal life.

Her fingers curled hard into the table. She could stay. She could slip into this life like a coat she'd forgotten she used to own. Become the girl who never begged for stories. Who never wished for more.

But her skull already throbbed with splitting pressure. Her father's voice warped again, his words bending into a stranger's pitch, and her scars pulsed hot under her skin, stars flickering like they were trying to warn her.

Her own thoughts turned vicious:

You begged for wonder.

You wanted more. Now you want to climb back into a cage of bread and routine?

Was Penny worth losing your father's voice? Worth losing everything?

Which truth will you keep, Maren? Which lie feels safer?

Her mother's hand brushed hers across the table, soft and flour-dusted. For a moment, Maren's resolve cracked wide. This was what she'd wanted: to keep them. To not lose everything.

But the warmth dissolved even as Maren clung to it.

The table under her palms warped, oak grain curdling into pale marble veins before knitting itself back into wood again. The window light flickered, gold to white to gold, like a candle about to gutter.

Her father's lips still moved, still shaping words she couldn't hear, only now the muffled sound underneath wasn't his at all. It was a stranger's voice, low and certain, layered atop the silence where her father used to be. A voice with no name, just authority:

You don't even know what he sounded like.

Maren's chest burned.

She tried to hold on, to memorize her mother's smile, but already the room was shifting. The walls breathed. The shelves emptied, then filled, then emptied again, each time with different jars, different handwriting, different years of her life stacked out of order.

Penny's laugh cut sharply across the shopfront.

Except it wasn't the plain-dressed Penny anymore.

Aprons bright with red, hair catching herbs like sunlight snagged in leaves, eyes lit with the same warmth that had anchored Maren through every sleepless dawn.

Her Penny.

The sight cracked something in Maren's chest she didn't know she had left. She looked more alive than Maren had ever managed. Radiant even.

And Maren wasn't in it.

She stood rooted to the floor, breath trapped.

The scene moved without her. Penny laughing at the bookbinder as he pressed flour across her nose. Penny smoothing dough into neat circles while children's hands tugged at her skirt. Miniature versions of Penny.

Penny turned toward the sunlight spilling through the bakery's windows, smile broad enough to warm the whole street.

Eldenwick glowed. The bakery thrummed with life. The tune Maren couldn't remember was absent, but the laugh. Gods, the laugh rang bright enough to fill the rafters.

Maren's scars burned hot against her skin. She staggered back, but the room followed her, expanding and multiplying. One bakery became two, became three, each one alive with Penny's laughter, Penny's children, Penny's life unburdened by chaos.

Her thoughts battered her from the inside:

You fought fire. You bled truth. For what?

Look at her. She never needed you. She thrives without you.

If you don't come back from the Court, this is the world that will grow.

Wasn't that what you wanted? For her to be safe? Happy?

The air thickened with the smell of cinnamon and rosemary, so strong it choked her. She pressed her hand to the wall. Marble, not oak. When she blinked, the shelves flickered between bread loaves and blank white stone.

Penny bent to kiss her child's cheek. When she looked up again, her eyes were…. golden.

Not warm gold. Not mortal gold.

Golden.

The laugh that spilled from her mouth twisted in pitch, sharpened too suddenly, a sound that belonged in the Court's throat, not Penny's.

Maren slammed her palms to her ears. "Stop. Stop!"

The cry tore her throat raw.

The bakery shattered like glass.

Light fractured, spilling into shards of sea-glass green and stormwater blue. The scent of cinnamon dissolved into cold brine. Shelves warped into masts. The oven crackled into a storm wind.

Her knees buckled. When she looked down, a book lay open across the floor, its pages bleeding ink. Words spilled like waves across the boards, soaking into her skin until they weren't words at all but… salt?

Salt on her lips.

Salt stinging her eyes.

She was no longer in the bakery. She was on a ship.

Wind slammed into her. Rigging snapped overhead. The sea reared up black and endless, swallowing stars. She stood on the deck in boots that weren't hers, sword belted at her hip, the taste of adventure cut sharp in her mouth.

She'd written this life once, half-dreaming at the bakery table when Penny teased her into telling stories. And now she was living it: the smell of brine, the pull of the tide, the creak of wood beneath her boots.

Her scars gleamed brighter, galaxies spilling across her arms like a map to somewhere else. The labyrinth had taken her parents, twisted Penny, but here, it offered her what she had begged for since she was a child.

Her heart kicked against her ribs.

This is yours. You wanted this. You don't need bread. You don't need Penny. You don't need anyone. You can live in a story if you just let go of everything else.

Sails snapped above. Men and women she had never met bellowed her name, voices raw with salt and wind. They shouted orders she somehow understood, as if the story had been waiting for her tongue.

She gave them back in a voice steady as command.

The storm tugged at her curls, tangling them wildly. The salt in her mouth wasn't fear, but a foreign sense of freedom. For one trembling heartbeat, she was captain of everything she had ever dreamed.

Ink bled down her hands, dark against the star-glow. She glanced at her palms and saw words etched there. They were stories she had promised she would write one day, if only the ovens would stop demanding.

If only the world would let her.

Now the words were alive. They writhed across her skin, spilled off her fingers, became lightning that forked through the storm.

Her lungs ached with exhilaration.

This was *hers*.

The labyrinth had given her *this*.

For a breath, she swore she saw her own reflection in the stormwater pooling across the deck, but it wasn't *Captain* Maren Greenbriar staring back:

It was the baker, soot-streaked, burns crawling her arms, mouth open in a silent scream.

She stumbled back, and her boot slipped.

The deck pitched hard.

The book slid across the planks, pages bleeding salt and ink. She lunged after it, but was too late.

The sea rose up, arms of black water curling like it had been waiting. It caught her by the ribs and dragged her under.

Salt filled her mouth.

Above, the ship dissolved into ink, the crew into echoes, the storm into silence. Only her heartbeat remained, hammering loud, then slower, then—

Her lungs screamed.

She kicked upward, arms flailing, but the surface kept retreating. The stars above her blurred and spun, constellations folding into shapes she almost recognized as her own skin until the water pressed down so heavily she couldn't remember which way was air.

She thought of Penny, bright as sunlight.

Of her father's voice, gone forever.

Of the bastard thief's coin flipping, endless and merciless.

This is how it ends. Not fire. Not names. But in the story, you begged to live.

Her chest convulsed. She opened her mouth, and the sea poured in.

Dark water swallowed her, then spat her into light.

Shards.

She stumbled forward, boots hammering on stone that wasn't steady, corridors spiraling out from under her feet like snakes. Walls surged up, slick as glass.

Mirrors.

She ran.

Instinct, not choice. Her body obeyed before her mind could claw words together.

Run or drown.

Run or vanish.

Run.

Every step splintered her reflection. A hundred selves flanking her, sprinting beside her, all of them her and not her. Faces that looked back with hunger, pity, rage. Hands clawing forward, some scarred, some clean, some jeweled, some slick with blood.

Her baker-self lurched with flour on her apron. Another grinned sharp with salt in her hair and stormlight on her sword. Another bore burns. Another wore a crown, stars crawling her skin like constellations had claimed her as their map.

And more. Too many. Too fast.

She tried not to look. Looking was poison. Looking was drowning all over again. But the mirrors bent close anyway, forcing her to see.

Their mouths moved together, a cacophony of her own voice weaponized:

You're nothing but your duty.

You wanted stories.

You abandoned reality.

You will fail them all.

You are nothing without her.

He will break you.

You will disappear here.

The voices tangled until she couldn't tell if they were hers or the Court's or the echo of the drowned sea inside her lungs.

Her scars flared hot, star-maps bleeding light that warped against the mirrors until whole galaxies unfolded around her. Some versions of herself reached for that light as if in worship. Others shrank from it like it burned.

The corridor split into three.

Then five.

Then ten.

She picked one, any one, sprinting until the glass warped again. She slammed her shoulder against it and was thrown into another hall of selves, another infinity of reflections.

No exit.

No end.

Just more Marens, layered, overlapping, eyes multiplying until she wasn't sure if her own gaze still belonged to her.

She screamed. Her voice fractured, broke apart into a dozen echoes, each one laughing back at her, cruel and familiar. The mirrors swallowed the sound, spit it back as new versions of herself, each worse, each truer.

Her lungs heaved. Her legs burned. Her thoughts tangled into knots too tight to slice open. What was she running toward? What was she running from? Did it even matter anymore?

All the mirrors whispered the same truth in different mouths:

You will never get out.

The corridor tightened. Glass angled in. Her own faces pressed closer, smeared across silver, mouths opening wide like they could bite her whole.

She bolted harder. She didn't know if she was chasing freedom or being chased by herself.

Maybe both.

The walls bent sharply, funneled her into a single narrow hall. Mirrors narrowed with it, compressing her reflection into a long, warped smear of light and shadow. For one dizzy second, she thought she saw not herself at all, but something waiting under her skin. Something she hadn't asked for, hadn't named. A shape with edges too bright, too human, too divine.

Her scars screamed light, and the glass shattered.

Shards rained down, cutting stars across her arms. She ran anyway, bare feet on razors, through splinter and gleam, through the wreckage of herself.

And still the labyrinth bent forward, endless, endless, endless—

Light.

At the end of the hall, past the ruin of mirrors and the echo of too many selves, light pooled bright and golden. Not the sterile white of marble. Not the warped gleam of glass. Gold. Warm.

An exit.

Maren's chest heaved. Her lungs begged. Her legs burned. She ran anyway, faster, the promise of release dragging her forward like a hook in her ribs. The closer she came, the more her scars blazed, constellations screaming against her skin.

The corridor widened into a chamber. Light flared from its center.

A cage stood there.

Not the plain black of iron, but the same gilded bars she had seen before, the Court's cruel ornament, twisted into spectacle.

Gold leaf still clung in patches, but most of it had blistered black, seams glowing faintly as if fire still licked through the filigree. Ash drifted at its base, smearing the once-bright shine into ruin.

Inside—

Penny.

She lay crumpled on the floor, hair loose, and herbs gone. Her dress was scorched to rags. Her chest didn't rise. Her eyes didn't open.

Maren's scream tore itself out before she could think. She slammed against the bars, fingers clawing raw metal. Heat seared her palms, but the cage held.

"Get up," she begged. "Please, get up."

But Penny didn't even stir. Only the faint curl of smoke rose from her body, the stench of charred cloth and skin flooding Maren's throat until bile surged bitter up her tongue.

Her scars flared so bright the chamber itself warped. And for one hellish second, she saw it wasn't Penny at all.

It was herself.

Charred. Burned. Her own eyes stared empty at the ceiling, mouth open as if she'd screamed.

The vision flickered, shifted, became Penny again.

Then Maren.

Then Penny.

Then both were overlaid like two and stitched together badly.

Her body folded. She pressed her forehead to the bars, sobbing ragged into the heat. All her endurance, all her scars, all her survival had led to this? To an ending where Penny lived radiant without her, or lay dead because of her, or worse, where Maren herself had never escaped the fire at all?

Her thoughts clawed at each other, incoherent, overlapping:

She dies because of you.

You never escaped the fire.

This is your ending.

The gilded bars groaned under her grip, but didn't yield. The smoke thickened. Phantom screams coiled in the air: Penny's voice and hers, indistinguishable.

Maren hit the floor.

Clink.

The sound of a coin spinning, slicing through the ruin like it had been waiting all along.

A voice followed, velvet and cruel, curling against her ear:

"Darling, you do make a mess of yourself."

27

Chaos Made Flesh

T he world broke.

The labyrinth shattered.

White marble cracked into ribbons of black. Fire guttered backward, smoke sucked into itself until the air tasted like ash and lightning. The cage stuttered, image splitting: Penny's corpse, her own corpse, Penny again.

All of them flickering on and off like broken lanterns.

And through the ruin, he stepped.

Not walking. Not striding. Simply *there,* as though the Court had folded space to make room for him. A coin spun lazily between his fingers, each turn warping the chamber's edges further out of joint.

Maren's breath clawed at her ribs. Too fast. Too shallow. Her scars flared so bright they hurt, starlight bleeding through her skin like it wanted out.

No.

No, not him.

Another trick.

Another mask.

Another cruel jest stitched out of her own want.

She pressed both palms to her ears, but it wasn't the sound she was blocking. It was his shape. His smile. His eyes.

Not real.

Not him.

Her chest convulsed. Penny's phantom scream still rang, underlain with her own. The image of her body, burned, blistered, abandoned in that cage, wouldn't vanish. She needed it to vanish. She needed *everything* to vanish.

Her nails raked across her arms.

Harder.

Harder.

Skin split. Blood welled. She clawed at the constellations stitched beneath, trying to rip them out, tear the light free before it mocked her again. She didn't want them. She didn't want to glow like the Court's pet survivor. She wanted silence.

She wanted *nothing*.

Her own voice tore raw from her throat. "Get out of me!"

The walls echoed her words back. A dozen versions of her voice shrieking in chorus. The sound drove her harder against herself, nails digging until stars smeared crimson.

The coin turned, and the room bent. His presence filled every inch of it.

And Maren screamed louder, because if she stopped, if she listened, if she believed for one second that he was real, then she'd break in a way she couldn't come back from.

She lunged at him. Not to escape, but to *hurt.* Nails slashed for his face, his throat. Her teeth snapped so close to his shoulder she tasted the heat of his skin.

He caught her wrists before she landed the blow. One hand clamped them both above her head, slammed into the marble so hard the crack spidered under her skull. The coin gleamed in his free hand, turning once, slow, as if the world itself pivoted on its arc.

She bucked beneath him, hips twisting, legs kicking wild. Fury foamed in her chest, more beast than woman. She spat, hot and bitter, straight at his cheek.

He only laughed. Low. Hungry. The sound of a predator finally entertained.

"Still fighting," he murmured, pressing her wrists harder until her pulse thrashed against his grip. His body caged hers completely, weight heavy across her hips, pinning her down. His face lowered until her spit smeared his skin, and he grinned through it.

Her breath rasped. She jerked her head sideways and bit. Hard. Her teeth sank into his shoulder, through cloth, sharp enough to taste iron.

His hiss was not pain. It was pleasure. He pressed closer, lips brushing her ear as his voice curled dark and velvet against the raw edges of her mind:

"I'm the only one allowed to break you, darling. Look at you, already in pieces."

Her scars flared, galaxies trembling against his chest where she fought to writhe free. She spat curses, hoarse and choking.

"You think the Court deserves this?" he whispered, coin spinning between his fingers, silver flashing with every syllable. "No. You're mine. My chaos made flesh."

She bucked again, frantic, teeth snapping at his jaw this time. He shifted easily, turning her head aside with a brush of his cheek, smiling when she tried to shred him with every part of herself.

He *adored* it.

The more she fought, the more tightly he held her. The more rabid she became, the softer his touch grew, his grip iron but his thumb stroking her pulse, memorizing the way it thundered for him.

Pinned beneath him, fury tearing her throat raw, she had never been more alive or more undone.

And he, with his coin flashing and mouth curved like a wound, looked down at her as if nothing in the Court had ever pleased him more.

* * *

The labyrinth howled as it collapsed.

Walls bent inward, mirrors split, white marble shrieking like bone ground to dust. Penny's corpse flickered one last time inside the cage before vanishing with a hiss of smoke.

He didn't flinch.

He rose in one fluid motion, hauling Maren up with him like she weighed nothing. She thrashed once, weak, then sagged against his chest, eyes wild and unfocused, lips still shaping curses that broke apart before they reached air. Her constellation scars pulsed frantic light across his throat, stars scattering against him like they knew their master.

He cradled her in both arms, princess-style, as though she were not a rabid creature who'd bitten his shoulder a breath ago but a prize he'd claimed from the ruin.

The coin spun in his fingers, catching what was left of the labyrinth's light, and every time it turned, the broken world stuttered harder: arches snapping, corridors folding, glass collapsing to ash.

He walked through it like a god, steady, inevitable, while everything else screamed and fell away.

The seam ripped wide. Court voices surged through the tear: a hundred gasps, shrieks, murmurs, the thunder of wagers overturned.

The Arbiter's voice cut above them all, hammered silver and iron: *"Interference. Trial abandonment."*

Whispers hissed into roars. Spectators leaned from their balconies, hungry and furious. Coral Head was already on her feet, coral crown jagged in the glow, eyes snapping with venom.

And the thief didn't stop.

He stepped onto the dais as if the Arbiter's law were nothing but air. His presence bent the Court's noise into a hush. The coin flicked from his fingers with a casual grace, and the Arbiter's decree caught mid-word, voice choking silent as if the law itself had been gagged.

Gasps rippled outward. Half the Court leaned closer, delighted. Half drew back, outraged.

Maren stirred weakly in his arms, a broken whisper scraping out: "Not real…not you…just another trick." Her nails dragged at her scars, but he held her tighter, tucking her wrists against his chest where she couldn't claw.

The thief's mouth curved as sharply as a blade. He looked up and smiled like a man who had already won.

"Mine," he said, coin flashing once more.

And with that, he carried her straight through the center of the Court. Untouchable, unstoppable, the spectacle of a god parading his chosen ruin.

He did not hurry.

He threaded through the Court as if the marble had been laid for his feet alone, coin ticking in his palm like a small, mocking metronome.

Maren fit in his arms the way broken things fit in the hollow where a hand should be. Her head lolled and he carried her as if she were weightless, as if she had never thrashed and bitten and spat at him. Her lashes fluttered; her mouth kept shaping breathless fragments of accusation and denial that never found purchase.

The coin winked once, twice, and for every turn the world around them hiccuped: tiles rearranging, a balcony folding away, a whisper unspooling into laughter. He walked through it all like a storm through paper.

By the time they reached his rooms, the Court had become an afterimage: a roar dimming behind glass. He set her down inside a chamber that smelled faintly of cedar and citrus. The door closed with a soft, certain click.

She lay where he put her, on top of his bed, eyes unfocused, hands limp at her sides. The constellation scars across her arms and throat pulsed slowly, then quickly, a constellation breathing until she could feel nothing but the light on her skin.

The room around her was strange. Sparse. Walls curved in ways that felt organic, like they'd grown into shape rather than been built. One sloped inward and was papered with sideways shelves of books, their spines mismatched and worn at the edges, titles curling in languages she didn't recognize.

Another wall shimmered faintly with soft, shifting color, like dawn trapped in water. A threadbare armchair slouched in the corner. A mug sat on the floor beside it, long since gone cold.

The whole room felt like him. Chaotic, but intentional. A kind of beautiful entropy. Every object was out of place and perfectly so: a map pinned sideways, a globe with constellations instead of countries, a coat flung over the back of a chair with pockets that probably held riddles.

In that light, the room recoiled into shapes: curtains like sails, a lamp like a distant lighthouse, but nothing held meaning long enough to be trusted.

She tried to make it stop by moving.

Her fingers flexed and found the map on her forearm. For a beat she reached for it without thinking, an animal act, reflex and defiance both. The moment she touched the heirloom light, the stars under her skin skittered. They did not sit like stitches. They rolled like living things, constellations unbraiding into threads that moved under her palms, threads that lived and pulled and whispered.

A hallucination—

No, not a neat one.

They were real in the marrow of her eyes. The stars swam and crowded, swollen and insectile, pinpricks rearranging into eyes that blinked without lids. When she dragged a fingernail across them, they stretched and hissed, the light fracturing into shards that stung like salt.

She saw her father's hand at the bakery counter, but his mouth was a hole that sucked sound away. Penny's figure moved beyond the pane of an impossible window, bright and alive and uncaring.

Terror uncoiled in her like an animal; she clawed down harder. Her fingernails buried into the map of stars until pain hot as brand came back at her. Blood speckled the pale light. She tried to tear the constellations free, to tear the Court's ownership out of her skin, because if she could strip the light, perhaps she could strip what made her theirs.

Her hands were trembling too much to do it cleanly. She dug at a seam near her wrist, voice a cracked rasp of something that might once have been a laugh and might now have been a sob.

"Get—out—of—me," she choked, and the words were little flung stones.

His hand closed over her fingers so suddenly she thought the bones would break. Not a grip that punished; a grip that stopped. He folded her fingers against her palm as if holding an animal that could not understand the shelter being offered.

His other hand pressed to the place where her ribs moved fast. The motion was minimal, domestic: a suppression of movement, the soft correction of a storm.

"Don't," he said. It was not a command so much as a careful hammer. "Stop."

The room tilted. For the first time since the cage, her brain hesitated enough to question whether this was safety or another bruise the world was offering.

Her eyes fixed on his face; it was too near, too present. He smelled of smoke. Old, not the fresh kind that left hair stiff and throat raw, but the slow, sweet ember he kept like a signature, and something darker underneath. He looked at her with an expression that made a place inside her ache in a way fury never had.

He did not let go. He did not look away. He bound her hands, but not with chains. He found a length of black silk on the bedside table: smooth and cool and ridiculous against the hot, sticky salt of her blood. His fingers moved with the economy of practiced gentleness, looping the fabric once, twice, knotting it so that it held but did not cut.

The motion was intimate in a way that should have made her recoil, but she was too raw even to feel indignation toward the restraint. The silk did not feel like bondage so much as a hand that would not loosen until she stopped hurting herself.

The silk bound her wrists above her head, his weight pressing her into the mattress. He could have smiled, could have laughed at her ruin. He didn't. His face hovered close enough that his breath warmed her temple, close enough that she could see the gold flecks in his eyes gleam when her scars flared beneath him.

Her voice was a ghost in her throat. "Let me go."

His thumb smeared the blood on her arm like he was memorizing it. His coin clinked once in his free hand, lazy, deliberate. "The Court wanted your pieces," he murmured, eyes drinking her in. "But I want all of you."

The words seared, heavy as a brand.

Her chest hitched. She tried to summon fury, her old fire, her teeth, her laugh, but the well was dry. Penny's face flickered in her mind, not sunshine, not rosemary, but radiant without her, radiant because she wasn't there. A bakery full of warmth that would never again smell like Maren.

And what was she now?

Not a baker. Not a daughter. Not a friend. Just a creature stitched with stars that wouldn't leave her skin.

Her breath cracked. "There's nothing left to want."

His smile curved, a blade with its tip at her throat. "Darling," he whispered, leaning close enough that the word scorched her ear, "you're only saying that because you've never been mine."

The coin spun once, flashing. For a moment, the stars across her body pulsed in rhythm, betraying her, answering him instead of her. She twisted against the silk, not to escape, but because the sensation of moving and failing reminded her she was still *here.*

"I'm not yours," she rasped.

His hand tightened on her wrists, pinning her deeper into the sheets. His mouth hovered a hair from hers, his laugh low, villainous. "You say it like a choice."

Her stomach twisted. This was the mischief of him: not gentle, not cruel, but something worse: *truth bent until it fit his hand.*

And yet the sting of it landed inside her chest.

For the first time, she wasn't fighting to get back to Eldenwick. She wasn't fighting to hear her father's voice or Penny's tune. She was fighting to prove there was still a self left under all this ruin.

That was when she realized: the self she'd clung to, with flour on her apron and laughter over bread, was already ash.

The girl who had walked into the Court was gone.

Her scars burned, light whirling dizzy, constellations shifting across her like the sky was remapping itself. She stared up at him, lips trembling, and for the first time, she did not spit, did not curse, did not laugh.

She yielded. Not to him, not to the Court, but to the fact that she was no longer who she had been.

His grin widened, savage and hungry, like he'd been waiting for this moment all along.

"You feel it now, don't you?" His voice was velvet-edged in iron.

"The ruin suits you."

28

Vile

The ceiling had kept moving without her.

Constellations slid slowly across the ceiling, spirals of faint silver light, like the Court thought a mortal girl could be tricked into wonder with stars painted overhead.

Maren hadn't asked what they were. She hadn't asked anything. Days had gone like this; her body stretched thin against a mattress that smelled faintly of cedar and citrus, her mouth dry from saying nothing.

The cot in her cell had been stone. This was softer, and somehow worse. The softness mocked. It implied she was worth preserving. That she hadn't already been gutted, rewritten, and ruined.

Her chest still carried the ache where the fire had torn her apart. Her ribs creaked with every shallow breath, stitched with scars that glowed faintly whenever the stars shifted. She hated that she could feel beautiful when she should've felt monstrous.

She hated that she felt anything at all.

So, she didn't move. Didn't speak. Just let the ruin sit in her like a stone in her stomach.

If Penny had been her anchor before, that anchor had snapped. The thought of dragging her back with herself felt poisonous now. Penny deserved more than tethering herself to someone already cracked open.

Maybe it had always been true: Penny's life would be better without her.

The door did not open. It never did. The air just shifted, bent, and she knew without looking that he was there.

The scrape of fabric, a breath of cedar and citrus, the faint rattle of chain at his belt.

And then, the chair creaked.

Maren almost laughed. A bitter, cracked thing. He'd lasted longer than she expected, pretending to be a gentleman. But the mattress dipped a moment later under his weight, and she stilled.

He didn't speak. Of course, he didn't. He moved like gravity itself had chosen his side: slow, certain, deliberate. He didn't ask permission.

Mischief didn't need it.

The bed listed under his body as he stretched out beside her, casual as if he were claiming a throne. One arm folded behind his head, the other sprawled loose, hand brushing his own stomach. He didn't curl small, didn't edge politely to his side. He sprawled, long and leonine, like a predator taking the warmest spot without question.

And gods help her, it felt inevitable.

Her throat worked. Air caught sharp behind her teeth. She hated the sound that scraped out of her: half-breath, half-word, and raw from disuse.

"Why?"

The silence after it was worse.

She could feel his grin in the dark without even turning her head. Finally, his voice slid low, velvet with mock-innocence.

"Why am I crawling into bed with you?"

Her head snapped toward him, curls tumbling into her eyes. Maren's chest hitched. "That—" Her voice cracked, sandpaper rough. She cleared it, forced the sound steady. "That isn't what I meant."

His grin widened like she'd handed him a game piece. "And here I thought you'd finally spoken because you missed me."

She bared her teeth. "I'd sooner miss a plague."

"Mm. At least plagues leave a mark." He rolled to his side, head propped on his palm, gaze dragging shamelessly over her scars. "And you're nothing if not marked, darling."

Heat licked her throat, anger burning against the coil of shame she carried. She yanked the blanket tighter around her shoulders, as though it mattered. "Why are you here?"

He shifted again, sprawling onto his back, hand flung wide across the mattress so that his knuckles brushed the space between them. "The chair was lonely. The bed is warmer. And you—" he tipped his head to her, "—don't seem in a hurry to leave my room."

Maren's nails dug crescents into the blanket. She could smell him: cedar, citrus, and smoke, curling close as heat. "You could have stayed away."

"And miss the moment you finally opened your mouth?" he smirked, pleased with himself. "Never."

Maren kept her eyes on the ceiling. The constellations shifted lazily above, mocking her silence with their restless glitter. Her throat ached from the words she'd given him, but she forced another out.

"Why did you save me?"

He hummed low in his chest, rolling toward her, elbow sinking into the mattress, so his weight tilted closer. "Clarify, darling. From the Arbiter's little maze? Or from yourself?"

Her jaw clenched. "Don't twist it."

His grin was maddening. "You're asking why I broke my own rules. Why the Court's Spirit of Mischief cheated the game." He tapped a finger against his mouth, as if considering. "Could be I enjoy the chaos you cause. You spark, they gasp, and I get to watch Order grind its teeth. Delicious."

"Self-serving, then."

"Always," he said smoothly, leaning closer until his shoulder brushed the blanket she'd wound around herself. "But not only."

Her stomach dipped. "Then what?"

He didn't answer at once. He studied her instead, eyes sliding across her face like he was trying to memorize the cracks. His hand drifted to the headboard behind her, palm braced so that he hovered without touching. Close enough that her pulse tripped anyway.

"There was another mortal once," he said at last, voice lighter than the words deserved. "She wanted too much. The Court rewrote her. A new toy in its collection." His golden gaze softened a fraction, "I thought I could wish against it. I failed. Order bound her tight."

Maren's lips parted. "Almost."

His smile sharpened. "You have been listening."

She turned her face away, curls shielding her. "So, you saved me because you couldn't save her."

"That's one story." He dipped closer, so near his breath brushed the curl at her temple. "Another is that I saw a mortal girl with more fire than sense and thought: how entertaining."

Her heart thudded. "You broke your court for entertainment?"

"For you." His grin curled slowly, devilishly. "Though I find those two things often overlap."

She wanted to shove him. She wanted to claw his grin from his face. Instead, she dragged the blanket higher, like it could smother the heat clawing its way up her throat.

"You're vile."

"Vile," he echoed, satisfied. "And yet, here you are, in my bed, asking why I couldn't let you destroy yourself."

Maren forced herself to breathe slowly, steadily. The ceiling above them refused to stay still, its stars bleeding into new shapes, new spirals. She clenched the blanket tighter around her shoulders, stubborn as if her fists could keep the whole world from rearranging.

"What is it?" she asked at last, "The ceiling. Why does it move?"

He tipped his head back against the headboard, lashes lowering in a lazy half-blink. "Ah. You've noticed."

"It's hard not to," she snapped. "They won't stop shifting."

"Not stars, darling. Stories." His voice curved with amusement, like he was explaining a trick to a child and waiting for her to bristle. "Every mortal choice. Every desperate wish. They drift, they spiral, they collapse. Most blink out before they can burn. But some…" He tilted his chin toward her, golden eyes gleaming. "…some blaze loud enough to rattle the Court itself."

Her pulse stuttered.

He didn't look away. "Yours was a beacon. I felt it the night you begged the world for wonder. A hunger loud enough to bend the firmament."

Heat clawed up her chest. "That wasn't—" She broke off, throat tight. "It wasn't supposed to matter."

"Everything matters when it's that loud." He shifted, his arm brushing her shoulder through the blanket, casual as a claim. "You wanted more, so Chaos listened. It always listens. What you see above us is the proof. A thousand lives burning themselves into stories." His grin sharpened. "And one mortal baker's want carving brighter than the rest."

Maren stared at the ceiling despite herself. Constellations slid into each other, blinking out, reforming. She thought she glimpsed flour dust curling into a star-trail, the crooked outline of a bakery roof dissolving into a fox's grin. She pressed her nails into the fabric at her chest, furious at the way it looked like her.

"Stop," she muttered.

"Stop what?" His coin winked in and out of his fingers, lazy as breath. "Telling you the truth?"

"That isn't truth. It's—" She swallowed hard. "It's spectacle."

"Chaos has never pretended otherwise." His tone was velvet again, low and coaxing. "But it's your spectacle now, darling. You lit the fuse. Don't be shocked when the fire spreads."

She tore her gaze away from the ceiling, back to him. His grin was too close, his body too comfortable in the bed, his words wrapped in cedar and citrus until they felt less like lore and more like seduction.

"You twist everything," she said, hoarse.

"Of course I do." His voice dipped, intimate, delighted. "I'm Mischief."

Maren's fingers clenched the blanket tighter. "That's not an answer."

"It's the only one that matters." He shifted, rolling onto his side so that the bed tilted toward her, his weight cutting the space in half. His knuckles brushed the pillow between them, close enough that the cedar on his skin chased her breath. "The gods carved six of us out of their own hungers. Cast us down like dice and told us to play."

Her pulse stumbled. "Six."

"And a seventh," he murmured, grin sharp as a secret. "The one they kept.

Selfish, wasn't it? They gave us courts, told us to gather mortals, let the little stories burn bright enough for divine amusement. Shrines, prayers, blood, bread, mortals never could resist dressing their fears in worship." He twirled his fingers idly, as though winding her along. "You built us with every wish you whispered into the dark."

Maren glared at the ceiling. "Sounds like exploitation."

"Sounds like living." His golden gaze cut back to her, molten and merciless. "Spirits burn. Mortals beg. And the gods laugh." He tilted closer, his voice brushing her jawline. "But don't look so tragic, darling. Mischief doesn't mind being begged."

Her breath caught. Heat spiked low in her stomach, infuriating. "Restraint must be new for you."

His grin widened, feral. "Do you know what it costs me to lie here and not take advantage of this bed?"

She turned on him, blanket clutched tight, cheeks burning despite herself. "Pig."

"And you're trembling again." He slid a fingertip down the pillow seam between them, slow as a taunt. "Is it exhaustion… or anticipation?"

"Try disgust."

"Delicious." He let the word linger, savored.

Her teeth ground together. "Stop calling me that."

"What, delicious?" His grin gleamed. "Or darling? Or baker? Mortal?" He leaned close enough that the heat of him pressed her lips numb. "My undoing?"

Her pulse thundered. "Don't."

His coin flashed once between his fingers, winked out. "You mortals used to call me properly, once. Whispered my name on thresholds, painted it in ash. Names are leashes. A true one binds. Why would I ever gift mine?" His voice dipped, rich as velvet. "I like yours better."

She bristled. "You don't even say it."

"I don't need to." He brushed a curl from her face, fingers hovering close enough to set every nerve alight. "Bastard. Thief. The way it drips off your tongue. Gods, it's intoxicating."

Her throat locked. The blanket slipped an inch lower. She didn't stop it.

He smiled, sharp and devastating. "Say it again."

She spat the word like venom. "Bastard."

His breath caught on a low, hungry laugh, his gold eyes molten in the dark. He leaned closer, slow enough that she knew he was enjoying every flicker of her reaction. "Ah. Music."

For one impossible moment, their mouths hovered a heartbeat apart. Her lungs forgot how to work.

For one breath, she let herself drown. The warmth of him, the gold in his eyes, the taunt still lingering in the air, her body betrayed her before her mind could shove it back into its cage. She leaned, reckless, a kiss trembling on the edge of her mouth.

But the bastard didn't meet her lips.

He slid sideways instead, slow enough to make sure she felt the denial. His mouth brushed her jaw, lower, teeth grazing the soft skin at her throat. A nip, light but devastating, right over the curve of her collarbone where the constellation scars shimmered faintly.

Maren's breath punched out, sharp and humiliating. Her hands tightened in the blanket like they could anchor her against the heat that flared low in her belly.

"Delicious," he murmured against her skin, velvet and merciless.

The spell snapped.

She shoved him hard, legs tangling in the blanket, foot kicking out like she meant to break his ribs. He laughed as he caught himself with a palm against the mattress, rolling back onto his side of the bed with obscene ease.

"Violent little thing," he drawled, stretching long across the mattress as if he hadn't just tried to devour her pulse. "I like it."

"You're insufferable," she spat, yanking the blanket back over her shoulder.

His grin spread slowly, wickedly, as though she'd just handed him a crown. "You didn't seem to mind a moment ago."

"Try dead."

"Darling, if I were dead, you'd miss me." He teased, lazy as sin, folding his arms behind his head like he'd just won something. "Almost as much as you wanted me just now."

Her cheeks burned hotter. "In your dreams."

"Mm," he said, sprawling wider across the bed, stealing more space with every inch. "In yours, more likely."

She turned away, furious at him, at herself, at the traitor heat still buzzing through her veins. He chuckled low, victorious, and let the silence fall back into place.

Above them, the constellations shifted restlessly, as if even the stories were leaning closer to see what happened next.

She had lived through the Court's trials. Now she only had to survive the Mischief Spirit.

29

Scandal

The first thing she registered was warmth.

Not the fever-burn of trial fire, not the ache of scarred ribs, but the quiet, human kind, the kind that came from another body pressed against hers.

Maren surfaced slowly, her skull thick with sleep, the ceiling's restless constellations swimming above like they'd been watching her all night. For one disoriented heartbeat, she thought she'd sunk back into her bakery bed, curled against feather-stuffed blankets and dreamless quiet. Then the rhythm under her ear betrayed her: steady, unhurried, too strong to be her own.

His heartbeat.

Her lashes snapped open.

Her cheek was pillowed against his chest, her arm curved traitorously across his ribs. His body was hot, solid, every line of him molded around her as though she'd crawled here willingly. She must have. She'd shifted in the night, seeking warmth, and tucked herself straight into the arms of the most dangerous thing in the Court.

A flush climbed her throat. *Careful,* she told herself. Quiet. If she moved slowly enough, maybe she could slip free before he—

"Good morning, darling."

The words vibrated under her ear before she even lifted her head. His voice was amused velvet, low and lethal, the kind of tone that already knew he'd won.

Maren jerked back, but his arm tightened immediately, banding her waist. "Ah, don't be shy. You practically crawled on top of me. It would hurt my feelings if you fled so soon."

Her head whipped up to glare, curls falling wild across her eyes. He was already watching, golden irises molten in the dim, hair tousled black as spilled ink across the pillow. His features were all fox-sharp lines and unfair symmetry; smugness etched into every angle.

"Bastard," she hissed, shoving at his chest.

He caught her wrist easily, grin widening. "Mmm. My favorite refrain. You sound so earnest in the mornings."

She tried again, kicking at his shin under the blanket. He only laughed, low and delighted, the sound scraping heat across her skin. His other arm slid higher, pinning her more securely against him until she was straddling the line between trapped and embraced.

"You didn't complain last night," he murmured, teeth flashing. "Quite the opposite. You nestled in like a kitten and sighed yourself to sleep."

Her face burned hotter. "I did not."

"Shall I mimic it for you?" His mouth brushed her ear, close enough that his breath raised goosebumps along her throat. He gave the softest, most devastating nip at the shell of it, then hummed in satisfaction when she jolted. "Ah. That's the sound."

She shoved again, half-panicked, half-furious, but his hold didn't slacken. His grin curved wickedly as he whispered, "The Court already thinks you've seduced me. Why don't we confirm their suspicions? Imagine Kipwick's face when he barges in."

Her pulse skittered wildly. "Let me go."

He arched a brow, fox-like, sharp, infuriatingly amused. "But you're so comfortable."

Her palm cracked against his chest in a shove that would've sent a mortal man tumbling. He barely shifted, only caught her gaze with that lazy, dangerous glint. "Careful, darling. Keep squirming like that and I'll start to believe you really can't get enough of me."

She bared her teeth. "Die."

His smile was devastating, all teeth and hunger. "After you."

Her shove landed square in his chest. He let her push him back just enough to think she'd gained ground, then shifted, fast as a trap.

The blanket tore loose from her shoulders in the scuffle, slipping low. She gasped, clutching at it, but the bastard was quicker. One hand caught the edge, yanking it aside as he pressed her down into the mattress. His weight pinned her, a thigh sliding deliberately between hers.

She froze, breath spiking hot. Every nerve screamed humiliation, nude under him, scars glowing faintly where the blanket no longer shielded.

"Bastard," she spat, twisting beneath him.

He lowered his mouth to her ear, a grin audible in his voice. "You say it like a prayer. Careful, darling, I might answer."

Her palms shoved at his shoulders, but he caught her wrists with insulting ease and pressed them to the pillow above her head. His hips pinned her firmly, his thigh blocking every kick or knee she thought about throwing. He leaned down, slow, deliberate, lips ghosting over her jaw, then lower, tracing the scatter of stars across her collarbone.

"Get off," she hissed, thrashing.

"Mmm. Off?" His voice was velvet amusement, "Say it slower, and someone might believe you mean it differently."

She bucked against him, fury blazing. "I'll gut you."

"Invitation noted." His grin curved sharply against her throat as he dragged his fingers down, brushing the scars etched faintly across her ribs, lower, to where the blanket barely covered her hips. He traced one constellation like a cartographer mapping his claim. "Gods, I could chart whole galaxies on you."

Her chest heaved. "Touch me again and I'll kill you."

He laughed, low and delighted, like she'd just offered herself up. "Darling, you do make murder sound so sweet."

He shifted his weight, pressing her deeper into the mattress, eyes gleaming molten. "Look at you. Naked beneath me, hissing death threats with every breath. If the Court thinks we're lovers, well, why not give them a scandal worth wagering on?"

Her head snapped to glare, curls wild, cheeks flushed crimson. "You wouldn't dare."

His grin was pure fox. "Try me."

And that was precisely when the door banged wide.

Kipwick froze in the doorway, tray in paw, eyes comically wide as he took in the tableau: Maren pinned, bare but for a twisted blanket, Mischief Spirit braced over her, golden-eyed and smug.

The fox slapped a paw over his face. "Oh, *stars above*. That's permanently burned into my retinas. I'll need holy water. And a stronger drink."

"Get off!" Maren roared, still pinned.

"Mm," the bastard purred, eyes never leaving hers, his voice pitched just loud enough for Kipwick to hear. "You're very insistent this morning. Want me to get off, darling? Or keep going until the fox faints?"

Kipwick groaned. "Oh, definitely a stronger drink." He stumbled back, muttering about bleach for his eyes.

Maren's fury crackled hot enough to light the constellations above them. "I hate you," she hissed.

The bastard only grinned wider, pressing just a little more weight against her wrists. "And yet, here we are. Delicious, isn't it?"

Kipwick did not flee. He made a strangled sound, peered through his paws like a child at a puppet show, and remembered he had a job.

"I am duty-bound," he announced to the ceiling, voice pitched high with trauma. "I cannot leave until I deliver the summons. Unfortunately."

"Deliver it to the hall," she snapped. "From outside the room."

"I tried that once. It does not count if the paper slides back under the door." He cleared his throat and refocused on the far wall. "By the Arbiter's authority, the Court is convened. Charges have been recorded. Both the mortal and the coin-flipping menace are required to present their regrettable faces at once."

"Regrettable," the bastard murmured against her jaw, perfectly pleased. "Flattering."

"Get off *me*," Maren hissed.

"Mmm. Still ambiguous." He eased a fraction of weight off her wrists, only to pin her hips more securely with his thigh. "Do you mean now, or soon, or never?"

"Kipwick," she said through her teeth, "if you are truly duty-bound, find me clothes."

Kipwick executed a bow that involved a ladle and averted eyes. "Already anticipated. I brought a robe. Then reconsidered. The Court would combust. So, I stole a shirt."

He pivoted, flung a black shirt toward the bed, and kept his face heroically turned.

It landed across her stomach.

The thief's gaze dropped to it, amused. "Ah. My favorite."

She yanked at the fabric. He did not move. The shirt stayed trapped beneath his hips. His grin sharpened.

Her patience snapped.

She twisted hard, hooked her ankle behind his, and used the momentum of fury. He let her roll him just enough to slide free in a tangle, then caught her again before she tumbled off the mattress. She snatched the shirt, dragged it over her head in a single violent motion, and ignored the way it fell past mid-thigh.

He watched the whole thing like a connoisseur. "Thief," he said, fond and sinful.

"Says the thief." She shoved off, hair wild, collar askew, bare legs daring the room to comment. "It is mine now."

"Is it," he murmured, eyes molten. "Then I suppose I should take it back."

Kipwick groaned softly. "For the love of the gods, stop flirting while I am present."

"I am threatening," Maren said.

"Semantics," the fox replied. He stretched a paw toward the door. "We are late."

The bastard slid to his feet with a predator's unhurried grace, coin kissing his knuckles as if it belonged there more than bone. Barefoot, hair in wicked disarray, he looked like every rumor Coral Head would ever need. He reached to smooth the collar of his shirt on her body, and Maren slapped his hand away.

"Touch me and I will break your fingers."

He smiled as if she had offered a glove. "Promises, promises."

Kipwick shifted his gaze between them like a spectator at a duel. "One last item before we parade the scandal through a crowded venue." He coughed. "The charges. Interference. Trial abandonment. Corruption of proceedings." He paused. "I added that last title because it sounds important. There was also a note about 'undue influence of the presiding Spirit via horizontal proximity.'"

Maren stared. "Horizontal proximity."

"I do not write the euphemisms," Kipwick said primly.

The bastard's smile turned lazy. "I prefer vertical proximity."

"Die," she said.

He tipped his head. "After you."

Kipwick slapped a paw against his own forehead. "I need holy water."

Maren shoved her feet into boots that were not hers and did not match the shirt because she refused to shuffle to judgment barefoot in his clothes. She tied the laces with shaking fingers and hated the shake more than anything in the room.

The bastard watched the tremor, then pitched his voice soft enough that only she would hear. "Stay close to me."

"Orders now?" Her laugh scratched. "How ruler of you."

"Observation," he said. "You enjoy getting lost. I enjoy finding you."

Heat punched low. She strangled it. "I enjoy your silence."

"Liar." He leaned down until his mouth was near her ear, not touching, a threat made of air. "You enjoy my attention."

Kipwick clapped once, too brightly. "If the prelude is complete, we really must waltz. The dais has a schedule."

Maren strode for the door before her own body could embarrass her again. The shirt hem brushed her thighs with every step. It felt like being branded. It felt like armor she refused to admit was armor. She caught her reflection in a crooked shard of mirror and almost laughed. Star-scarred legs. His shirt.

The Court deserved the show.

The door widened obediently. Cold air licked her knees. A whisper rose from the stones beneath like a bet already placed.

Behind her, the bastard fell into step, coin silent for once, presence loud as a storm that had decided on restraint. Kipwick scuttled ahead, tail held high as an ungodly banner.

"Reminder," Kipwick said, switching to a tone that meant he cared more than the joke allowed, "do not give them anything true."

Maren set her jaw. "They can choke on spectacle."

"Excellent," he said, cheered. "You are learning."

They reached the threshold where the corridor thinned and the audience of portraits leaned in to listen. Voices drifted up from the chamber beyond, hungry and gilded. Somewhere a bell chimed twice, sweet and cruel.

The bastard's breath warmed her neck. "If rumors must live, why not feed them?"

She did not look at him. "Because you are gluttony in a body."

"Incorrect," he said, amused. "Should we go back to our history lesson last night?"

Kipwick threw the door wide with a flourish that would have insulted a lesser stage. "Presenting," he sang sweetly, "the mortal disaster and her favorite catastrophe. Do try to keep your clothing on."

The room beyond hushed like a mouth closing on a bite.

Maren stepped through in his shirt, bare legs, and too-big boots scuffed. The Court inhaled. The bastard smiled like he had planned it. Kipwick sighed like a martyr who had at last earned his drink.

"Summons delivered," the fox said, finally official, and tucked the ladle under his arm. "Now, please go break hearts and precedents. I am parched."

30

Corruption of Proceedings

The chamber waited like a mouth.

Stone teeth of tiered balconies leaned inward, packed with creatures and courtiers draped in smoke-bright silks. Murmurs raced along the walls like rats, feeding on rumor before she even crossed the threshold.

Maren did not shrink. Not this time.

Her legs were bare, constellation scars glowing faintly across her skin, the hem of his stolen shirt brushing mid-thigh like both scandal and armor. Every step in her scuffed boots cracked the hush wider.

She had walked into this room once before, hollowed, trembling, desperate to clutch at her anchor. That girl was gone. Burned in trial-fire. Lost in the maze. Starred over with scars the Court could never peel away.

Now the Court saw what the labyrinth had left behind.

The Arbiter's voice fell from the dais like iron dropped on stone. "Mortal." The word rang, too heavy to be only syllables. "You return altered."

Maren tipped her chin, silver-blue eyes catching the chamber's half-light. Her pulse throbbed, steady with fury. "I return alive."

The audience hissed. Some delighted. Some wary. All hungry.

Behind her, the thief ambled in, coin rolling lazily across his knuckles as though the summons were a jest written for his amusement. He looked like sin interrupted: shirt unlaced, hair a tousled crown of ink, grin already barbed. The whispers rose to a fever; accusations confirmed by spectacle alone.

Maren's jaw set. She felt the Arbiter's weight press down on her ribs, a judgmental gravity meant to pin. But the Court had already burned her, hollowed her, stitched her back with fire. She straightened under it, let the scars glow brighter, and met the Arbiter's faceless decree head-on.

This time, she did not flinch.

The Arbiter's voice split the chamber.

"Count I: Interference. The Spirit of Mischief bent adjudication."

The sound rattled the balcony stone, a hammer on bone.

"Count II: Abandonment. The mortal fled her labyrinth."

The chamber hissed, delighted.

"Count III: Corruption of Proceedings. The mortal seduced the presiding power."

A wave of laughter rippled sharp, cruel, hungry.

Maren did not bow.

She did not shrink.

She kept her chin tipped high, shoulders squared, fire etched into her skin. The shirt brushed her thighs with every breath, scars beneath glowing faint and defiant. Her fury burned steady, not the reckless blaze of a baker desperate to claw her way home, but something much colder and brighter.

She could feel him behind her, the thief, with a lazy grin sharp as a knife's reflection, coin sliding across his fingers. He didn't answer the charges. Didn't need to. His presence was provocation enough.

The Arbiter's decree pressed harder. *"Balance is not theater. One mortal entered. One mortal must pay. The choice is yours, but the price is certain."*

Before Maren could draw breath, a voice cut across the chamber like glass through silk.

Coral Head rose, jeweled hairpins sparking like sea-fire, smile brittle as glass. "She is no balance," she purred. "She is infection. And while she writhes in his bed, mortal cities burn."

Murmurs rippled sharp as razors.

Maren's breath caught.

Coral Head's voice sweetened, dripping venom. "Tideglass, little baker. Gone in wish-fire. The streets melted bright as glass. Shops, houses, and prayers all burned. We hear of such things even here. Flames scream loud enough to rattle the Court." Her eyes slid to Maren, thin and cruel. "Perhaps your lamb forgot to tell you. Or perhaps her family is ash while you play pet to Mischief."

A gasp cracked through the balconies, half horror, half glee.

Maren's ribs locked. Penny's aunt. The shop with the best herbs. Gone. Possibly gone before the Arbiter caged Penny. And Penny might not even know.

Her scars flared hot, as if the accusation had burned straight into her chest.

She forced her voice steady, though it scraped her throat raw. "You sit in jewels," she said, eyes locked on Coral Head. "I walked through fire. I crawled from ash. If you think I seduced survival, then let me be guilty."

The chamber hushed.

But the steadiness cost her. Beneath it, a seed of doubt writhed. She had begged for wonder once, alone in her bakery. What if that hunger had reached farther than her own skin? What if Tideglass was her fault?

A voice from the balconies hissed: "She abandoned her ovens. Her mother's work lies cold."

Her chest pinched sharply. Her mother's hands in flour. The bakery hearth, dead and dark.

Her throat went raw, but she forced the sound steady. She turned toward Coral Head, not with petty rage, but with a gaze that glowed faint silver-blue, light bending wrong around the constellation scars at her collarbone. For one heartbeat, she felt larger than her body, her fury threaded with something too vast.

"I did not beg to be saved," she said, quieter now, silver-blue eyes catching torchlight. "But I will not be ashamed of living. If Tideglass is lost, then may its dead burn brighter than you ever will."

Gasps. Some clapped. Others hissed. Coral Head's smile cracked, saltwater fury seeping through the break.

Behind her, the Spirit laughed low. Velvet-dark, intimate, carrying across the chamber. "Delicious." His hand twirled the coin, a sound that hushed even the boldest whispers. His grin was wicked triumph, as if her fury had been his plan all along.

Maren's pulse hammered. She stood steady, but inside, the bakery crumbled; Penny vanished, and Tideglass screamed in flames. She felt hollowed, carried only by the fire the Court had stitched into her.

Gasps rippled again, sharper, unsettled. Some clapped. Some hissed. Coral Head's mouth pinched thin, fury seething like saltwater on iron.

The Arbiter's voice fell like a stone dropped into still water. *"Choice remains. Door A: the mortal stays, the lamb goes free. Door B: the mortal attempts the trial anew. Under Sight, with no interference. Decide."*

Maren's chest ached with the weight of it. Penny's face burned behind her eyes. The Court's hunger licked at her skin. And the thief's presence curled close, promising crown and ruin in the same breath.

She stood straight, fire in her scars, voice steady, even as devastation hollowed her ribs.

The Arbiter's decree still echoed. *"Decide."*

The chamber leaned in; every balcony tiered like a mouth full of teeth waiting to chew her choice. Bets whispered, odds reshaped. Two doors, both lined with fire.

Behind her, the Spirit only smiled.

The coin flicked once into the air, a glint of silver cutting through the torchlight. A hush fell, not commanded, but pulled, as though the sound of metal spinning claimed the air itself. The chamber's torches guttered in unison.

The coin did not fall fast. It hung in its arc, lazily revolving, and every eye in the room followed.

The thief's gaze was fixed not on the Arbiter, but on Maren. His mouth curved sharply as if they were the only two players at the table. His fingers caught the coin, closed over it with a snap like a gavel.

The Arbiter's iron voice faltered, just enough to notice. "The terms are—"

"Flexible," the bastard purred, lazy as luxury, voice rolling across the chamber like silk over blades. "Door A, Door B… what's a door but wood to burn?"

The Arbiter's faceless form shivered. Not fear. Not anger. More like a thread yanked taut. "Spirit of Mischief. You will not—"

The coin flicked again, caught between two fingers, a blur and a pause, the simplest sleight of hand. Only it wasn't simple. The floor rippled beneath them, obsidian slabs rearranging like a deck shuffled at speed. A column of spectators gasped as their tier stretched half a foot higher. A lantern fell upward instead of down.

Chaos bent around the sound.

Maren's stomach lurched with the shift, but the Court only cheered, delighted at the trick. To them, it was a spectacle. To her, it was smugness. To the Arbiter, it was defiance.

The coin spun again.

"Clause it in silver," he said, golden eyes molten, grin like blasphemy. "Bind me. Restrain me. Let the mortal choose her trial without my touch. Do you think I mind?" He caught the coin and pressed it flat against his palm. "I don't mind. But you will say it how I want it said."

The Arbiter stiffened, voice distorted, dragged. "The Spirit… is bound… by clause of restraint. The mortal may claim trial."

Gasps hissed sharply from the tiers. Even the Court knew this was no simple bargain. The Arbiter did not bend. The Arbiter spoke. Yet now its decree had been cracked and remade.

The Spirit bowed mockingly, coin vanishing between his fingers. "There. Order appeased. Balance intact. Chaos amused."

Maren's heart slammed. She did not fully understand what she'd seen. Only that his coin was never just a toy.

The Arbiter steadied its form, voice colder. "If you break this clause, Mischief, you are unmade."

He laughed, rich, velvet, devastating. "Try."

The coin winked back into existence, flicking lazily, catching torchlight like a blade. It was nothing. It was everything.

Maren's nails dug crescents into her palms. The Court roared approval, drunk on spectacle. But beneath the roar, a knot of dread wound tight in her stomach. The thief had played the Arbiter like a string, and the Court had applauded.

The Arbiter's decree still stood, reshaped: two doors, one choice. But the terms were his.

The Arbiter's voice hardened, clipped. *"The mortal has until dusk."*

The chamber exploded into wagers.

The bastard leaned down behind her, coin whispering across his knuckles, his voice silk at her ear. "See? I told you. It listens when I want it to."

Maren kept her chin high and her body rigid. She did not ask what he meant. She would not give him the satisfaction.

But the coin winked once more, a silent promise of power in his palm.

The Court rippled with delight, coins flashing, ledgers opening, wagers thrown like bones into a pit. Some bet on her surviving. More bet on how she would die. The noise pressed at her ears until it blurred, a hive gone feral.

Maren stood in the center of it, spine taut, scars bright. She did not let them see her tremble.

The Arbiter had said it plain: Penny or trial. One door chained to sacrifice, the other to ruin.

The choice should have been easy. Penny was her anchor, her promise. But Penny's song had been silenced, her roots in Tideglass possibly ash now. And Maren herself was not the baker girl who'd walked in clutching for rosemary and warmth. That girl had died in the fire, been scattered in the maze.

What remained was something stranger, fiercer. A girl carved by want and wonder, luminous where she should have been broken. A mortal, the Court now called "star-blessed".

The Court's laughter followed her. Coral Head's venom echoed, "Tideglass, gone in wish-fire." Penny's braid. Her mother's ovens. Eldenwick's cobbled streets.

If wonder had cost Tideglass, what would it cost next?

The realization hollowed her even as it steadied her. She had wanted so badly to go home. Now the thought of flour-dust and bread felt like trying to fit herself back into torn skin.

She wanted to be sick.

She wanted Penny safe.

She wanted… too much.

Behind her, the Spirit prowled lazy circles, coin flicking as if nothing were at stake. His grin stretched cruel and confident, the Court's golden villain basking in scandal. He wanted her here. Wanted her caught between doors, caught between fury and longing.

She clenched her fists until her nails bit blood, holding herself upright through the quiet devastation. She would not weep for Coral Head. She would not kneel for the Arbiter.

The Arbiter's final word rang flat: "Dusk."

The chamber dissolved into laughter, applause, and bets tallied. The Court smelled blood and wanted spectacle.

Kipwick's paw touched her elbow, gentler than she deserved. "Come, star-girl," he murmured, whiskers twitching with sorrow beneath the jest. "There's someone who still hums your name, even if you can't hear it."

Her chest ached raw. *Penny*.

She let him lead her out, boots heavy, the shirt brushing bare thighs, her scars glowing in the gloom like constellations scrawled by gods. Behind her, the Spirit followed, every coin flick a reminder that he had bent law itself for her and called it play.

Maren did not look back. She only gripped the thought of gilded bars and rosemary hair and prayed she still had words to give.

31

Beautiful Cages

The corridors coiled.

Walls bowed inward, stone veined with shifting light, every surface rippling faintly like breath beneath skin. Gilded sconces burned without flame, exhaling smoke that curled into shapes of faces: some laughing, some weeping, then dissolving before she could focus.

Maren's boots scuffed against the black obsidian, each step echoing longer than it should, as if the Court wanted her approach to sound like a march to execution.

Kipwick was a few paces ahead, tail rigid and ears pricked back. His jaunty whiskers drooped with the weight of the silence. For once, no quip came. The foxling only glanced at her over his shoulder, eyes glinting, then returned his gaze forward.

Behind her, the bastard sauntered. His coin whispered across his knuckles, bright silver catching the sconces' light. He didn't bother hiding his grin; it curved easily and cruelly, as if he had already read the scene ahead and decided it was comedy.

Maren's stomach twisted.

The deeper they went, the more the hallway shifted: arches bending like ribs, iron doors slick with gold leaf, floors swelling underfoot in small, deliberate pulses. The Court of Chaos had never been built. It breathed. It rearranged itself like a host leading her by the elbow, every shadow urging her forward toward a cage she both craved and dreaded.

Her pulse thundered, ribs aching with each beat. Penny waited ahead, her anchor, her undoing, the last scrap of *her* before-fire self.

And yet: Maren's steps dragged.

She wanted to run. To barrel through the next door, rip the bars open, throw herself against her friend, and never let go. But part of her wanted to turn back, to flee before she saw the truth of what weeks in the Court had done to Penny.

The thief's voice slid over her shoulder, velvet and taunting. "Afraid of what you'll find, darling?"

She did not answer. She only clenched her fists tighter until her nails cut her palms, and walked on, deeper into the Court's hungry heart.

The corridor widened into a hall that was more of a reliquary than a room.

Pillars of bone-white stone rose like organ pipes, arcing to a ceiling lost in shadow. Veins of gold webbed through the stone, glowing faintly as if molten beneath the surface.

At the center waited a cage with spun bars of gilt filigree. They curled upward in twisting patterns, delicate enough to resemble lace, but strong enough to hold gods' amusement. Stars glowed faintly in the gaps between each curl, as if the bars themselves had been pulled out of constellations and hammered into shape.

The sight rooted Maren in place.

Because inside—

Penny.

Her apron was now faded, dulled to a wine color, stiff with old flour and dust. A braid still hung over one shoulder, sprigs of thyme caught in the plait, but it had dried brittle and gray-green. She was thinner, her cheeks hollowed, and her lips were cracked and pale. Her hands twitched against her thighs as if kneading dough in some dream she couldn't wake from.

Her eyes were open but glassy, pupils drowned wide. A hum slipped from her throat: soft, tuneless, and endless.

One note.

Like a song only meant to keep her alive.

Maren's chest locked. The scars across her ribs seemed to blaze hotter, too tight for her lungs. She reached for the bars, metal cool against her fingers, though her body burned.

"Penny."

No answer. The hum droned on.

Her pulse slammed harder, panic rising sharply in her throat. The Court had gilded her bright, beautiful friend and set her to wilt like decoration. A sunbeam caged and left to wither.

Maren's vision blurred. Horror swelled sharply, breaking through the stone wall she had built around her heart since losing her parents. Cold fury couldn't save her here. This was Penny, and she looked already half-devoured.

Maren pressed her forehead to the gold, nails scraping. "Penny, it's me."

Nothing changed. Not the hum, not the glass of her eyes.

She felt the bastard's presence at her back, coin whispering lazy, his grin stretching cruel. And in that moment, stone-hard fury cracked into raw panic.

Because what if Penny was already gone?

Maren's throat burned. She gripped the gilded bars until her knuckles blanched. "Penny, look at me."

The hum went on, steady as a whetstone, pupils wide and unblinking. No flicker of recognition. No spark.

Maren's breath came sharp. She slammed her palm against the bars. "Penny!"

The sound echoed too loudly in the chamber. For a heartbeat, it seemed to swallow even the hum. But Penny's mouth only parted again, the same note spilling out, endless.

Behind her, the thief sighed. Not bored, but *amused*.

"You mortals do dream cages so beautifully," he murmured. The coin clicked once against his knuckle, a soft chime swallowed by the room.

Penny faltered. The hum stuttered, caught in her throat, then broke into silence.

Maren's breath hitched. "Penny?"

Blink. Slow, dry. Another blink. Her glassy gaze cleared by fractions, like frost melting from a pane. Her lips trembled, and the sound that came out wasn't a hum but a whisper.

"...Maren?"

Her knees buckled. Relief and devastation slammed through her ribs, molten-hot. She pressed closer to the bars, tears blurring the faint glow of her scars. "It's me. I'm here. I'm here."

Penny's eyes darted, wet now, confusion laced with dawning horror. She pressed forward until her forehead met the gilt between them. "You... you came back."

Maren choked on a sob. She caught Penny's fingers through the narrow space, thin and cold, clinging tight. "Always."

Penny's grip trembled, but it held. Her breath shuddered, as if speaking cost her more than singing had. "Mar," she whispered, voice breaking on the old nickname. "I dreamed of you."

The word split something open inside Maren. She pressed her forehead to the bars, salt burning her eyes. She hadn't been Mar in weeks. She hadn't been that girl since the fire, since the maze. Hearing it now was like being dragged back into herself, only to realize she no longer fit.

"What did you dream?" she rasped, though she wasn't sure she wanted the answer.

Penny's lips quirked, weak but still sunshine trying to break through the storm. "The bakery. Our bakery." Her thumb brushed over Maren's knuckle through the bar, small and reverent. "I kept sweeping the flour from the floors, but it never stayed clean. You scowled at me for fussing, then stole half the loaves off the rack before they cooled."

Maren's throat closed.

"I saw rosemary sprigs over the door," Penny went on, her eyes shining now. "I saw children pressing their noses to the window to watch us bake. I saw you swearing at the oven when it smoked, and me running for water."

Her voice cracked, then steadied, bright with a desperate joy. "I dreamed it until it felt real, Mar. Like we already built it. Like we already lived it."

Maren's body shook. She wanted to believe it. Gods, she wanted to crawl through the bars and fold herself into that impossible warmth. But the scars across her ribs burned hot, sharp reminders. "Penny…"

"You don't know what it was like," Penny whispered, tears slipping now. "Stuck in that song, waiting. Dreaming was the only way I remembered myself. And every dream, every one, was you. Us."

Maren broke. She wept against the bars, her shoulders hitching, her hands clutching Penny's as if she could stop time by sheer force. She had survived fire, madness, loss of self. But this: this gentleness, was what undid her.

"You'd be happier without me," Maren whispered hoarsely, half to convince herself, half to break the tether before it strangled her. "You don't need me to build that bakery. You'll make it brighter without me weighing you down."

Penny shook her head fiercely, braid fraying, thyme scattering like brittle leaves. "No. It was never going to be just mine, Mar. It was always ours." Her tears slipped through the bars to wet Maren's wrist. "I don't want the bread without your homicide in it."

Maren cried harder, grief hollowing her chest. The labyrinth had shown her a Penny who thrived without her, who smiled brighter without chains of chaos and fire-scarred friends. She had clung to that vision like proof she could let go. But here, through the bars, Penny dreamed of her. *Always* her.

The weight of it tore her open, made every choice ahead bleed raw.

Penny's fingers trembled against hers, thin and desperate, anchoring Maren to the bars. She would have stayed there forever, forehead pressed to gilt, tears wetting Penny's skin, if not for the voice curling from the shadows.

"Sweet," the bastard drawled, velvet rich, "but you do make such tragic lovers' vows in unfortunate venues."

Maren froze. Penny stiffened, eyes darting past her shoulder.

The bastard stepped closer, coin whispering between his fingers. The lamplight gilded his sharp features, ink-black hair tousled, mouth curved in a grin. He prowled toward them.

"Tell me, darling," he purred, gaze sliding over her hunched frame at the cage. "How many mortals weep like this for their anchors? Whisper promises through bars?" He leaned closer, voice dropping until it slithered hot along her ear. "Or is it only you who makes despair look so… desirable?"

Maren's back went rigid. She pushed to her feet, but Penny still clung to her hand, confused, frightened.

"Stop," Maren said, raw.

He ignored her, eyes glittering, grin sharp. "Don't look so scandalized. It's a compliment. Your tears shine brighter than your little bakery's ovens ever did." His coin flashed once, catching Penny's wide stare. "No wonder the Court can't stop watching."

Penny gasped, horrified. "Maren…"

Maren's pulse thundered. She turned fully to face him, shoulders squared. "You don't get to—"

"Oh, I think I do." He stepped closer, the cage's glow brushing his jaw, his breath skimming hers. "You've never looked more alive than now, in my shirt, clawing for a girl you'll never keep."

Heat seared her throat, fury licking higher.

He tilted his head, fox-sharp, savoring her reaction. "Does she know how close you've come to burning for me? Or should I paint it for her?" He mimed a brushstroke in the air with two fingers, his grin slowly widening. "Her Mar, wrapped in Mischief, begging to be ruined."

Penny made a strangled sound, eyes wide with horror.

Maren's fist moved before her mind caught up.

Knuckles met bone with a sound too sharp to be flesh alone, like striking flint against steel. The impact jolted up her arm, rattled her shoulder, and cracked through her ribs. The bastard's head snapped sideways, ink-black hair flying, coin slipping from his fingers in a flash of silver.

For a heartbeat, silence reigned.

Then he straightened. Slowly. Deliberately. Blood slicked the corner of his mouth, a ruby smear against a grin that hadn't faltered. His golden eyes gleamed molten, bright with something worse than rage: *delight*.

"Gods," he said, voice roughened with the hit, wicked with laughter. "I could kiss you."

Maren's chest heaved, breath ragged, fist still trembling from the blow. She wanted to swing again. She wanted to claw his grin off his face. She wanted—

She didn't know what she wanted, only that the fire in her blood had found its target and refused to let go.

He leaned into it. Literally. Tilting his jaw back toward her, his cheek swelling faintly where her knuckles had landed. "Is that all?" His voice dipped to a taunt; velvet wrapped in barbed wire. "One spark, and you think you can burn Mischief?"

Her pulse roared, drowning thought. "Try me."

Behind her, Penny's gasp tore the air open. "Maren—" Her voice cracked, horrified. "...what did they do to you?"

Maren froze.

Penny's hands were trembling. Her wide eyes darted from the faintly glowing constellations seared across Maren's skin to her balled fist, then to the Spirit she had just struck; a being no mortal should have dared touch. "You're... glowing. You're not just snarky and surviving anymore. You just punched him like—like—" Her throat bobbed. "Like you're not even human."

Maren's stomach dropped, fury and grief tangling until she didn't know where one ended and the other began.

The bastard licked the blood from his lip, slow, savoring. He leaned closer, bracing his hand on the cage so his body blocked every escape. "Not human," he agreed, eyes flicking between them, grin all sharp teeth. "Not baker. *Mine.*"

Maren swung again. He caught her wrist this time, grip steel and grin feral. The tension between them crackled electric: violence and want, indistinguishable from each other.

"Careful, darling," he murmured, voice low enough that Penny couldn't hear. "Every time you hit me, I fall a little harder."

Maren yanked free, chest heaving, eyes blazing silver-blue. Penny flinched at the sight, pressing her back against the bars.

"Mar," Penny whispered, voice trembling like the braid unraveling at her shoulder. Her hand clutched through the bars, catching at Maren's wrist as if sheer grip could drag her back. "Please. Look at you."

Maren's chest still heaved, scars pulsing faint light across her collarbone and ribs. She wrenched her wrist free from the Spirit's hold, but her fists stayed balled, ready to strike again.

Penny's eyes shimmered, wide and wet. "This isn't you. My Mar would have snapped something clever, rolled her eyes, called him a bastard, and gone back to her bread." Her voice broke on a sob. "She wouldn't have lit up like—like stars—like something I can't even recognize."

Maren's breath shuddered. She turned back to the bars, forehead pressing against cool gilt, shame burning alongside fury. "I didn't choose this."

"I know." Penny pressed forward, so close their foreheads nearly touched through the bars. Her tears wet the metal between them. "But you're still you. You're still the girl who bartered with Old Keld, who cursed every morning when the dough didn't rise, who swore she'd never leave me alone with the dough because I'd ruin it."

Maren let out a wet, fractured laugh. "You always did over-salt it."

Penny's lips quirked, just for a heartbeat. Then her face crumpled. "Come back to me. To us. To the life we were supposed to have." She reached up, fingertips brushing the glowing scars at Maren's throat as though she could wipe them clean. "Please, Mar. Remember your mother. Remember the bakery." Her voice cracked. "Don't let this place take it from you."

Maren's vision blurred, tears spilling unchecked now. The weight of her mother's legacy pressed hard against her ribs.

She hadn't told Penny yet. The choice. The doors.

Her voice came ragged, splintered. "They've given me a choice. One trial, alone, with no interference. If I succeed… we walk out together. If I fail… they keep me. Or, I can stay here in your place. And you go free."

Penny's breath caught, eyes widening with horror. "No." She shook her head so hard the thyme crumbled from her braid. "No, Maren. You can't just give yourself to them. You can't stay."

Maren swallowed hard. "I can't survive another trial. You don't know what it did to me. Fire, forgetting, the maze..." Her voice broke, sobs choking it. "I'm not whole anymore."

Penny's hand pressed hard against hers, desperate. "You're stronger. I can see it. You made it through, Mar. You can do it again." Tears streaked her cheeks, shining in the dim. "Please. For me. For us. Don't trade yourself away."

Maren shook her head, trembling. "I can't. I can't go back to who I was. I don't want to. You deserve the bakery. You deserve the legacy. You'll live a better life without me weighing you down."

Penny sobbed, shaking her head furiously. "No. It was never just mine. It was always ours. I dreamed of you, Mar. Every single night in this cage. Our bakery. Our laughter. Our life. I can't lose you."

Her voice dropped, breaking into a whisper: "Please. Please fight. Please come home."

Maren wept harder, forehead pressed to the bars, Penny's tears dripping against hers, their hands tangled tight. Her body shook with every sob, her fury spent and her grief laid bare.

Maren's sobs slowed, but they didn't stop. They came quieter now, deep tremors that shook through her ribs until her whole frame ached. Penny's hands clung through the bars, desperate, as if sheer grip could hold her together.

Maren raised her head at last. Her eyes burned red, swollen, silver-blue shining through the haze like fire beneath ash.

"I *can't*," she whispered.

Penny's lips parted. "Mar—"

"I can't go back." Maren's voice cracked sharply, then softened, each word trembling. "I've seen too much. Felt too much. Fire in my lungs, stars under my skin. If I walk out of here, I'll spend the rest of my life haunted. Baking bread while my hands ache for chaos. Measuring flour while my body remembers the taste of wonder."

Penny shook her head fiercely, tears spilling fast. "Then we'll bake and laugh and—"

"It won't be enough!" Maren's shout ripped through the chamber, her voice raw. She pressed her forehead to the bars again, eyes shut tight. "It will never be enough again. I'll rot wishing for more. I'll ruin us both."

Penny's sob wrenched out, high and broken. "You don't mean that. You're just scared. You're tired. Please, Mar. We can still—"

Maren lifted her head, tears cutting tracks down her cheeks, face etched with certainty even as it broke. "The labyrinth showed me. You don't need me. You thrive without me. You'll build the bakery brighter. You'll marry the bookbinder, fill the shelves with children's laughter, and keep my mother's legacy alive. You'll live." Her breath hitched hard, ribs seizing. "And I—" She swallowed, words tearing like glass in her throat. "I'll burn here, because I can't stop wanting."

Penny's hands slid higher, clutching Maren's face through the narrow gap, trembling hard. "No, no, no. You're my best friend, my sister, my everything. You can't just—" Her voice collapsed into sobs. "You can't just give yourself away."

Maren wept, leaning into Penny's touch as if to memorize it, to brand the shape of her hands against her skin. "I'm not giving myself away. I'm trusting you."

Penny froze, breath sharp.

Maren pressed harder against the bars, desperate, clinging. "I'm trusting you with her bread. With her legacy. With the dream we made together. Because I can't carry it anymore. But you can. You will."

Penny's tears fell fast, dripping onto Maren's wrists. "Don't do this. Please don't do this."

Maren broke again, sobbing into the bars. "I already have. The moment I begged for wonder, I traded everything else."

They fell silent, clinging tighter, foreheads pressed together through gilt. Their breaths hitched in the same rhythm, one breaking against the other.

Behind them, the soft whisper of silver rolled once, barely audible, just a flicker of sound as if a coin danced through fingers and then stilled.

Penny flinched, though her eyes stayed locked on Maren's. "Promise me something."

Maren's nails bit into the bars. "Anything."

"Don't let them take you away from me. Not completely. Even if you stay here… even if you burn." Penny's lips trembled. "Don't let me wake up one morning and not remember your spark."

Maren sobbed, clutching her tighter through the bars. "Then remember it now. Hold it. Braid it into your loaves. Keep me there."

Penny nodded, broken, still clutching. "I'll save you a seat at the table."

Maren kissed her fingers through the bars. Salt and thyme and gold. "And I'll save you in every star I light."

Another faint click behind them. A coin settling against a palm, as if sealing something.

Maren didn't turn. She couldn't.

32

The Hollow

Kipwick led her only so far.

Past the gilded cage, past the watchful doors that pressed inward like listening ears. When the corridors began to twist in on themselves, fox and mortal parted ways. His paw brushed her ankle once, whiskers twitching with something like blessing, then he melted into shadow.

That left only her and the bastard.

He did not speak at first. His coin whispered between his fingers, the sound soft, steady, the only measure of time in a place that warped it. Maren walked stiff, every muscle in her body still raw from Penny's tears, from her own. Her cheeks burned with salt. She tried to swallow it back, to press herself into stone again, but each step forward only made the hollow inside her larger.

"Where are we going?" Her voice rasped, brittle.

He didn't look at her when he answered. "A place I keep for when I've too much on my mind." His grin tilted sharply. "Which isn't often."

She almost scoffed, but the grief in her ribs weighed her down. He had been alive since the beginning of mischief. What could trouble him?

He held out a hand. Not demanding, just expectant. When she didn't take it, he curled his fingers around her wrist instead.

The world tilted.

Stone dissolved beneath her feet, corridors peeling away like shed skin. The Court's perfume of smoke and honey thinned, replaced by an air cool enough to sting her lungs. Her stomach lurched as if she had been pushed sideways through reality itself.

Then it steadied.

She stood beneath a sky that wasn't a sky. Stars spiraled in deliberate curls above them, slow as water beads sliding across glass. They shifted when she blinked, rearranging into new constellations the moment her eyes slipped. Green and gold and violet pulsed across the horizon like a living aurora. The ground beneath her looked stitched from shadow and light, luminous threads weaving through grass that bent toward her ankles as if it recognized her.

Maren gasped despite herself.

"The Unmade Hollow," he said, his voice almost ordinary, as if it were just another tavern. "Where stories go when they're half-forgotten. Or half-true."

She turned in place, curls whipping, eyes wide. Even her scars seemed to glow brighter here, catching stray starlight. The laugh that escaped her chest startled her. It scraped her throat raw, as if it had forgotten how.

"It's... beautiful."

Her chest ached with the thought: *Penny would've loved this.*

"Unstable," he corrected, though his gaze lingered not on the horizon, but on her. His grin curved, quiet, fox-sharp. "But yes. Beautiful."

She walked a few steps ahead, boots sinking into grass that shimmered like it had been embroidered with silver thread. The blades bent toward her when she passed, brushing her still-bare calves like they wanted to be noticed.

"Where stories come to die," she muttered, crouching to drag her fingers along a glinting seam in the ground. The light pulsed under her touch, too alive to be a grave. "Looks more like where the world coughed up its secrets."

His chuckle slid from his chest, dark and low. "Mortals do tend to mistake endings for messes. Your ruin at least looks deliberate."

She shot him a sidelong look, still crouched, curls falling into her eyes. "Says the one who spends eternity spinning coins, hoping no one notices he's alone."

His grin faltered for a breath, then returned, sharper. "Careful. Sound like that again and I'll start believing you want me."

She straightened, brushing starlight from her palms. "If I were flirting, you'd know."

"Oh?" He strolled closer, hands loose, coin vanishing somewhere in his sleeve. "And how would I know?"

"Because you'd smile less like a fox circling dinner and more like a man who still believed in something."

His laugh was low, genuine this time, like velvet torn. "Darling, I haven't been a fool in centuries."

She tilted her chin up at him, eyes bright despite the exhaustion dragging at her bones. "Everyone's a fool for something."

He arched a brow. "And you?"

The question cut deeper than she wanted. Her mouth snapped shut, throat raw. For a moment, she almost said nothing. Almost let silence keep her safe. But he was still watching, grin sharp, waiting like he knew the weight would make her speak.

She exhaled hard, smirk cracking. "Fine. A story for a story. You first."

He gave a mock bow, then leaned against a tree that flickered into a tower and back again. "Once, mortals whispered prayers to me at shrines. Mischief was sacred. Necessary. My name was painted on thresholds. 'Mischief that blesses. Mischief that breaks.' They fed me coin, wine, kisses, all to keep me pleased… I cared for none of it."

"Then why tell me?"

His grin curved, slow and wicked. "Because you'd look better kneeling than any priest they ever offered me."

She rolled her eyes and shoved his shoulder hard enough to make the tree behind him flicker. "That's not a story. That's you bragging."

"You wanted truth. Mischief does not lie."

That earned a scoff.

She sank cross-legged into the grass, fingers worrying at the silver-thread blades until they bent under her touch. Her throat felt scraped raw from everything she hadn't said. "You want a story? Fine. Nineteen years old, parents already gone, Penny not in the picture yet. I wrote my own obituary."

The Spirit stilled, grin faltering for the briefest beat before sharpening again. "Go on. I like funerals."

Her mouth tugged into a smirk, but her voice came thin. "Every day at the bakery, gossip came in faster than flour. Births, weddings, deaths. It was all anyone talked about, and I—" She cut herself off, jaw tight. "So I slipped a parchment under the chapel door. Said: 'Maren Greenbriar, town nuisance, perished tragically of boredom.'"

He laughed, sharp and delighted, golden eyes catching light. "Boredom. You picked the cruelest death. Fitting."

"The priest read it at Sunday mass. I had half the town weeping, and the other half wondering why the bakery still smelled like fresh rolls."

His grin sharpened, golden eyes gleaming. "And when they found you very much alive?"

She shrugged, mock-casual, though her hands twisted grass into knots. "I told them it was a resurrection. Clearly, the gods were so desperate for entertainment that they sent me back to keep ruining everyone's day."

He barked a laugh, head tipping back. "Of course. Even then, you made a spectacle of surviving."

"After that," she said, smirk curling, "no one looked twice when I mouthed off to customers. Or when I charged a lord extra for sweet buns. If they complained, I said, 'You're arguing with a ghost. Do you really want that on your conscience?'"

The Spirit prowled a step closer, grin all teeth. "So that's why you walk through my Court like it belongs to you. You've been haunting mortals all your life."

"Exactly." She leaned back on her hands, eyes glittering with challenge. "What's one more afterlife, bastard?"

He studied her a beat too long, grin quieter now, molten with something unreadable. "Convincing. Almost dangerous."

Her brows arched. "Almost?"

"Baker," he said at last, savoring it like he might bite.

She snapped back without missing a breath. "Thief."

His grin curled sharper. "Undoing."

Her pulse lurched, but her tongue stayed quick. "If I were your undoing, you wouldn't still be on your feet."

His laugh rolled low, dark velvet. He tipped his head, gaze gleaming. "Careful. Every threat from your mouth sounds like an invitation."

She pushed herself up from the grass and turned toward the pool. It shimmered just beyond them, still and glowing like liquid moonlight, each ripple catching starlight and scattering it in colors too bright to belong to water. Stones ringed its edge, pulsing faint warmth. The air above it smelled sharper, like rain hitting hot iron.

Maren tipped her chin toward it, smirk twitching. "Keep smirking, and I'll toss you in with the rest of the Hollow's mistakes."

He let out a low hum, closing the space until her pulse jumped. "Darling, you'd have to touch me first. Don't pretend you're not thinking about it."

Her eyes narrowed. "Don't tempt me."

He prowled nearer, close enough that his shadow brushed hers, close enough for the glow of the pool to climb the cut of his jaw. "You've been tempting me since you were in my bed."

She rolled her eyes, even as heat curled low in her stomach. "That was survival." Her throat tightened. "And you let me."

"That was a scandal," he corrected, grin widening. "And this—" he gestured to the pool, to the shimmer tracing her scars, to the Hollow bending toward her like it wanted her more than him, "this would be sacrilege. My favorite kind."

She folded her arms, smirk sharp. "So you admit I'd win?"

His laugh was low, dangerous, delicious. "You'd lose, darling. And you'd enjoy it."

Her breath hitched before she could stop it. The pool glimmered at the edge of her vision, every ripple promising consequence. And for the first time, she wondered which of them would drag the other under first.

The pool was too bright, too perfect. Maren hovered at its edge, arms folded, pretending the glow didn't tug at her like a dare.

"You'd hate it," she said, smirk twitching. "Bet it would muss your hair."

The Spirit's grin widened. "Try me."

She bent, plucked a pebble from the stones, and let it drop into the water. Ripples fanned out, catching stray constellations. "See? Even the Hollow wants me to."

He crouched low, his golden eyes catching the light, a predator's amusement sharp. "That wasn't throwing me in. That was foreplay."

Her cheeks heated, but she met him head-on. "For you, maybe. For me, it's just warming up."

"Darling, if you wanted me wet, you only had to ask."

Her jaw dropped, then snapped shut. "You're impossible."

"Unstoppable," he corrected, stepping close enough that his boots touched the shimmer of water. He tipped his head, fox-sharp, grin lazy. "So. Who goes in first? The baker with too much bravado? Or the spirit who invented it?"

She lifted her chin, pulse racing. "Easy answer." And before he could blink, she shoved.

The pool hissed when he fell, stars bending like they wanted him under. He came up waist-deep, his shirt clinging to his chest, his ink-black hair slicked wildly across his face. His grin was unscathed, devastating, as if she'd only baptized him into something worse.

"You'll pay for that," he promised, voice molten.

Maren had barely backed a step before his wet hand shot out, seizing her wrist. She yelped, tried to wrench free, but the glow lit her scars, betraying the hitch in her breath.

"Don't—" she warned.

He tugged.

She toppled forward with a shriek, water swallowing her whole. It burned cool, fizzing across her skin like being kissed everywhere at once. She came up spluttering, her curls plastered, her shirt clinging scandalously, and he was already laughing, his rich, low voice.

"You bastard!"

"Accurate." His grin sharpened as he wiped water from his mouth, eyes trailing over her with infuriating calm. "But admit it, you wanted in."

She shoved him hard. He didn't budge. She splashed instead, sending arcs of starlight against his chest. He only laughed harder.

"Stop looking at me like that," she snapped, though her lips betrayed a smile.

"Like what?"

"Like you won."

"Darling," he drawled, stalking closer through the waist-high glow, "I always win."

"Not this time." She lunged, but his hands locked around her waist, iron and heat both. The Hollow spun, stars fracturing above them, and in the next breath, she was pinned against him, water thrumming at her back. Too close. Too easy to forget the bars, Penny, everything.

Her breath caught. His grin lingered, but softer now, dangerous in a different way. "Careful," he murmured. "You play, you pay."

Maren lifted her chin, smirk wobbling but holding. "You sound awfully sure for someone dripping like a drowned cat."

His laugh was rich, devastating. "And yet," he said, fingers tightening just enough at her waist to remind her he could pull her under without effort, "you can't seem to stop looking."

Her stomach fluttered, and damn him for noticing. She forced her mouth to sharpen. "Maybe I'm picturing how satisfying it'll be to finally throw you under."

"Mm." He leaned closer, nose almost brushing hers. "Or maybe you're picturing something else entirely."

Her pulse slammed, water fizzing against her thighs. His grin stretched, fox-like. "Are you afraid, darling?"

"Of you?" she scoffed, though her voice shook.

"Of what happens," he murmured, lips brushing the space between breath and skin, "if you stop wasting energy pretending you hate me. Imagine what you'd do if you admitted it."

The words hit harder than his grip. Maren's breath caught, sharp. Because yes, she had been pretending. Pretending her heart didn't sprint toward him with every barb. Pretending she hadn't leaned into his bed like a coward seeking warmth. Pretending she hadn't searched for him in every shadow while Penny faded in her cage.

He waited, smile curved but quiet, a predator indulging prey with the illusion of choice.

Maren swallowed, fury and longing tangling hot in her chest. "Maybe," she said, voice low, "I'd rather prove you wrong."

"Then do."

The space between them collapsed.

His mouth claimed hers, searing and inexorable.

Their mouths met like a spark striking dry tinder: instant fire, crackling, impossible to smother. His lips curved into a grin even as he kissed her back, wicked and savoring, like he'd been waiting for this moment since the first insult she'd thrown his way. Her hands fisted in his soaked shirt, dragging him closer, refusing to let him set the pace.

His tongue teased at her mouth, coaxing rather than demanding, mischief even here. He kissed like he ruled: reckless, consuming, and shameless. Every movement was a claim, every grin was a threat disguised as pleasure.

And she answered in kind, biting back, taking as much as he gave.

Maren gasped against him, and he swallowed the sound whole, one hand sliding up her spine, fingers splaying hot against her bare skin beneath the shirt. The Hollow pulsed brighter, stars overhead flaring, as if it too leaned closer to watch.

Her knees buckled, and he caught her, laughter hot against her mouth. "Clumsy."

"Shut up," she muttered, dragging him back into another kiss.

This one was deeper, hungrier, a clash of teeth and breath that stole every ounce of air she had. She poured her fury into it, her grief, her longing, until she didn't know which was which. He met it all with equal heat, devouring her like mischief incarnate, but his hands on her waist trembled just enough to betray restraint.

The pool tipped beneath them. Starlight shifted, water pulling. In the frenzy of mouths and hands, balance broke.

They toppled under, the Hollow swallowing them whole. Cold light fizzed across her skin like a thousand sparks, tracing every scar like the Court itself was hungry to taste her.

She broke the surface with a gasp, water streaming down her face, hair plastered wild. He surfaced a breath later, grin wicked, dripping, eyes blazing.

"You kissed me into drowning," she gasped, half-accusation, half-confession.

"Darling," he purred, water dripping from his grin, "I haven't even started."

And then he kissed her again, harder, dragging her against him in the glowing water. She tasted starlight, felt her body melt into the rhythm of his mouth, his teeth grazing her lower lip in a promise that was equal parts threat and worship. Her thighs brushed his as they struggled for balance, the shirt clinging scandalously, leaving her almost bare in his arms.

It should have humiliated her. It should have terrified her.

Instead, Maren kissed him back, reckless, alive. For the first time since the Court swallowed her, she stopped fighting wonder. She wanted it. Wanted him.

Wanted too much.

The Hollow sang with it. Stars flared, water rippled outward in luminous rings, and trees flickered into towers of light. The place itself seemed to bend around their mouths.

He broke away just enough to rest his forehead against hers, grin crooked, breath ragged. "Unstable," he murmured, voice hoarse.

Her lips trembled, swollen, her chest aching with everything she'd lost and everything she wanted. "Beautiful," she whispered back.

33

Until Dusk

They spilled onto the bank in a tangle.

Grass bent flat beneath their dripping bodies. The Hollow itself seemed to ripple around them, shifted by the heat they'd poured into it. Stars spiraled tighter overhead, curling like smoke rings; the grass shimmered brighter where her bare calves brushed it, threads of silver tangling in her skin.

Maren lay flat on her back, breath sawing, curls plastered wet across her cheeks. The shirt clung indecently, her scars glowing faintly through the fabric, which had become sheer. She pressed her palms to her ribs as if she could hold her chest still. She couldn't.

Beside her, he stretched onto the grass like he owned it, grinning slowly and lazily, golden eyes gleaming with the arrogance of someone who had just stolen the world. His ink-black hair clung wild to his forehead, dripping star-water into the grass. He looked less like a spirit and more like a man born for ruin.

She turned her head and glared at him. "Don't look at me like that."

"Like what?" He rolled onto his side, propped his head on his hand, the picture of indolent amusement.

"Like you've won something."

"I have." His grin cut sharper, coin whispering between his fingers even here. "Until dusk, you're mine. And I intend to exploit every ounce of it."

The words slid hot down her spine, both promise and threat. She sat up too fast, water dripping down her thighs. "I need to change. I can't walk into judgment looking like… *this*."

His gaze tracked the shirt clinging to her, soaked and translucent. His laugh was low, velvet. "On the contrary, darling. Walk in like this and half the Court will collapse before the Arbiter says a word."

Maren's cheeks flamed. She shoved her curls back, half from fury, half from the heat crawling up her throat. "I'll need clothes."

"My room's open," he said, casual as if offering her tea, though his grin told her exactly what he pictured. "You seemed to like it there."

She turned away, fists tightening in the damp fabric, every nerve sparking with the memory of his mouth. He was right. She *had* liked it there. Too much.

She lowered herself back into the grass. The blades glowed faintly where her body pressed them flat, silver threads coiling upward like they wanted to hold her down. Her breath still stuttered, every inhale pulling the Hollow's charged air into her lungs until she swore it might set her blood alight.

The thief sprawled a few feet away, one arm behind his head, coin balanced on the other palm as if gravity had nothing to do with him. It spun lazily, gleam and shadow flashing across his knuckles, catching starlight as though the Hollow itself wanted to watch. He wasn't watching the coin.

He was watching her.

She hated that she knew it without looking.

Maren turned her face upwards. The stars above swirled in spirals too slow to see and yet too fast to feel real. Whole constellations bent, unhooked themselves, drifted apart, as if even the heavens couldn't keep their shapes straight here. She wondered what Penny would have thought. If her friend would have gasped, or pointed out the goat-shaped cluster, or laughed herself breathless at the sheer absurdity. Maren bit her tongue hard enough to sting. She wouldn't cry. Not now.

"It changes," he said suddenly, his voice rolling soft and dangerous across the grass. "The Hollow bends to what you bring it. Fury. Desire. Grief."

Her throat locked. She felt the ache of all three scrawled across her bones.

"Then it should have torn itself apart by now," she muttered.

His laugh was quiet, sharp at the edges. "It nearly has. You're a dangerous guest."

Her lips curled into something that wasn't quite a smile. "I'd rather be dangerous than pitiful."

The coin spun again, bright, then vanished between his fingers. "So you've proven."

The quiet stretched, heavy, almost unbearable. The stars swirled above like they were being pulled into some hidden drain. Her chest ached with it. For one brief moment, she wanted to say it aloud: *I don't want to leave. Not after this. Not after wonder tastes like this.*

Instead, she pressed her nails into her palms, hard enough to ground herself. "Don't look so pleased," she snapped, not turning her head. "You act like I kissed you because I had no other choice."

His grin curved against the silence, audible even if she didn't see it. "Didn't you?"

Her lips still burned from the memory of it, and she hated how easily she could replay the exact moment. She had leaned in first. Her. Not him.

He hadn't stolen it. He had waited.

The thought curdled in her chest, equal parts fury and want.

"You think I kissed you because I wanted to," she muttered, eyes on the shimmering pool. "But I didn't have a choice."

Grass hissed faintly as he rolled onto his side, propped on one elbow, grin slow and devastating. "You kissed me like someone who'd run out of weapons."

Her head snapped toward him, face burning. "Weapons?"

"Your wit. Your fury. Even your grief." His eyes caught on her mouth, wicked. "When those failed, you kissed me. Like surrender. And you enjoyed it."

Her pulse slammed, outrage tangling with want. "I didn't—"

"Oh, you did." His voice was silk over a blade, merciless. "You kissed me because you couldn't think of anything sharper."

Her throat closed around the denial. Damn him, damn his accuracy.

Because part of her knew it was true: her fury had bled dry, her grief had cracked her chest open, and he'd been there, smiling, waiting, a flame she couldn't stop herself from reaching for.

She spat the only defense she had left. "If that was surrender, then I hope you choke on it."

His grin widened, fox-sharp. "Choke me, then."

Her breath hitched. Heat crawled low and shameless through her belly, and she hated that he could see it in her face. She hated more that he liked seeing it.

Maren shoved upright, glaring down at him where he lounged, coin now idly flipping between his knuckles. "You're insufferable."

He leaned back on one elbow, all lazy provocation, golden eyes glowing like molten sun. "And you're still here."

Her hands balled into fists at her sides. "Because I have until dusk."

His grin curved slowly and devastatingly. "Until dusk, you're mine. And I intend to exploit every ounce of it." He rolled the coin across his knuckles, leaned closer, voice low. "Admit you want to stay, and I'll reward you properly."

Her stomach lurched at the double edge of the words: threat, promise, *and* temptation.

She forced a laugh, sharp as shattered glass. "That's your play? Bribe me with another kiss?"

"Darling," he murmured, leaning close enough that his breath brushed her ear, "I could bribe you with ruin, and you'd still come willingly."

Her breath faltered.

He smiled like he'd already won.

The coin winked once across his knuckles and vanished. He didn't reach for her, not yet. Just leaned back into the grass like a man entirely at ease, as if the Hollow itself had been spun into a net designed to catch her.

Maren stayed rigid, every nerve lit raw. She needed air, needed distance, needed to stop remembering the way his mouth had pulled hers open like it had been inevitable. Her shirt clung obscenely, water dripping down her bare thighs into the glowing threads of grass. The Hollow had grown brighter since their kiss, stars spiraling faster overhead, as if the whole place had tilted in response to the rush of her pulse.

She should have been cold. Instead, she burned.

"Dusk," she muttered, forcing the word past her lips. "I should change before then."

"Change," he echoed, tone smooth as poured wine. He rolled back onto his side, bracing on one elbow, close enough that her breath caught. "Into what? A ghost again?" His gaze skimmed deliberately down her soaked shirt, scars glowing faintly beneath. "Or something far less modest?"

Her stomach lurched. She snapped her head away, curls dripping into her face. "I meant clothes. Actual clothes."

"Mm." His grin curved. "And here I thought you were finally comfortable in mine."

Her hands fisted in the grass. "I can't face the Arbiter like this."

"You could," he said lazily, twirling the coin into existence again. It spun silver, reflecting light that painted her throat, her cheek, and the swell of her lip, still bitten from his kiss. "You'd silence every wager before the first decree. They'd all drown themselves just to look a little longer."

Her chest burned. "You're vile."

"And yet," he murmured, leaning close enough that his damp hair brushed her shoulder, "you're still damp with me."

The words slid under her skin, hot, dangerous. She should have risen. She should have shoved him away, gone dripping into the dusk to face whatever waited. Instead, she stayed. Her chest heaved with a laugh that never came. "You'd love that, wouldn't you? Me dressing in your clothes again."

His eyes glittered, gold molten bright. "Love?" His mouth curled wickedly. "No, darling. I'd worship."

The air caught in her throat. She hated that it thrilled her, hated that he could make the word sound like blasphemy and prayer in one breath. Penny's face flashed behind her eyes, the smell of rosemary and thyme, bars between their fingers. Guilt clawed sharply across her chest. What kind of monster kissed her captor? What kind of friend drowned in wonder while

Penny wasted in silence?

He laughed low, velvet rich. "Come. You want clothes? My room will do."

"I'm not staying in your room again."

"You already did." His grin widened, devastating. "And you didn't seem eager to leave. What was it you told yourself? Survival?"

Her jaw clenched so hard it ached. He was right, damn him. She had stayed. She had curled into his bed like a coward, and he had let her.

The Hollow shimmered with her silence. Grass bent toward her calves, bright and wanting. Stars overhead seemed to tangle, tugged by something she didn't understand.

Dusk pressed at the edges of her chest like a closing fist. A choice. Penny, or wonder. Duty, or this.

She swallowed hard. "It doesn't matter."

"Oh, but it does." He reached, slow, deliberate, and brushed a drop of water from her collarbone with the pad of his thumb. His fingers traced lower, brushing the glowing line of a scar. "It matters, darling. Even the Hollow thinks so. Look at it, unstable already. Beautiful because of you."

Her breath came sharp, traitorous. Heat coiled low and shameless. She should have shoved his hand away. Instead, she stayed still, rigid, her pulse battering her ribs.

His fingers skimmed lightly over her scars, pausing when they glowed faintly under his touch. "Chaos looks good on you," he murmured.

Maren froze. She should've shoved him away, but the Hollow itself seemed to lean with him, stars curling brighter above, the pool pulsing as if echoing her heartbeat.

Her chest ached. Penny's hands had been so cold. And here she was, burning under the touch of Penny's captor.

She swallowed hard. "Flattery? That's new. What's next, flowers? A serenade?"

He laughed, low and devastating. "If I sang, you'd beg me to stop. If I brought you flowers, you'd burn them. Kisses, though—" his grin sharpened, eyes wicked, "—you never waste those."

Her cheeks burned. She shifted back a fraction, nails digging crescents into her palms. "Keep talking like that, and you'll find out exactly how sharp my teeth are."

"Mm." His hand lingered against her side, not forcing, just resting there like a claim. "And you're still letting me touch you."

Her throat burned. Fury tangled with want until she couldn't tell the difference. "I need to change."

"And I've already told you," he purred, leaning so close his breath brushed the shell of her ear, "my room is open. Until dusk, you're mine. Let me prove how ruinous that can feel."

The words tangled hot in her stomach, twisted into something she couldn't name. Want. Fury. Guilt. *Wonder.*

Maren clenched her fists tighter, desperate for the ground to anchor her. She told herself she'd move; she'd snap something biting. Instead, she whispered, "You really think you could ruin me?"

His smile curved against her skin. "Darling, I already have."

Her chest fractured on the truth of it. He wasn't wrong; he never was when it mattered.

She shivered. He didn't miss it. His laugh curled smug and dangerous against her neck. Her nails dug deeper crescents into her palms. She hated him. She wanted him. She wanted the Hollow to stop spinning, wanted Penny's face to stop haunting her, wanted to stop tasting starlight on her lips. Dusk was coming, and the world would burn one way or another.

He pulled back, grin sharp enough to cut. "Come, little mortal. Let's see if you can walk through my Court wearing me before you've even decided whether you'll stay."

Her pulse slammed, equal parts horror and heat. And still she rose, dripping, unsteady, because the truth was simple and damning: she would follow him.

The Hollow bent with their steps, stars dragging downward until the sky collapsed like fabric torn from its seams. Grass hissed underfoot, silver threads snapping, and the shimmer of water curled upward into smoke. One blink, and the pool was gone. Another blink, and she stood before familiar walls that hadn't been walked to so much as conjured.

His room.

The door hadn't opened. It hadn't needed to. The Court folded around his whim.

Maren's stomach pitched. She hated how easily she could be carried from wonder to captivity with nothing but the flick of his intention. Hated more that part of her wanted to stay caught in it.

She crossed her arms tight over her chest. "You could have warned me."

He leaned against the bedframe, hair still dripping, coin whispering lazily between his fingers. "Where's the fun in warning?"

Her glare slipped lower against her will. Water had plastered his shirt to his chest, every line of muscle a provocation. He knew it. Smirked like he'd dressed for the occasion.

She forced her voice steady. "Clothes. Now."

He prowled closer, coin whispering across his knuckles. "Say please."

Her stomach twisted. "You're annoying."

"And you're wet," he said, devastatingly casual. He flicked the coin once. Fabric shimmered into existence on the bed: clean, soft clothes, dark skirts, and a blouse finer than anything she'd worn in Eldenwick. "For you. Mortal modesty, if you insist."

Maren snatched them up with a glare, backing toward the dressing screen. "Turn around."

He didn't move. "Why?"

"Because I said so."

"Mm." He tilted his head, golden eyes molten, grin fox-sharp. "You forget whose shirt you were writhing in five minutes ago."

Her breath caught hot in her throat. She ducked behind the screen, cursing him, herself, everything.

The blouse whispered softly over her damp skin, clinging faintly at her collar where water hadn't dried. Her scars glowed faintly beneath, constellations just visible. She tugged at the skirt harder than necessary, as though strangling fabric would strangle the thought of his mouth on hers.

His voice curled lazily over the screen. "Need I remind you how little you were wearing in that pool of starlight?"

Maren's fingers stilled, her cheeks scalding. "You're… vile."

"You're slow." His grin was audible. "Do hurry. I've only claimed you until dusk."

Her heart slammed against her ribs. The words landed like a hand at her throat, not cruel, but claiming. *Until dusk.* She yanked the skirt into place, stepped out, chin tipped high.

He was still lounging, coin spinning, gaze dragging over her in open appraisal. "Better." He smirked. "Though I admit I preferred the shirt."

"You would." She crossed her arms, but heat crawled up her throat at the way his eyes lingered. "What exactly do you think you've claimed?"

He rose in one fluid motion, closing the space between them until she could feel the warmth radiating from his damp skin. The coin danced between his fingers, then vanished like smoke. His grin hooked wickedly as he leaned down, voice a promise pressed to the shell of her ear.

"Until dusk," he murmured. "I claim your time. Your mouth. Every shiver you pretend not to feel."

Her breath caught. Fury and want tangled sharply in her chest. "You can't keep me."

His teeth flashed, devastating. "I don't need to. You'll stay. And when you do, I'll reward you properly."

She shoved at his chest, only half-heartedly. "You're insufferable."

He caught her wrist, brought her knuckles to his lips, brushing a kiss just faint enough to sting with restraint. "And yet you're still here."

Her pulse thundered. For one fleeting, damning heartbeat, she wanted dusk never to come.

Her throat tightened. Penny's voice, her plea through the bars, flickered at the edges of her memory. Duty clashed hard against the heat low in her belly, and for one brief second, Maren almost hated herself for wanting both.

He leaned closer, close enough that his breath teased her damp curls. Close enough that if she tilted up just slightly, his mouth would be on hers again.

Her chest heaved. The words tangled in her throat: *I don't want to leave.*
And then—
A rap on the chamber door.

34

Choose

A rap on the chamber door broke through the air like a blade. Maren jolted, breath caught high in her throat. His mouth was still close enough to brush hers if she leaned the smallest fraction, and for a heartbeat, she almost hated whoever had the gall to interrupt.

The bastard's grin soured sharply. "Perfect timing." He flicked the coin once, catching it lazily, but irritation clung to every line of him. His shirt still clung wet to his chest, hair ink-dark and disheveled, droplets trailing down his jaw. He looked like a scandal in progress, yet the knock had soured his appetite.

Another knock, firmer. Kipwick's muffled voice leaked through the door. "Summons."

The Spirit leaned back just enough to glance at her, molten eyes narrowing with amusement and something more complex. "You took too long behind that screen," he murmured, voice velvet over razors. "I could've peeled those wet things off you in half the time."

Her cheeks burned hot. "Shameless."

"Efficient," he corrected smoothly, grin fox-sharp. "Don't confuse the two."

Maren shoved past him, pulse hammering, but the heat low in her belly betrayed her. His words sank like claws: half-tease but also half-truth. He didn't move to open the door. He just watched her, coin sliding lazily across his knuckles, irritation still curling in the edges of his smile.

The door rattled again. Kipwick, more insistent now. "By the Arbiter's decree, both of you are required at once."

Maren pressed her nails into her palms, forcing composure, though her body still ached from his nearness. Dusk was closing in, her choice waiting like a blade, and the Court would not let her stall forever.

The Spirit sighed. He did not look hurried. He never did. He prowled to the door with predatory ease, coin winking once more between his fingers. "Come, darling. Time to parade your mortal ruin before the Court."

The corridors of the Court writhed with light. Obsidian dark as ink stretched underfoot, veined with gold that pulsed like veins under skin. Torches guttered sideways as if unsure which way gravity pointed, shadows bending toward her steps.

Maren's stomach knotted tighter with every pace. She told herself it was the Court of Chaos twisting around them, not her own chest tightening. But the thought of dusk, the choice waiting for her like a blade, gnawed until she wanted to double over.

Kipwick paced at her side, whiskers twitching, waistcoat a little more rumpled than usual. He glanced up at her, then at the dripping spirit beside her, then back again, expression caught somewhere between pity and amusement. "You know," he whispered loudly enough to echo, "I'm not saying I approve of what I just walked in on, but if you two want to keep… ah, writhing in his shirt, maybe do it when the Arbiter doesn't have the whole chamber waiting."

Maren's face burned hotter than the torches. She jerked her gaze away, but the bastard beside her only smirked wider, coin whispering across his knuckles.

"Careful, fox," he murmured, golden eyes cutting sidelong toward Kipwick. "Jealousy doesn't suit you."

Kipwick scoffed, tail lashing. "I'm not jealous. I'm nauseous." He twitched his whiskers with mock severity. "And you owe me a bottle for the trauma."

The Spirit's grin stretched sharp, but he said nothing more. His silence was almost worse, the way he prowled just behind her shoulder, shirt plastered damp against his chest, hair still tousled from the Hollow. He carried irritation like perfume, thick and intoxicating, every stride reminding her that he had been denied something he fully intended to collect later.

The Court seemed to notice. Its bones hummed. Balconies unfurled like petals above them; courtiers draped in smoke-bright silks leaned over to watch. Coins clinked, bets whispered sharp as knives. The walls themselves rippled faintly, as if leaning in to taste the tension.

Maren tried to keep her pace steady. Every instinct screamed to bolt, but there was nowhere to run, not from the Arbiter, not from Penny's cage, not from the gnawing truth in her chest.

Her scars burned faintly under the new blouse, constellations glowing through thin fabric. She pulled the skirt tighter around herself, as if modesty could stitch her back together. It didn't.

Kipwick's paw brushed her arm, grounding her for just a moment. "Chin up, star-girl. If you're doomed, at least doom with flair."

Maren almost laughed. Almost. The sound snagged in her throat, half a sob.

The Spirit leaned down just enough for his voice to curl hot against her ear. "Keep walking like that and they'll think you're eager for the gallows."

Her nails bit crescents into her palms. She didn't give him the satisfaction of a reply.

Ahead, the chamber doors yawned open, carved marble etched with spirals that pulsed faint gold.

Dusk was waiting.

Maren's boots rang against the floor as she crossed the threshold. She felt the sound in her ribs. A thousand eyes bent toward her, hungry, delighted at the mortal dragged back into the mouth of judgment.

And then she saw it.

Penny's cage had been pulled forward, set like a centerpiece in the chamber's glow. Gilded, terrible, every bar humming faint with light. Inside, Penny clutched the bars with thin fingers, apron smeared and wrinkled, eyes red from crying.

Alive. Awake. Desperate.

Maren's chest cinched so tight she thought she might crack open. She looked once, only once, before wrenching her gaze away. Because Penny's tears were worse than fire. Worse than the maze. Worse than every decree the Arbiter had ever flung.

She had survived trials that burned and hollowed, but this, the grief in Penny's eyes, twisted the knife deeper than any Court punishment.

A low ripple of laughter broke through the crowd, heads turning toward the Spirit sauntering in behind her. He didn't hurry. Didn't even look like he belonged to the same trial.

Shirt plastered scandalously to his chest, hair tousled like he'd just crawled from a storm and liked the attention. The coin flashed lazily across his knuckles, catching firelight, bending every gaze toward him.

He grinned wider, as if the chamber had been built for his entrance alone.

Maren stiffened, refusing to look at him. His presence prowled close, heat brushing the back of her neck, every coin flick loud enough to scrape her nerves raw.

The Arbiter's faceless form shifted on the dais, iron voice booming over the chamber's roar. *"Balance calls. Charges weigh. One mortal entered. One mortal must pay."*

The hush that followed pressed down heavy as stone.

The Arbiter's voice rang out:

"Door A: the mortal stays. The lamb goes free.

Door B: the mortal attempts the trial anew. Under Sight. With no interference."

The words echoed through the chamber, each syllable reverberating in her ribs.

And then the doors appeared.

The first, Door A, was tall, narrow, wrought of black metal shot through with veins of gold. Its surface shimmered with every coin flick in the room, rippling as though tossed into a bottomless pool. Flames licked faintly at the hinges, smoke bleeding from the seam. Behind it was a suggestion of torchlight and shadow, voices whispering, and eyes glinting hungry in the dark.

The second, Door B, was shaped of weathered oak, bound in iron bands. Its edges flickered with hearth light, faint smoke curling from the seam as if bread had just been pulled from an oven on the other side. The faint toll of a market bell echoed.

Maren's breath came sharp, shallow. Her scars flared faintly beneath her blouse, as though they recognized both paths and wanted to pull her in opposite directions. Her mother's bakery. Penny's laughter. Eldenwick. The Hollow's wonder. The Spirit's grin. Revels.

The chamber leaned in around her. Coins clinked, voices hissed bets, silk sleeves rustled. Every sound stacked on top of the next until her thoughts drowned under the weight.

She pressed her nails into her palms, grounding herself in pain, but the choice still loomed, pulsing bright and dreadful in the space between those two doors.

One life left behind. One life forever chained.

The Arbiter's faceless gaze bore down, voice grinding the silence flat.

"Decide."

Maren's scars prickled under her blouse, constellations burning faintly as if Chaos itself tried to claim her body, tugging her between the two paths. Her knees wavered, chest squeezed tight, breath scraping raw. It wasn't just choice; it was gravity, yanking her apart.

And then Penny's voice cracked through it.

"Mar—" Her hands clutched the gilded bars until her knuckles blanched, face streaked with tears. "You can do this. You survived fire. You survived that maze. You can survive again."

Her words broke, uneven, frantic. "We'll go home. Together."

Maren's chest locked.

Penny pressed closer to the bars, eyes wide, desperate, her voice raw with a hope that shook. "I'll take over the bakery if I have to. I don't care. You don't have to hate it anymore. I'll keep it. I'll keep everything. Just—" Her shoulders shook, thin frame rattling in the cage. "Just come back. That's all I want. You. Alive."

The plea tore through Maren worse than the Arbiter's decree. Worse than the Court's jeering hunger. Because it was Penny. Penny, who still believed there was a way back. Penny, who thought that survival was enough, that if they clawed out together, then everything else could be sorted later.

The chamber quieted. The Court tilted forward in their balconies, silks rustling, coins clinking softer now, wagers whispered in tones sharp with curiosity. They smelled blood, and hope, and wanted to see which one the mortal would bleed for.

On the dais, the Spirit sprawled across his throne as if he had written this script himself. His grin curved sharp as a blade's reflection, golden eyes fixed on Maren like the doors were nothing more than props to amuse him.

Maren's knees nearly buckled. Because for one sickening heartbeat, she wanted to believe Penny. That she could step through Door B, endure, and wake in flour dust again. That she could let Penny's hope be enough for both of them.

But the Hollow still sang in her veins. The taste of wonder still burned on her tongue. And the thief's shadow lingered at her back, golden eyes catching every tremor.

Maren's chest rose sharply, shallow. The oak door wavered with warm and familiar hearth light. Eldenwick. A return. A chance to hold her mother's legacy in flour-dusted palms again. She could almost feel the wooden counter beneath her hands, Penny humming at her side.

And yet, her throat closed around it.

The thought of stepping back into that life now, after fire and labyrinth, after wonder had seared her bones, felt like trying to fit her body into a child's dress. Too small. Too *suffocating*.

The black-gold door shimmered at her other side. Chaos. Fire. Wonder. Power. The promise of never going back to a world that had only ever half-seen her.

Penny's voice cracked the silence.

"Maren—look at me!" Her fingers clutched the bars, knuckles white. "We can go home. You and me. We'll start over."

Maren's chest twisted. Penny's braid was coming undone, apron smudged with grime. Her face was wet, streaked with tears, but her eyes still glowed with that same steady brightness that had always steadied Maren, too.

"You don't have to stay here!" Penny's voice rose higher, raw. "You survived. You can do it again. We'll go back. We'll laugh at this someday. Please just choose the door home."

The chamber leaned in, hushed, greedy.

Maren shut her eyes. She could almost believe it, the way Penny said it; like survival was inevitable, like home would still feel like home. But her scars burned bright under the blouse, glowing constellations, a reminder carved in her flesh: she was not the same girl who had walked into this place.

She felt him. The Spirit lounging on his throne, coin flashing lazily between his fingers. He said nothing. His presence pressed hot against her spine, every flick of that coin whispering like a promise, or a threat.

Penny's sob cut through her thoughts. "Don't let them keep you. You're stronger than this."

Maren's lips parted, but no sound came. Was she? She had clawed through fire, crawled from ash, staggered blind through a maze until she forgot her own name. She was alive, but not whole. And here, in this chamber, with those two doors gaping like jaws, she wasn't sure what strength even looked like anymore.

The oak door smelled of bread. The black-gold door smelled of starlight. Both made her sick with want.

Her mother's voice whispered in memory: *keep the ovens warm, keep the hearth fed.*

Her own voice whispered in rebellion: *I want wonder. I want more.*

Penny's hands rattled the bars. "Mar, please. Don't leave me like this. Don't let me walk out alone. You promised we'd always be together."

Her knees buckled. She gripped her skirts, grounding herself in the press of fabric, the sting of nails in her palms. Her head spun with too many wants, too many fears.

She thought of Penny's optimism, her hope, the way she believed Maren could survive anything. She thought of the bastard's grin, the way he had leaned close and said *until dusk,* as if time itself bent around his coin. She thought of Eldenwick, and how it might already be ash with Tideglass burning down the coast.

Her breath came fast, ragged. One step would decide everything.

She heard the soft clicking of the coin.

She didn't look. She was too tangled in the ache of Penny's voice, the way it pulled her like gravity. But she felt it, deep down, the world tilting minutely, the doors shimmering faintly, as though someone had pressed a thumb on the scale.

"Maren!" Penny's voice cracked again, frantic. "Door B! Please, you can come home with me. You'll hate yourself if you don't!"

Maren's throat tore with the words, raw and steady. "I can't."

The Court gasped. Penny sobbed, shaking the bars until her fingers bled. "No! You can! You're stronger than this!"

Maren stepped forward, knees trembling, eyes fixed on the black-gold door. "Door A."

The Arbiter's decree fell like iron on stone. "Door A chosen. The lamb goes free."

The cage dissolved with a shudder of light. Bars melted into air, scattering like dust motes caught in a draft. Penny stumbled forward, apron stained, braid half-fallen, eyes wide and wet.

"No." Her voice cracked so loud it echoed off the chamber walls. "No, no, no!"

Maren lunged instinctively, reaching for her, but the space between them had already grown into something impossible. Penny's hands clutched at nothing, still reaching for bars that were gone.

The Court roared its approval, silk sleeves clapping, coins showering down onto stone. They cheered like gamblers at a fight, delighted by ruin. The sound swelled so loud it made Maren's teeth ache.

But Penny's cry cut sharper, clean through the revelry.

"Mar!" Her scream shook the balconies. "You can't leave me! You can't!"

Maren's throat tore. She pressed forward until she was chest-to-chest with her, holding her face in both hands, tears burning down her own cheeks. "I'm not leaving you. I'm setting you free. You have to live for both of us."

Penny sobbed, ugly and raw, clutching Maren's wrists like she'd never let go. "I don't want freedom if it's without you."

Her body shook against Maren's, small and breakable in her arms. For a moment, Maren could almost believe they were back in the bakery, laughing as they stacked loaves too high, fighting to balance it all before it toppled. But here, in the Court's gilded teeth, there was no laughter. Only ruin.

Maren kissed her forehead hard, like sealing something into her skin. "Go. Please. You'll bake, you'll laugh, you'll have mornings and nights again. You'll have a life."

Penny shook her head frantically, tears slicking her cheeks. "Not without you. I can't—I can't—"

Her voice cracked so loud it silenced even the boldest bettors. A scream that made the chamber hold its breath, if only for a heartbeat.

Maren forced herself to let go, though every tendon in her body screamed not to. Her hands fell useless at her sides, fingers trembling. "You'll live," she whispered. "That's all that matters."

The Arbiter's faceless form shifted, unseen hands dragging Penny backward, away from her. Penny clawed the air, nails scraping sparks against nothing, sobbing Maren's name until her voice shredded into hoarse silence.

Maren stood frozen, scars glowing faint and terrible, her face wet with grief she hadn't shown since her parents' burial. The chamber erupted back into revelry, a feast of noise and hunger, but she heard none of it. Only the hollow absence where Penny's cry had lived.

The sound of Penny's last scream hadn't finished echoing when Maren's knees buckled.

Her body hit the marble floor hard enough to knock the breath from her lungs. The impact rang through the chamber; one hollow, human sound swallowed by the laughter still rolling through the balconies.

The Court was still clapping. Still cheering. Coins rained from upper tiers, chiming bright against stone. A thousand voices rose in delight at the mortal who had chosen ruin, as though it were a sport.

But Maren didn't hear them anymore.

Her palms flattened against the cold, slick surface of the floor. The same floor where she'd just stood clutching Penny. The same floor where she'd bartered her soul for wonder. It was too cold, too smooth, too alive. She could almost feel the Court's pulse under it, throbbing with her own.

A sound tore out of her throat, half sob, half something wordless and feral. It startled even her.

She folded in on herself, hands clutching her skirts, gasping as if she'd been stabbed. And in a way, she had been. Not by steel, but by the absence left in Penny's wake.

Images flooded her. Memories, but like bleeding, color and warmth spilling out of her all at once.

The bakery at dawn, windows fogged with steam. Penny's laugh as she knocked flour from Maren's hair. Mrs. Aldren scowling at flax seeds on the loaves. Goats bleating on cobblestones slick with rain. Old Keld at the market stall with his crooked smile and bent squash.

Her mother's voice, gentle: *A baker's first scar. Wear it like a badge.*

All of it came at once; the weight of living; the small, ordinary miracles she'd taken for granted. The feel of the sun on her arms as she kneaded dough. The smell of cinnamon and smoke. The ache in her hands after a long day, and the comfort that followed.

Gone.

All of it *gone*.

She had thought the Court had taken her body, her name, her laughter. She hadn't realized it would take her memories too, not by force, but by distance. That every recollection would unravel the further she stepped into wonder.

Her chest heaved, ribs tight, as if her lungs had been replaced with ash. Tears streaked down her cheeks, scalding trails that made her vision swim. She pressed a hand to her sternum, as if she could hold herself together by will alone.

Around her, the Court's joy crescendoed. Courtiers threw wine from upper tiers; laughter rained like broken glass. The chamber was alive, writhing with sound and color, feeding on the sight of her ruin.

Maren's fingers trembled against the stone. She looked at them, at her own hands, and saw flour dust that wasn't there. The pale ghosts of calluses from rolling dough. Her mother's ring missing from its place, lost somewhere between fire and shadow.

Her breath came short, sharp, ugly. The sobs broke through now, unstoppable, gasping. She tried to stifle them, but the effort only made them louder.

She bowed forward, forehead against the cold floor, shoulders shaking. It wasn't reverence. It was surrender. The kind that came when there was nothing left to fight for.

Her tears pooled on the white stone. The light shimmered under her palms, swallowing the salt, the grief, the remnants of who she had been.

She choked on a breath, a memory, a word. *Penny.*

And then more spilled: Eldenwick. Mother. Goat. Dawn.

Every name is a wound. Every memory is another thing slipping away.

She felt hollowed. Flayed. Remade.

When she finally lifted her head, her cheeks were wet and her throat raw. Her scars glowed faintly through her blouse; constellations pulsing slowly, like a heartbeat. Her breath caught at the sight of them. She looked unrecognizable. Not mortal, not goddess, just something that had been burned clean and left behind.

The laughter kept roaring above, oblivious.

She whispered to the floor, voice breaking on each word.

"I've baked nothing but ruin."

35

Work Proposal

The revel had rolled elsewhere.

Laughter bled down the corridor like spilled wine, distant and tinny, the kind of sound that made joy feel obscene. The chamber itself was empty now, save for one mortal girl folded on the floor and the slow drip of candle wax pooling beside her hand.

Maren hadn't moved. Her face was pressed against the cold stone, breath coming in shallow hiccups. The marble reflected her in fractured pieces: her blurred eyes, trembling mouth, scars glinting through the fabric of her blouse.

The torches burned low, guttering in the draft left by the departing crowd. Far off, music swelled from the ballroom; the bright, wild sort of tune that begged for feet and forgot the price they'd danced on.

"Star-girl."

The voice was soft, edged with the click of a cane. Kipwick paced in from the hall, whiskers singed at the ends, waistcoat dusted in glitter. He stopped a few paces away, ears flattening at the sight of her. "You're leaking saltwater on the Lord of Chaos' floors. Bad look. He'll charge extra for the stain."

Maren made a sound, half-laugh, half-choke. It hurt coming out.

Kipwick sighed and padded closer. "Honestly. You survive fire, a monster, a labyrinth, a lunatic deity, and this is what does you in? A *choice*?"

Her voice rasped raw. "It wasn't just a choice."

"I noticed," he said. "You looked like someone being digested."

She swiped at her cheeks, "They're all still celebrating."

"Of course they are. Court of Chaos loves a good tragedy. Especially when it comes dressed like you." He offered a paw, "Come on. Up you get."

She didn't move. The floor felt safer. Cold. Honest.

Kipwick tilted his head, eyes narrowing. "You planning to root here permanently? Because if so, I'll fetch a nice moss for cushioning."

A weak, wet laugh slipped out before she could stop it.

"There it is," he said, smug. "The sound of the living. Keep that up and they'll stop thinking you're a ghost."

He hooked his cane gently under her arm, levering her upright with more patience than grace. She swayed; he steadied her with a muttered curse. "Saints of mischief, you're heavier with sorrow than you look."

Maren wiped her face again, uselessly. "Where do I even go?"

"Your chamber. Preferably before someone decides to repurpose you as center decor." He started walking, tail flicking for her to follow. "Come on. I'll escort. I'm feeling charitable and marginally sober."

They crossed the empty hall. The echoes of laughter followed them like ghosts, bright, cruel things.

Kipwick glanced up at her, tone softer now. "You did what you thought you had to."

"I ruined everything."

He shrugged. "Then you're finally speaking the Court's language."

Her breath hitched, halfway between a sob and a snort.

He smiled faintly. "There. That's better. Cry on your own time, star-girl. No sense feeding the vultures."

By the time they reached her chamber door, the music had swelled again. The flutes were shrieking, glasses were breaking, and delight devouring its own echo. Kipwick rapped the door with his cane, the sound small against the noise of revelry.

"Wash the grief off, Maren," he said quietly. "Let the Court think you're untouchable."

She looked down at him, eyes rimmed red. "And if I'm not?"

He sighed, tipping his head. "Then fake it. Chaos loves a performance."

Her lips trembled, but she nodded.

When the door closed behind her, the noise of the Court dimmed to a distant roar, and for the first time since the choice, silence felt heavy enough to drown in.

The room smelled faintly of citrus and cedar, and in the far corner, the copper tub already waited: steam coiling lazily from its brim, perfumed with something floral and sweet. The Court of Chaos knew what she needed before she did. It always did.

Maren stared at the tub a long while before her legs moved. Her body felt foreign, bones borrowed, and skin too tight.

She climbed in fully clothed. The water hissed against fabric, swallowing her with instant heat. It burned at first, both purifying and punishing. She sank until it reached her collarbone, arms limp, hair fanning across the surface. The water lapped faintly, reflecting the candlelight in shivering halos.

For a moment, it was enough just to be submerged. The warmth dulled the ache in her chest. She closed her eyes, tried to pretend she was washing it all away: the Court, the choice, Penny's scream that still ricocheted inside her skull.

But the heat crept higher, seeping through the cloth until the fabric clung heavily and suffocatingly. The weight of it tipped from comfort to restraint.

Something in her snapped.

With a sudden, raw sound, half sob and half snarl, she grabbed at the blouse, ripping the seams down her shoulder. The fabric tore like paper. Buttons scattered across the tile, little silver echoes. She yanked at the skirt next, shoving it down under the water, furious at it, at herself, at the Court that kept deciding what she was allowed to feel.

When the last scrap of cloth slid away, the heat hit her skin directly, shocking, almost tender. Steam curled around her bare shoulders. She let out a shuddering breath and finally folded forward, arms braced on her knees.

The tears came quietly at first, sliding unnoticed down her face. Then harder.

Ugly.

Violent.

The kind that left her gulping air that didn't fill her lungs. She pressed a hand to her mouth to stifle the sound, but her body betrayed her, trembling with every sob.

The tub's surface quivered with it. The heat fogged the edges of the room until even the walls seemed to breathe with her grief.

She slid lower, desperate to hide the sound from herself. The water closed over her ears, muting everything.

For a heartbeat, it was peace. A dark, heavy, and final peace.

Then the memory hit.

The ship from the labyrinth, the freezing pull, the taste of salt and fear, the way her lungs had filled, and her vision had gone white. Her hands shot up before she thought, thrashing for the surface.

She broke through with a ragged gasp, coughing water, dragging air into her lungs like someone trying to relearn breathing.

And that was when she saw him.

He was already there, seated on the rim of the tub like he'd been waiting all along. Elbow braced on one knee, coin rolling idly between his fingers, shirt half open, finally dried from before.

Golden eyes caught the candlelight, molten and unreadable.

"Evening, darling," he said softly.

He watched her for a breath, gaze taking in the torn fabric she'd flung aside had settled in a heap by the wall, half-submerged, thread edges curling like singed petals.

The coin clicked once against copper, light skating over his knuckles.

"We were interrupted," he said, voice quiet. "I came to claim what I was owed."

Her throat worked. The words did not reach fury. Nothing reached fury. Everything inside her felt scraped clean, like a pan left too long in the fire. She was aware of heat on skin, of water lifting her hair, of breath that would not settle. The rest was dull hum.

"Until dusk," he added, almost idly. "You offered me that."

She stared at the far wall, past him, past the candle slumped in its brass lip. "I offered nothing." Her voice rasped. "I chose."

He considered that, coin stilling. "You did. And you bled for it." His eyes tracked a line of water along her collarbone. "Let me have the easy part."

He slid the coin into his pocket and leaned forward, palm braced on the rim near her knee. The tub creaked a protest. Steam rose between them, fragrant with the scent of orange peel and green. He kept his gaze on her face.

"May I?" he asked.

The word jarred. Consent, placed gently where she had expected command. Maren blinked hard, then gave the slightest nod.

He did not touch her first, where it would have been easy to take. He reached for the copper pitcher and dipped it into the water. He rose, moving to her side of the tub, and poured in a slow sheet over her scalp. Warmth slid through curls, along the nape of her neck, down the ridge of her spine.

His free hand gathered her hair, careful fingers combing until knots surrendered. The cadence was almost domestic. She hated that her eyes wanted to close.

"You ruin every outfit I gift you," he said, conversational. "Perhaps I should stop bothering with buttons."

"Perhaps you should stop bothering with me." The retort landed thin.

"Unlikely." He set the pitcher aside and used both hands, working through tangles with patient pressure. "You walked into my Court and made it look smaller than your hunger. I noticed."

Her mouth pulled, a ghost of bitter humor. "Your Court already ate me."

He slid thumbs to her temples, slow circle, then back into her hair. "It chewed. You lived. Different verbs."

The tenderness of it confused her more than any wickedness. He should have been knives. He was a blur of suds and steam, the weight of his knee against the rim for balance. When his fingers found the small scar behind her right ear, he paused just long enough to say, softer, "Here too."

She boxed an arm around her chest, not from modesty but to keep the ache from spilling out again. "What do you want, really?"

"Quiet," he said. He gathered her hair, wrung water through his fist. "And your attention while I speak."

"To what?"

"Work." A smile touched his mouth. Not kind. Not cruel. Interested.

"The Court needs a keeper of stories. Someone who decides how they're told. Someone unafraid to change the endings." He dipped the pitcher again and poured a finer stream along the curve of her neck. "The Arbiter tells and punishes. You revise. You always have. Margins on your storybooks. That false obituary when you were nineteen."

Then he grinned, small, less wolf and more secret. "Be useful to me. Be terrible to everyone else."

Steam prickled her lashes. "You made the Arbiter."

"I did." His fingers moved to the curve of her jaw. "Tools rust. Stories renew."

"So, you want a scribe."

"I want a knife that looks like a pen."

The tub hummed with the faint rattle of copper settling back to heat. He had shifted while he spoke. He sat now at the long side. His sleeves were rolled, forearms wet, veins dark under pale skin. He smelled like cedar and smoke and whatever lived between them.

Her scars pulsed faintly through the steam, constellations low on her ribs, thin lines at her hips. His gaze tracked them but never dropped. It felt like restraint and like calculation. Both fit him.

"You think I would sit beside you and bless your mischief," she said.

"I think you would sit beside me and break the right things." He reached for the soap, worked it into a lather, then set it down, empty hands returning to her hair. "You chose to stay. Let the choosing mean something."

"Penny will hate me."

"Penny will live." His tone did not shift. "That is the gift you bought. Take yours."

She wanted to argue. The words would not shape. The water's surface wobbled with a tiny quiver. He saw it and, for once, said nothing.

He drew her forward by the crown of her head, just enough to tip her toward his chest without forcing contact. The distance between their mouths was a breath, nothing more. He did not close it. He pressed a soft kiss to her temple, tasting the salt from the tears that still haunted her.

"Until dusk," he murmured. "I keep what is mine."

Heat crawled low and treacherous through her belly. She hated the way her body answered him. She hated the truth braided into the words. He had been the one to say them first. She had been the one to stay.

"What if I refuse your work?" she said.

"You will not," he said, simply. "It was always you. The Court already bends toward your wanting. Even the Hollow followed your emotion."

"Do not make me a god."

"I will not." He eased a hand to the back of her neck and pressed a slow circle that sent a line of warmth down her spine. "I will make you necessary."

Her eyes closed. The candles hissed. On a table by the hearth, a stack of books that had not been there when she entered thumped into being. Familiar spines. Thumbed corners. The ones she had stolen from the chapel shelf and scribbled in by lamplight.

She stared at them, stunned. "Those are mine."

He did not look at the books. He watched her see them.

"You pry," she said.

"I collect." He tipped her head back, rinsed with care, and kept his touch steady when her breath snagged. "You rewrote endings that did not serve. Do it again. For me."

"For you," she repeated, dry.

"For us," he corrected. The word sat in the air like a baited hook. "Say yes, and I will give you what no mortal has been given since they painted my name on thresholds."

She went still. "Your name."

His smile thinned. "You wanted it. You still do."

She stared at the ceiling. Candle smoke drew a crooked line across plaster, then vanished. Trust was a word that lived like a bruise inside her. He knew it. He pressed on it lightly, not to heal, only to remind.

"Not yet," he said, almost kind. "Earned things hold longer."

She swallowed. "And you think this is earning."

"I think this is you walking out of the tub and choosing a place at my side while the Court is full and hungry." His thumb grazed the faint scar at her collar. "I think you will like who you are when you do."

She laughed once, a broken sound that still had teeth. "You are very good at this."

"I am mischief," he said. "You knew that when you climbed into my bed."

Silence settled. Not peace. Something with an edge.

He leaned in, close enough that his breath warmed her mouth. "Until dusk."

Her pulse stuttered. She let herself lean the smallest amount, not a surrender, not a kiss. Something between.

"Help me out," she said.

He stood at once, hands braced, forearms tense. He did not look away when she rose, water breaking off her skin in bright sheets. He reached for a towel without being asked, wrapped it around her with an efficiency that felt like claim and like care.

The Court breathed on the other side of the door. The books waited. The candles guttered and held.

He tucked a wet curl behind her ear. "Work first. Rewards after."

"Villain," she said, softer now.

"Always," he answered, and offered his hand. "Come."

He guided her out of the steam as if escorting someone half-dreaming. The towel trailed behind her in a soft gold line, steam still rising from her skin. The books waited, a small crooked tower beside the hearth. He bent, plucked one from the pile, and thumbed its swollen spine.

The cover was one she knew, blue once, now gone gray from years in a flour-dusted shop. *Tales for Small Gods and Lost Children.* She'd read it under the counter when trade was slow, copying its endings into the margins when she disliked how they closed. Seeing it here made her heart stutter.

"Stolen. From the chapel shelf," she choked in disbelief.

He smiled, "You left it open to my favorite page."

He flipped it, slow, until the parchment breathed between his fingers. Ink glimmered where the candle caught it: a child's hand drawn in the act of stealing a coin from a god's table. Beneath it, the text, half faded: *the mischief spirit, unnamed, who blessed the thief and broke the altar.*

Her stomach twisted. "You knew this story?"

"I wrote this story." He touched the line where the ink had bled. "You rewrote it."

She blinked hard. "You were the god who lost the coin."

"I was the coin," he corrected. "Mortals always lose the right pieces."

He reached for another towel, draped it over her shoulders, tucking the edge just above the curve of her collarbone. The contact was maddeningly light. "Hold still," he said, though she wasn't moving.

He took a fresh garment from the air. Silk darker than wine, soft. The Court made things too fine for mortals to earn.

"Arms," he murmured.

When she hesitated, he laughed under his breath, not cruelly. "You ruin every outfit, and I keep supplying them. There's a lesson buried in that."

"Don't tempt me to find it," she muttered, but she lifted her arms. He drew the fabric over her shoulders, the brush of his knuckles tracing a path of heat up her neck. The silk clung to the damp at her spine; he smoothed it there, fingers flat, deliberate, neither shy nor greedy.

"There," he said. "Less ghost. More legend."

"I don't feel like either."

"You feel," he said. "That's the start."

She turned toward the books, toward *Tales for Small Gods*, still open on the table. The smell of wet parchment hit her: salt, dust, the faint metallic tang of ink.

"Why show me this?"

"Because it remembers what names forget." He moved behind her, his breath warm against the damp crown of her head. "Every myth leaves a door cracked. You just need to read between the lines."

His hand slid past her shoulder, resting lightly on the page. The text shifted as she watched, letters bending like metal in heat. Hidden beneath the printed words, faint and older, another script glowed through. Her pulse jumped.

"What is it?" she whispered.

"The part your priests erased." His voice was low enough to vibrate against her spine. "The name they stopped painting on their thresholds when they grew tired of chaos."

She stared as the letters aligned, black over black, until they formed a single word.

Sevryn.

The sound of it in her mind made the air tilt. The candles bowed their flames inward, as if listening.

He leaned close, mouth near her ear. "Say it."

She almost couldn't. Her lips parted anyway. *"Sevryn."*

The room breathed. The copper tub rippled behind them; the window fogged over.

He smiled, and the expression was half triumph, half relief. "There. You found it where it's always lived. Between lines. Between breaths."

Her throat felt scraped raw. "Why give it to me?"

"Because you already hold the rest." His fingers traced the inside of her wrist, where her pulse stuttered. "Because a Story Keeper needs the story's true name."

She turned to face him fully. He was close enough that she could see each droplet of water still clinging to the hollow of his throat. His eyes burned like coins in candlelight.

"What happens now?" she asked.

He tilted his head, a grin curving slowly and dangerously. "Now you decide what you'll write with it."

Her breath shook. "And if I write wrong?"

"Then we'll rewrite together," he said, and brushed the damp curl at her temple back into place, gentle as promise, wicked as invitation.

The candles guttered low. She should have sent him away. Instead, she let him stay; one lie of comfort between dusk and dawn.

36

Adornment

She woke to warmth.

The slow, drowsy kind that lives in another body. Silk tangled around her legs; her cheek rested against the smooth plane of his chest. His skin still carried his signature, intoxicating scent.

For a moment, she didn't move. The world outside their chamber hummed with distant revel: with laughter, clinking glasses, and the endless song of Chaos, but here it was quiet. His thumb traced slow circles on her hip through the thin silk, an idle rhythm that felt almost human.

"Still breathing?" he murmured.

Maren's eyes opened to the curve of his grin above her. "Unfortunately for you."

"Tragic." His voice was a low drag of amusement. "I was beginning to enjoy our domestic phase."

She pushed herself up on one elbow. "We don't have a phase."

He caught a curl of her hair between his fingers, twisting it lazily. "We have mornings. That's a phase."

She tried to pull away; he didn't let her. The motion only drew her closer, her knees brushing his thigh. His lips found the hollow beneath her ear, a slow press that turned to a kiss, then another, a trail up the curve of her throat.

"Stop," she said, breath unsteady.

"You don't sound certain." His mouth curved against her skin. "I could spend the day proving you wrong."

"Could," she echoed, "but shouldn't."

He laughed softly, the sound rumbling through her ribs where their bodies met. "Mortal logic. You've been corrupted by routine."

"By sleep," she corrected, though her head tilted despite herself, granting him another inch.

He kissed that inch. "Sleep later. The Court's waiting to meet its new Story Keeper."

Her pulse jumped. "They know?"

"They suspect." He drew back just far enough to look at her, golden eyes still dark from the night. "You'll want to look the part when I confirm it."

She blinked, still half caught in the haze of touch. "You could at least let me wake properly before parading me."

"That was the plan." His grin was wicked, tender at the edges. "You woke too soon."

He brushed his thumb across her lower lip; it lingered, and her breath faltered. "You're insufferable," she whispered.

"I'm inevitable." He kissed the corner of her mouth, gentle enough to feel like mercy, then sat up, stretching. The movement sent a scatter of light across the sheets; the gold in his eyes caught it, bright as the coin that never left his hand.

She watched him, drowsy and conflicted, wondering how ruin could look so much like grace.

He glanced back, smile sharpening. "Get dressed, darling. The Court grows impatient, and if we stay in this bed another minute, I'll make us both late for the next catastrophe."

"Threat or promise?"

"Both."

Maren sat there a moment longer, fingertips brushing the places his mouth had been. For the first time since fire and maze and grief, her heart didn't hurt. It beat: steady, foolish, and believing.

A flick of his wrist, and silk shimmered into existence at the edge of the bed. A deep red threaded with gold, regal, fine enough to make her pulse stutter.

"Wear that," he said, lounging against the bedpost as if he'd been waiting for her reaction. "The Court's still celebrating you. It's terribly impolite not to attend your own legend."

Maren groaned, dragging a hand down her face. "It's still going?"

"It's Chaos," he said with mock solemnity. "We don't stop until something breaks."

"Then I'd hate to disappoint," she muttered, snatching the dress.

He grinned. "You'd hate to, yes. But you never quite manage it."

Maren turned her back to him as she pulled the gown on, but she could feel his gaze tracing every movement; an awareness that prickled like heat along her spine. The silk clung cool and heavy to her skin.

His reflection appeared in the mirror before she saw him: golden eyes, tousled black hair, the half-smile of someone who'd always been standing too close.

He held a thin chain between his fingers. "You forgot this."

She frowned. "I don't—"

He stepped closer, looping it around her throat before she could protest. The metal was warm, pulsing faintly. In the mirror, she caught a glimpse of the pendant: a single coin, smaller than his, etched with something she couldn't quite read.

"What is it?" she asked, voice low.

"Adornment." His tone was almost gentle. "Every Story Keeper should have one."

"Is that what I am now?"

"You'll see soon enough." His breath brushed the back of her neck as he fastened the clasp. His fingers lingered there, tracing the curve of her skin, until her reflection blurred with the rush of her own pulse.

"Careful," she said softly. "You're going to make people think you like me."

"I do like you," he murmured. "You're chaos pretending to be order. My favorite kind of lie."

Her mouth twitched into something that wasn't quite a smile. "You sound awfully sure of yourself."

"Would you rather I sound nervous?"

"Yes."

He laughed, low and genuine. "Impossible. It's difficult not to be pleased when the story's going exactly to plan."

The words caught at her, faintly wrong, like a snag in silk. "Your plan?"

"Our plan," he corrected instantly, meeting her eyes in the mirror. His grin softened just enough to look like sincerity. "You survive, you stay, you rule. That's the story, isn't it?"

She wanted to argue, to point out that she hadn't agreed to any of this, but his hands were still at her neck, and his reflection was all heat and golden light. The air between them pulsed with that familiar, dangerous pull.

"Ready?" he asked, voice dipping low, almost tender.

"For what?"

He smiled. "For the world to kneel."

The doors swung open on a storm of light and sound.

The revel had not stopped, but it had evolved. It grew larger, louder, hungrier.

A thousand chandeliers hung from invisible ceilings, swaying like glass fruit on unseen branches. Petals of fire drifted through the air, never burning, only scenting the room with smoke and something sweeter: wine, maybe, or *madness*.

Music writhed through the space, too complex to follow, woven of heartbeat and laughter. Dancers spun barefoot across the marble, their feet leaving trails of color that melted and reformed into new shapes.

The Court of Chaos was a living thing, its beauty always one breath from collapse.

Maren stopped just inside the threshold. The noise, the color, the heat; it pressed against her like the inside of a fever dream. She had seen the Court before, but never like this. It was intoxicating. *Terrifying*.

Beside her, Sevryn looked perfectly at home.

He caught her hesitation and smiled, that slow, dangerous curl of a mouth that had ruined a thousand promises. "Breathe, darling. They're applauding you."

She blinked. He was right. The room had shifted. Heads turned, conversations faltered. Whispers rippled outward like shock waves, carrying her name on their tongues: *Star-blessed. Fire-girl. Mortal chaos.*

Her pulse stuttered. She wanted to shrink back into the shadows, but Sevryn's hand settled at the small of her back: light, possessive, and steadying.

"Walk," he murmured. "They should see what wonder looks like when it refuses to die."

She did. Her skirts whispered over the marble, catching light with every step. Nobles and courtiers parted to make way, bowing or smirking or simply staring. She had never been more aware of her own heartbeat.

A blur of rust-red braids and tabby ears caught her eye. Her heart warmed a fraction at the sight. Tamsin, perched on the back of a floating settee, licking what suspiciously looked like icing off his thumb.

The dais waited at the far end of the hall, carved from marble that reflected everything except truth. Above it, the constellations on the ceiling shifted restlessly, like they, too, wanted to see what came next.

When they reached the steps, Sevryn released her only long enough to flick the coin across his knuckles. The crowd hushed instantly, drawn by the gleam.

"Beloved chaos," he said, his voice carrying easily through the hall. "We have new stories to tell."

Laughter and applause answered him, wild and eager.

Maren's stomach twisted.

He turned toward her, holding out a hand like a gentleman at the end of a dance. "Come."

She hesitated only a moment before taking it. His fingers closed around hers. Together they stepped onto the dais.

The marble beneath their feet shuddered, once, twice, and then flared with light. The revel's music faltered.

The Arbiter's form shimmered into existence above the dais. Its faceless head bowed low, voice echoing through the hall like the toll of a great bell.

"Spirit of Mischief," it intoned. *"Balance is not yours to command."*

The crowd gasped, delighted. Conflict was better than song here.

Sevryn only smiled. "Then whose is it?"

"Order's," the Arbiter said, its voice splitting the air. *"Not yours to unmake. Not hers to hold."*

Light fractured across the chamber, lines of gold and silver forming a cage around them. Maren staggered back, heart slamming. "Don't—"

But he had already flicked the coin.

It spun lazily upward, caught the light, and froze mid-air. The room bent toward it. Dancers stopped mid-step, torches leaned. Even the stars above seemed to tilt their faces downward.

When the coin fell, it struck the dais, and the golden cage splintered.

The Arbiter staggered, its form flickering. "You cannot—"

"I can," Sevryn said softly. "And I have."

He caught the coin again, rolled it across his knuckles, and smiled like the universe had just told him a joke only he understood.

Maren stared as the Arbiter's light bled away, unraveling thread by thread until only smoke remained. The glow raced along the edges of the hall, taking with it the faint sense of boundaries she hadn't realized existed. The Court sighed in collective pleasure, like a beast being stroked.

In the sudden silence, Sevryn turned to her, still smiling. "There," he murmured, almost tender. "Balance restored. Order dismissed."

The room erupted into cheers. Glasses shattered. Fireworks bloomed from nowhere, bursting into colors that had no names.

Maren stood in the middle of it all, dizzy. She looked at the empty air where the Arbiter had been and then at the coin gleaming in Sevryn's hand. *What had he done?*

He leaned close, his breath warm against her ear. "Smile, darling. You're being worshiped."

Her lips trembled, but she managed a faint curve of a smile, the kind that could be mistaken for awe.

Applause crashed like thunder. The Court surged toward them, ribbons of light coiling through the air, and someone began to play a waltz too wild to have steps. Sevryn turned to her, palm outstretched in invitation.

"Dance with me," he said, voice low enough that only she could hear.

Maren hesitated. The place where the Arbiter had stood still shimmered faintly, an afterimage burned into her sight. The Court of Chaos, untethered and roaring, looked ready to swallow itself whole.

He didn't wait for an answer. His hand found her waist, guiding her into motion before her breath could catch.

The dance swept them into the revel's orbit. Dancers scattered like sparks around them, skirts flaring, hair aflame with light. Music pulsed under her skin; her pulse followed it helplessly. Sevryn's grin was bright and dangerous as ever.

"What did you just do?" she finally asked, voice barely a whisper between turns.

He spun her, caught her back against his chest. "I gave Chaos its teeth back."

The words slid into her ear like silk over knives.

She looked up at him, searching his face. The gold in his eyes caught the torchlight, molten, unreadable. "You destroyed the Arbiter."

"Destroyed?" He chuckled. "No, darling. I merely unmade my mistake."

Her steps faltered. "Your mistake?"

"Order," he said, as if the word itself were distasteful. "It was meant to leash Chaos when I tired of watching mortals crumble under it. But leashes chafe, even on gods."

He twirled her again, faster this time, until the room blurred and her breath came shallow. She could barely think over the whirl of light and sound. Still, her mind snagged on the glint between his fingers, the coin, rolling lazily across his knuckles even as he danced.

The coin.

The image of it spinning through torchlight burned behind her eyes. She remembered the book he'd shown her the night before, the myth of the mortal thief who'd stolen a coin from the gods, a coin that could rewrite intention itself. She had thought it was another story, one of the hundreds she hoarded. He had looked at her and said, *I was the coin.*

Her stomach turned cold.

Maren let him spin her again, forced her smile to match his, but her gaze caught the coin every time it flashed. Always in motion. Always turning.

"What does it do?" she asked, too softly for the Court to hear.

He laughed, a sound of pure pleasure, not mockery but triumph. "It listens," he said. "And obeys the will that deserves it most."

The Court around them howled approval. Firelight rained in curtains. The floor rippled like water beneath their feet, but Sevryn moved as though he'd written the rhythm into existence. He bent her backward in one smooth arc, his hand at her spine, his mouth so close she could feel the promise of another kiss.

"Smile," he whispered. "They're watching their Story Keeper learn her role."

Her heart pounded so violently she thought it might split her ribs. The revel's beauty pressed in, dizzying. The laughter, the smoke, the thousand colors shifting faster than she could name, but all she could see was that coin glinting between his fingers, carving the air with every flick.

Every story needs a hand to hold the pen.

That's what he'd said. She hadn't realized until now that he'd never specified whose hand.

Sevryn drew her upright again, their chests flush, their breaths tangled. Around them, the Court roared her name, chanting it like worship, like warning. He smiled down at her, and she felt the world tilt, not the floor this time, but something deeper.

The music swelled.

Maren met his eyes, gold swallowing gold, and for one impossible heartbeat, she thought: *Maybe this is how stories end. Not with peace, but with surrender.*

37

Wonder

The music didn't stop when the world started coming apart.

It only changed key.

The revel swelled, gilded and gorgeous, the chandeliers dripping molten light, violins screaming joy. Maren stood in the center of it: red silk, flushed cheeks, his hand at her waist.

They were still laughing, drinking, bowing before their glittering god.

Sevryn's thumb traced idle circles along her back. Warm. Familiar. *Lethal.*

The sound of it: the silk, the heartbeat, the music, fused into something *wrong.* A rhythm she recognized but couldn't name.

Her pulse.

The coin.

The faint, metallic click. It echoed through her bones as if her blood itself had been keeping time with him. Every spin she'd ever watched, each lazy flick, each arc of silver, was buried somewhere beneath her ribs.

She looked up at him. He smiled down like he'd been carved for it. Light caught his eyes and turned them molten. She thought, absurdly, that he looked almost human when he smiled like that.

Then the chandeliers wavered.

The room tilted, barely perceptible at first, like a ship listing to one side. Wine spilled across marble in delicate streams; color bled at the edges of faces. A dancer's laugh stretched too long, became a scream pitched as joy.

Her stomach lurched.

"Something's wrong," she murmured.

His hand tightened at her waist. "You're drunk on victory."

But she wasn't. The air itself was sick with sweetness, heavy enough to choke.

Everywhere she looked, silver. Silver in the chandeliers. Silver in the goblets. It bled from him, that same burnished hue that haunted every dream she'd had since Eldenwick.

And suddenly, she couldn't unsee it.

The color threaded back through her memory, bright and cold.

The coin glimmering in her bakery the night the thief came.

The coin flashed a sliver of moonlight as she first stepped into the Court.

The coin's glint as she burned in the fire.

The melody swelled around her, too bright to bear.

He brushed a curl from her face, tender as a lie. "Stay with me."

Her breath stuttered. She could smell him, cedar, citrus, smoke, the same as the day everything began. The scent that had followed her through every trial, every fall.

And she understood, in a quiet, slicing way, that it hadn't been following her at all.

It had been leading.

The chandeliers trembled. Petals of fire drifted from the ceiling, dissolving before they reached the floor. Her knees nearly buckled.

"You've been here before," he said softly, as if coaxing a memory.

A whisper inside her ribcage: Every step, every breath, every choice—

Her own voice, from this morning. "Our plan," he had said in her chamber, eyes bright in the mirror. She had laughed then.

She didn't now.

The truth crept up her spine like frost.

The music. The revel. The trials. The gifts. All of it spun from that same quiet rhythm. The rhythm of his coin, of his control.

Her wish for wonder had been granted too perfectly.

She looked at him, the man she'd almost loved, and saw only pattern. A design that stretched back through every impossible thing.

The air thickened, ringing with a hum she could no longer tell apart from her heartbeat. The chandeliers blurred into halos of molten gold.

Maren's lips parted, but the sound that came out wasn't a word. It was a breath caught on realization.

He leaned closer, smiling the same smile he'd worn the day she sold her soul.

"Dance with me," he said.

And she did, one step. Only one because her body hadn't caught up to the betrayal yet.

But the music had. It twisted, beautiful and dissonant, and in its broken rhythm she finally heard it for what it was: *a song written for her to break to.*

One step, two, her pulse syncing with the wrong rhythm.

Maren's gaze snagged on the chandeliers. Gold pooled down their arms, dripping light like wax. The air thickened, slow as syrup. Each violin note sliced thin, stretched too far, warping into echoes of memory. The coin's sound.

Always the coin.

She blinked, and the floor wasn't marble anymore. It was black glass. Her reflection stared up: mouth open, whispering things she couldn't hear. Silver light crawled under her skin, tracing the constellations he'd stitched there. Her scars burned cold.

And then came the flash.

A hand slick with blood, silver thread pulled through it. His voice: *Never.* Her own whimper answered it. The bakery dissolving in steam. The fever, the cot, his coin glinting between fingers, made gentle for the sake of cruelty.

She stumbled back into the revel. But her body didn't feel right. It moved as if strings tugged it.

Every blink was a different scene, stacked wrong.

The courtroom.

The coin, hung midair in its arc, refusing gravity, catching torchlight while the Arbiter's voice faltered.

The labyrinth mirrors swallowing her reflection. Hundreds of Marens screaming, "You wanted this."

The Unmade Hollow, the grass glinting silver, his coin spinning while he smiled and said, "Until dusk, you're mine."

Her mind flickered like candlelight in a wind. Each flash was a blade.

Her father rolling silver across his knuckles, eyes gold instead of brown. The scent of cedar and citrus wrapped around her as the copper tub steamed and the note burned, "Wear it. Indulge me. *I want them to see what I claimed.*"

He'd always been there. In every place she thought she'd stood alone.

The wish-fires.

The trials.

The laughter.

Her stomach heaved.

The revel blurred into heat and static. The dancers flickered like mirages, laughter skipping in place. The chandeliers swayed, spilling molten reflections across her dress until she looked like she was burning again.

Maren's hand shot to her throat. Her pulse was frantic, and not hers. It was his coin's rhythm. She felt it deep within her, the steady, merciless click of a decision.

"You're trembling." Sevryn's voice slid against her ear, low and amused.

She turned, face pale. "What have you done to me?"

His grin deepened, soft as sin. "Done? Darling, I've made you extraordinary."

The words split her. Something cracked behind her ribs; an awful sound she realized was her own breath breaking.

Flash.

Coral Head sneering, *She writhes in his bed while cities burn.*

Flash.

The Arbiter choking on its own decree.

Flash.

Her fist connecting with his jaw, the coin slipping from his fingers in a flare of silver as he whispered, *I could kiss you.*

Flash.

Penny's hands reaching through bars. *You're not even human.*

Each memory fell like a hammer, and she couldn't tell which hit harder: the lies or the tenderness?

The music stuttered again. Then stopped.

The Court froze mid-spin, marionettes caught in their bow. Only the torches breathed.

Sevryn's hand lingered at her waist, patient, unbothered. "Breathe," he murmured. "You're remembering out of order."

Her palm slammed against his chest. "You planned this."

He didn't flinch. "I granted it."

The sound that left her throat wasn't a scream. It was lower. Broken. A sound scraped from the bottom of something too human to be divine, too divine to be human.

Her knees almost gave, but the fury hit first: white-hot, precise.

Every flicker of silver in her vision coalesced into understanding.

The coin hadn't followed her. It had *written* her.

The baker. The survivor. The lover. Every version built by his hand, spun from her wish and sealed with his grin.

The chandeliers shattered.

The shards caught light midair, spinning. Tiny coins, every one of them.

And Maren, heart beating too loud for the silence that followed, realized the music had never been for the revel.

It was a dirge.

Her own.

Maren swayed, breath shuddering. Her reflection split across the shards: one face, then another, each flickering out of sync. One version still in the bakery apron. One with her trial burns. One crowned in gold light.

She didn't know which was her.

"When?" she whispered.

Sevryn cocked his head, coin dancing between his fingers again. "When what, darling?"

"When did you start rewriting me?" Her voice rose, raw. "Was it when I wished? When I died? When you pulled me out of the fire?"

He smiled, slow and catastrophic. "You make it sound so deliberate."

"Was it?"

He laughed. "Mortals are always so obsessed with timelines. As if knowing when helps them undo the thing. But you—" He stepped closer, coin flashing like a second heartbeat. "You were pliable from the start. I barely had to touch the thread."

Her stomach turned. "You used me."

"I refined you." His tone was silk drawn over razors. "Do you think you survived the fire by chance? You think Almost let you leave because of grit and cleverness? Every trial bowed for you because I told it to."

Her hands shook. "You told it—"

"—to love you," he finished, delighted by the horror blanching her face. "Even the maze. Even the fire. Everything wanted you, darling. I just… tuned it."

The words hit harder than any blow. She staggered a step back, but the floor bent with her. The Court had warped around them: the walls curving inward, dancers still frozen mid-bow.

"I don't even know what was real," she said.

He smiled wider. "That's the beauty of it. You don't need to."

Maren pressed her palms to her temples, nails digging crescent moons into her skin. "When did you stop being you?" she asked herself, but the question bled out loud. "When did I?"

"Somewhere between *want* and *wonder*, I'd guess." His voice dropped low, rich with mock sympathy. "You were quite poetic when you begged."

Her vision blurred with heat. "You bastard."

He grinned. "Your favorite word. Do you even remember learning it? Or did I put it in your mouth the night you tried to curse me and failed?"

Her knees went weak. She stumbled again; he caught her elbow before she could fall, as if the gesture were mercy.

"Don't touch me!" She tore free, breath rasping. "You made me—"

"Yes." His gold eyes flared. "I made you magnificent. A story worth burning a Court for."

Her throat burned. "You made me a puppet."

He tilted his head. "Strings are just structure. You wanted purpose, didn't you? All that kneading, all that small, mortal ache to matter. I gave you eternity instead."

She wanted to claw at him, to break the perfection of that grin. "I don't even know which parts of me are mine anymore!"

His grin sharpened to cruelty. "None worth keeping."

Something inside her cracked open. It wasn't tears, but laughter, brittle and wrong. "You enjoyed this," she said. "Every moment. Watching me think I had a choice."

"Oh, I adored it." He spread his hands, theatrically innocent. "You should have seen yourself. Brave little mortal, arguing with destiny, baking bread as if it meant anything. I almost envied you, believing you mattered."

She shook her head, whispering, "Stop."

"But you don't, Maren." His tone softened, almost tender. "That's what makes you exquisite. You're what happens when a wish learns it's hollow."

Her breath hitched. "You said you—"

"What?" He stepped closer, the air darkening with him. "That I cared? That I could love?" His grin flashed like a blade. "Spirits don't love. Different emotion. We *use*."

Her pulse slammed.

He leaned in until she felt the heat of his breath at her ear. "And gods, you were useful."

Her hand flew before she knew she'd moved. The slap cracked the still air. His head turned with the force of it, a curl of black hair falling into his eyes.

For a heartbeat, nothing.

Then he laughed. Low. Dangerous. The laugh of something that had never been human and had never wanted to be.

"You finally look like what I made," he said. "Ruin."

"Go to hell."

"Lead the way, darling," he said, and smiled like the world bowed to him.

Her vision swam. She couldn't tell where the marble ended and her own reflection began. The gold dust rose around them like smoke, curling into shapes: coins, eyes, her own hands trembling.

He reached into the air; the coin reappeared, bright as a wound. "Here's the trick, darling," he murmured, flipping it. "You think you want answers. But what you want is control. That's always how mortals break."

The coin spun, bright and endless.

Maren stared at it, the glint refracting across her eyes. "When did I stop being me?" she whispered.

Sevryn smiled. "You didn't stop. You *changed hands.*"

She couldn't breathe. The gold dust hung thick as fog, and every inhale tasted like him.

Her pulse thrashed under her skin, a wild, traitorous drum. She wanted to claw her chest open just to see if there was a coin spinning inside.

He watched her, lazy as ever, the revel burning quietly behind him. His Court was still frozen, a painting mid-brushstroke, every dancer locked in adoration. The entire world held its breath for his cruelty.

"Why?" Her voice was thin, jagged. "Why do all this? Why *me?*"

Sevryn's smile was exquisite. "Because you asked for it."

Her stomach dropped. "What?"

He strolled a half-circle around her, slow, conversational, like a lecturer explaining an art piece. "Oh, don't tell me you've forgotten your bedtime prayer. The one you whispered into the storybook by candlelight. What was it again?"

Her throat locked.

He snapped his fingers, pretending to recall. "Ah. *I wish for wonder.*"

The words hit like a strike to the ribs. Her entire body flinched.

"You were so naive," he said, voice gone silken with mock nostalgia. "Sitting there in that dim little bakery room, hands still dusted in flour. You'd read the same story three times, the one about clever girls and kings. And then you said it." His grin sharpened. "You said my name without knowing it."

She shook her head, trembling. "No—"

"Oh yes." His coin spun once, catching light from every direction. "You wanted *wonder.* Such a vague, delicious word. It could mean anything. It could mean everything. I couldn't resist."

Her pulse went ragged. "You stole that wish."

"I interpreted it," he corrected, gold eyes bright as a forge. "You never specified what form wonder should take. Fire? Chaos? Death? Me?" He spread his arms. "Darling, ambiguity is consent in the language of the divine."

"Stop—"

"Why would I?" His voice rose, brighter, crueler. "You said you wanted your life to change. You wanted more than bread and boredom. You wanted stories. So I gave you stories! I burned your town, shattered your soul, delivered you trials that made the gods themselves lean forward to watch."

Her heart seized. "You destroyed everything I loved."

"And you loved the wrong things." He smiled, perfect and merciless. "So I replaced them with better ones."

Maren's voice cracked. "You replaced me."

He tilted his head, amused. "You make it sound like a loss. You're not lost, Maren. You're immortalized. You're the Story Keeper of Chaos, the first mortal to co-rule the Court. Do you know how few get rewritten that well?"

"I didn't want to be rewritten!"

"Oh, but you did." He stepped closer, coin flashing between them. "Every time you begged for meaning. You think you're angry because you lost yourself. You're angry because I gave you exactly what you asked for, and it's uglier than you imagined."

The words landed like blows.

Her breath came shallow, broken. "I didn't wish for this."

"No?" His grin deepened. "You wished for wonder. I made your world wondrous. The bakery that baked itself. The fire. The friend. The Spirit who could ruin you and still make you grateful for the ruin."

Her vision burned white-hot. "You tricked me."

"I *am* the trick."

Her fury snapped like a tether breaking.

The sound started small, a vibration through her teeth, a hum under her ribs. The Court around them shuddered. Gold dust shot upward in a slow, glittering cyclone. Her gown lashed in an invisible wind.

"Careful," he said softly, almost delighted. "You're leaking."

"Don't patronize me."

"Don't insult my craft." He leaned close, voice dipping into a dangerous purr. "You didn't climb to power, darling. You were built for it. Every thread of emotion you've ever had, every petty mortal ache, is mine now. You wanted to be part of something greater? Congratulations."

He pressed a hand to her chest, over her heart. "You're the heart of Chaos itself."

The touch scorched. Her scars flared beneath his palm, constellations pulsing with light. She gasped and struck him away, but the air trembled with the force.

The torches bent backward. The marble cracked under her feet.

He laughed, low and delighted. "Ah, there she is."

"Stop calling me *she* like I'm your creation."

"But you are."

Her hair whipped across her face. "I hate you."

"Good," he murmured. "Hate is stronger than love. Hate keeps the story burning."

"You think this is a story?" she spat.

"It's the only thing that's real." He gestured to the motionless dancers, to the twisted chandeliers, to the endless feast frozen mid-cheer. "They don't exist without it. You don't. I don't." His voice rose, godlike now, layered with something vast and echoing. "Every heartbeat in this Court is a story, and you, my darling, are the keeper of them all. I didn't chain you. I exalted you."

The wind surged, ripping at her gown. "You exalted yourself!"

He grinned. "Same thing."

The fury in her chest split wide open. Power licked the edges of the room: wild, radiant, and red. The chandeliers reformed upside down. Flames climbed the walls in reverse.

"You wanted wonder?" he whispered. "Here it is."

She screamed.

The Court exploded in light.

Every frozen reveler shattered into motes of gold. The marble floor buckled, rippling like water. Her own reflection fractured, multiplying around her until she was surrounded by hundreds of Marens, all screaming the same thing—

You asked for this.

The air caught fire with it.

He stood in the center, untouched, still smiling. "Beautiful," he murmured, voice reverent. "You finally understand."

"Understand?" she rasped, stepping through the ruin toward him. Her eyes were fever-bright. "No. I finally see you."

<h1 style="text-align:center">38</h1>

<h1 style="text-align:center">Beautiful</h1>

The ceiling kept changing its mind.

Chandeliers lay on the floor like sleeping beasts while their twins still burned in the rafters. Frost glazed the velvet steps. Fire ran beneath it, a red vein under ice. The marble bled ink that crawled toward the dais and then crawled back out again.

Sevryn stood in the middle of the carnage. Reverent, almost gentle, like a man watching a cathedral collapse in perfect symmetry.

"Beautiful," he said again.

The coin necklace at her throat woke.

Not a jingle. A pulse. A trapped bird behind bone. It hit the beat of her ribs, missed, then hunted it down until they matched. Heat climbed her scars in a slow, bright tide. The star-maps beneath her skin lit one by one.

She took a step. The floor rippled as if something under the stone had turned over to look at her. Cold stung her ankles. Heat licked her calves.

"Careful," Sevryn murmured, smiling into the ruin. "It is hungry."

The Court had *always* been hungry. Today it bit its own tail.

Maren tasted smoke and iron. Her throat hurt. Her reflection kept appearing where no surface should catch it. Three steps away, the marble wore her face, eyes fever-bright, mouth set like a promise. Behind her, another Maren staggered through rising frost with the same stubborn chin.

She touched the coin necklace.

354

Cedar and citrus still clung faintly to the metal. His scent. His hand giving it, careless as an ornament, voice all velvet: *Every story needs a hand to hold the pen.*

Not a gift. A tool. Worse, a handle.

"Tell me you did not plan this," she said, dry as ash. Her lips were numb. Her voice held anyway.

"Plan is such an orderly word." He cocked his head, gold eyes lit like hearth coals. "I preferred to invite."

The ceiling cracked. The crack stitched itself with golden thread, then unstitched. A chandelier on the floor rang like a bell. Twice. Sweet, cruel.

Her scars warmed where his teeth had once found her collarbone. The memory flared, and she crushed it. Heat traveled regardless, mapping her ribs, crossing her breastbone, a diagram she had never agreed to wear. When the warmth reached her throat, the Court paused.

She let out a breath. The pause let out with her. The room moved again, frantic, joyful, suicidal.

Oh.

He watched her, coin rolling against his knuckles, lazy as a pulse he did not need. Not looking at the collapse. Looking only at the way the collapse bent when she breathed.

He had always enjoyed an audience. Now he had an axis.

"You stitched it," she said, and the words felt like needles. "Into me."

He did not blink. Only tipped his chin a fraction, the fox who had already swallowed the henhouse and was admiring his shine. "You survived a fire that breaks most mortals. I helped you keep the heat."

Not an answer, but close enough.

The first trial. The ring that woke hungry. The place where her skin was rewritten with stars. It had saved her. It had branded her. The Court had written itself under her skin so it would not forget how to breathe if the roof went. And he had held the needle.

If the Court fell to ash, the constellation inside her would keep some sliver humming. If she lived, it lived. If it lived, so did he.

Insurance, wearing her face.

Rage spiked, clean as a knife. It steadied her better than the floor did. "You wanted chaos unbound," she said. "You brought the knife to its throat and called it worship. And now you need my breath to keep your altar from dying."

He smiled like she had recited his favorite poem. "You hear me very well."

Another chandelier tipped out of the ceiling and decided to hang sideways instead. Glass chimed. A ribbon of water ran up the wall, met a ribbon of flame coming down, and shook hands in steam. The balconies tilted toward her, then away, like flowers that could not agree on the sun.

Beneath it all, the coin at her throat beat. Her scars kept their quiet glow. The room answered them in small, ridiculous ways. A column that had begun to fall reconsidered. A line of cracked marble paused until her next inhale. An overturned chair righted itself and burst into frost.

When she touched the pendant, the steadiness sharpened. Not peace. Not safety. Alignment. A moving thing put into a groove.

Every story needs a hand to hold the pen.

He had given her one. He had expected to hold the wrist.

"Is this what you wanted?" she asked without looking at him. Her eyes tracked the ink spilling across the floor. Letters rose out of it, tiny and legible, then slumped back into a puddle. Names. Places. Some she knew. Some she would hate to learn.

"Yes." His answer came soft, easy, cruel. "You, here, with the sense to be furious. The Court of Chaos honest enough to stop pretending at balance. The Arbiter eating silence. The story is alive because you refuse to die inside it."

"And if it eats everything," she said. "Including you."

He laughed. It curled around her like smoke. "Then we will find out how far your scars stretch."

"Leash a dog," she said, quiet, mostly for herself. "Pretend the hand holding it is a gift."

"Darling," he said, with the soft amusement that had ruined more nights than wine, "I would never call you a dog."

"Try chain, then." Her smile bared teeth. "Or bridal ribbon. Something elegant for the witnesses."

The smile he gave back had heat under it, and a kind of hunger that had nothing to do with the Court. "You always did look best bound to me."

If the Court died, a piece would survive under her skin. If he died with the Court, he would not let it die. Which meant he would not let her.

She met his eyes. The gold inside them burned bright and steady. No fear. No hurry. The only calculation she should have noticed sooner.

"You trust me to keep breathing," she said.

"I trust you to hate suffocation." He smiled. "You are dependable in that way."

She set her palm over the coin. The pendant trembled. In the brief quiet of its shiver, she saw it: the way the Court settled toward her touch, the way dough settled under a hand that knew what it was doing. Not obedience. Technique.

Every story needs a hand to hold the pen.

The coin steadied. Her breathing did not.

It sat beneath her palm like a small, obedient sun, heat pooling where skin met metal. The Court of Chaos leaned toward that meeting. A pattern wanted to happen.

Pattern. In Chaos.

She looked at Sevryn. He watched the contact, not the ruin. Coin whispering over his knuckles, fox-quiet, pleased with himself.

His coin flicked. The spinning chandelier slowed as if it had remembered to be graceful. A line of ink on the floor picked a direction and flowed toward the dais as if given a purpose beyond puddling. The air itself seemed to lean.

Intention.

His coin set the want.

Then what did hers do, besides pulse like a captured thing and calm the room when she let it?

She pressed harder. The pendant thrummed, answering with a beat almost too steady to be hers. Marble cracks softened at the edges. A shattered goblet on the steps decided to be a bowl. The chandelier on the floor rang once and went quiet, like a child told to hush.

Not want. *Outcome.*

Resolution.

The thought hit and refused to move. She tried to push past it, and it just sat there.

He raised a brow, small and infuriating, as if he had heard the thought form. Maybe he had. The Court wore her breath now. He wore the Court. It was not a comforting triangle.

"Keep your toy," she said, fingers still on the pendant. "You already have too many."

"My favorite is the one in your hand," he said softly. "You make it interesting."

Her mouth tasted of ash. Interesting was his word that had a habit of a double meaning.

She looked down. The pendant was deceptively dainty. Silver on a thin chain. Pretty as something bought from a stall with market bells and rosemary bunches on the table.

Every story needs a hand to hold the pen.

Pen, not plan. He did not plan; he invited. He set want in motion and watched it crash. Then he laughed like a god who had never learned to apologize. The Arbiter had been the apology. He had unmade the apology. Now he wanted a neat hand to finish the mess into something he could keep.

Her pulse kicked. The Court felt it. Balconies trembled, then caught themselves. The chain at her neck lay cool, ordinary, almost pretty. It hid what it was, the way he hid cruelty under charm. She had always hated jewelry. Too much shimmer begging to be looked at.

She stared at the little disk until the light on it turned cruel. A pen, he had said. Not a crown. Not a lock. A tool…. for endings.

She had always ruined endings.

The memory rose with a soured sweetness. Old storybooks on the bakery shelf. Pages foxed at the corners from flour and fingers. Her father, with a voice she could no longer remember, was reading the neat, careful finish that the chapel approved.

The princess forgave.

The thief gave back the gold.

The village was safe because it did not ask questions.

No.

That was not how it lived in her head.

She had taken a charcoal stub and written in the margins. Sometimes a knife did the job, a thin slice along the seam so she could insert a scrap of paper like a stitch. A better last line. A different door. The wolf apologized with his teeth still wet. The girl took the road through the dark and made a map of her bruises. The baker refused to marry a prince who liked the idea of bread but not the work of kneading.

Small acts of vandalism. Survival, in a town where everything ended the way someone else said.

She had been practicing.

The thought tasted like humiliation. Practicing for what? This stage. This audience. This man with his coin and his grin, who had guessed exactly how much she would hate the ending he had written for her and dared her to fix it on his terms.

Heat crawled back up her scars. The pendant vibrated against her palm, as if pleased at the recognition. She wanted to tear it free and hurl it into the nearest convenient abyss. The Court would fetch it back on a platter.

The pendant's pulse quickened, matching her heartbeat like it was mocking her for finally catching up. The Court tilted with it: walls quivering, air thickening with light until breathing tasted like copper.

Maren stared at the ruin around her, at the story refusing to end, and felt something hot and raw split open inside her.

"This is what I get?" Her voice scraped the air. "All of *this* and it ends in pity?"

The chandeliers trembled. Frost and flame froze midair like the room itself didn't dare interrupt.

She laughed once, a sound too thin to stay upright. "Oh, I can see it now. The moral." She lifted her arms to the collapsing ceiling. "The mortal forgives the monster. They fix the world together. Balance restored. Order and Chaos walk hand-in-hand into the sunset." Her voice cracked into a snarl. "How original."

Sevryn didn't answer. He just stood there with his coin and his calm, his perfect, empty patience, like the portrait of a god pretending to be human.

She *hated* him for it.

Because if he flinched, even once, maybe she could still believe he was a story worth salvaging.

But he only smiled, faint and waiting, as though he thought this rage was a performance.

It wasn't.

She'd performed enough.

Her pulse burned through her scars, down her arms, until her fingers shook with it. "You wrote me into this," she said, voice low. "You took everything that was mine. My town, my bakery, my friend, my dreams. My grief bartered and my skin branded and called it character development."

The Court shuddered.

Maren kept talking because stopping meant surrender.

"I should've known it was a story," she spat. "The patterns were too neat. The hero's trials. The big speeches. The tragic kiss. All of it tidy enough to entertain an audience and call it profound."

The air rippled. Somewhere in the rafters, the ceiling muttered, echoing her last word like a confession.

Profound.

"Lazy," she corrected, staring up at the crack of gold light bleeding through the plaster. "It's lazy. The kind of ending I used to rip out and rewrite because it wasn't honest."

The ink on the floor shifted, listening.

Sevryn's grin faltered for the first time. "Careful, darling. You're talking like an author."

"Maybe I am."

The words came out sharp, defiant, alive. "Because I've spent my whole life fixing endings written by people who never bothered to ask how it felt to live them. I know what happens next. The heroine forgives the monster. She stays. She learns that ruin and redemption make a balanced meal." Her hand clenched on the coin, its edge biting skin. "I'm supposed to call that growth."

A low hum built beneath her feet, the sound of the Court thinking.

She tilted her head, eyes bright with fury. "But that's not growth. That's surrender in pretty language."

The pendant seared against her palm. The floor pulsed once, twice, like a heart trying to sync with hers.

"I *hate* this story," she whispered. "I hate that you think I'm small enough to stay inside it."

Her reflection blinked back from the ink pools: the dozens of Marens staring, waiting for someone to choose the line that stuck.

She drew in a ragged breath. "You want a heroine who forgives. Who kneels. Who thanks you for the cage because it taught her something about herself." Her laugh broke like glass. "But I was raised by a storyteller. I know what this is."

The chandeliers began to swing overhead, each one glowing with the fever of a word about to be spoken.

"You build stories to trap people in morals. To teach lessons they never asked to learn. But I don't believe in morals."

The Court creaked. The world leaned in.

"I believe in revisions."

The air went still enough to hurt.

Sevryn's coin stilled mid-spin, caught between his fingers. For the first time, he looked uncertain.

Maren's lips curved, not soft, not kind. "You wrote this story wrong."

And then, quieter, like a promise only the world was meant to hear:

"I'm going to take the pen back."

The coin at her throat flared white-hot, the chain burning against her skin. The Court's walls rippled, edges of reality softening like wet parchment.

It was listening.

Finally, after every trial, every bargain, every false ending—

Maren Greenbriar stopped being the heroine.

And started being the author.

The Court flinched.

~~Mercy is the only answer.~~

Agency is.

The chandeliers struggled to agree. Half settled into neat rows. Half swung wider, clattering glass-like teeth.

Sevryn's coin flicked; the air leaned toward him, hungry for a direction.

~~She forgave him because love was stronger than pride.~~

She remembered pride was only a word men used when they meant obedience.

His mouth curved, patient and pleased. "Rewrite, then," he said, as if this were a game he had always intended to watch.

She did not look at him. She put her palm flat over the pendant until the thin chain cut her skin. The Court listened. The marble tried to resolve into a hall of two rulers, equal, smiling. She dragged the sentence sideways with the weight of her breath.

~~A coronation of balance lit the room.~~

The room burned with unfinished want.

Letters bled up out of the floor and climbed her boots, begging to be read. She kicked through them. They lost their shapes and slumped back into pools.

The page fought back.

Paragraphs slid their chairs politely into place, then shoved each other for the center. The ceiling spoke in couplets. The floor answered in lists. The Court began to chant its own stage directions.

Stand.

Stand.

Stand as if this were the lesson.

Do not leave.

Do not leave or the story fails.

Maren lifted her chin. "Then let it fail."

The pendant burned brighter. The line of gold inside the crackled ceiling went white. Words blistered on the walls, peeling like paint.

~~She saw his face without the coin's light, and it was a man's face, flawed, wanting, capable of change. She took his hand. The Court sighed with relief. The story closed itself like a book put gently away.~~

She saw the coin first. Then the hand that taught it to move. The Court held its breath because it did not like what came next.

Sevryn's coin flashed. The toppled pillars aligned an inch toward ceremony. The overturned chair righted and offered itself like a kneeling place.

Her pendant answered with a pulse that rattled the glass. The chair cracked down the middle and remembered it was kindling.

The prose stuttered.

She tried to pull a sentence into a shape that would carry her out. The sentence tried to bite her. They wrestled.

She wrote.

~~The door opened to~~

The door has no right to open for him.

Ink hissed. The floor smudged. A chorus of well-meaning morals tried to crowd into her lungs. She coughed them back up, ugly and honest.

Verse pushed through the cracks:

no lesson,

only cost.

no tender closing,

only breath and heat and feet that still know forward.

Sevryn stopped smiling. The coin paused between two fingers. "Be careful," he said. "You are not built to hold it that long."

"I am not built to be *held*," she said.

The pendant flared. Her scars answered, constellations white as cut bone. The chain shrieked against itself. The prose blurred at the edges as if the page were being sanded down from the outside.

~~He stepped to her; she met him halfway.~~

No.

The word landed like a hammer. The sentence below it buckled.

The Court panicked. The chandeliers rose with a clatter, insisted on symmetry, failed, and crashed into rhyme.

Shine and settle,

Shine and settle.

Do not break the pattern.

The pendant refused to dim. The light ate adjectives. Lines thinned to their spines. When she reached for a verb, it came hot and bright and exact.

Run.

The prose recoiled, then snapped a leash of narrative around her ankles.

~~But first, she forgave, because that is what saves a heroine.~~

~~But first, she chose the throne, because that is what saves a world.~~

But first, she chose herself.

Maren changed tactics. She stopped pushing sentences like furniture. She cut them. Fast. Clean. She turned the clauses into doors and walked through before they remembered to slam.

The pendant went white. The prose could not describe it. Lines singed off into silence mid-word, the way parchment chars when a candle tips.

She reached for a line that wanted to be a vow and ripped it into a map.

~~We will rule together, and~~

stairs. left. cold air.

The page staggered. Paragraphs shuffled themselves, tried to recover elegance, failed into jagged stanzas. She heard the Court hissing in margins she had not known could speak.

stop

stop

stop breaking what holds us

Sevryn's voice chased her from a distance that kept refusing to stay measured. "You cannot author a world and keep your hands clean," he said. He was closer now. Farther. Both. His coin kept throwing intention after her like a net. Archways turned toward her path. Floors softened to keep her gentle. Doors loved the idea of opening for the heroine who forgave.

She was no heroine.

She fed the page a simpler diet:

Run.

The world blurred. Titles tore. Chapters bent their spines and tried to make new numbers out of pain. The Court's scrollwork peeled off the pillars and beat its wings once, twice, like trapped birds.

She grabbed the last coherent phrase before the light cooked it.

Run.

39

Unstable

You were expecting a conclusion, weren't you?

There isn't one. Not yet.

I am done being finished by other mouths.

I am not done.

The pendant cracked. A hairline. Light bled through and burned a thin kiss into her palm.

Good. Cost.

The Court howled. It threw one final neat paragraph in her path:

~~He reached for her hand without the coin. A man, not a spirit. A choice, not a trap.~~

I let the sentence stand for a breath. I wanted to. Then I put my knife through it.

The crack in the pendant widened. Power hissed. The chain snapped and bit her throat. The coin fell against her chest and went from white to dull silver to something quieter. A tool spent.

Good. No godhood. No crown. Only a path.

The Court bucked one last time, flinging images like bribes. A warm bed. A throne at her height. A kitchen with steam and laughter, so clean it hurt. The pictures shattered on impact and fell as harmless glitter.

I held the last word I trusted.

Run.

Sevryn said her name. It sounded like hunger and history and a door she would not use.

I turned my back on the page.

She ran.

I ran.

Epilogue

Sevryn

The realm screamed when she tore it open.

The tear wasn't a wound so much as an insult, a mortal-made slash through a place that had existed before languages learned how to name themselves, and as Maren vanished through the blazing seam. Her silhouette was a smear of firelight.

The Court of Chaos convulsed around her exit like a beast denied its due. The chandeliers swung wide in panic, the marble buckled, the constellations in the ceiling blinked out one by one, and the air itself folded in the wrong direction.

Sevryn stood at the center of the ruin, untouched, haloed in the gold dust that fell from a ceiling that no longer obeyed gravity. The Court tore itself apart around him. Reality trembled. Story buckled.

He watched her run.

Because he was patient. And because the mortal girl thought herself free in the way children think shadows cannot follow them into the dark, unaware that parts of the Court still clung to her bones. Those little threads of mischief woven through her blood, slivers of Chaos stitched beneath her ribs, a rhythm not fully her own pulsing in her chest like a second heartbeat that had always belonged to him.

She would run far.

Mortals always did.

But one does not outrun what lives stitched beneath their skin.

He exhaled slowly, and the Court trembled.

With a thought, he stilled the chandeliers mid-swing. With a blink, he sent the splintering marble slithering back together. With a whim, he forced gravity to remember itself. Order was not his nature, but he wielded it like a knife when he needed to. Just a brief correction to keep the realm from collapsing entirely before he was ready for it to suffer.

The tear sealed enough to stop bleeding, but not enough to hide where she'd gone. A scorch mark remained, faint as a whisper. *Her* mark. Her defiance.

Sevryn stepped toward it, and the entire hall bowed around him.

He touched two fingers to the charred stone. Heat bled up his skin, not her heat, but the coin's. The lesser one she'd burned into nothing. A clever trick. An unanticipated variable.

A thrill.

He almost laughed.

Mortals were at their most beautiful when they ruined carefully crafted plans.

He withdrew his hand, flexing his fingers, feeling the hum of the true coin tucked neatly in his palm. Silver, whole, older than the architecture of ambition itself. He rolled it across his knuckles, and the metal shimmered with a pulse that was not entirely its own. It vibrated once, sharp enough to sting.

Then the whisper came.

A pressure, ancient and cruel, curling through the coin's metal in a language older than Mischief, older than want, older than the gods who cast Spirits into shape because they feared the weight of their own emotions.

Sevryn stilled.

The whisper repeated, threading through the coin like a needle through flesh, forming meaning by force rather than clarity.

He approaches.

The great hall shuddered, as though the floors remembered a name they'd never been taught. The chandeliers dimmed, their light bending as if something unseen had brushed past their flames. Storylines etched into the walls flickered, losing pieces of themselves: half a sentence erased here, a detail unmade there.

A warning.

A promise.

An invitation to war.

The Storybreaker.

He did not stand in the Court, but his influence crawled through the seams of reality like frost across glass.

Sevryn's jaw tightened in a slow, deliberate curl.

"Not yet," he murmured, and the coin went still.

The Storybreaker would not enter his realm without consequence. And when he came, he would look at Maren with a hunger carved from a different kind of ruin, a different kind of promise.

And Sevryn would tear out his throat for it.

But that was a story for later.

She was running into a world that would not recognize her anymore. A world she would rewrite simply by breathing in it. A world that would bend, willingly or unwillingly, to the shape of her hunger.

She thought she'd escaped him.

She thought she'd broken free.

She thought the ending was hers.

He let that belief live. Let it bloom like a new, fragile page.

Because Mischief liked games.

"My darling mortal," he whispered to the empty, trembling hall, "run while the story is kind."

He flicked the coin.

The Storybreaker was coming.

So was she.

And the next story would ruin them all.

Acknowledgments

What a reckless, holy whirlwind this has been.

Maren and the Mischief Spirit will forever live inside me, not because it is my debut novel, but because it was born from the places I nearly did not survive. Maren's story is close to my heart because she is stitched from my own questions, my own defiance, my own hunger for wonder in a world that often felt too small.

I grew up in a very small town in northwest Georgia, the kind of place where dreams are often expected to be practical or quiet. I was neither. I wanted to be a "starving artist". I wanted to paint and write poetry in the margins of my life. I wanted to go to art school. I wanted to live off whatever I could make with my hands and my mind.

Then, in my senior year, I was told I would not even be accepted into my local community college because I had dropped a chemistry class.

To the school counselor who said that: thank you.

Your doubt became kindling.

As it turns out, I was accepted. It was the cheapest option. Sensible. I planned to transfer to a larger university once my core classes were finished. Although it wasn't an art school, I had a timeline. I had control.

Life, however, did not consult my timeline.

I became pregnant in my first semester of college, immediately following the worst mental health crisis I had ever experienced. I was eighteen. I was drowning in daily suicidal thoughts. The world I thought I had carefully constructed collapsed before I had even learned how to steady it.

To the teacher who failed me during that season, ironically in English, while I was pregnant and barely holding myself together: thank you.

You taught me something I could not have learned from praise. You taught me that I could survive humiliation. That I could fail at the only thing I thought I still had control over. That I could survive being underestimated. That I could survive even when I was not at my best.

You were part of the fire.

I married my husband three months later. We were young. We were terrified. We were stubborn enough to believe love could outpace fear. We were wrong about many things, but not about each other.

To my husband: thank you for choosing me when I was not easy to choose.

You watched me rage. You watched me unravel. You watched me write my poetry in the middle of breakdowns. You stayed when I did not even know how to stay with myself. When I begged you to let me work because postpartum was swallowing me whole, you said yes without ego, without resentment, and without hesitation. You have never once tried to shrink my ambition to make it more comfortable. You have only ever handed it back to me and said, "go".

I had my daughter in July 2023. Twelve weeks later, I found out I was pregnant again. I was still in college. I was still trying to understand my new role of becoming a mother. I was still trying to remember who I was outside of survival.

And still, I did not slow down. I didn't know how.

I graduated from that community college in December, months pregnant, holding a four-month-old baby and a degree in one hand, and fear in the other.

To my professors who saw something in me even when I felt like a walking contradiction of potential and chaos: thank you. Especially to the professor who guided me through creative writing and reminded me that stories are allowed to be messy before they are meaningful. Thank you for the opportunity.

I transferred into an online bachelor's program the following January. This is where *Maren and the Mischief Spirit* truly began.

In a short story workshop, exhausted beyond reason with a newborn and an eleven-month-old, I wrote about a mother who wished for a break and accidentally magicked her children away. She immediately misses them and wakes up from a dream sequence. In hindsight, this seems like a confession more than fiction, but the core lived on.

Motherhood did not erase my creativity. It sharpened it. It terrified it. It made every story about loss and longing feel personal. My daughter, Ophelia, has sat beside me through more drafts than most "friends" ever will. She now insists she wrote this book. She taps away on her toy laptop beside me, announcing she is "writing like mommy."

Let it be known: I am merely the scribe. She is the true architect.

To my children: thank you for anchoring me to the real world when my mind wanted to escape it. You are the reason I fight. You are the reason I write about love as something dangerous and worth choosing anyway. I hope one day you both will be proud.

To my sister: thank you for reading the messy first screenplay and daring to say, "This should be a full book." Thank you for pushing me toward fantasy when I would have settled for small. Thank you for introducing me to stories that reminded me that chemistry on the page matters. Thank you for believing that Maren and Mischief were not finished. You saw what I could not.

To Katie Reed, my developmental editor: thank you for telling me the truth. You told me my writing was strong, but my conflict was not. You told me to dismantle the comfortable version of the story and rebuild it with stakes. You helped me push Maren into reluctant heroine territory. You helped me deepen Eldenwick. You helped me understand that trials should cost something. Your counsel was invaluable in making this story truly come alive.

To the courthouse where I worked full-time while drafting chapters in stolen minutes between case files and hearings: thank you for shaping the Arbiter. Watching justice unfold, watching power move in rooms heavy with consequence, changed this book. Real life bled into fantasy, as it always does.

To my students, in the practical life I've shoved myself into: If I ever tell you to take yourself seriously, to write the thing anyway, to believe that your voice deserves space, understand that I am not speaking abstractly. I am speaking from experience. Thank you for letting me teach you. Thank you for reminding me why language is power.

To my town, the one that has always felt too small: thank you. You gave me texture. You gave me monotony to rebel against. You gave me stories hidden in plain sight. You taught me what it feels like to want more and to feel guilty for wanting it.

To the version of me who almost did not make it: thank you for staying.

There were days I did not believe I would see nineteen. Days when the future felt like a cruel joke. Days when I was angry at everyone who tried to help me. I spit on grace more than once. I rejected kindness out of pride and pain.

And still, here I am.

This book is not just about wonder. It is about surviving your own mind. It is about wanting more than the life handed to you. It is about making reckless choices and living with them. It is about grief. It is about power. It is about refusing to remain small because someone once told you that you were.

To every person who doubted me: thank you.

To every person who loved me anyway: thank you more.

And to the darkness that followed me for years: we have come to an understanding. I no longer run from you; I write you into shape.

With love and chaos,
  RS

About the Author

Rhianna Sylver is a romantasy author with a soft spot for sharp-tongued heroines, magic, and slow-burn romantic tension. When she is not writing, she is usually juggling the beautifully chaotic life of being a young mom, a full-time English teacher, and a storyteller with too many ideas and not enough hours in the day.

Her debut novel, Maren and the Mischief Spirit, introduces her signature blend of emotional stakes, mythology, and character-driven romance. Her stories are built for readers who love banter, longing, and worlds on the edge of unraveling.

Rhianna lives in Georgia with her husband, two children, and an ever-growing TBR pile she fully intends to conquer someday.

You can connect with me on:

🔗 https://www.instagram.com/rhiannasylver

Subscribe to my newsletter:

✉ https://tr.ee/tKcNb-lxNe